I0593555

Joseph Alfred Scoville

The Old Merchants of New York City

Joseph Alfred Scoville

The Old Merchants of New York City

ISBN/EAN: 9783337419219

Printed in Europe, USA, Canada, Australia, Japan

Cover: Foto ©Andreas Hilbeck / pixelio.de

More available books at **www.hansebooks.com**

THE OLD MERCHANTS

OF

NEW YORK CITY.

BY

WALTER BARRETT, Clerk,

SECOND SERIES.

—The harvest of the river is her revenue, and she is a mart of nations.
—Whose antiquity is of ancient days.
—The crowning city, whose merchants are princes, whose traffickers are the honorable of the earth.

Isaiah xxiii. 3, 7, 8.

NEW YORK:
CARLETON, PUBLISHER, 413 BROADWAY.
MDCCCLXIII.

To

ARCHIBALD GRACIE, Esq.

You were really the first merchant that the author ever met, and it was to you that he was indebted for his first knowledge of the rudiments of commerce, and his early acquaintance with the names and persons of the leading merchants of the period, among whom none ranked higher than yourself.

The author also came upon the stage sufficiently early to know *that* ARCHIBALD GRACIE, Senior, your venerable father, who, about the period of the passing of the last into the present century, was among the first merchants of this or any other country,—his ships visiting every port of the world. When, in writing in these chapters of "Old Merchants," about the loftiest commercial integrity, spotless private character, the innocence of a child, of grand commercial views bounded only by the latitude and longitude of the globe, the dignified presence, the philosopher in overwhelming misfortune, patience in waiting through long weary years for the wrong to be made right, the venerable white hairs and the soul of goodness,—to write correctly of all, the author had only to recal to memory that same father of yours, whose remains he saw placed in the family vault more than a third of a century ago in St. Thomas churchyard.

What, then, more proper, than that the author should respectfully dedicate this volume to yourself, bearing a name doubly honored in mercantile annals?

PREFACE.

The extraordinary success that followed the publication of the First Series of THE OLD MERCHANTS OF NEW YORK, was quite unexpected. Many editions have been exhausted, and it is still in active demand. This, the Second, is the continuation of the series in regular order, and may be found more interesting even than the first.

The material is as correct as it was possible to make it up to the time of the publication. The chapters will be fully revised and corrected in subsequent editions, and the author will cordially thank any one who is better informed than himself as to particular merchants or their families, alluded to in any of the series or chapters, if they will send their corrections, or additional information, to the residence of

WALTER BARRETT, Clerk.

No. 27 West 27th Street, New York.

THE OLD MERCHANTS OF NEW YORK CITY

SECOND SERIES.

CHAPTER I.

Among the many powerful names enumerated among these " Old Merchants " since their commencement, who have lived and moved in this great commercial city for seventy years, who had added to its glory and prosperity, who have given names to families of which their descendants may well be proud — who have been remarkable for their extended commerce, their wealth, their bold operations, embracing a world — as remarkable for their intelligence as for their integrity, for their capability and their correctness in every relation of life ; of vigorous intellect, of a continued perseverance for years and years, of unwearied diligence ; yet · of how little consequence beyond their own sphere, or " off change," have any of them been ?

How very few have wielded party influence, or obtained political power ? The exceptions to this rule are so remarkable, that one can count upon his fingers the names of almost every prominent man, who in the last half century, among merchants, has been elected to the lower house of Congress, or even to either branch of our State Legislature.

J. G. King was in Congress, but from New Jersey, where he has resided while he was alive.

1*

Moses H. Grinnell, of Grinnell, Minturn & Co., was once in Congress, lower house, but years ago.

John I. Morgan and Gideon Lee were both in Congress.

Fernando Wood was in the lower house. He was formerly of the firm of Wood & Fairchild. He has also reached the mayoralty, as have a few other merchants, such as A. C. Kingsland, Gideon Lee, W. H. Havemeyer, Philip Hone, D. F. Tieman and others. John Broome, was Lieut. Gov. of the State.

But two merchants of this city have reached the governorship of a State, and of these two, I have to record a very curious fact. One came from Connecticut a poor boy — become a merchant, and afterwards became twice Governor of the State of New York. This one was Edwin D. Morgan.

The other was a Connecticut boy originally, but before he came to New York to be a merchant, had been secretary of the treasury to General Washington in 1795 to 1799, and then established himself as a merchant in New York city, and when he retired from business went to Connecticut, and was twice elected Governor of that State, as E. D. Morgan has been of New York. I allude to Oliver Wolcott, Jr. He was the son of the first Oliver Wolcott who was Governor of Connecticut in the Revolutionary times. Young Oliver, when Washington became President, took a position as " Comptroller of the Navy," of which Alexander Hamilton was Secretary. In 1795, he succeeded Hamilton as Secretary. Shortly after, Thomas Jefferson became President, in 1801 — Oliver Wolcott Jr., came to New York, and went into business at 52 Pine street, under the firm of " Oliver Wolcott & Co." In 1802, he was elected president of the Merchants' Bank, chartered that year,

and was surrounded by such grand old fellows as Joshua
Sands, Richard Varick, Henry A. Coster, Lynde Cat-
lin, Henry Wyckoff, William W. Woolsey, Peter Jay
Munro, and other great names of the city. To be a
bank director in this city, when there were but four
banks, " New York," " Manhattan Company," " U. S.
Bank," and " Merchants," was an honor, and it gave
a great financial power.

He resigned the presidency of the bank in 1805, and
devoted himself especially to merchandizing, keeping his
store at 52, and his residence in an old-fashioned dwelling house, 26 Pine street. He did business until 1814
at the old store, 52. In 1816 he gave up his house, 26,
and went to Litchfield, Conn. It was after that he became Governor of Connecticut.

While living at 26 Pine street, his beautiful daughter
married (in that house,) William Gracie, of the firm of
Archibald Gracie & Son (1810). Never did bridal
couple enter into married life with more brilliant prospects of happiness than these two. She was beautiful
beyond compare. At this time Archibald Gracie owned
a country seat, near Hurlgate. It was called " Gracie's
Point." It overlooked Blackwell's Island — a large,
yellow, wooden building, on the East River, and almost
on the bank. Thither the young couple repaired on
the evening of the day they had been married at 26
Pine street. The festivities were kept up until a late
hour. The bride retired with her bridesmaids, and the
happy husband was sent for to see his young bride —
die. She had ruptured a blood vessel. It was a melancholy affair. Never was there a more high-spirited gentleman than Colonel William Gracie. He (many long
years afterwards) entered into marriage with Miss Fleming, a beautiful girl, scarcely less lovely than his first

bride. When he died, about twenty years ago, he left a daughter.

Governor Wolcott died at Litchfield, Connecticut.

Thus much for our first New York merchant, who became a Governor. Now for the second, E. D. Morgan.

He, too, was a Connecticut boy, born in Hartford, the adjoining county to Mr. Wolcott, who was from Litchfield. Young Morgan was placed in a very subordinate clerkship in a store at Hartford city. His duty was to sweep out the store, go of errands, and do a little of everything. While he was acting in this capacity, his employer sent him to New York city, a place he had never been to before, of which he had no previous conception, and probably no idea of the important figure he would bear in it. While looking about the city, he met with a cargo of corn that was for sale. It occurred to him that there was money to be made by it. He at once acted upon the idea, purchased the cargo, and sent it to Hartford. When he reached that place, he went to work and sold this lot of corn at a round price, realizing for his employer a very large profit. After this somewhat bold operation by the junior clerk, the partners came to the conclusion that there were other ways in which young Morgan could be made more serviceable than in sweeping out the store, and they promoted him to more important duties. Not many months after the visit to New York, he began to think that Hartford was rather too circumscribed for his growing mercantile ambition (he had no political thoughts then,) and with his usual promptness he decided to go New York city. His acquaintances in Gotham were limited, but this did not daunt him. He possessed the irresistible perseverance and indomitable industry that would enable him to surmount anything, and he determined to try his fortunes here. To this city he came in 1830, I think. I do not remember the name of the house in which he became a clerk ; but he lived in John street, at No. 57, with David Hale, who had just started *The Journal of Commerce*, but not being sure of success, aided on his enterprise by keeping a boarding-house of a high character.

Among other youths from Connecticut at that time, George Collins, Morris Earl, John J. Phelps and Amos R. Eno accompanied Edwin D. Morgan. At any rate they came here about the same time, and one or more boarded at David Hale's.

Later in life, in 1836 or 1837, E. D. Morgan formed a partnership with his old crony and townsman, under the firm of Morgan & Earle, at No. 61 Front street, and their business was the wholesale grocery. Of course, their means were very limited, and it was some time before their credit became fully established, and their custom was for a long time principally from the section whence they came.

They added to their profits by being agents of Hartford Fire Insurance Companies, and as the latter took risks at a very low rate, they did a heavy business.

Morris Earle continued in business with Mr. Morgan a year, then the firm was dissolved, and Morgan was so heartily sick of all partnership arrangements, that he determined to have no more partners. He continued business at the same store one year, and then moved from 61 to 63 Front. His residence was at 45 Pearl, First Ward, and he now commenced to take an active part in primary politics.

This, after all, is the grand secret of a man's success in political life. No matter what party he belongs to, he must, to hold a position and obtain nominations, be able to hold his own in the primary work, and do a little for himself. Good and great men are not so scarce, that they have to be sought after among the secluded men. When a princely merchant of any party is sought after, it is because a party or men wish to use him, either for money, respectability, or some other selfish purpose. No man continues to be before the public any length of time, unless he is able to control the primary meetings in his own party, in his own ward; nor could he keep in public life if he had the eloquence of Clay, or the profoundness of a Calhoun, without the same foothold.

Many a merchant of both or all parties has waited in his counting-room for a nomination to Congress. Such a man may wait until doomsday before he is nominated for that or any other position. Did such a man stoop to mix with the rank and file of the people, serve on ward committees, half elect them, get on general committees, know the masses, learn to pull the strings, he could eventually be elected anywhere, if his party had power. An outsider, however high his rank, cannot make up his mind to buy a nomination, and succeed. He will be cheated.

Morris Earle, after he left the house of Morgan & Earle, continued in the same business on his own account. He died ten years ago, worth $100,000. He was a hard working merchant. He went to his store before seven o'clock, A. M., and staid there until late at night. He made his clerks do likewise. In this manner he shortened his own days, and destroyed the enjoyment of his life.

Edwin D. Morgan was a very different person. When he was left alone in business, he commenced speculating in the great articles of sugar and coffee, and made no efforts to extend his wholesale grocery business.

In prosecuting these plans, he for many years spent his winters at the South, particularly at New Orleans. He visited all the great plantations, and not unfrequently purchased all the sugar of a planter before it started for market. Being calm and shrewd, he was very successful in all such purchases, and made money very rapidly. I should suppose he was now about fifty years old. He is a fine looking man, large and tall, and worth half a million of dollars. In 1844, Mr. Morgan moved his residence to 85 Lafayette Place, Fifteenth Ward. Little did he dream when he took that house, that upon so trivial an act, hung his future advancement to an Assistant Alderman's birth, a State Senatorship, a Governor, and perhaps a President. *Quien Sabe?* as the Spaniards say.

The success of Governor Morgan teaches a great moral lesson, and it is this — to have a great political success in after years, you must be faithful and true in the first position the people give you.

In 1849, the Whig party in the Fifteenth Ward nominated Edwin D. Morgan for assistant alderman. He was elected of course. He was upon the Sanitary Committee of the common council that year of cholera epidemic. He was remarkable for his attention to his public duties as a member of that committee. He never failed once to meet with it, during the whole period of its existence. He made himself very popular with all classes during the short period he was assistant alderman.

In the fall of 1849, assistant alderman Morgan was transplanted from the common council to the state senate, by being elected senator from the sixth senatorial district. He entered upon his senatorial duties at Albany, January 1st, 1850. He held it two sessions

and in 1851 was re-elected, and served two sessions
more until July 21, 1853.

While senator, he was one of the most influential
persons at Albany. A good merchant must necessarily make a good legislator. The patient examination
that he is obliged to bring to bear upon his mercantile
transactions, he continues to apply to legislative actions.

Mr. Morgan was a very heavy operator in railroad
stocks and interests. He was deeply interested in the
Hudson River railroad company. He was also a large
holder of the Troy and Schenectady road, with his
friend James Boorman (already on our list of published
American worthies.) When the Central railroad stock
was consolidated, the T. & S. road was consolidated with
that stock ; he and his friend realized a large sum by
it.

In 1858, the name of Edwin D. Morgan, New York
merchant, was brought forward in the Republican State
Convention as a candidate for Governor. There were
several other candidates, and his name was not apparently as prominent, or his chances of success as good
as some others.

James M. Cook, the knowing ones all said, would be
the Governor nominated. But they underrated Mr.
Morgan, his sagacity, and his management. Messrs.
Schoolcraft and Weed, of Albany, were among his
backers. He had all the Albany influence in his favor.
As a matter of course he bore down all opposition in
the Convention, was nominated, and triumphantly
elected.

As the expiration of his first term of two years approached, it was expected, or, rather, it was supposed,
from the course which he had pursued in vetoing the
Susquehanna railroad, that he could not obtain strength

enough in the convention to get renominated. Many
of his former political friends had deserted him, and for
a time it really appeared as though his old opponent,
James M. Cook, of Saratoga county, would be the successful man in the Convention of 1860. But again
events showed that Mr. Morgan was too shrewd and
stood too firm to be easily beaten even by his most
powerful opponent. He triumphed over all opposition,
and was again nominated, and again elected — and the
last time by a majority of over 50,000.

Luckily too is it for the state and nation, that in this
year of gloom and rebellion we have an enlightened,
patriotic New York merchant for our governor. Notwithstanding he has been tied up by foolish legislation,
he has worked wonders, and made the people and the
State proud of him. In spite of red tape, he has displayed great executive qualities, and such as will forever,
while we are a nation, and New York a state, command
the admiration of mankind.

Our New York merchant can map out his own political future. He has only to say that he will accept
political advancement, and he will get it.

Merchants as a class, should feel proud of the prominent advancement of one of their own class — and his
faithful performance of duty, leads to the advancement
of others.

If the merchants of New York acted in harmony,
they would rule the world.

With the vast amount of money they control, if it
was used with sense, not a member of Congress, Legislature, or even a Ward constable could be elected without their consent.

If the men they sent to Congress from this city were
sensible and well supported, not an act of legislation

could be passed by Congress without the consent of this city.

Not an ambassador or foreign consul to any nation or part of the world could be appointed without the consent of the merchants of New York.

The merchant members of Congress could say to any Administration or any Congress — " Do this, or the banks we represent, will do so and so. You shall not have a dollar unless you do as the city of New York, her merchant princes and bankers speaking through us, say you shall do."

Did New York city exercise and express her just rights, a Secretary of the Treasury could not hold power an hour.

Her members in the House have only to say " *her* will," and it would be done, or no more funds would be given for Government use, and it would break when in conflict with Wall street, the banks and the merchants.

But what sort of members does proud New York — the greatest commercial city of the Western world send to represent her mighty interests — her property of five hundred millions of dollars in specie that she can raise in a week ?

Does she send her money kings or her merchant princes ?

Does she send a Howland, a Goodhue, a Boorman, a Belmont, a Perit, a Minturn, a Murray, an Astor, a Law, a Griswold, a Westray, a Vanderbilt, a Taylor, a Thompson, a Marshall, a Livingston, a Barclay, a Stewart, a Gracie, a King, a Duer, or any of our grand, good, honest merchants, or financial names ?

No !

Who does the queen city send ?

Ben. Wood, the policy dealer and lottery vender, and men fit to be his associates.

I thank God that we have got one merchant from New York as governor, who does the city honor in return for being honored. A little salt, to save a bad lot.

When the merchants of New York are true to themselves, and the high destiny of the city, no such men as some of those who now represent her will do so then.

Until she sends her best merchants and her experienced financiers, her true power in the world will never be felt.

I omitted to mention that Edwin D. Morgan was for some time a director in the Bank of Commerce ; and this calls to my mind a very curious fact about that institution, with its immense capital. Some years ago a law was passed, that in all banks of issue the stockholders should be liable to double the amount of stock they held. For instance, if I owned $1,000 in the Bank of Commerce, or any other, and it should fail, I could be called upon to pay $1,000 more. The stockholders of the Bank of Commerce at once refused to go into any such responsibility. It at once ceased to be a bank of issue, and has an arrangement with the Bank of the State of New York for such bank notes as the former requires to carry on its business.

I believe Mr. Morgan still carries on business in his own name, and has a son, Edwin D. Morgan, Jr., in business.

CHAPTER II.

Stephen B. Munn will be recollected by many in this generation. He lived in Broadway, No. 503 — on the same block where the St. Nicholas Hotel now stands, as late as 1856. He died in that year.

Stephen B. Munn was a Connecticut boy. He lived and worked upon a farm until he was 17 years old, and then he went into the " tin peddling " business, as thousands of others have done, and made their first step on the road to fortune. A tin peddler is a traveling merchant. He generally connects himself with a " tinner," who also has a store to supply his " peddlers." The peddler first secures a horse and a tin-peddler covered wagon. The latter is judiciously divided into various receptacles, and a great many tin boxes, to contain needles and small articles of merchandise. These goods are peddled out by the " tinmen," who calculate to make a large profit. A " tinner " of means would frequently have out twenty tin peddlers." These wagons and peddlers took different routes in the Eastern and Western States, and some have boldly gone to the Southwest and South. Besides a large assortment of tinware, these wagons carried a regular assortment of merchandise — a real variety store on wheels. A smart Yankee tin peddler was sure to make money, and be sure to acquire a sharpness in trade, that prepared him for the shrewd New York merchant of after years.

Such an education was given to Mr. Stephen B. Munn, who was born in the northern part of Connecticut. He reached this city in 1794, and commenced operations upon a small scale at 100 Maiden Lane. He afterwards removed to 103 Maiden Lane, between Gold and Pearl streets. His stock was principally dry goods, but he kept an assorted stock of goods—a sort of peddler's wagon stock, too, on a large scale.

Notwithstanding his small capital, young Munn worked wonders with it. He attended auctions of every kind, and bought for cash. He was never successful in buying goods at private sale. He always said so. Probably his knowledge of dry goods, acquired in his peddling operations, was very superficial, and he was taken advantage of at private sale, which he could not be at auction, where he could use the sagacity of shrewd buyers, and duplicate their purchases. However that may have been, it is evident that Mr. Munn coined money up to 1800, for then he was able to buy the store No. 226 Pearl street, (near where Platt street has since been opened in.) He bought this place, and occupied the lower floor as a store, and lived in the upper part with his family. It was his store until 1821 — and his residence also until the war of 1813; that year he moved into Broadway, and in 1823 he moved his family into the handsome house he had built at No. 503 Broadway, where he died.

Property in Pearl street, in 1800, could not have been worth a great sum. The rent of a three-story house and store beneath did not exceed $400, and the cost of the building and lot, 25x100, was not over $4,000.

There are several good reasons why rent was reasonable and real estate was low. In 1800, the taxes were comparatively nothing. There was no water rent. People swept the streets. The lamp-lighters used the oil given them for street-lamps, and did not (as was done in after years) use dirty, cheap oil, and sell the costly city article.

There was no army of 2,000 policemen to support, costing tax-payers at least $2,000,000. On the contrary, one hundred steady and brave watchmen did duty at night, and earned their one dollar. These " good old leather-heads," with their clubs cost the city $25,000 a year. Not a dollar more,— and how few robberies, rapes and murders were committed in those good old days. The population was smaller in 1800 than in 1861, and of course more honest. The early people did not know anything about swindling sewer and other contracts. Street opening was not expensive, as people not interested did not have to bear the expenses, as is now done. For instance, Chambers street was extended for no special purpose except to benefit a few, at an expense to others, of a million dollars, and many houses taxed from two dollars to twenty-two hundred dollars, that do not receive twenty-five cents benefit. Over 6,848 houses were taxed for this scheme. Also, look at opening the Bowery from Chatham to Franklin Square, at a cost of $600,000. Over 800 pieces of property assessed for this purpose. These assessments are made from Old Slip to Fourteenth street. Even the projectors of that scheme have realized no benefit from it.

Such things were not done in 1800, consequently it was safe to own real estate in those days.

After S. B. Munn got established in Pearl street, he became a very bold operator, and bought largely. During the war, or rather towards its close, he had filled his

store with goods at war prices. He had bought " invoices " of goods at a fabulous percentage. When war
closed and peace was declared, he was one of the largest holders, and evidently destined to be ruined. Not
so. He was an exceedingly shrewd man, and he at once
concentrated all his energies to aid him in disposing of
his high cost merchandise and large stock, with as little
loss as possible. One of the plans to which he resorted,
was to exchange his merchandise for soldiers' land warrants. He was about the only man in the city who had
pluck enough to make the exchange, as the warrants at
that time were deemed of very little value ; but Mr.
Munn believed that no species of property could be
worth less than his dry goods at war prices. By pursuing this course, he reduced his stock very materially,
and he also accumulated a large amount of land warrants.
But even this shrewd scheme barely saved him from
bankruptcy. He weathered the storm, and continued to receive land warrants as long as he dared, but at
last they became so depreciated that he declined to exchange his dry goods for any more.

Finally he went West, and located all the " soldiers'
land warrants " he had become possessed of, taking up
an immense tract of land either in Ohio or Illinois.
The number of acres was immense. Still, this did not
appear to be a well planned operation. The western
lands were of no value. For years and years Mr. Munn
was using every exertion to raise money to pay the taxes and expenses upon this heavy land investment. It
kept him in hot water. He was always financiering —
always short ; he was obliged to keep heavily mortgaged
property that he owned in the city, and by such means
he was able to pay the western taxes ; he was however
one of those men said to be born under a lucky star.

What would have proved ruinous and beggared others, bettered him.

When the great land speculations of 1835 to 1836 commenced, a company of moneyed men, headed by Knowles Taylor, the son-in-law of that excellent man and merchant, Jonathan Little, conceived the idea of purchasing the lands of Mr. Munn.

J. Little & Co. kept store at 216 Pearl street, near Fletcher, and in the neighborhood of Mr. Munn's old place. Taylor was the partner, and lived in Bond street in pretty good style. The family was from Connecticut, and Knowles was a brother of the celebrated Jeremiah H. Taylor, who lived at 235 Pearl, and was a quiet, religious man, already alluded to in these pages.

Jonathan Little & Co.'s was a large silk importing house in its day. He was the President of the Marine Society of this city in 1817.

When this company commenced negotiating for the lands, they offered Mr. Munn a large price, half cash and half the price to remain on bond and mortgage. He knew his men too well. They were all rich, and he turned a deaf ear to the offer. He had fixed in his own mind, upon a just price for the lands for cash, and he would not submit to any deviation; therefore he named $200,000 cash. There was a short delay; but the spirit of speculation was abroad with spread wings, and flying all over the land, and this company paid the price demanded in cash, and received a deed of the lands.

That sale was the greatest god-send of his life. It relieved him from his embarrassments; and shortly after, when land fell in the city, he was enabled to make some splendid purchases, in localities that trebled in value. He was always engaged in lawsuits.

Stephen B. had a brother named Patrick Munn, who

was in the fur business in this city many years, commencing as early as 1800 in Burling slip; and I think that
brother was in business as late as 1830, but of this latter fact I am not certain.

I think the wife of Stephen B. Munn was a Connecticut girl, and came here with him. They had a large
family of children. Some of his daughters were magnificent girls, and greatly sought after, both for their
beauty and their probable wealth.

There were some runaway matches. One married
Captain Russell Glover, and it came under that head.
They are both living. Another runaway match was
with Captain Jack Pierce — handsome Jack, as he was
called. I must say that when he aired one of Wheeler's fashionable suits, he was a gay looking man. He
was captain of one of the Havre packets. He is dead.
There were three or four children from this marriage.

William A. Munn was another son. He lived with
his father at 503 Broadway, many years.

One son went West, and became a large merchant at
Ithica, N. Y. His name was Stephen, and the old man
bought the stock of goods for him, and paid for them
too. That son, I think, failed and made a bad thing of
it, and died. He left a son, Stephen, that I have not
seen for some years.

A daughter married Thos. F. Cornell, who was in
the pot and pearlash business at No. 7 Coenties Slip
many years, — once, I believe, with his brother Alexander and once was of the firm of Cornell & Cooper.

Mr. Cornell lived at No. 505 Broadway, next door
to his father-in-law, for a few years. Old Stephen
owned that property. Mr. Stokes married one daughter. John B. Borst, a broker in Wall street now, married a daughter, but she was the widow of Mr. Stokes,

when B. married her. A Mr. Beebe married a daughter.

I think one of his son's-in-law was a doctor — Marshall, it may be. Once the old man said to a friend : " When I left business, about 1820, I was worth, clear of the world, $800,000. I have not got half of it now. It has been eat up — drank up — squandered — spent — all used up — by all except one — that is the doctor; he has never drawn a cent out of me, and he shall have it all when I die." Who the doctor was I do not know. It is pretty certain that when Mr. Munn died, in 1855, or 56, his property would not have sold for a quarter of $800,000. But property rose in value greatly after his death. He left four executors to his will. One was Dr. Cheeseman, another was John A. Collyer of Binghampton, and the other two names I do not recollect. Under the judicious management of Mr. Collyer, his property realized more than it was ever expected it would do. Of the real estate on Broadway, that portion upon which Lord & Taylor's store stands brought $250,000. The two lots next to the St. Nicholas Hotel, extending through to Mercer street, brought $75,000 each. The estate produced a large sum.

He was a very shrewd man in every respect. A very good financial story is told of him. At one time, when he was closely cramped up, he made up a large package of " notes," and offered them for discount at the Mechanics' Bank, where he kept his heaviest account. He at once drew checks for all in the bank. He soon after received a note stating that his " account was overdrawn." He hurried to the bank and showed the note to the cashier. " What does this mean ? " he asked.

" Why, it means that you have overdrawn your account, Mr. Munn."

" I have done nothing of the sort, sir. See here, sir ; here is my account, and by it I have not overdrawn by several hundred dollars."

The teller was called, and the moment he cast his eye over the items, he exclaimed, " Why, Mr. Munn, you have credited yourself with notes that the bank has not yet agreed to discount. They are not *done* yet."

" Then why the devil don't you do them ? It is not *my* fault," replied Mr. Munn.

The notes were discounted by the bank, and it is not at all likely they would have been had not Mr. Munn been up to this financial *dodge.*

Stephen B. Munn in early life was excessively dissipated, but he afterwards reformed and became not only an extremely good business man, but a leading man in the Broome street Baptist Church, where the Rev. Dr. Cone preached so many years.

He was a man who did not regard time or place, when he wanted to make a strike. When the mother of Henry Laverty died, her funeral took place from her residence in Pump street.

Several solemn looking old citizens were present. Presently Mr. Munn arrived. He was greeted with mournful looks ; and finally, as he took a seat, he turned to an old crony.

" Well, Jack, what is the news in Wall street ? "

Once in Wall street he saw on the opposite side of the street, conversing with some highly respected friends, a man who owed him $25. Mr. Munn hailed him.

" B——, when are you going to pay that $25 you borrowed long ago. Promised to pay it several times. Never have seen it yet. Can't you pay five at a time ? Got any now ? Take a dollar on account."

It is unnecessary to say, that persons in the highest

walks of life were not at all anxious to become debtors
to Stephen B. Munn.

Once when he was passing along South street, in
front of Thomas H. Smith's great store, as it was called
thirty years ago, he saw several casks of Jamaica rum
just delivered from a custom house cellar, and ready
to be received by a prominent grocer, who had purchased the lot. He was an acquaintance of Mr. Munn's.

"Smith, I'll give you five cents a gallon more than
you paid, if you sell me a single cask."

The bargain was struck. Munn was to send for the
cask, in about an hour. He marked it very carefully.
A short time afterward, he was passing the grocer's
store, and he saw a negro pumping something out a
cask.

"What are you doing?" he asked of the darkey.

"Pumping out twenty gallons of this rum, and I'se
goin' to put in fifteen pure spirits and five gallons water. Don't stop me. I got to take the cask up back to
de great store in South street."

Stephen's eyes glistened. It was the cask he had
bought pure. He took a seat. Presently the grocer
arrived. Munn opened — told the whole story — at-
tracted a mob — and finally the mortified, cheating grocer ran off up the street, and eventually closed his business, and removed away.

In the days when Mr. Munn was in business, postage
was enormously high. He received an account sent to
him by a merchant in Cincinnati. There was an error
of four cents in the account. So soon as Stephen's book-
keeper, Mr. Hoyt, discovered it, he pointed it out to
Mr. Munn. The latter at once wrote the merchant
about it. The postage on the letter was twenty-five
cents. Indignant at such a payment, and determined

to punish Munn, he enclosed him by mail a package containing several old newspapers, and Stephen had to pay $2. He returned by mail a package which cost the Cincinnati man $5. This was continued to benefit the post office fund, to the extent of $80, when Cincinnati sent by mail the "log book" of a ship, for which Munn had to pay $17. He then concluded to confess beat, and stop that fun.

, He had another wealthy correspondent in St. Louis. The two had been *kiteing* along for several years, and there was a heavy interest account that had never been settled. It was always put off. Finally Mr. Munn said to his book-keeper, " I will give you a hundred dollars if you will go to work and make out the " interest account " of Mr. So-and-so." He agreed. The account was made, and showed a balance in Mr. Munn's favor of $4,300. Shortly after the St. Louis merchant arrived here very unexpectedly. Mr. Munn called his attention to that account. " I want it settled."

" Really, Mr. Munn, I came on here this trip for a family matter — not to do any buying, and I brought no funds with me," said St. Louis. " Well, I want the account settled, and it shall be settled. If you don't settle it at once I'll have you arrested," said Munn. The St. Louis man laughed, and walked away. Before night closed, sure enough he was arrested, and he called upon Munn with the deputy sheriff. At that time, to get out of prison one had to have common bail put in, and also special bail. " This is strange conduct, Mr. Munn, to a friend," said the indignant St. Louis man.

" Is it, indeed ? I told you I would have you arrested if you did not settle up that interest account, and I want to show you I am as good as my word. Now, old fellow, I'll go your common bail, and I'll be your spe-

THE OLD MERCHANTS

cial bail, and I'll lend you money to pay that account,
and $40,000 more if you need it, but *I'll have that ac-
count settled.*" It was settled to the satisfaction of that
odd genius, Mr. Munn. He hired Mr. Hoyt, his book-
keeper, from the navy yard. His duty was to keep books
and also the "petty cash." This cash is used to pay
small bills — postage, petty expenses, and amounts it was
not worth while drawing a check for.

Mr. Hoyt kept this cash, and every night found himself short two or three dollars. This, as an honest
book-keeper he charged to his own account, or made it
good out of his own pocket. Mr. Munn, very likely,
helped himself. At last the book-keeper said to him,
"Mr. Munn, I would feel obliged if you would leave a
memorandum in the drawer, stating amount and purpose, when you take money out of the drawer."

No attention was paid to this request. At last the
book-keeper found it was becoming a very serious loss.
So he got a lock-smith, and had a patent lock placed
upon it. He went to his dinner. When he returned,
he found Mr. Munn furious. "I can't get that drawer
open." Mr. Hoyt explained the reason. In a rage,
Mr. Munn went to a neighbor. "What sort of a book-
keeper do you think I have got? He wont let me take
my own money! It is my money. What business has
he got to lock it up?" His friend saw the matter clear-
ly, and explained it to Mr. Munn, and told him he ought
to be thankful that he had a conscientious cash keeper.

CHAPTER III.

The last chapter related especially to Stephen B. Munn, but I did not finish with all I recollected about him.

On one occasion, he called into a large " stationery " store down town, and there he espied a large cask of black sand. No one was in the store but a lad, who wished to be very smart, and make a large sale.

" What is the price of that barrel of sand ? " asked Stephen B. The boy put on a pretty stiff price, about double the cost, and watched with anxious eyes the suspense of his probable customer. Finally he spoke. " Young man, I will go home and make a calculation how much my bill will come to. " I will take half a pint of the sand." The lot ordered would have amounted to about a mill and a half. The old joker never took it.

A rich merchant with whom the relator was a clerk, held a mortgage upon the property owned by Mr. Munn, corner of Broadway and Grand street. It ran along Broadway several hundred feet. The property was worth ten times the amount for which it was mortgaged, but there was often delay in getting the interest. On this occasion, Stephen was in. The question was asked, or rather the object of the visit was stated as follows : " I called to get the interest on that mortgage of Mr. P.'s."

Mr. Munn — "Did you, indeed? Can you read the Bible, young man?"

" Yes, sir."

" I want you to read this chapter in the Book of Job."

Young man read a chapter, and Mr. Munn listened with the greatest attention. It was about a horse being clothed with thunder. After the chapter had been read, Mr. Munn observed : " Job was a great old fellow — wonderful genius. Now I'll give you a check for the interest money ; and, mind you, hereafter when you call I'll always give it to you ; if I do not, write me a note if I'm out, and I will leave a check when I come in. You read Job first rate."

For several years he paid the interest promptly, and at last relieved himself from calling by paying the principal.

When Mrs. Munn died a few years ago, at the residence 503 Broadway, her body was laid out in the house. Old Stephen could have been seen apparently measuring the width of the street all day. He set everybody to work conjecturing what he was trying to do.

His brother, Patrick Munn, was in the fur trade many years.

When Christian G. Gunther, the head of the fur house of C. G. Gunther & Son, arrived in this city forty-two years ago, he hired out to John G. Wendell, a brother-in-law of John Jacob Astor, and to this Patrick Munn. From these two he acquired his knowledge of furs. Wendell kept a furrier store at that time at No. 77 Maiden lane, and Munn at No. 291 Greenwich street. Stephen B. Munn was a heavy subscriber to the free school when it was first started.

" Thomas Suffern, h. 11 Washington sq.," says the Directory of 1861, at page 832.

If the " Tax book" was consulted, very likely his name would appear as paying taxes on one half a million of real estate, and half as much more on personal. Yet who would imagine what an active career that same man has had in this city, and how greatly he has added to its wealth and prosperity, while pursuing and achieving it for himself?

Ask nine men in ten who that apparently very aged man is, with such marked features, showing great energy and determined purpose, and they will tell you it is Mr. Thomas Suffern, an Irishman.

Mr. Suffern is an Irishman, but he reached this city very young — at least fifty-five years ago.

His uncle, George Suffern, kept a tobacco store at No. 2 Depeyster street, as early as 1792. The next year he moved to Nos. 4 and 6, where the store was kept as late as 1801, when Thomas removed to 166 Pearl street. There he kept until 1827, when he removed to 244 Pearl street, and remained there until he left business in 1837.

The old George Suffern did a tobacco business until 1810, when Thomas succeeded to that business. The entire family lived at No. 59 John street. The old gentleman had two nephews — Thomas, who took his business, and Edward, who was a lawyer at No. 29 Pine street, about the time of the war, 1814; all the rest died or retired, except Thomas, who kept the old store at No. 6 Depeyster, and lived at No. 59 John street.

Of the circumstances that led Mr. Thomas Suffern into a different business, I am not aware, buthe was for years largely engaged in the Irish dry goods importing.

2*

In 1827, or thereabouts, a French teacher came out from France, and settled at No. 29 Murray, corner of Church, north side. It was a modest two-story house. There he taught French by classes, and he also taught at private houses and in schools. Poor, modest Joseph Bœuf! He went back to France in 1836 with lots of money, and there, I believe, died. How many thousands, male and female, must recollect the mild, amiable Frenchman! He also took boarders, and taught them to eat French. He was the French teacher of his day. He taught 10,000 persons in this city the French language. Among his pupils, were Thomas Suffern, Walter Barrett, George McBride, Richard Tucker, John S. Hunt, S. P. Judah, and 500 more of solid New York names.

I confess my amazement even now at witnessing the energy with which Mr. Suffern went into French. He must have been fifty-six years old then (1834.) I believe he contemplated giving up business, and traveling in Europe.

He resided at that time in Park place, No. 23; the next year he moved up to Washington square, No. 11, where he yet lives. He lived at 80 Greenwich street for many years.

Thomas Suffern married a daughter of William Wilson a very wealthy merchant. Mr. W. lived to a very advanced age. He was an intimate friend of old George Suffern, the uncle of Thomas, and it was probably this intimacy that led to the marriage between the heir of the one and the daughter of the other.

Old George Suffern never married. His property descended to Thomas, his nephew.

William Wilson was such a man and merchant as I love to write about. He was a Scotchman. I do not

know when he came to this city ; but it must have been
soon after the Revolutionary war, for he was a member
of the St. Andrew's society in 1786, when old John
Mason was chaplain. He kept a store in 1790, at 215
Queen (Pearl) street.

I do not know what year William Wilson left business. He was a heavy importer of British dry goods.
His correspondents in Manchester, England, was the
firm of " Peel, Yates & Co." That Peel was the first
Sir Robert Peel, and father of the great Prime Minister,
About 1799, a son of Yates came out to this country.
At that time Mr. Wilson kept his store at 217 Pearl
street, near Fletcher. Young Yates came out to get
up a large business for Peel, Yates & Co. He was
fearfully dissipated, got in debt, and was finally locked
up in the debtor's jail, a square building that stood
where the Register's building now stands, in the Park.
It was a pleasant spot to live in. There was a bell in
the tower, and a railing around the cupola, where the
prisoners went to sun themselves. I believe young
Yates died there.

Mr. Wilson when he retired up town, gave up house-
keeping, and went to boarding. Among his most intimate cronies were John I. Glover, who had a country
house out of town, William Renwick, and Thomas Buchanan, a great merchant — Scotch too. He lived in a
house that stood where the Merchant's Exchange now
stands, in Wall street, and Thomas Pearsall married a
daughter of Mr. Buchanan. Mr. Gilfert died only a
year ago. He has a son, a doctor, in the city.

Leonard Kip, a lawyer, married a daughter of William Wilson, and is a brother-in-law of Mr. Suffern,
and has attended to his legal business for many years.
1 believe Mr. Wilson had no sons.

Mr. Wilson attended Dr. John Mason's church in Cedar street, until Mr. Mason left it for his new one. Dr. McElroy afterwards preached in that church. There were three of these Scotch churches in this city. One in Pearl, between Elm and Broadway; another was McElroy's; and the new Murray street Presbyterian church, where Dr. Mason removed. Mr. Wilson furnished the money to build the church in Murray street. He was originally connected with it, through its venerable pastor. The church in Murray street was finished about 1812, and I think that about that time Mr. Wilson went out of business. He was treasurer of the church. Mr. Suffern also attended that church; so did old tobacco George Suffern. It is singular, too, that an Irishman should be a warm Scotch Presbyterian; yet such was and is Mr. Suffern, for he is now eighty years old, at least.

The Murray street church was taken down in 1842, and removed to Eighth street, near Broadway, its present location. Though it looks to be the same church, yet it is really much smaller. The church occupied four lots in Murray street, and only three in the present locality. The pews, and so forth, are all smaller. It has been sold for a Catholic church, and that denomination now occupy it.

Mr. Suffern ceased to attend the Murray street church long before it was moved up town. He joined Dr. Hutton's church, next to the University building, and the corner of Washington place, facing the Parade ground, and near his residence.

Mr. Suffern has become a large real estate owner, and is immensely rich. He inherited from his uncle and his wife very large properties from each. He is liberal to his church, and frequently gives it $1,000 or $1,500 to help it along.

I believe his only son, a young man of twenty-two years, died a few years ago. He has daughters. One he sent to a Catholic school to finish her education, and she became a Catholic in earnest, much to the annoyance of her father. His business was an importer of Irish linens, diapers, &c.

A stranger who visits Depeyster street to-day, can form no idea of what it was in 1800, and a hundred years previous. It is a narrow street extending from Water street to the water (South street.) It is a fair sample of Dutch streets in New Amsterdam, and also of streets in Old Amsterdam and in Rotterdam (where the author lived a few years) to this day.

One of the Depeysters lived on the corner of Pine and Depeyster streets, and the mansion is still there with its tile roofs. It is occupied now by John D. Hennesay, builder.

It was built at least a hundred years ago. In the Revolution, the house adjoining of same age, was kept as a crack hotel, and British officers boarded there. The upper part is now a tenement house.

William Wilson was one of the " old school " benevolent old gents. He was one of the few that met at the City Hotel, Nov. 29, 1816, to start a " Saving's Bank." They did it too, although the bank did not commence operation until the 3d of July, 1819. Mr. Wilson was one of the first trustees. So was George Arcularius, the baker so many years in Cortlandt street. He was born in the old house that stood until recently at 11 Frankfort street, now occupied by the *Leader* building.

Old Philip I. Arcularius, a tanner and currier, put up the old building, No. 11 Frankfort, about 1794. Ex-mayor James Harper married Miss Arcularius, the daughter of Philip I., in the same building, and glorious old times have come off on the premises.

The author of this book has an arranged list of merchants that he intends to write about sooner or later. Among the names of firms in his portfolio, is that of " Bogart & Kneeland," one of the oldest and most respected commercial houses in this city. They started in business at 71 South street, in the year 1804.

The attention of the author has been called to this " firm," by a most melancholy occurrence that happened at 49 William street, on the afternoon of the 2d of August.

The firm is still Bogart & Kneeland, and continues in the cotton business, although the partners of fifty-seven years ago must have been dead long since. The sign over the present locality is 55 years old.

Fifty-eight years ago, Henry Kneeland, of the firm of Bogart & Kneeland, had his private residence at No. 183 William, near Beckman street. He resided there some years, and probably in that same house, young Kneeland, who killed himself, was born. Here is the story :

" *Suicide of a Merchant in William Street.*—Coroner Gamble was called upon yesterday to hold an inquest upon the body of Henry Kneeland, a brother of Mr. Kneeland, of the firm of Bogart & Kneeland, cotton merchants, No. 49 William street, who committed suicide on Friday afternoon, by shooting himself in the head with a pistol. Henry K. Bogart, the partner of deceased's brother, testified that Mr. Kneeland came into the office as above about three o'clock on Friday afternoon, and closed the door. Mr. Bogart asked him why he closed the door, but deceased took a seat and made no reply ; deceased then made use of some inco-

herent language, in which the word " dishonorable " occurred, and drawing a pistol out of his coat pocket, shot
himself through the head. Witness ran for a physician
immediately, but all medical skill proved of little avail,
as the unfortunate man lived but a few moments; deceased never threatened to commit suicide, nor had the
witness any idea that he contemplated such a thing;
deceased had been pecuniarily embarrassed for some
time past, and it is supposed that the derangement of
his financial affairs led to the commission of the rash
act. The jury rendered a verdict in accordance with
the above facts, and the body was handed over to the
friends for interment. Deceased resided at Fairfield,
Ct., where he leaves a large family to lament his un-
timely end. Mr. Kneeland was a native of New York,
and was fifty-four years of age."

The Mr. Kneeland who founded the great cotton
house was the subject of scandal connected with Rosina
Townsend, in 1836, when Helen Jewett was murdered.
It was said that when he died, proofs were found among
his returned checks and papers that he had paid $30,000
to suppress publications about the matter.

CHAPTER IV.

The most interesting class of merchants for these chapters, are those that connect the small port, and the mammoth city — the New York after the war, with its 12,000 population, and forty years later, when it was the greatest city of this continent, and had fairly commenced to be the greatest city in the world.

The personal history of the merchants of such a period has a charm at the present time, eighty years later. There are aged men in this city, yet alive, who were boys here in those days, 1780. Many who remember quite distinctly events of ten or twenty years later, and who on holidays were permitted to make country excursions from this city. A favorite one was to cross the fields, jumping brooks and little streams, from where Chamber street touches the Park north, north-west to a country tavern, about where Spring street market, on the North River, now is.

It would be a fine thing to know the exact nature of the kind of business of the different merchants in those days. Before me are two bills for hollow ware, £10, October 3, 1771, and receipted by Edward & William Laight. William signed that in his small, lady-like handwriting. Another is dated April 28, 1772, and signed by the coarser handwriting of Edward.

Another receipted bill is dated New York February 25, 1766, and signed Walter & Thomas Buchanan — a great old firm in our infant New York. I know it was Thomas who signed that receipt, because I have another dated May 17, 1780, for £339 11*s.* 3*d.* in full, for checks and calicoes. That is signed Thomas Buchanan & Co., and it is the same bold, old English writing of 1766. So I know that Thomas signed both. The firm had changed ; Walter had not died, but had gone out of business probably, for his name is down as a resident member of the St. Andrew's Society in 1786.

Then I have another for £607, an account of bill of spirits, dated June 21, 1780. That is signed for Thomas Buchanan & Co., by John B. Coles. Of course I know by that, that John B. Coles was a clerk with the great commercial firm of T. B. & Co.

Only a few years later, however, Coles went into business on his own account, at No. 12 Dock street (it ran from Broad to Hanover square, in what is now Pearl street.) He was a large flour merchant in 1795. He moved from No. 82 Pearl (No. 39 Great Dock street) to No. 1 South street, where he had his store, and No. 1 State street, where he resided.

If in the whole city of New York, such a combination of convenience, health, pleasantness, and near to business, can be found, I do not know where it can be. No. 1 State street and No. 1 South street. At both places he could look upon the ships passing up both the North and East rivers. The slip at Whitehall must have come up within a few feet of his house. He could stand on his handsome door steps, whistle or hold up his finger, and in an instant he would have had three or more of the original Whitehall bargeman rowing up to him. Then he could go out with one, and have a

row all around the harbor, at that time without being
run over by anything more furious than a slow moving
horseboat ; for in those days, sixty years and odd ago,
there were no steamboats racing up and down, and but
few ships entered the harbor.

Then, too, our wealthy old merchant could get up at
daybreak, look out of his window, and see what old
cronies were walking upon the Battery.   Then he could
stroll there before breakfast, and while drinking the
glorious breeze fresh from the salt sea, could shake hands
with his constituents, for John B. Coles was alderman
from 1797 to 1801 — the period I now write about,
as he was again in 1815 to 1818, also alderman of the
good old-fashioned first Ward.   In these days, all the
wealth, aristocracy and dignity lived in the first Ward,
and it was an honor to be its alderman.

After breakfast Alderman John had only to walk
down the east side of Whitehall street (for he lived at
the corner of State,) a few rods, and then he found his
flour store all ready to receive him.   " Boy, give me the
spy-glass," would he say to the junior clerk, and raising
it up he would peer over Governor's Island, to see if the
vessel telegraphed to the signal on the Battery was coming up or not.

John B. Coles must have loved that locality.   He
lived at No. 1 State street until 1810, when he moved
to No. 2, giving up No. 1 to one of his boys.   He had
several.   U. C., Isaac U., B. U., W. F. and one John
B. Jr.   The last lived at No. 1 State street, and in the
year previous kept a flour store at No. 32 Stone street.
I think that one died in 1811 or 1812.   Oliver kept at
29 Old Slip, and afterwards Isaac U. kept there, but
finally all the sons kept at No. 1 South street.   Then
they took in a Mr. Morris, and for a few years the firm

was Coles & Morris. From 1812 until 1825, I do not
think old John B. Coles meddled with business much,
but left it entirely to his sons, and son-in-law, for Mr.
Morris married a daughter, but in 1825 and 1826 the
business was carried on under his name, and those of
his sons do not appear to have been connected with him.

I think he died in 1826 or 1827. He probably was
eighteen or twenty years old in 1780, when he signed
his autograph as clerk to Thomas Buchanan & Co.,
and if he had lived until to-day, would have been a hundred.

I notice that there is a John B. Coles in the present
day. If he is a descendant of the old New Yorker that
I write about, I will cheerfully give him the document
I have alluded to signed for six hundred pounds. It is
worth keeping. At least so I should regard it, if anybody would give me " Walter Barrett's " signature dated 1780, and he was to be a great-grandfather of mine,
or even a grandfather. It is not everybody who can go
back on an ancestor in this town, and find that he was
a worthy old Knickerbocker, and particularly exhibiting
such uncommon sense as to select a store at No. 1 South
street, and a dwelling at No. 1 State street.

In 1827, his sons Isaac U. and William T. Coles,
kept on the old business, and like their father showed
great good sense in keeping in the old vicinity for residences. Isaac lived at No. 1 State, and William at No.
2, next to each other, for on the opposite side of State
street is the Battery, and of course the numbers are
continuous. There they lived and continued in business together at No. 1 South street until 1832, when
Isaac U. left his brother, and started business at 28
Front street. In 1833 William left business and State
street. I am not certain that he died there.

Isaac kept on business until 1834, when he moved from No. 1 State street to 50 Bond, then becoming aristocratic. He gave up his store in Front street in May, 1835. He resided in Bond street until 1851. It was occasionally a marked house, from the fact that year after year, it was hermetically sealed. From 1836, on a few years, I do not believe it was ever entered. It was as solemn as if a dozen murders had been committed there. The memory of such men as John B. Coles ought not to die. But where has aught been written about them, save my Old Merchants?

These will not perish, in this handsome book. It is for this reason we ask our readers, and the friends and relatives of the names mentioned, to correct them when they see errors, and send it to me.

I do not claim to be perfect, or any way near it, but this I do claim — I have done more to rescue from oblivion the names of New York merchants, than any other author that has ever lived.

I would do more if I had the materials. There are many that exist which could be placed at my disposal, and be made to serve a useful purpose. How many have family record, — documents connected with commerce, — statements of trade, lying useless, from 1700 to 1800, that would be to Walter Barrett invaluable.

I would use such material, sift out chaff from wheat, and work it up into a form that will be imperishable, as I have this.

I have said that Mr. Coles did a flour business. He was in it, or his sons, for a period of over forty-six years. He was a man much respected. He was one of the directors in the Bank of New York. He was elected in 1806, and continued year after year until 1820, and how much longer I do not know. This is an endorsement not fully appreciated. A merchant may be once elected a director of this time-honored old bank, the first started in the State, in 1784, when Mr. Coles commenced business; but to be re-elected year after year, is paying the highest tribute to any man's capacity, integrity and character; for to be a director in that bank long, one must possess all these.

It would be difficult to say what benevolent society or moneyed corporation Mr. Coles was not connected with. He gave his name to every good work, and when he gave his name he worked for the institution.

Mr. William Neilson married a daughter of John B. Coles, and his children have married to some of our first people. Robert Gracie married a daughter of Mr. Neilson. So did Charles E. Borrowe.

With this digression finished, I now return to the original receipt.

Thomas Buchanan was a king among merchants. He did a very large business, and his firm must have been in existence for full fifty-five years. I know it was in 1766 as Walter & Thomas Buchanan. Between that date and the close of the Revolution the firm changed, and it became Thomas Buchanan & Co. It is likely that Walter was the partner, although for some cause unknown to me ninety-five years later, his name does not appear.

They separated in 1772, and Thomas then continued his mammoth business on his own hook at 41 Wall street. Walter started a separate concern in Liberty street. He kept there some years and then moved to his son Walter W.'s residence at 4 Duane street, where I think he must have died about the close of 1804. That son, Doctor Walter W., was a remarkable man. He lived in Hudson street not far from Duane, No. 45, until the war. Then he moved away and was gone until 1825. He came back to the city that year, and lived at 114 Grand street, corner of Broadway. Again he disappeared, and I have no track of him.

Thomas Buchanan became very prominent on his own account from 1792 to 1809, when he took in his son George, and the firm was Thomas Buchanan & Son. The firm kept at 44 Wall (just below the present Exchange) as late as 1816, when they removed their counting house to 4 Slote lane (now Beaver,) and his residence to No. 64 Broadway. George lived at the home of his parents. In 1819 old Thomas died. Notwithstanding, the firm was kept up until 1824, the business being conducted by George Buchanan. At that time it was not necessary to change the style of a mercantile firm when a prominent partner died. That year too, George disappeared from commercial life. The old lady, Almy, the widow of Thomas Buchanan, continued to reside in the old mansion, 64 Broadway, (just above Beaver) as late as 1832. I do not know when she died. She was a fair sample of an old New York merchant's wife.

Two of the sons of Peter Goelet, Peter P. and Robert Ratze, married daughters of Mr. Buchanan, and consequently Peter Goelet of 1861, that lives in Nineteenth street, is a grandson of both the noble old merchants.

Margaret Roberts, formerly Margaret Buchanan, I believe is still alive. His daughter Almy married a Mr. Hicks, and his youngest Thomas Pearsall. Thomas Buchanan was buried from 64 Broadway, as Peter Goelet was from 53 Broadway, when he died.

There are no such funerals in these days. Grand old funerals — it was worth living in those times, jus. to have the pleasure of going to the stylish, comfortable

funeral of an old Knickerbocker. Nothing of that kind
can be got up now. In the first place, we lack the negroes. In those days the servants were all colored, and
when their master was to be buried, they were dressed
in black, with white towels on their arms. All the
rooms in the house were flung open. Everybody received scarfs and gloves, and such wines! There are
no such wines now in existence as were to be had at an
old Knickerbocker funeral. Both Peter Goelet and
Thomas Buchanan had Maderia wine in their cellars
one hundred years old. Dust, an inch thick, upon the
bottles. All the friends went to such funerals. So did
acquaintances, for it was only on such occasions that
people could get wine to drink — the best, even in those
days of cheapness, $10 per bottle. Could it be had now,
it would be worth $100 per bottle; but it is not to be
had. Such wine is not in existence. Thomas Buchanan was in business when this city had but 10,381 souls.
He was here through all the dark hours of the Revolution, and he lived to see it grow to 120,000. He, modest merchant, little dreamed that it was he and such as.
he, kings of commerce, that had made it grow so greatly, and increase so vastly in wealth.

Where are your Clintons — your Tompkins, Jays
— your Burrs, Hamiltons, and the names that adorn
history — mere politicians or so called statesmen, when
compared with the creators of the wealth and the glory of the great commercial city.

The merchants were the bees that made the honey —
the drones were the statesmen that made the noise.

De Witt Clinton has all the glory of the canal. He
was the fly on the coach wheel. The merchants of
whom I spoke were the spokes, the axles, the wheel
itself. They had made money by commerce, and they

lavished it in building the great canal, destined to return its cost a hundred times to the generous city and
the generous merchants who planned and built it.

It is such names that I am placing on an imperishable record. Even tradition, in a few years, will forget the very names of the true founders of this city,
and such I rank those alluded to in this chapter.

It is almost impossible to tell how closely in every
way, manner and shape, Thomas Buchanan identified
himself with the interests of the city, in commerce,
finance, charity, and every benevolent society.

As early as 1792, he was one of the governors of
the New York hospital.

In 1834 he was a director of the old United States
Branch Bank in this city, and continued so for many
years.

Another old firm in 1780 was John and Francis At-
kinson. They did a very heavy importing business.
Their store was at No. 223 Queen (Pearl) street,
about Burling slip. They kept on during the war, and
Francis was among the founders of the St. George's
Society, in this city (1786.) In fact, he belonged to a
St. George's Society that existed before the war. His
brother John became a member in 1788; and his neph-
ew, John Jr., in 1809. They kept their firm at 123
Pearl street as late as 1795. In 1801, John Atkinson
& Son kept on the business. Francis had retired.
Their store was at 132 Pearl street, and they lived at
No. 20 Courtlandt street many years. As late as 1819
the firm was kept up at 167 Pearl street, and that year
changed to J. Atkinson Jr., and G. H. They lived
upon Hudson square. Next year it was Atkinson &
Fleming. I think Augustus Fleming had joined the
brother,— the old John had died. The firm of A. & F.

was kept up as late as 1825, when John Jr. removed to Wall street. He lived at No. 152 Greenwich street. The widow of old John lived at No. 126 Chambers street many years, as late as 1830, and then they passed away from my memory.

Twenty years ago I knew a tall man, who lived at 534 Pearl street, and who was named Atkinson. He was a naturalist, and talented. I was well acquainted with him then. Last night I met the same six-foot iron-gray head, coming down Hudson street, and I have an idea that same man is a descendant of the ancient English Atkinsons, the merchants before the Revolution.

3

CHAPTER V.

The old book-keepers (and there are thousands of this class in the city, regulating the financial records of the merchants,) have had some remarkable men among them. An extraordinary one I remember, named Pierpont, who was book-keeper for many years to G. G. & S. Howland. Another was Richard Wilson, who had been book-keeper in London for the great bankers "Smith, Payne & Smith." He came on here and kept books for Oldfield, Bernard & Co., and Gracie, Prime & Co., and finally went to Baltimore, where he became Secretary to the American Life and Trust Company, started there some twenty-five years ago, and of which a branch was established in this city under charge of Morris Robinson, one of the best financiers of his day. He was a long time cashier of the U. S. Branch Bank in this city. The building stood next door to the Custom House, Wall street, and is now occupied by Sub-Treasurer Cisco.

In the first volume of this work I mentioned Charles Henry Hall, who was book-keeper to Thomas H. Smith & Son, the great tea merchants. I mentioned that his successor as book-keeper was William Roberts. Afterwards Mr. Roberts carried on business under his own name at the great store of Thomas H. Smith & Co.,

166 South street. He was there two years up to 1829, then established himself at No. 1 Wall street, corner of Broadway, in the basement. Probably there was never a finer stock of choice brandies and wines than he kept ; and he did a very large business, for he was well known to nearly all the leading business men in the city. His residence in those days, from 1831 and on, was at No. 2 Vesey street, where the Astor House stands. He rented it from John Jacob Astor, whose book-keeper he had been until he went to keep the books of Thomas Smith & Son, the tea importers.

Speaking of this firm, puts me in mind that I met and shook hands with young Tom only two weeks ago, under St. Paul's statue, and a hearty greeting we had. I never have seen young Tom look better. He invited me to his country house down on Long Island, and seemed quite distressed when I refused to go and drink with him to the memory of the dead, with whom we have both been more or less connected in this and the last century.

I do not know the precise day when his father, old Tom, started business in New York city, but it must have been before 1800. His name was Thomas Howell Smith, and he was in 1801 at 196 Front street. He kept a wholesale and retail grocery store. The next year after he took in a son-in-law, George W. Bruen, as a partner. The latter was a son of Mat. Bruen, of the firm of M. & J. Bruen, merchants at 177 Broadway, sixty years ago. It was in 1803 that the firm of Thomas H. Smith & Son began to be generally known. From grocers they rose to be the greatest tea importers in the United States.

I suppose in the thirty years that followed, Thomas H. Smith was one of the greatest of the old school mer-

chants. He had some of the most extraordinary men
with him as clerks.

Peter G. Hart was one, but it is a very curious circumstance that when Thomas H. Smith & Son moved
from their old store, No. 196, in 1806, that Hart
should have left their employ, and started the wholesale
grocery business in the same place, and there he continued standing for twenty odd years, gaining daily, and
becoming very rich, while old Mr. Smith branched out,
and became ruined. Peter G. Hart had his store at
No. 196 Front street as late as 1827, when he died.
He resided at 35 Beekman street, and the family were
attendants of Dr. Milnor's church. He left several
charming daughters. The widow, after his death,
moved to No. 127 Hudson street. She afterwards
moved to 535 Broadway, two doors this side of John
G. Coster's house (now Chinese building.) I think
that property was left to Widow Peter. She afterwards
went to East Sixteenth street.

Mr. Roberts was a very methodical man in his business, very precise and careful, and was very reliable in
all matters of accounts. Long after he had left Mr.
Astor's employ, that gentleman used to go and see him
to consult about accounts. The famous lawsuit, " Ogden vs. Astor," was settled up by Mr. Roberts, who
died only last year (1863,) and was living at the time
in Prince street, next door to Mr. W. B. Astor's office.
Mr. Roberts gave up active business about 1840. He
has a son, Dr. Roberts, who lives in University place,
corner Thirteenth street. He married a daughter of
Martin Hoffman, who was a great auctioneer in his day,
and father of L. M. Hoffman who died a few days ago.
Martin Hoffman was a great merchant once. He was
of the house of Hoffman & Seton, auctioneers. Old

Hoffman married a Miss Seton. If I was to write all that I could about those Hoffmans, I should have to commence back as far as 200 years ago, when Martin Hoffman was an auctioneer in 1661. I can't swear positively that he was an auctioneer, but I know he was a large tax payer in that year, and of course decidedly Dutch. He lived (the 1661 gent,) in *De Heere Straat.*

Of all the Hoffmans, I am more pleased with the Martin Hoffman who flourished just after the Revolution, and who was father of several children, among them, Lindley Murray and Martin, I remember very well. There was a daughter, Sarah. I think she married a Roberts ; she was born in 1783. L. M. Hoffman was born in 1793. He had an elder brother named Daniel M., and another named Martin.

Martin (of 1790 memory) was a public-spirited man and took an interest in everything that was going on in New York then. He made three of his children Tontine stockholders, and it is curious that out of 203 shares, based on 197 lives, Lindley Murray Hoffman was born last, 1793. He died a few months ago. Martin Hoffman was in everything. He belonged to a fire-company, 1791. In 1792 he was a Sachem of Tammany Hall, and in business on his own account at No. 67 Water street that year. He was captain in the first Regiment of Infantry, 1792. He was master of St. Andrew's Lodge (Free Mason.) In 1795 he founded the auction and commission house of Hoffman & Seton ; the store was at No. 67 Wall street. His partner was one of *the* Setons. It was a great family sixty years ago. The head was William Seton, cashier of the Bank of New York, when it was first chartered, 1784. There was Andrew and William, Jr., and James and Charles. William, the older, was of the great house of Seton, Maitland & Co., they did business at 61 Stone street, and old William lived over the counting-room. His partner was William Maitland. I think Charles Seton was the partner of Hoffman & Seton, afterwards H. S. & Co.

In 1808, Mr. Hoffman took in a Mr. Glass as a partner, and did the same business at 67 Wall street, under the firm of Hoffman & Glass. That concern continued in business under that style until 1822, when they took in L. M. Hoffman a partner, and added a Co. to it. Old Mr. Hoffman lived up Broadway, near Jones street. In 1823, Mr. Hoffman took in his son L. M., and a Mr. Pell, and the firm was Hoffman, Son & Pell, at No. 65 Wall street. The other son, Martin, Jr., did an auction business on the corner of Wall and Pearl, but lived with his father, while L. M. was keeping house at No. 113 Grand street. In 1826, both of these sons joined their father, and kept on the auction business at No. 63 Wall street, under the firm of M. Hoffman & Sons.

Mr. Pell kept the old store at No. 65, and did business under the firm of W. F. Pell & Co. Never lived in this city a handsomer race of men than those Pells. Old William was a noble old fellow, and his sons William and Waldron were also splendid fellows. I think the old gentleman, Mr. Hoffman, died in 1827. He was buried from No. 691 Broadway, but the firm was not changed for some years, or until the law was passed to the effect that no name should be used in a firm, unless it really was in it. In 1834, the old firm was changed to L. M. Hoffman & Co. — Martin, Jr. being the company — and they moved from the old store near Pearl, down to No. 83 Wall. Some years later, they moved to No. 111 Pearl, in Hanover square, and this firm was not changed, but was there down to 1861. Martin, the brother of L. M., I believe died some years ago at Maranoneck; and I think young L. M. Jr., was in the dry good business. Now these younger ones, grandsons of the famous Martin of 1790, still keep up the old business, under the firm of L. M. Hoffman's, Son & Co., at No. 111. Next door to them, at No. 109, under the style of Pells & Co., are these old neighbors of thirty-five years ago, when one house was at No. 63 and the other at No. 65 Wall street.

When L. M. Hoffman died, a few weeks ago, the journals were filled with notices of him. The Chamber of Commerce passed resolutions of condolence. He de-served them all, for he was an honorable merchant, and a useful citizen. He was as mild and gentle as a lamb. I do not know that he ever spoke an unkind word to any one in his life. He never did a mean action since he was born.

I had an idea that he would be one of the seven per-sons that would have inherited that property. His chances were far better than others who still live. There is a curious history yet to be written about that Tontine building, if one could get at all the facts. Here are some of them. The building now standing, and which is the second erected, stands at the north-west corner of Wall and Water streets, and was com-menced in 1792 by an association of New York mer-chants, and completed in 1794. There had previous-ly been no proper place where the merchants could meet to do business. By the constitution, 203 shares were subscribed for $200 a share. Each share entitled the holder to name a *life* of each sex. Each nominee had his or her age and parentage stated by the nominee. During such nominee's life, the subscriber received his equal proportion of the net income of the establishment. Upon the death of the nominee, the subscriber's interest ceased, and his interest became merged in the owners of the surviving nominees.

The original shares were assignable and held as personal estate, and the whole property was vested in five trustees, who were to be continued in trust, or by succession, until the number of nominees was reduced to seven, when the holders of these shares, contingent upon these surviving nominees, became entitled to a conveyance in fee of the whole premises to be equally divided between them.

The nominee himself did not necessarily have an interest in the association ; for each subscriber, in naming a person, generally a child, looked to such as had a promise of length of days.

For instance, old Martin Hoffman nominated before March, 1795 — three of his children — one born 1791 — 1792 — and 1793. L. M. was the latest date — none later. His chance was good for many years. One nominee was born as early as 1752. Martin was born between 1778 and 1790. William Gracie was a nominee. There are now alive Chas. King, born 1789 — John, born 1787 — and Archibald Gracie born 1791, and others whose names I don't know. The constitution was signed November 4, 1794.

All the meetings of citizens were held in the Tontine Coffee house. All the famous charities of the city were born there. So were banks and coporations. A grievance was remedied by a meeting at the old Tontine Coffee house, and it decided everything.

It was a hotel, too. George Frederick Cook died there in 1812.

The Merchants' Exchange was kept in this grand building in the large room, until 1825.

It was thirty feet square.

I remember how Colonel Gracie used to walk to the looking-glass, pull up his shirt collar, and say :

" Don't I look as though my chance for the Tontine, one seventh, is as good as any one else ? "

Alas, his chances died with him in 1840 — twenty years and more ago.

I presume the men of that day named all their children who were born then. Rufus King subscribed heavy. So did Archibald Gracie. He named William and Archibald.

Among the males yet left, beside those named are G. C. Verplanck, 1786 ; William Bayard, 1791.

It was called the Tontine Coffee House ; but the subscribers, when the Exchange opened, got a decree of Chancery authorizing them to let the premises for general purposes, in 1834.

In 1843, the legislature altered the title to " Tontine Building."

On the 4th of June, 1861, it had existed sixty-seven years.

Originally there were 137 males and 66 females, 203 ; 3 females and 3 males were duplicated, so that really only 197 names were mentioned.

Some parties, a few years ago, made a new proposition. They agreed to put up a new building, which should revert to the seven left, provided they, the builders, had the rent of it for the balance of the time. For this they agreed to pay the Tontine trustees the sum of $20,000 per annum: The new building, it was agreed, should not cost less than $40,000.

I now return to William Roberts. He adopted a

young lady as his daughter, who afterwards became the
wife of the celebrated Doctor Alexander F. Vaché, who
was an old New Yorker, and loved it too, as he did his
own soul. Though not a merchant, yet it will not be
out of place to mention the son of an old New Yorker,
who was old John Vaché, and was the first artificial
flower merchant and manufacturer that ever lived in
New York. He commenced his business at 28 Liberty
street in 1790, and he continued it there until he moved
to Newark in 1827. •

I do not know where the old gentleman died, but I
believe his family reside in Newark. Yet Alexander,
the doctor, was born at 28 Liberty street, before this
century. It was upon the old house, No. 28, that he
mounted his first shingle in 1826, " Alexander F. Vaché,
M. D." That was a proud hour for the young medical.
He had been a favorite pupil with the celebrated Dr.
Mott. He was a graduate of the College of Physicians
and Surgeons of the University of the city of New York.
He was also a great friend of the celebrated Professor
Samuel L. Mitchell, who thought the world of the
young surgeon. He persuaded young Vaché, in 1821,
to join a scientific expedition, and sailed from here for
the Pacific Ocean in the U. S. ship Franklin, Commodore Charles Stewart, (was is yet living, and the oldest
Commodore in the American Navy.) When the party
got out to the coast of Chili, mercantile events arising
out of the revolutionary condition of the country so
limited the field of sientific observation by confining the
ship to that immediate coast, that Dr. Vaché joined the
frigate Constitution, Commodore Ridgeley, and returned to the United States, after an absence of two years.
In 1825, the Doctor again went to sea with Captain J.
H. Clark, U. S. navy, in the double capacity of mess-

mate and surgeon, on a voyage to the river Amazon.
The object was to ascertain its navigability, and connections with the interior of the South American provinces. The Emperor of Brazil would not permit any
outsider to do what he could not do himself, and he ordered them off, refusing positively permission to ascend
the Amazon. On her return the ship stopped at several ports and places. In this experience among tropical
diseases, the Doctor was fitting himself in an admirable
manner for the office of Health Physician at the Quar-
antine ground, that he afterwards filled.

Dr. Vaché was very much beloved by all who knew
him. He was an active politician in the Sixth Ward.
He was a great friend of William Leggett, Richard
Adams Locke, Ulysses D. French, and others. The
doctor was one of the original Loco-Focos of 1835 and
'36. He was a prominent member of the County Convention of the latter year. He was one of the signers
of the letter to Colonel R. M. Johnson and to Mr.
Van Buren. The course pursued by Dr. Vaché elected Edward Curtis and James Monroe to Congress that
year.

The doctor was the most ingenious casuist of the
Loco-Foco party. He spoke at all the meetings in an
earnest tone of voice, smooth, low, and he used the
nicest words and a style to fastidiousness. The doctor
was a great favorite with the highest leaders in the party. All knew him personally. He left a fine family
of children, one daughter and several sons. He died
some years since.

Charles Henry Hall, who in later years was book-
keeper to Thomas H. Smith & Son, had been brought
up by the old house of Murray & Mumford, alluded to
to before this, and was a clerk with them as late as 1804.

My friend Thomas Quick, suggests that I should give a full description of Mr. Humphreys, who once owned the house of Phil. Hone, in Broadway, next to Park Place (save one door,) and occupied by the commercial firm of young Fred. Tracy. His name was William Humphreys, and sixty years ago he lived at 311 Broadway, in 1804, and was of the firm of Humphreys & Whitney in Burling slip. They lasted many years.

CHAPTER VI.

There have been many merchants of great celebrity in this city, named Lawrence, but among all the Lawrence race, none have been more remarkable than the brothers John and Isaac Lawrence. John was in business during the war, and lived and did business at 162 Queen street (Pearl.) In 1795 he took in his younger brother Isaac, who had been clerk with him for two years previous, and the new sign was placed over the store 154 Water, corner of Fly market. Isaac had received a collegiate education at Princeton College, and intended to become a lawyer, but his health was poor, and he went into business with his brother John. The firm of John & Isaac Lawrence continued until 1803, when the brothers separated after doing a very prosperous and extended commerce. They were owners of vessels, shippers of goods abroad, and importers. They did a very heavy West India business. This was owing to their having relations established in the West India Islands. In fact, they had a brother named William, who owned a plantation in Demarara, where he died. Another brother named Richard was also an eminent merchant in New York, and died at Hell Gate, where he owned a country seat in 1816.

When the house of J. & I. Lawrence dissolved, the

store was at 208 Pearl, and Isaac lived at 40 Courtlandt street. Isaac continued on with the business at
the same place, 208 Pearl, until 1814. He was out of
business until 1817, when he became President of the
United States Branch Bank, that had been established
in this city. The office was then kept at 65 Broadway.
His residence at that time was at 480 Broadway. He
afterwards moved into a handsome house he had built
at 498 Broadway, above Broome.

John Lawrence, the partner of Isaac, lived at 82
Murray street. He was a great man in this city, and
engaged in all the benevolent projects. He was a Governor of the New York hospital, a Trustee of Columbia College, and a Member of Congress. There were
several John Lawrences living in New York at the close
of the last century, but the one I am now describing,
who died in the summer of 1817, if I am not mistaken,
had been in Congress. He left several daughters.
They married into some of the first families. One married John Campbell, another Benj. F. Lee, one John P.
Smith, another Timothy G. Churchill. After he
moved from Murray street, Mr. John Lawrence lived at
391 Broadway.

Isaac Lawrence was a merchant in the most extended
sense and meaning of the word. From 1795 to 1815
there was not as great a chance to make extended operations as a few years ago. He had been a director in
the old United States Bank that was located in the city,
and so also was his brother John. That old Bank of
the United States commenced operation before 1792.
I think its charter expired in 1811. The president of
the bank, in this city, was old Philip Livingston at its
commencement, and at its close Cornelius Ray. The
directors were such men as I have written about —

Thomas Buchanan, John Atkinson, Thomas Pearsall, William Laight, William Bayard, Jacob Le Roy, and Archibald Gracie. Jonathan Burrell was its cashier from 1791 to 1811. He lived in a fine old mansion at 49 Pine street.

When the Bank of America was chartered in 1812, the leading merchants who got it up had an idea that it would take the place of the United States Bank. Hence its comprehensive name, Bank of America. They made the late cashier of the United States Bank, Jonathan Burrell, cashier. He afterwards became vice-president, and he continued so until 1819. He lived then up at 388 Broadway, where, I think, he died.

Jonathan Burrell was a great patron of one of the most extraordinary characters of his day. I mean a New York barber named John B. Huggins. He flourished his razor for many years, about the commencement of this century, and as late as 1808. Mr. Burrell believed in the United States Branch Bank, and in the Bank of America ; he would have trusted either with untold millions, and he would have trusted Huggins with a more valuable article — viz., his throat. Mr. Burrell was not alone in his faith in this barber. He shaved Archibald Gracie, Col. Richard Varick, William W. Woolsey and William Coleman of *The Evening Post*, Governor Oliver Wolcott, and Thomas Buchanan. His shop was their favorite resort. He was an oracle of news. People regard Robert Bonner as having carried genuine advertising and its humbug style to an extravagant pitch in this age. He was not a circumstance to John Richard Desbrosses Huggins, Empereur de Frisseurs, Roy de Barbers, Autocrat of Fashions, &c., &c. In 1806, there were more daily papers than now. They were *The American Citizen, The New*

York Gazette, The Mercantile Advertiser, The Morning Chronicle and *The People's Friend,* morning papers. The afternoon dailies were *The Commercial Advertiser, The Evening Post* and *The Public Advertiser.* Two of the first named dailies are now flourishing. Of the weekly papers there were the *Republican Watch Tower,* the *Spectator,* the *Express,* the *Herald,* and the *People's Friend,* printed from the daily offices. The regular weekly papers were the *Museum, Price Current, Visitor, Republic* and *Spy.*

In all of these papers did Mr. Huggins flourish, both in poetry and prose. He had the cleverest writers of the day to aid him. He paid them like an emperor. He commenced advertising in 1801. Hamilton wrote some of his articles, and they were very clever. His place, during the last years, was at No. 92 Broadway, opposite Trinity Church. Previous to that, from 1794 to 1800, Huggins kept his shop on the basement floor of the Tontine Coffee house, then kept by Mr. Hyde. Here is one of his cards:

> " JOHN RICHARD DESBROSSES HUGGINS,
> Knight of the Comb,
> LADIES' AND GENTLEMEN'S HAIR DRESSER,
> Tontine Coffee House,
>
> New York."

In these days the ladies had their hair dressed with great care, and sometimes it was the case with gentlemen. Many of our old merchants have kept awake and not laid down their heads, for fear of disarranging their hair after it had been fixed (perhaps two days previous) for a great ball.

At No. 92 Broadway, Huggins kept a store, also, with trunks of perfumery, essences, " lavender water, with amber perfume," " best pomatum, high scented," fine smelling water," "milk of roses," "English honey water," "bags. and pin cushions," "Spanish skin," " coral powder," " Venetian sponge," " pastes," " washes," " cosmetics." One of his pupils was Maniort, who kept at No. 90 Broadway many years, and his pupil was George Meyer, who keeps at No. 17 Park Row, under Power's hotel.

The Bank of America was chartered for twenty years, with a capital of $4,000,000. This was twice the capital of any other bank then chartered. It was the sixth bank chartered by the State of New York. The president was Oliver Wolcott, afterwards Governor of Connecticut, and who had been Secretary of the Treasury under General Washington, and the first president of the Merchant's Bank in this city, in 1803. The directors were Jonathan Burrell, Archibald Gracie, William Bayard, Stephen Whitney, George Newbold, and others who had been old United States Bank directors.

They did not succeed in making the Bank of America take the place of the United States Bank ; and in 1816, Congress chartered that institution with a capital of $35,000,000, to last twenty years. It did last that time, and then General Jackson crushed it. The branch in the city had its office at No. 65 Broadway, and its cashier was Lynda Catlin. Its president and principal man was Mr. Isaac Lawrence, who until 1836, presided over its destiny. He only lived four years afterwards, and died July 12, 1841. He was one of the real aristocracy of the city, and was among the first. There are two legitimate kinds — one descended from the old Holland Dutchmen that came here in 1630, and thereafter, and another of English who came here in the same century, although a few years later. John and Isaac Lawrence were of that stock. Three brothers came out to this country in the troublesome times of King Charles the First. They were passengers on board the ship " Planter," and landed in Massachusetts in 1635. They were named John, William, and Thomas. From Massachusetts they emigrated to Long Island in 1644, and took a patent of land from worthy old Governor Kief. Old John afterwards moved to New York city, then New Amsterdam, and was a great man among the Dutch and English. He was a merchant. He was alderman from 1665 to 1672, and mayor in 1673. He was again alderman from 1680 to 1684, and mayor again in 1691.

One hundred years later, another John Lawrence, also a merchant, and great grandson of the old one, was alderman from 1762 to 1765.

The eldest one was made Judge of the supreme court in 1693, and held it until he died in 1699. He was born in 1618, in England. His will, in his own handwriting, made when he was eighty years old, is still on file in the county clerk's office.

From one of these brothers, John and Isaac Lawrence were descended — a good old New York stock, by the English breed.

Isaac Lawrence married Miss Cornelia Beach. She was a daughter of the Rev. Abraham Beach, one of the ministers of Trinity church, and a man of note in his day. Mrs. Lawrence was a very remarkable woman — an exemplary Christian, and a perfect lady. She was charitable to all that came in her way. She had many children — one son and several daughters. She brought them up in the right way, and they took pattern after her.

They used to go to St. Thomas' Church, corner of Broadway and Houston street, in its palmy days, when

Dr. Hawks preached there, and there never lived in this city such a family of beautiful daughters. They were the prettiest girls in the city. They are all married to prominent men. Cornelia married James A. Hillhouse, of New Haven. Harriet married John A. Post. Isaphene married Dr. Benj. McVicker. Julia Beach married Thomas L. Wells; Maria, the Rev. W. J. Kip; and Hannah, the pride of the family, married Henry Whitney, a son of the late Stephen Whitney.

Isaac Lawrence had but one son, William Beach Lawrence. He received all the advantages of an excellent education, and was intended for a public career. He became Secretary of Legation at London, shortly after Mr. John Quincy Adams became president of the United States, in 1825. While in London he was extremely popular with all classes. Upon the accession to power of General Jackson, Mr. Lawrence was supplanted by a partisan of that gentleman. Mr. Beach Lawrence removed to Rhode Island some years ago, and was adopted there by the democrats. He was elected Lieutenant Governor of the State. He would have made an excellent merchant, had he entered upon the career. He married a daughter of Archibald Gracie, the great merchant, alluded to so frequently in these pages, and thus became brother-in-law to James G. and Charles King, who had married sisters, and to the brothers Gracie. No man was ever placed in a pleasanter position in life than " Beach," as his relations called him. Surrounded by loving sisters, a doting father who left him rich, he has known or felt but few of the thorns of life ; and even now is quite a young man, and no one who meets him would suppose for an instant that he was over forty years old. He has children. One of them, William Beach Lawrence, Jr., is a young man of un-

common promise, and bids fair to keep up the reputation
of the race he springs from.   There was one very painful matter connected with "Beach," and his father, I
allude to the father's indorsement for the son, and his
final ruin in consequence.   In 1834 a lot of lots on
Murray hill of Isaac Lawrence were sold to pay Beach's
debts for some $50,000, that last year were worth
$800,000.

I omitted to mention in my sketch of John B. Coles,
his extraordinary activity in his younger days whenever
any affairs of benevolence were concerned — wherever
suffering humanity was to be relieved.   Probably there
was never more suffering in this city than in the yellow
fever of 1798.   From 29th July to 29th November,
2,086 died, and at that time the city contained about
55,000 inhabitants.   Its very first victim was an old
merchant, named Melancton Smith, who was taken
sick in his store in Front street, near Coenties Slip.
His death was followed by several of his neighbors being
taken ill, among them were Peter A. Schenck, the
father of Peter H. Schenck, of modern times.   Almost at the same time it broke out in Cliff street and
Burling Slip, Ryder street, and Eden alley, at Golden
Hill street (since John.)

It raged greatly in Eden alley and Ryder street,
where not a family escaped it ; and it terminated fatally
to one or more members except in two houses — one
of Dr. Hardie, and the other Mr. McMaster, the grocer.   All the other families suffered fearfully.

Ryder street ran from Gold to Fulton, forming the letter L ; it is now called Ryder's alley.   When called Ryder
street, Dr. James Hardie and several of our most respectable citizens lived in it.   At No. 1 Ryder street was a large
printing office.   It seems almost incredible now.   The

east corner of Ryder street, facing on Fulton street, No. 67, is occupied by an old New Yorker, named Edward Evans, for an extensive clothing establishment. The only merchant in Ryder street is a young man, who keeps an extensive establishment for old books. I frequently patronize him. From Fulton street Ryder runs up a turn and goes out into Gold street. In this section the fever raged fearfully. Eden alley was on the opposite side of Gold street.

At that time there was a prospect of a foreign war, and everybody was engaged in making preparation. Companies were being formed, batteries were being erected, subscriptions were being raised for the purpose of building vessels of war to protect our commerce, when the yellow fever broke out. At once all the war views were suspended. Speedy death was the only prospect. Parents were deprived of their children, husbands of their wives, wives made widows in a few hours, and from happy independence made beggars. Infants cried for dead parents. Whole families were cut off. Half of the houses were empty, and the frightened occupants fled to the country.

It was at such a time as this that John B. Coles evinced qualities that made him a benefactor to his race and to the city. He was ever where suffering was to be relieved, and he passed from one to another getting aid and using it to the best advantage. He collected from the following persons: From General Horatio Gates, who was then a resident here, $50 ; from Archibald Gracie, $50; from Moses Rogers, $50; from Thomas Pearsall & Co., $100 ; from Tracy, $50 ; from a man in Staten Island he got two sheep, ten bushels of potatoes, six bushels turnips and twenty-five pumpkins. From Teunis Quick, Mr. Coles received $40. From

Charles L. Camman, $100. " A man," gave Mr. C.
$100, he was a man. Henry Seaman, $50. Herman
Le Roy $50. From Mr. Griffin in Newark, 480 lbs.
of beef. William Bayard, $100. Boonen Graves
gave Mr. Coles $100. Isaac Torboss gave five barrels
of flour. John McVicker gave $100. Thomas Lown-
der gave 100 loaves of bread. Thomas Pearsall & Co.,
gave Alderman Cole $100. Hubert Van Waggenen,
$50. Dominick Lynch gave one ox, two pigs, two
lambs, eighty chickens and sixteen bushels potatoes. All
the country towns sent down something. Walter
Bowne gave $10, G. G. Bosset gave twelve bottles
syrup of vinegar, and two bottles of " vinegar of *four
thieves*." Pots of West Indies sweetmeats, lambs,
fowls, carl, cigars, loaves of bread, cart-loads of herbs
and roots, potatoes, beets, turnips, cabbages, carrots,
radishes, thyme, barrels of pork, ducks, butter, apples,
hams, Indian meal, rye meal, corn, straw, catnip, seven
dozen castor oil, bag of beans, two cheeses, three pair
of shoes, cords of wood, barrels of cider, 1000 eggs,
two barrels shad, four geese, and parsley. Such
were the articles that poured in every day from different sections of the State and New Jersey.

Good old merchant Thomas Buchanan sent in $100
and ten barrels of oatmeal. John Watts too, sent in
oxen, sheep, and forty barrels Indian meal. Sir John
Temple gave 100. Dirck Ten Broek gave fifty fat
sheep. Of course, in a time like this, another of our
old merchants could not have been idle. I allude to
John Murray Jr., brother of Lindley Murray, the
grammarian.

The common council, when the yellow fever broke
out, borrowed a small sum of money, to be appropriated

to relieving the poor and distressed. In September, John Murray Jr. came forward with $10,000 more.

It seems incredible to us now, the horrible accounts of yellow fever. It was at one time a regular scourge to the city. Every few years it visited New York and Philadelphia. In 1793 Philadelphia lost 4,041. In 1795 New York lost 732 ; in 1798, 2,086 ; and Philadelphia 3,056. In 1803, New York lost 609 out of 1,369 cases. In 1805 the yellow fever cases were about 600, and deaths 202. In 1822 it raged here with unusual violence. The cases were 601, and deaths 230. The citizens all fled ; part of down town was boarded in. The custom house, post office, banks, insurance offices, and principal merchants, all moved up into Greenwich village. Down town all the places of public worship were shut up ; but for this precaution the deaths would have been as great as in 1798, when John B. Coles was so active. Mr. Coles himself was buried in Trinity churchyard. How quickly good works are forgotten. If I succeed in rescuing from oblivion such acts as his, I regard myself as having performed a good work. Had De Witt Clinton done any thing so creditable, it would have been heralded over the world ; but done by an insignificant merchant, it was hardly worth mentioning in old times.

CHAPTER VII.

Last Sunday evening I was walking up Greenwich street, and when I reached No. 337, I stopped and looked at the old house, once in a fashionable locality, and occupied by one of the first merchants of the city. Opposite was a block of handsome three story brick buildings (between Jay and Harrison streets) and there also lived the first people. But now, how changed! Low tenement houses, dirty, out of repair, and daily witnesses of scenes that shock humanity. It is only twenty years ago since the occupant of No. 337 moved away from that house to Bleecker street. I allude to Schuyler Livingston. I saw him only a few weeks since, as he tottered along the street to his counting-house in Beaver street, and complained of rheumatism. On Monday, the 2d of September, he died at White-stone, Long Island. He was 58 years old.

Mr. Livingston was very much pleased with what I had written about him. I do not think he ever had as much said about him before or since. Schuyler Livingston was a true New York merchant. He was educated to it, serving a regular clerkship of five years, as nearly all of our great shipping merchants have done.

In 1819, when S. Livingston was sixteen years old,

he entered the counting-house of Henry & George Barclay. This house had been in business about five years, having commenced just after the war. Their office was at No. 3, in the famous Phœnix stores, that stood at the corner of Water and Wall streets, as late as 1830.

There were three of the Barclay brothers, — Henry, George and Anthony. They were sons of Colonel Thomas Barclay, who was Consul General of Great Britain for the Eastern States, appointed after the War of 1812.

This firm was continued for some years. In 1824, when Schuyler Livingston became of age, he was taken in a partner, but his name did not appear, nor was the style of the firm changed from H. & G. Barclay until 1834, when it became Barclay & Livingston. This change was owing to the law passed, and no name of a person should be kept in a firm when he was not in it. Henry Barclay had removed from New York to Saugerties some years previous, and the brother Anthony, (afterwards British Consul,) with George Barclay, made the firm of Barclay & Livingston.

The last firm has continued to this day, George Barclay being in it.

They were the agents of " Lloyds," London. For nearly half a century this house has done business, and for forty years Schuyler Livingston was its main pillar.

That man's whole life, from boyhood, was devoted to the mercantile profession. He had no ambition outside of it. In forty-three years, since he swept out the " office " as under clerk, he has not probably been out of New York over a week at a time.

To rise early in the morning, to get breakfast, to go down town to the counting-house of the firm, to open

4

and read letters, — to go out and do some business, either at the Custom house, bank or elsewhere, until
twelve, then to take a lunch and a glass of wine at
Delmonico's ; or a few raw oysters at Downing's ; to
sign checks and attend to the finances until half past one ;
to go on change ; to return to the counting-house, and
remain until time to go to dinner, and in the old time,
when such things as " packet nights " existed, to stay
down town until ten or eleven at night, and then go
home and go to bed, — this for forty-three years had
been the twenty-four hour circle for Mr. Livingston, as
it is for thousands.   The credit of the house — its standing at home and abroad — was dearer to his heart than
all the national difficulties of Europe.   He thoroughly
understood his business.   He never neglected it.   He
was careful, prudent and just ; but the moment a merchant failed, then good-bye to any further feeling of
equality on the part of the managing partner of the old
and respected firm of Barclay & Livingston.   He might
give charity to such a man, but never his countenance.
To fail, and not pay one hundred cents on the dollar,
exhibited in the eye of Mr. Livingston something wrong
— a lack of moral qualities that Schuyler could not
comprehend.   He never failed — why should other
people fail ?   He was a specimen of hundreds, that are
great men on change.   His routine of thoughts and of
action was precisely like them.   It is not wealth —
mere gold, bank stock or real estate that such men worship.   His business connection brought him constantly
into correspondence with old English merchants and
firms.   Those he worshipped, and he modelled his
own counting-house as far as possible after theirs.

Mr. Schuyler Livingston would not have accepted
the presidency of the United States at any period of his

long mercantile career, unless its duties could be performed as secondary to those of the great house of
Barclay & Livingston. If by taking the presidency or
governor of the State he could have extended the business connections of the "firm," he would have accepted the office, the same as he became a director in a
bank or insurance company. It helped him in business
facilities.

In a thousand ways and all unconsciously, this modest man, but true and thorough-bred merchant, such as
New York only can produce, loved her, and added to
her wealth and her greatness. He has passed away
from the scene of 15,000 days of labor. In his new
surroundings, he will be a faithful man and do his duty,
and but one thing will confuse or disappoint him. It
will be to find in Heaven merchants who have allowed
their names to go to " protest " on earth.

The Evening Post says a few kind words, viz: " He
was a man of great intelligence, probity, and kindness
of heart. In politics he was always a staunch demo-
crat ; and though always refusing office, he was for many
years prominent in the councils of the party.

" By his death the city loses another of those merchants of the old school who made her name and her
wealth and enterprise known the world over."

The firm of Paulding & Irving was a very old one.
Ebenezer Irving was of the firm, and lived many years
at No. 41 Ann street — the lower part of Ann street,
approaching Gold. Ryder street, and Gold between
John and Fulton, are at this day fair samples of the
streets of old New York, and even of Rotterdam and
Amsterdam, after which they were modelled. He was
a son of William Irving, who was a merchant at No.
75 William, and did business as early as 1786 ; and he

continued there until 1795, when he moved to No. 128 William street.

I remember the modest two-story wood and brick house as well as possible. Old William lived there as late as 1803. In later years, this house was occupied as a milliner shop, 1826, and when it was torn down, a splendid building was erected there, now occupied by Tiemann & Co., as a paint warehouse.

There was Washington, Peter, and William Irving; Ebenezer and John T., of the young children.

Peter was educated as a physician, and kept a drug store at No. 208 Broadway; he had with him young William. This was as early as 1795. The two kept there until 1803, when the old William and William Jr., founded the firm of Irving & Smith. They kept in Pearl for twenty odd years, first at No. 162, and afterwards at No. 145, as late as 1820.

Old William Irving must have died some time in 1807, at No. 157 William street, to which he had removed from No. 128.

Ebenezer Irving, the son, who was a partner of Nathaniel Paulding, lived at No. 157, until a year previous to the old gentleman's death, when Peter, Washington and Ebenezer all lived at No. 294 Greenwich street. Peter kept at No. 67 Water street.

The firm of Paulding & Irving was extensively engaged in the wine trade. From 1801, the firm did business at No. 162 Front street. Niel McKinnon was a clerk with them for many years. They did a wholesale as well as retail business, and kept the choicest stock of wines, porter, brown stout, and imported liquors and ales, that could be found. Both wrote a bold, old-fashioned handwriting. I have accounts before me made out by both partners. Ebenezer continued with

Mr. Nathaniel Paulding until about 1811, when they dissolved. Mr. Paulding kept in the same store, No. 162 Front street, until 1819, when he moved to No. 168. There he kept his splendid stock of wines until 1835, when he, with thousands of others, was burned out in the great fire. That event broke the old gentleman's heart. How well I remember his remarkable appearance, and his honest countenance. After the fire, Mr. Paulding started business at No. 35 Vesey street. He gathered there a fine lot of wines, but there was none that he prized as he did those in his old store. In Vesey street, Mr. Paulding kept as late as 1847 ; he seemed to be alone. He boarded at No. 81 Murray street, and I think he died about that time. He was an aged man, and much respected. In 1811, when the firm of Paulding & Irving was dissolved, Ebenezer and Peter went into business together at No. 135 Pearl street, under the firm of P. & J. Irving & Co. Peter was the doctor, and I think the company was Washington Irving. The last, with Peter and John T., kept at No. 3 Wall for the three previous years. The widow kept house for them at No. 108 Liberty, until she moved to No. 41 Ann where she lived as late as 1817.

In 1808, when he and Peter were at No. 3 Wall, when he was " Attorney-at-law," Washington planned the " Knickerbocker History of New York." In a preface, dated " Sunnyside, 1848," to the author's revised edition, published by G. P. Putnam for the proprietors in 1859, he says: " The following work, in which at the outset nothing more was contemplated than a temporary *jeu d' esprit*, was commenced in company with my brother, the late Peter Irving, Esq. Our idea was to parody a small hand-book which had recently appeared, entitled ' A picture of New York.' Like that, our work was to begin with an historical sketch, to be followed by notices of the customs, manners and institutions of the city; written in a serio-comic vein, and treating local errors, follies, and abuses with good-humored satire.

" To burlesque the pedantic love displayed, our historic sketch was to commence with the creation of the world; and we laid all kinds of work under contribution for trite citations, relevant or irrelevant, to give it the proper air of learned research. Before the crude mass of mock erudition could be digested into form, my brother departed for Europe, and I was left to prosecute the enterprise alone.

" I now altered the plan of the work. Discarding all idea of a parody on ' The Picture of New York,' I determined that what had been orriginally intended as an introductory sketch should comprise the whole work, and form a comic history of the city."

For years after I read that preface, I hunted after " the Picture of New York." That of course, must have been published about 1807. I could get no one to tell me about it. A book that Washington Irving would condescend to parody must be a valuable book. It is only a few days ago that I found the genuine book. No wonder that Irving noticed it. The title-page reads as follows:

THE PICTURE OF NEW YORK:

OR

THE TRAVELLER'S GUIDE

THROUGH THE

Commercial Metropolis of the

United States,

By a Gentleman residing in the city.

NEW YORK:

Published by J. RILEY & Co.

Sold by BRISBAN & BRANNAN,

City Hotel, Broadway.

1807.

The book contains 223 pages. The author, " a gentleman residing in the city," was no less a person than
Samuel L. Mitchell, as I have evidence in the handwriting of the late Dr. Vaché.

It needs no evidence of its authorship, save what is
found upon every page, in the ponderous quotations
that Washington Irving so happily hits off. Mr. Samuel L. Mitchell was a wonderful man, and to show how
quickly a man in political life is forgotten, while Mr.
Mitchell is remembered for other matters, very few are
aware of the fact that he was United States Senator
from 1804 to 1810 from this State, and a member of
the House of Representatives from 1800 to 1804.

Any one who will read the picture of New York —
its preface, giving " authorities," " situation," " size and
configuration," " discovery," " Long Island," will at
once recognize the resemblance between Knickerbocker's
first chapters and it.

To return to the business firm of the Irving Brothers.

Irving and Smith continued in business until 1816,
when they separated their auction from their commission business, keeping the former firm at No. 142 Pearl
street until 1818, when it took in Robert Hyslop, and
it was Irving, Smith & Hyslop.

The auction business was carried on at No. 133
Pearl street, by Irving, Smith & Holly. They all
closed up previous to 1825.

Even the house of Peter & Ebenezer Irving & Co.
was dissolved about 1820. It was kept about ten years
at 123 Pearl street. Ebenezer lived at No. 3 Bridge
street, and kept store at 127 Water street. He was
burnt out in the great fire of 1835, but he did business
as late as 1841. I think he died about that time.

William Irving, a son of the old William Irving,

was of the firm of Irving & Smith. He lived at one
time at No. 17 State street, and also at No. 3 Hudson
square. I think he died about thirty-five years ago.

John T. Irving died a judge. He lived in Chambers
street. At one time he went into partnership at No. 10
Pine street, in a " loan office " with John Nitchie.
The firm was Irving & Nitchie. They had an office at
60 Wall street. Mr. John Nitchie was public admin-
istrator, and his house was in Broad, just below Exchange street.

The Irvings of the olden time added greatly to the
wealth of New York, to her commercial reputation, and
two of them to her literary names and fame.

CHAPTER VIII.

There will be more knowledge conveyed in these chapters of the antecedents of prominent merchants of New York, than in any other manner yet attempted. How many will be informed for the first time that familiar names in the haunts of commerce, and merchants in this generation, have been familiar names among the same class for three or four generations back, and the fathers, grandfathers, great grandfathers and double great grandfathers, of men now known on " change," have been known in their day respectively.

The London Times recently alluded to the fact, that there was no aristocracy in this country except that of wealth. There never was a greater mistake. There is as distinct an aristocracy here as in any land upon earth. Since the power of entailing has been cut off, there is no way of keeping property in the eldest son from generation to generation, and consequently an aristocracy of wealth would have a brief existence. Wealth has power, and can make itself exclusive. But it has no affiliation with the family aristocracy, or of old descent, or of hereditary mercantile enterprise. Old Henry Astor, the butcher, and John Jacob, the cake peddler, who became a sagacious and far-seeing merchant, possessed great wealth; but there were and are

4*

hundreds of families in this city, whose portals as an
equal John Jacob with all his wealth, nor Henry either,
could not have crossed.

We look back in this city 200 years, and not more.
Before 1662 not much was known about it. It was a
small town, with few records. There are few tombstones
in our old churchyards recording names much before
that date. After 1665 there were two classes of the
community — those that had come here from Holland,
or that were descended from the original Dutch.
Another class was those of English descent. Such a
one as I described the Lawrences, John and Isaac, were
of that family. Of the Dutch there are families older
by ten or fifteen years. The important persons here
from the date of settlement were merchants. Old
Wouter Van Twiller, the first governor, was a merchant, or rather a merchant's clerk, being regularly
brought up in the West Indian Company's counting-
room, and that fact ranked him as the equal of an ordinary merchant. Wouter was born in Nieuwkirk, and
probably when he ceased to be governor of our ancient
New York he went back there. I do not know of any
Van Twillers that have kept up the name, and been engaged in mercantile employment in this city ever since.
Had they done so, they would have been regarded as aristocracy, and would have moved in the very first circles, as the Stuyvesant family has always done, whether
poor or rich. The Stuyvesant family would not have
been quite as ancient by a few years. The descendants
of old Peter have always been engaged in commerce
and trade. Their land titles cannot be disputed. In
this country none but fools look across the water for
an ancestry.

Old Van Twiller who used to get the people before

the door of the fort in the spring of 1633, break in the head of a barrel of wine, and get all hands drunk, drinking toasts "to the health of the Prince of Orange and me," may have been a left hand son of the old Prince, or his father may have kept a dance house in " New Church " village,— we don't care about that. The Van Twiller family would in New York in 1861, only be allowed to date back to the 16th of April, 1633, when their ancestors landed from the ship " De Zout-burg," the first vessel of war that ever entered this harbor. People here don't care what the ancestry was on the other side.

In my sketch of the head of the Isaac Lawrence family whom I knew, and whose ancestors I stated to have landed in 1635, I might have added with strict truth, that across the water, in England, the ancestors of those I named, spelled it " Lanrens," and that the first of note of that race was Sir Robert Laurens, of Ashton Hall, who accompanied King Richard (Cœur de Lion) to Palestine, and at the siege of St. Jean d' Arc, Robert Laurens planted the English banner of the Cross on the batteries of that town, for which King Dick slapped him on the shoulder, and thus made him a knight.

That would not do. It would make a family claim 670 years old, and here we do not stand any such nonsense. We will go back to the landing in America, and give credit for 220 to 226 years to a Lawrence or a Van Twiller — to a Dutchman or an Englishman, from the above old stock, and when I mention these names, I use them as *samples* of hundreds of families in this city who can claim the highest social ancestry known here.

There is no ancestry known in this city higher than that of a merchant, for it is the only business that is *hereditary:* and as hereditary descents give crowns and coronets in Europe, so in America hereditary merchants have their claim to honor.

We have had eminent men in professions in this city during 200 years. They have blazed out in their day and generation as lawyers, physicians, clergymen, inventors, and then died without leaving a successor. It is a rare occurrence that even a son has succeeded a father in his profession, not so with merchants. There are mercantile houses who have father to son succeeded each other in business from 1661 to 1861, and scarcely conscious of it themselves. This seems singular and impossible, though I have frequent evidences of it in my researches.

It is easy to see how this can happen. We will take a merchant named Jacob Kierstede, in 1660. He is doing business in Beurs street (Exchange street;) it has been since 1637. He was born in Holland in 1615. He has a son named Martin, and a clerk named Jan Cregiere. Jan Cortse Neetje, the daughter of the older Kierstede, marries him. The firm becomes Kierstede & Zoon, in 1670, and continued for twenty years. In 1700, old Kierstede dies, and the firm becomes Jan Cregiere.

Young Martin Kierstede was placed in the store of Peter De Groot, in the Hoogh straat (part of Pearl,) as a clerk to learn the business, in 1670, when fourteen years old. Seven years later, he became a partner with De Groot, and married his niece. He succeeded to the business, and when De Groot died, in 1700, he used his own name, and was in business until 1730. He died in 1742, aged eighty-six years. He was succeeded in business by two of his own clerks. His own son Abraham, born in 1679 was apprenticed as a clerk to a Mr. Abeel, in 1695. In 1702, he became a partner, and the firm was Abeel & Kiersted. He died in 1760. His business firm was merged into Abeel & Co. (a son of the old partner in 1703 being its head,) in 1750.

A grand nephew of this Abraham was in business in 1784, and kept in business under his own name. Long after the Revolution, in 1790, he died.

At that time other descendants of the old race were in business. Simon was pawnbroker at 285 Broadway ; James was a brass founder at 2 Chambers street ; and John kept a hat store at 23 Courtlandt street, on the identical spot or lot of ground where Horace H. Day, the celebrated India-rubber dealer, erected a fine store a few years ago, and which he occupied until he gave up business altogether. He still owns the property.

John Kiersted, the hatter, had a son named John Jr., and the firm was John Kiersted & Son. As late as 1806, the old man kept the store, and the son moved to Greenwich village.

Between 1810 and 1860, there have been two prominent Kiersteds that I have known personally. C. N. became a partner with Warner & Kiersted, dealers in paints, at 33 Broad street. 1820, the firm was Warner & Platt. Christopher N. Kiersted was a merchant in 1812, at 245 Duane street ; then in 1817 he kept book accounts, as did many merchants, if unfortunate in business. He afterwards went in with Warner. Thirty years ago he lived at 58 Broadway, and they kept at 33 Broad street. In later years they moved to 68 Broad, and changed the firm to Kiersted, Warner & Co. The same business, although partners are changed is, I believe, still carried on in Beaver street, near Broad. C. N. Kiersted is dead. He was a fine old man, and thirty years ago was a most energetic and useful citizen.

Henry J. Kiersted must have started in the drug business, in my old favorite Fifth Ward, during the last war. At that time, or in 1812, Luke Kiersted was a great man in the Fifth. He was a very red-faced man, and was a pewterer and plumber at No. 4 Jew's alley, and in the rear of No. 40 Charlotte street.

James Kierstead was an old Fifth Warder, and lived at 35 Walker street, in the rear, and also in Lispenard street. Another, Hezekiah, was a grocer at 9 Vesey street.

Henry T., started in 1814 in Murray street, near Broadway. Then he moved to 38 Hudson, corner Anthony. In 1820, he moved up to 529 Broadway corner of Spring street. He was there until 1856. I think now he is at 1339 Broadway, and that the firm is Henry T. Kierstead & Son. The senior must be a very aged man. The Christopher N. of the old paint house must have left a family. There are several eminent physicians of the same name. I suppose they are his sons.

I now return to the fact that there are many in the city who know nothing of the actual business of their ancestors, or of such a statement as that one of the name and blood has been in continuous business in New York from 1637. That is, there never was a time one of the number of the same name was not a merchant or trader. There are fifty and perhaps one hundred such cases. It applies to the Hoffman family — originally spelled Hofman. If the firm was kept on direct from father to son, through a long course of years, there would be curious old books and writings to show. In Europe, Holland — itself for instance, or Amsterdam, many firms can show account-books kept with their correspondents 200 years previous in New Amsterdam and New York. There the same firm is kept up, and the law sanctions it. Here it does not. But that is not the true reason. In New York the " house " and the " store " are two distinct concerns. Probably Mrs. Goodhue, the wife of Jonathan Goodhue, never saw, except by accident, the vast accumulation of books connected within the years that her husband was the head of Goodhue & Co. A young Goodhue succeeded his father in the same business. Of course he is aware of the fact that his father founded a house. But suppose he had been brought up in another commercial house, and become a partner in that, and his father had died, he would not have succeeded to the books and papers of his father's house. They would have gone to Mr. Perit, the successor in business of Goodhue & Co. Now we have records ; two hundred years ago there were no newspapers. Hence, there are many names that are directly descended from a highly respected name, but of whom little is said, because they have not like the Stuyvesant, De Peyster, and other families of wealth, kept a record, and traced every one of the name.

I have used one or two imaginary changes to show how easy it was for a scattered business not to be traceable. I have never spoken to a Kierstead in thirty years, that I know of. Yet I will venture a heavy wager, that all of the name are directly descended from the original Kierstede (spelled with an *e*,) one of whose daughters (Blandina) married worthy *Pieter* Bayard, a dweller in *de Breede Weg* (Broadway,) a son of Nicholas Bayard, and nephew of old Peter Stuyvesant, who arrived here May 27, 1647, and ancestor of Peter Bayard, who can daily be seen on Broadway, between St. Paul's Church and the Astor, after three o'clock, with a book in his hand.

The Kierstedes are but one of many such. Even of those who kept records in their families, they tell nothing about the business or labors of the merchant citizen.

I will venture to say, that at this moment the home of the most eminent merchant in New York does not contain sufficient records of his passing a career as a merchant, to light a cigar with. And should he die and his business be closed, his " books, accounts and correspondence " of a life, will become the property of the clerk or person who " liquidates " the " business."

I make use of all such information as is sent to me about old merchants, or living merchants of the present day. I add to it — for there are very few who have done business in this city of whom I do not know somewhat. The more I know, the more interesting will be the sketch. If any one is disposed to carp because I do not know *all* about the history of a merchant, they should reflect upon the difficulty of actual knowledge of affairs that most men keep a secret. The most secret class in the world, and the most opposed to any sort of publicity about himself, is the great merchant. Why should it be so? While the politician, and the army and navy officer, are anxious to keep their names constantly before the world, why should the merchant who brings nations in every quarter of the world into constant communication, and is opening up new sources of wealth, be afraid of having all known about himself?

Among the class that I may safely call hereditary merchants, is Peter A. Schenck. His father, Peter A. Schenck, was an honorable grocer merchant in Fly Market, No. 26, before and after the Revolution in 1782 ; in 1795 he moved to 66 Front street.

Young Peter H. was placed as a clerk in the counting house of Lewis Simond & Co., who were among the heaviest houses after the Revolutionary war. In 1792 they kept in Queen street, and when young Schenck was their clerk, the store was kept at No. 4 William street, near Hanover square.

Very few merchants of the old school brought up their own sons to business in their own stores. A business education was a severe one in old times. Every duty, from sweeping out the office to book-keeper, was minutely exacted. It was a regular apprenticeship to commerce, and it resulted in making thorough merchants. The progress was as regular as clock work. Sweeping out office, doing errands, taking letters to post office, copying letters, copying accounts, entering goods at the Custom House, delivering goods sold, taking an account of goods received from the ships, keeping the store-book, making sales, assisting the book-keeper, going out supercargo to East or West Indies. I may add, the system of neatness and correctness in reference to copying letters, when once acquired, follows a man through his life. Old Archibald Gracie took ten times more pains with his clerks than is taken in Columbia College. When they were set to copying letters, it was read to the first blot or error and then destroyed, and the unhappy clerk was set at his task again, and made to copy correctly. This achieved, he was promoted to making " duplicates," and even triplicates of letters, and he had the honor of knowing that his " fist " went to ports in the uttermost parts of the earth, — for on the days of sailing ships, while one ship took the " original " letter, succeeding vessels carried " duplicates " and " triplicates," and not unfrequently the last reached their destination first.

If I had a son, whom I wished to make a thoroughbred gentleman — a man of the world and a man of

business, I would send him to college three years, and
then let him spend five more in the counting-house of a
heavy merchant, where he should sweep out, and end
by being a thorough book-keeper.

The discipline of the modern merchants is nothing
to what it was fifty years ago.   Our merchants of great
eminence before the Revolution, had been brought up
in English or Scotch counting-houses, and sent out here
to conduct business.   Such was the case with Archibald
Gracie, Thomas Buchanan, Theophilachte and Richard
Bache, Robert Murray, Francis Lewis, John and Francis Atkinson, Lewis Simond, and other eminent merchants, between 1720 and 1820.

CHAPTER IX.

In a previous chapter I wrote about the two Peter Schencks — father and son. I now return to young Peter H. Schenck. At that time, a grocer looked up to the great merchant. Consequently, a man of this stamp aimed to place his son where he would rise to the highest rank of merchant. Buying largely of the great merchants, he was a man not to be refused ; consequently, when old Peter A. Schenck asked Lewis Simond to educate young Peter, it was granted. He remained with Simond & Co. until 1798. That year the yellow fever prevailed, and Peter A., whose store was at 66 Front street, near Coenties slip, when Smith died, was the second person taken. Young Peter was sent for to conduct the business of the old man, and I have before me an account for " Scythes &c.," made out by young Peter H., and signed for his father while the latter was laid up with yellow fever — viz., " 7th of August, 1798." I have also another receipt which he signed for seventy-five dollars, in full for one year's wages, 1792. Peter A. lived and carried on business as a grocer many years after in the old store, and residing in Pearl street No. 92. In 1802, he took in young Peter H., and the store was kept at 49 Front street, under the firm of Peter A. Schenck & Co., young Pe-

92   THE OLD MERCHANTS

ter also being with his father.   At this time Martin W.
Bull was a clerk with the firm.   They continued on in
business together until 1806, when Peter A., the father,
was appointed surveyor of the Port of New York.   At
that time David Gelston was collector and Samuel Os-
good was Naval Officer.   The business was now conducted solely by Peter H. Schenck at the old place.
Old Peter was kept in office through the Jefferson and
Madison administrations until 1815, when he went to
Washington.   The young Peter H. kept the old store,
49 Front street, and did business as Peter H. Schenck
& Co. until 1824.   Then he moved to 40 Fulton street,
and lived at No. 2 Bowling Green.   The next year he
moved to 123 Maiden Lane, and I think the character
of his business changed.   His partner's name was Samuel G. Wheeler.   He was father-in-law to D. B. Allen,
who is son-in-law to Commodore C. Vanderbilt.

Peter H. Schenck, in the last war of 1813, gave
Government $10,000.   About that time he built a cot-
ton factory at "Mattewan," and when New York was
blockaded, they carted cotton by land from Charleston
S. C., to Fishkill Landing, N. Y., about 900 miles distance.

He had added greatly to the wealth of the city of
New York.   Few men have done more than this.
Who represents the name and race now I know not.

James De Peyster Ogden is an old merchant of this
city.   None have been more eminent than he.   I have
before me writing of his in 1805.   At that time he was
a clerk with Van Horne & Clarkson, merchant, of high
standing, shippers and importers,   Their counting-house
was at 129 Pearl street.   The senior of the firm was
old Garret Van Horne.   The junior partner was David
M. Clarkson.

Old David M. Clarkson was in business at 73 King street (Pine) as early as 1784. A few years after he formed the partnership with Garrit Van Horne. The signature of Van Horne & Clarkson, as written by old David, is the bold, large, old-fashioned hand-writing, so prevalent among the merchants of the Revolutionary period. It has a world of character and meaning in itself.

Even " James D. P. Ogden," as he signed himself fifty-six years ago, wrote a bold, open hand, and one that evinced character.

I have no means of knowing the age of the noble old merchant, but, in 1805, to be trusted with nine hundred dollars, he was not likely to have been under fourteen or fifteen years old. If so, he cannot be far from seventy now.

Fifty-four years of active mercantile life in this and other counties! What a life! What scenes he must have passed through! What an experience of commerce, happily, has been his!

Mr. Ogden received a regular education in the counting house of Van Horne & Clarkson. He went out to the north of Europe, where he remained three years, acting as the agent of the New York house of Le Roy, Bayard & Co. I do not know precisely when the noble old firm of Van Horne & Clarkson dissolved, but I think it was about 1809 or 1810.

Garrit Van Horne, the merchant, lived at No. 31 Broadway (where the counting house of Van Horne & Clarkson had been in their last years,) as late as 1825. I think he died about that time. The next year it was occupied by David Clarkson, and for many years after. Long David they called him.

Thomas S. Clarkson lived next door at 33 Broadway.

David (long) was the son of David M., although the
partner of Mr. Van Horne in 1790, who lived at No.
16 Courtlandt street, some seven years after he dissolved
with Mr. Van Horne. Old David Matthew (father of
David and Matthew,) I think died at No. 16 Courtlandt
street, about 1817 or 1818.

Never was there a nicer family than these old fashioned Clarksons. Not only the male members, but the
female members of it were splendid specimens of the
human race. I do not know why it was so, but they
always seemed to me to be in mourning. It was a
sight to see them all go to Trinity church, as they
moved slowly and dignifiedly up Broadway thirty or
forty years ago.

James De Peyster Ogden went into mercantile business in this city in 1820. His store was at 24 Broad
street, near the corner of Garden, and he lived at the
City Hotel. He continued business at that place for
some years, and then went abroad to Liverpool, England.

While General Jackson was President, Mr. Ogden
acted as United States consul at that port for a short
time.

After his return and for twenty-five years, his course
in this city was one that is to be envied. No man is
more respected and more esteemed, and no one deserves
it more. His family on both sides is coëval with the
settlement of New York. Father and grandfather
were eminent in their day and generation. His father
was a cotemporary of the celebrated Dr. Hosack, and
they were students together in the office of the eminent
Dr. Bard. Dr. Ogden was intimately known and esteemed by the great Washington.

The remark quoted from St. Paul, " All save these

bonds," Morgan Lewis says, was original with Dr. Ogden.

The committee of public safety in those days had a grudge against him. They took Dr. Ogden to General Washington's head quarters. " What," said Washington, " is that you? How are you ? " " Well, I thank you, General," said Dr. Ogden, "*save these bonds,*" looking very contemptuously upon the fellows of the committee who had brought him there. Washington replied, " Ah, those bonds were not intended for you, Doctor, and they knew it, but I am very happy to profit by the occasion to say how glad I am to see you, and to repeat my respect and esteem."

James D. P. Ogden is a grandson of this spirited old gentleman.

As a merchant no man has been more esteemed during the long life spent in this city, only relieved by the occasional absence upon important matters alluded to above, in Europe.

He has been one of the most prominent and esteemed members of the Chamber of Commerce for years. In politics, he has always occupied a prominent position in this city. It would have been fortunate had he been more identified with it, officially. He has always been a national whig of liberal principals. He was one of' the most active and prominent members of the Union Safety committee. He greatly dreaded the effect of the warfare waged against slavery, as it existed under the Constitution.

His speech, when he presided at the great meeting at the Cooper Institute, January 8th, gave his views of the then existing state of affairs, with his opinion of the necessity of passing the " border state resolutions," as prepared by Mr. Crittenden.

No man so deeply deplored the civil war that afterwards broke out, and that is now raging in our own
prosperous land.   But friendly as he always was to the
South, no man could more sternly recognize to its full-
est extent, the duty of opposing Secession, which is but
another word for Revolution, and of maintaining the
Union, the Constitution and the laws, as the only safe-
guard of every section of the Republic.

Few men can realize the honest city pride of such a
man as J. De Peyster Ogden.   No man can realize how
deep and abiding the interest that New York city has
in the momentuous issues of the passing hour.   He has
for more than half a century been a merchant here, and
he knows that commercially and financially our city is
destined to exert a paramount influence upon the peace,
the prosperity and the character of our common country.

If ever there was a time in the history of New York
when she should prepare to be the empress or mistress
of affairs, no matter how complicated they may become,
it is now.

It was an unfortunate hour for the nation when the
capital was removed from New York to its present location.

Had General Washington agreed to let it remain
here, millions would have been saved, and the Union
would have been perpetual.

But he and other leading men had become scared at
seeing at Paris the French Government overawed by a
mob, and they thought a village location for the American capital would prevent that ever happening here.
It was a bad hour when they did it.

When General Ross burned Washington forty-eight
years ago, it was a blessing in disguise.   Had we, then,
in New York, refused to give a dollar to the General

government unless the capital was removed back to New York, it would have been better, and saved the nation a thousand million of dollars, many lives, and prevented rebellion, and, perhaps general anarchy hereafter.

Even now the dirty hole that nature spurned for her capital, while she made her pet city the real capital of a continent and of the western world, is in danger. It has cost us thousands of lives; 200,000 men stand ready to protect what, save in honor, need not and ought not to have cost us a life or a penny, for it is worth neither; and if rebellion is happily subdued, it is to be hoped that the wisdom so dearly bought will be practised at once, and that regarding the penny-wise policy that built Washington, we may consult the pound policy that will make us destroy it, and remove the national capital back to the city of New York, where it legitimately belongs. The Central Park is the proper place for our national buildings, and there they will be safe.

Perhaps upon New York city at this moment depends the safety of the country. All are sanguine, but let us suppose for a moment that the rebels should capture Washington?

New York city will then be forced to be the seat of government even if events do not force her to take the helm of government. It is here the millions of gold are to be raised to carry on the war. It is here that exists the great power of the nation.

A thousand Washingtons, a hundred presidents and congresses may be cut off, and yet all is not lost, so long as New York is safe. They are the big and little toes, fingers and hairs of the great political body. New York city is the heart — the seat of vitality. Stop her beat

ings, and the prosperity, the liberty, aye, the existence
of the United States is ended.   The nation will die.

How united, then, in such an hour ought the citizens
to be?   How quickly they ought to prepare to place at
the head of our powerful municipality a man who may
in the course of events, if disaster comes, be found not
only to be chief of the city, but chief of the nation !

How important, under any circumstances, it is that
the mayor of this city, in such a fearful emergency as is
gaping before us, should be a man that has the entire
confidence of the various powerful classes of the city !
of the merchants, of the bankers, of the large property
holders, of the great mechanic and other interests, of
the rich and poor, of labor.   How utterly important it
is that socially, morally, and financially, he should be
without a stain.

Before his term of office expires in 1863, the mayor
of the city may be called upon to wield more power
than ever the Cæsars of Rome did in her palmiest days.

The " Old Merchant " articles are read and pondered
over by the wealthy, the merchants, and time-honored
old citizens.   It is them I address.   Why not take one
of this class and and make him mayor ?

Where among them will they find such a man as
James De Peyster Ogden ?

When will the city have ever had such a mayor,
combining, as he does, qualifications and experience that
will enable him to occupy any position that events may
force the city of New York to fill ?

She must not sink, and though anarchy and confusion
may flit, like death, in and out among sections and states,
she and her two grand seaward islands, Long and Staten, that make her a Trinity on earth, must stand as a
landmark for sections and states to re-annex to ; and
even if the present four years government is rendered

important by the probable clash with military chieftains, New York must stand as a rallying point once more for the whole Union.

She needs, then, a Chief Magistrate capable of ruling a nation, as well as city, in case of emergency, and in case of danger. With a mayor at her head that has the confidence of the capitalists of the city, New York can not only protect herself, but protect the rest of the continent.

New York city alone, unemburdened by Washington city, could have put down this rebellion six months ago ! Left to herself, she could put it down now in six weeks ! Her great strength cannot be destroyed, but it is injured in protecting Washington by millions of men and money — a place so useless, so dead, so demoralizing, so expensive, that if God Almighty would give time to a few human lives to escape, and then destroy it by fire and brimstone, as He did Sodom and Gomorrah, before a week, it would be the greatest blessing He could confer upon the American nation, and it would re-unite the thirty-four states ; for then the capital would come back to New York, and here it would rest forever. Here it belongs. To this point all the great public interests and vast private interests tend. There is not a palace or public building lofty, nor a hut, low and poor, in any part of the United States, that has not in it some one interest, human or pecuniary, in the city of New York.

She should prepare for her great destiny, by electing for her chief officer and men to her councils those who are equal to the task of conducting her affairs.

Among all the men I have written about no man comes so thoroughly up to the high standard of fitness for mayor of New York as James De Peyster Ogden.

Louis Simond, of whom I have spoken, as the house that gave a mercantile education to Peter II. Schenck, continued in business from the period I have written — about 1792 — until the war. At its commencement, L. Simond & Co. was at No. 65 Greenwich street. They did a heavy West India business, and sold 1,000 puncheons of rum every year. Henry Garnett was a clerk in that house many years. Then in 1814 the house dissolved, and Mr. Simond lived at 57 Broadway. I am not aware that the house failed, but it is most likely. All those who were extensively engaged in foreign commerce in 1813, found their connections and resources cut off, and were obliged to close up their business. Some, like Henry C. De Rham, went through safely.

Another eminent merchant was Jose Rois Silva. In the war his store was at No. 1 Beekman street. He afterwards removed it to No. 79 Front street, and resided at No. 9 Beaver street. He was doing a large and successful foreign trade as late as August, 1798, when the yellow fever seized him, and he died at 28 William street.

His book-keeper was Thomas T. Gaston, a regular " accountant " of those days, and who lived at No. 4 New street. Mr. Gaston kept books for perhaps twenty other large houses.

CHAPTER X.

I write about clerks, to give my experience. Fathers
are generally willing that their sons or connections
should do without salary for three or four years to have
them acquire a knowledge of business. Almost all of
the great merchants prefer to take boys from out of the
street or from the country — New England boys especially — and give them $50 or $75 the first year. The
merchants want aid — they prefer a boy without any
friends or rich relatives. The reason is obvious : a boy
from the country will work like a hero — do anything
he is told to do — acquire a thorough knowledge of
business — become a confidential clerk, a partner, and
never have alliances outside of the great house that has
brought him up. A man like the late Gardner G. Howland, doing a business of millions, when he gives a
check to one of the boys in the office to go to the bank
and get the money for it, or his coat to take to the tail-
or's to be mended, has no time to argue the matter with
the boy, that the one is a legitimate order to a clerk and
that the other is a servant's duty, as he would be told
by an aristocratic city boy. The country boy would
do what he is told, if it were to black his employer's
boots, and never think of such a thing as doing what he
ought not. Such a series of years of faithful obedience

is rewarded by a perfect knowledge of business, unity of purpose, and a partnership. This is the reason why nine out of ten of our principal American merchants are New England born. They enter the counting room to get their bread and get ahead. The New York boy of " prospects," enters it because it's genteel — if nothing is given him to do.

I would say that there is nothing impossible in this world — at the same time very few merchants wish to take a young man of eighteen as a beginner.

There are always a large number of applicants of friends of the larger merchants. Probably Goodhue & Perit, and the Howlands and Aspinwalls have each to decline, annually, a thousand such applications from wealthy parents and friends, who are willing that their young connections should enter the counting-room. Fourteen to sixteen years of age is their favorite limit. An uncorrupted boy from a New England district school, in ordinary times, is much more likely to get a foothold in a large counting-room than any other, and he can tell his own story better than a thousand letters of introduction, if he deals directly with the merchant. An applicant of three days' residence would be successful, while a three months' residence would be fatal.

The late Schuyler Livingston was generally supposed to be a very liberal man. So he was when it was his interest to be so. He was not always just. In one case he acted the part of an unjust man to two young and unfortunate merchants.

In a former chapter I have alluded to the fact that about thirty years ago, General Jackson sent out a merchant named Edmund Roberts to make a treaty with Japan, Muscat, and Siam. Mr. Roberts succeeded in making a treaty with the two last named nations, but

failed with the former. He went out on a second expedition, and died. Judge Amasa J. Parker, one of the
purest and best, as he is one of the most sagacious democrats of the state, married a daughter of Mr. Roberts.
At the death of the diplomatist, Mr. Parker, who was
then a Member of Congress from the Delhi district,
published a book at the Harpers. It contained the life
of Mr. Roberts, and many valuable papers connected
with the expedition he made by order of President
Jackson.

Based upon the information conveyed by Mr. Roberts,
a commercial house in this city opened a trade with
Muscat and the Imaum. This continued a long time.
Among other matters, some very valuable presents were
sent to the Imaum himself. One agent of this New
York house resided at Zanzibar Island, and another at
Muscat. The Imaum is himself not only a priest, but
indulges in merchandising when he finds a good opening
He loads one of his own ships in the early part of 1840,
and sends her to New York, consigned to this house,
that had been doing business with him for some time.
The New York house had failed, and the consignment
of the Arab ship and cargo passed into the hands of
Barclay & Livingston, who made a nice thing of it —
perhaps $5,000 or $6,000. Did the house of B. & L.,
who would have been puzzled to have told in what part
of the globe Muscat was located, divide the commission,
or make any return to that young house of Scoville &
Britton, who had toiled and spent money for years to
work up that trade? Not a dime. Schuyler Livingston told Mr. Britton, the only partner who was in the
city at the time the Imaum's ship arrived here, to kiss
his — foot. Mr. Britton long ago left mercantile business, and met with the greatest success in another line ;

he being the head of the house in this city of Britton &
Warner, bankers.

That was not all.   The " Sultanee." brought presents
from the Imaum to the president of the United States,
and also to Scoville & Britton, his New York correspondents.   An Arab chief returns present for present.
The President of the United States had sent the Imaum
valuable articles, and he sent back Arab horses to him.
Scoville & Britton had frequently sent presents to the
Imaum, among other things a Colt's rifle and pistol
mounted in ivory, and several other fire arms.   In return to S. & B., the Sultan sent camels-hair shawls
and certain articles.   Barclay & Livingston never had
sent the Sultan any presents, but they got his, and poor
Scoville & Britton never received one of them.   Mr.
Livingston claimed that the presents belonged to Barclay & Livingston, as consignees of the vessel.   Power is
right, and there was never any redress, nor never will
be in this world.   Satan in the other may say : " Schuyler, that was a clever dodge of yours in 1840 — keeping
those Arab shawls."   As the Sultan is dead, he can explain that they were intended for his friends — his correspondents — those who had made him presents in
1839, and not for a couple of names the Imaum had
never heard of, but who became consignees of the vessel, because they were the agents of Lloyds, London, and
by consent of Lloyd L. Britton.

Charles Henry Hall, the old book-keeper of Thomas
H. Smith & Son, became of great note afterwards.   In
1822 he kept at 44 John street, and in 1824 he lived at
576 Broadway.   This simple number, standing by itself,
would not attract attention.   It conveys the idea of a
dwelling-house on Broadway — nothing more.   But in
1823 it meant an entire block far up town, bounded by

Prince, Crosby, Houston, and Broadway, now occupied by the Metropolitan hotel, Niblo's theatre, Smithsonian hotel, and half-a-dozen other places. Standing alone in the centre was a two-story double house, No. 576. I see it now as it was then. In the rear were the most superb stables ever erected. The building was very large. Over the stall of each horse was his name painted. The property belonged to the Van Rensellaers of Albany, who had leased it to Mr. Hall. Here he resided until 1829, when in the Spring of that year, Charles Henry Hall moved himself, his family, and his magnificent horses to Harlem. His business office he kept at 20 Nassau street.

The house and ground was rented by William Niblo, who up to that time had kept the Bank Coffee House, corner of Pine and William streets, in the rear of the Bank of New York. It was a famous place. All the principal people of business dined and gave dinner parties there. Niblo opened it during the war in 1814, and made it very popular.

I think Mr. Niblo had been once in the employ of Daniel King. At any rate, he married his daughter. King was a noted publican of his day. As early as 1799 he kept a tavern at No. 9 Wall street; he kept in the same spot as late as 1811. In 1815 he moved his tavern up Broadway, near Prince street. In 1816 he moved down to 6 Slote Lane, near Hanover square. He kept there several years, or as late as 1820, when he moved up to Varick street, where he kept a boarding house. I think he died about 1825.

When Mr. Niblo leased the Hall house up at 576, he intended to keep a branch of his down town hotel. His customers were among the very first class of citizens. He was not disappointed. Within a week after the

5*

upper town house was opened, it was filled with eminent merchants and their families, who preferred such a
residence to house-keeping. Among this class, was
Archibald Gracie, Jr. and his family. He had recently
married Miss Elizabeth Bethune (1828) of Charleston,
S. C. Niblo pursued a modest career for a few years,
when some one suggested that he should open a sort of
garden for the higher classes, — as " Vauxhall," that
extended from the Bowery to Broadway, above Fourth
street, was too far out of town, and was too common
also. Niblo adopted the idea, and small alcoves with
tables inside, and plenty of flower pots, were introduced
as a feature. The next improvement was to move
Hall's old stable building around to a more central part
of the " garden," and then it was altered into a theatre,
almost open at the sides.

The first performance of note was Herr Cline's. He
was a brother of F. S. Cline, the actor. He is now living somewhere in this city, I believe, and has long been
forgotten, except his name. There has been an immense improvement since those days. Mr. Niblo's
theatre is a feature, and the hotel Metropolitan still
more so.

There is one feature that has been lopped off long
ago. In former years, old New Yorkers would sit in
the bar-rooms and adjacent spots, and talk over old
New York. Most of them are dead. One of them I
met not long ago, alive, fresh, and with as smiling face
and genial manners as he had thirty years ago, and not
a bit older. I allude to Edward Sanford, who holds a
responsible position in the bureau of the city inspector,
Colonel Delevan.

Now to return to Charles Henry Hall. He was
brought up by Murray & Mumford. I have his writing

before me of 1805, large, clear and distinct. This
house was started before 1786, as Murray, Mumford &
Bowen, at Crane wharf, foot of Beekman street. They
did an immense business in 1791. Bowen went out,
and Murray & Mumford continued the business at 73
Stone street. Old John B. Murray was the head of
this house. John P. Mumford was the other partner.
They were the heaviest merchants of the period, and
dealt heavily in teas. Robert Aldrich was a clerk with
them in 1797. They brought up many young men.
James Watson was with them in 1805, and was a fellow clerk with C. H. Hall. At the close of this year,
the house was dissolved, and in 1806, John P. Mumford, one of the partners, carried on the business in his
own name. He was assisted by his son, Peter J. Mumford. The store was at 42 John street. But of these
Mumfords, I shall make especial mention in a future
chapter.

At Niblo's coffee house a society of merchants went
regularly. It had a president and other officers, and its
members were the most prominent merchants in the
city. Of the society I shall write in one of the succeeding chapters.

There are many merchants who have succeeded in
this city, acquired fortunes, and moved away, leaving
nothing but their names. Others come here from
abroad, make fortunes and die, and their families move
away.

Of the latter class was Joseph Hopkins, an Englishman, who was a crony of John J. Glover ; John Ellis,
Thomas Buchanan, all English, and William Wilson,
the Scotch merchant, of whom I have said something in
former chapters.

Mr. Joseph Hopkins is a name well known to our

readers. The old "Pewter Mug," now being torn down, was for many years identified with the name of Joseph Hopkins — " Major Joe," " old Joe," " Major " " our Joe," and other familiar cognomens. He went to the land of gold many years ago, and I hope is rich. I am not aware that Joseph Hopkins of the Pewter in 1848, is any connection of Joseph Hopkins, the old merchant, of whom I now write. He was an Englishman, and commenced business in this city after the Constitution was adopted in 1787. He opened his store at 213 Queen street (that is, the 221 Pearl street of to-day, near Platt street.) At 221 Pearl street he lived and did business until 1803, when he died there. His wid‑ ow continued it until 1807, when she went to No. 36 Beekman street, where they had formerly resided in 1798, until in 1801 he built a fine brick store. His dwelling had previously been at 36 Beekman street, and I think he owned it, as in 1808 — four years after he died — his widow moved back to it.

John J. Glover was next door at No. 223 Pearl. He also bought the lot and erected a brick house, but long previous to the erection of the three below him. William Ellis lived on the opposite side of Pearl street, at No. 218. His brother John Ellis lived next door to Mr. Hopkins, at 219. He built a house also.

The three houses No. 217, 219 and 221 were after the same models, and in 1801 were regarded as superior to any dwelling houses in that or any other section of the city.

Stephen B. Munn, of whom I have written, lived at 226 Pearl, almost in front of these houses.

It was the custom of those days to have the stores of the merchants on the first floor and in front of the din- ing or sitting-room. Up stairs was the drawing-room.

It occupied the whole front of the house. Back of that was the bed-room of the merchant and his wife. The sleeping room of the children or other members of the family were on the third or attic floor.

Along in that vicinity were several Quaker houses. Richard R. Lawrence was at 251 ; Richard T. at 269 ; John and Isaac at 207 ; John B., the druggist, at 199 and 245 ; Jas. Parson & Sons were at 267 ; the Bownes, Robert, Robert L. and Robert II. were at 252 and 256 Pearl ; William Hicks was at 276 ; Clendening, Adams & Co., at 209, and the Franklins were scattered all along Pearl from 227 to Franklin square. Sixty years ago there were sixteen firms of the name of Franklin. Where are they all now? There was Samuel at 279 ; Thomas at 282 ; Franklin, Robinson & Co., William Franklin & Co., at 309 ; Franklin, Newbold & Co. ; Henry Franklin & Co. at 227 ; John Franklin Jr., 337 ; there was Abraham, Henry P., William and Matthew. Martin W. Bull, who was a clerk with Peter A. Schenck & Co., in 1804, is an old family here.

There was one of them, Francis, who was a translator of languages in the commencement of this century, and the first that I know of having existed here.

I have one of his 1806 cards :

FRANCIS BULL,

NO. 24 WILLIAM STREET,

Thankful to his friends and the public for past favors, informs them that he continues translating the following languages :

GERMAN,	SPANISH,
DUTCH,	PORTUGUESE,
IRISH,	ENGLISH,
FRENCH, and	ITALIAN,

and *vice versa*, with correctness and dispatch.

He settles accounts, ever so intricate, for masters of vessels and others — all on the most moderate terms.

He did that business only a few years, and I think he died about 1810.

There was an old house as early as 1795, " Michael & Thomas Bull," that did a very heavy business in this city for many years. They went out of business about 1800. Soon after, William G. Bull used to sell teas annually in this city. At that time he went out as supercargo to China every year, and was more or less interested in the venture. He was in this city as a merchant many years; in fact, he was regarded as the best judge of teas in the United States, until he died a few months ago. Another branch of that family were engaged in the saddlery business as early as 1806, and they have continued it ever since.

CHAPTER XI.

The founder of the firm of Goodhue & Co., was Jonathan Goodhue. He commenced business in this city in 1808, under the firm of Goodhue & Sweet, at No. 34 Old Slip. The store was afterwards removed to No. 44 South street. This building belonged to Theophilacht Bache. Goodhue & Sweet did a very heavy regular commission business for three or four years, and sold largely of foreign dry goods, and acted as agents of Salem ship owners. In 1811, the house was dissolved, and J. Goodhue carried on business upon his individual account until 1816. It was then Goodhue & Ward, and the store was kept at 44 South street. In 1819 it became Goodhue & Co., and Mr. Perit became a partner. He had formerly been of the house of Perit & Lathrop. Goodhue & Co., kept at 44 South street until 1829, when they removed to 64 South street where the same large house is still located. I have written about this firm in several previous chapters, but not so much of their first start as now.

Mr. Goodhue was born in Salem. Mr. Perit was born in Norwich, Connecticut, and received a collegiate education at Yale College. This is not often the case with merchants in this city.

In the first partnership of Mr. Perit with Mr. Lathrop, his brother-in-law, he was not successful, and during the war he was connected with an artillery company, and performed military service in the forts that protected the harbor.

After he went with Mr. Goodhue, his commercial good fortunes returned, and their house coined money. In 1833 or 1834 the health of Mr. Perit declined, and he conceived the idea that it was necessary to take more active exercise, and in order to insure that daily, he he purchased a piece of property on the North river, lying between Burnham's and the Orphan Asylum. It may have cost him perhaps $10,000. He sold it about two years ago. I suppose it is worth now half a million of dollars. This is a comment on persevering mercantile life. By a mere accident Mr. Perit buys a small lot of land, and makes more money than Goodhue & Co. ever made in fifty-three years hard work! Probably no house has done a larger business with all parts of the world than Goodhue for the fifty-three years that it has existed in a continuous business. This house, so eminent, commanding means to an extent that an outsider has no conception of, has made merely moderate earnings in comparison with some lucky land hit, made by unknown and uncredited persons, that has realized millions.

Mr. Goodhue died a few years ago, and his funeral — at his own request — was attended only by the members of his family and a few of his most intimate friends.

Since Mr. Perit sold his property in New York, he has removed to New Haven, Connecticut, to a magnificent house in Hillhouse avenue. He married Miss Coit, a very lovely girl, and still living, the ornament of the circle in which she moves. They have no children. He has done more than most merchants do for the benevolent enterprises of the day. He is unequalled as a merchant, and has been for many years honored with being president of the Chamber of Commerce,

The house of Goodhue & Co. ought to last, for the honor of the city, a hundred years more.

F. Varet & Co., French importers, did a very large business at one time. For years this firm was one of the heaviest in the silk trade. They imported and then sold heavily at auction through John Hone & Sons. The old man was named Francis, and the son Lewis F. They did a heavy West India shipping business. The old Varet was a French refugee, and settled in New York as early as 1797, at 26 Reade street. In 1804 he took his son into partnership, and kept at 112 Chatham street. In the war they kept their store at 94 Bowery.

Perhaps the heaviest business they did was in 1830, and for some years prior to that date. Though the firm was Francis Varet & Son, as it had been for twenty-six years, I am not certain that old Francis was in it actively. The son was an old man in 1830, and his private residence was at No. 36 Beach street.

The house employed their own buyers in France, and he was under engagement not to buy for any other New York silk house. At one time James R. Icard was their banker at Paris. John B. Viele of Lyons, France, was a partner of this house.

This house, established in 1798, is still in existence under the firm of Oscar Varet & Co., 21 Murray street. They yet deal in silks and have Paris connections. I think the names of the young men are Oscar and Emil.

I now return to the old house of F. Varet & Son. Their store was at 147 Pearl street for a long time. Lewis Varet was a very close business man ; He kept his affairs to himself and his own book-keeper, whose name was Durival. He made out all the entries of goods, and attended to the custom house business himself. He did not confine himself solely to dry goods ; on the contrary, F. Varet & Co. received cargoes of sugar, beeswax, &c., &c., from Matanzas. In Lyone he had large manufactories, monopolized in making little lacets braids, one sixteenth of an inch in width.

He also imported woolen gloves and mittens in hogsheads, and at first used to make immense profits, selling them at public sale ; but after a while the market got overstocked, and these goods became a drug in the market.

It is about eighteen years since Mr. L. Varet died.

Mr. Joseph Hoxie came here as a school teacher about 1818. He taught school in the Fourth Ward, where he is kindly remembered by many of his old pupils still.

When he first began to meddle in politics, it was as an active partisan of Tammany Hall ; but I believe he left the shade of the Wigwam about the time when Moses H. Grinnell and others, now prominent Republicans, left it.

Mr. Hoxie kept school as late as 1829, when he went into the mercantile business, having determined to follow the example of A. T. Stewart, and widen the sphere of his activity and usefulness.

He taught many years at 208 William street. It was at the old church that stood on the corner, where the Globe hotel now stands, of William and Frankfort streets.

He began in business about 1829, at 83 William street, and in 1834 removed to 101 Maiden lane, which locality, at that period, was regarded as the most favorable for the business in which he was engaged — viz., cloths.

Wilson G. Hunt was also in that neighborhood for a long time, and made money there. He had formerly been in the retail dry goods business in Pearl, near Chatham, where he was unfortunate, and was obliged to compromise with his creditors ; after which he commenced in the cloth business, under the auspices of his brother Thomas, at the corner of Pearl and Chatham streets. This new business to Hunt was successful, and he coined money. Here I must stop to narrate a most honorable transaction of Wilson G. Hunt. Although he had settled with his creditors for a certain sum on the dollar, and had received a full release from all his indebtedness, yet on a certain New Year's day he invited all of his creditors to dine with him; and judge of their surprise, when they had taken the seats allotted to them, they each found under their plates a check for the full amount of the balance of their original claims, with interest to that date. No wonder that Peter Cooper selected such a man for one of his trustees.

I have a full sketch yet to write of Wilson G. Hunt. I now return to Mr. Hoxie. His genial disposition did not qualify him for the intricacies of mercantile life. " Profit and loss," was an account he could not rightly understand. Although popular with the clothing trade, and exceedingly industrious, yet the disasters of 1836 and 1837 forced him to quit merchandizing. He had become a prominent politcian in the Whig ranks previous to that period. In 1837 he was elected Alderman of the Seventh Ward. The next year he was elected county clerk for a three years term. He came up again for nomination at the expiration of his term, but was defeated by the nomination of Revo C. Hence, who was defeated by the democratic candidate at the election.

Shortly after he was elected Judge of the Fourth Ju-

dicial District for four years. The difficulties of others
being constantly brought before him, he did not like it,
and when his term expired he sought employment
another way.

He was truly a friend of Henry Clay, and openly acknowledged as much by the great Kentuckian for many
years of his life. While on a visit to Ashland, after the
expiration of his Justiceship, he formed such an acquaintance with leading Western men as to secure to him
the agency of two or three Western fire insurance
companies. He then opened his office as an underwriter agent at the corner of Wall and Pearl streets.
Some years after, when fire insurance companies' stock
became a very profitable investment, and under the new
insurance laws, permitting the formation of insurance
companies without any special act, he with Hugh Maxwell, Moses Taylor, the late J. Hobart Haws and others,
associated themselves together and formed the present
Commonwealth fire insurance company, of which Mr.
Hoxie is the President.

He was one of the early members of the Whig party, and when that broke up he became one of the most
active spirits in the Republican party, but not an Aboli-
tionist. Mr. Hoxie is one of the most venerable looking men in the city. He is a popular speaker, for he
never speaks long so as to weary his audience, and his
speeches are always interspersed with such anecdotes as
bring down the house. This also applies to his social
life. He is one of those great friends of humanity who
do kindness by making men laugh. He is an honest
man. He is opposed to corruption both at Albany and
at Washington, and denounces them whenever he gets
a chance. In the campaign of 1840, when public sing-
ing was in vogue, Mr. Hoxie was one of the best vocal-

ists of his party. He is now an officer in the Market street church, and still a resident of the Seventh Ward, ,that first elected him to public life. His anecdotes, although perfectly chaste in language would hardly bear, my repeating them, except one as a sample. I have said nothing about the nativity of Mr. Hoxie. Of course, he is from the East, or he would never have been president of the New England society.

A friend once met him in Wall street and asked " Judge, where were you born ? " Hoxie cocked his eye in a very peculiar way, and replied : " There was once a man residing in the south-western part of this country who prided himself upon his judgment of human nature, and that he could tell the State in which a person was born, if he heard him speak a few words. Being seated in a tavern in Kentucky, on a turnpike road, frequently resorted to by travellers from all sections, he amused himself by his discriminating observation upon men who entered, as to the whereabouts of their birthplaces. On a certain day, a traveller on horseback approached the tavern. After alighting, he asked the landlord, ' Have you any oats ? ' ' Yes,' replied the landlord. ' Give my horse two quarts.' ' That man,' said the observer, ' is from Connecticut.' Shortly after another traveller arrived. ' Landlord have you any oats ? ' ' Yes.' Give my horse four quarts.' ' That man,' said the observer, ' is from Massachusetts.' Presently, a third traveller arrived and asked ' Have you any oats ? ' ' Yes.' ' Give my horse as many oats as he can eat.' ' That man,' said the observer, ' is from Rhode Island.' ' Now,'— says Mr. Hoxie,—' I come from the State where they give their horses all the oats they can eat.' "

Another of these old dry good merchants now retired,

and a resident of the Seventh Ward, is Abner Chichester. He made a large fortune by steady devotion to business, and lives to enjoy it, without changing his habits of life or moving into the Fifth avenue. He was in business in Pearl street, near Fulton, of the firm of Chichester & Van Wyck, for a long period.

He is one of the few of that successful class of dry good merchants that have done honor and added to the wealth of the city.

One of his daughters married Jackson S. Schultz of the firm of Jackson Schultz & Co., the large leather dealers in Pearl street. Mr. Schultz is a director in the Park bank, and has lately distinguished himself by his active exertions in putting down this war.

Another daughter married Robert M. Strebeigh, principal business manager and one of the wealthiest and most liberal stockholders of *The N. Y. Tribune*, who has a fine mansion in East Thirty-fifth street.

CHAPTER XII.

While I take pleasure in writing a chapter about an ordinary old merchant, who has merely his individuality to distinguish him, I take a double pleasure, when I can strike out with one who not only represents one of a class, but who is a type of a grand old race. I have had the New England class, such as Jonathan Goodhue represented, or G. G. Howland ; the old English race, represented by Thomas Buchanan ; the Scotch by Archibald Gracie. Noble old Francis Lewis, who was a merchant, and signed the Declaration of Independence, was afterwards an insurance broker, was of the Welsh class. I have yet to write his history. I have had the old Dutch merchant and his descendants, and their characteristics. I now take up one of a more ancient class, who, in all ages, and in all nations have seemed to have had a double nationality — their own, and that of the country in which they lived.

I have now before me the venerable form of Bernard Hart, who died about six years ago, at the advanced age of ninety-one. At all times, and in all countries, the Israelites have been the leading merchants, traders and bankers of the world. Mr. Hart was born in England in 1764. He came to this country in 1777, during the war, and was then thirteen years old. He made a visit to a relative in Canada for three years, and then, in 1780, settled down for a life in this city, and that life was prolonged seventy-five years more !

From 1780 until 1786, Mr. Hart, although quite young, was making purchases and sending goods to Canada, for the establishment of his relative, and this he continued to do until he made a commercial house for himself.

At that time, 1786, this city had 23,614 population of which 2,103 were blacks, and the taxes £6,100 —or about $15,250. If Mr. Hart had lived a few years longer he would have seen them as many millions as they were thousands when he started business. The city had been incorporated just ninety years. Since 1696. Its outskirts were Chambers street, although there were some scattering farm-houses — among them was that of Mr. Lispenard, who afterwards became a partner of Mr. Hart, under the firm of Lispenard & Hart. Standing where the northwest corner of the Park now is, you could see the chimneys of the dwelling of Mr. Lispenard among the trees, over towards the North river, where Desbrosses street now enters Hudson. Broadway ended where the Park now ends. To get off the Island north, you had to take the road outside of what is now the Park, pass up the Bowery, and wind around to where Madison square now is. There Kings road separated ; and old trees in Madison square yet mark the Boston road. Broadway commanded an uninterrupted view of the Hudson river, and the promenaders up it could look down at the sail boats and ships.

Wall street was then quite a wide street, and filled with costly edifices. Hanover square and Dock street (Pearl street between Hanover square and Broad street,) was the great place for business, and had many hand-

some houses — the families of the great merchants living over head, and the stores beneath. William street
was a good street, and it was the place for retail dry
goods stores. There were other streets, but they were
narrow and irregular. The City Hall, an old brick
building, stood in Wall, overlooking Broad street. The
Battery had pleasant walks. The old city was the gay-
est place in America in 1786. Water was much needed
in those days, and there were very few wells in the city.
There was a pump near the head of Queen street (Chatham and Pearl,) which received water from a spring
about a mile from the city. Carts conveyed water to
the doors of people in casks filled from the pump. At
the time too, the Israelites had a synagogue in the city,
and the minister was the Reverend Gershon Mendes
Seixas, who officiated half a century, and lived until
1816. Among the early settlers of New York city,
there were some families of Israelites. As late as 1686,
they were not allowed to have a place of worship.
They were allowed a burial place on the west side of
Oliver street, opposite the Baptist meeting house, the
gift of a few gentlemen. It is hemmed in with buildings,
but monuments were there bearing date 1652. Forty
years later, however, things changed, and a modern synagogue was built in Mill street. In 1729 it was rebuilt
of stone, and there the congregation worshipped until
1818. But at the close of the last century, the Israelites
were not powerful or prominent. There were a few
strong names, and among them were Mr. Bernard Hart,
Benjamin Seixas, T. and M. Seixas, Isaac Moses and
Son, Simon and Joseph Nathan, Benjamin S. Judah,
and Bernard S. Judah, Uriah and Harmon Hendricks,
and a few others. What a contrast between the
commencement of this century, 1800, and 1863 ?

6

The Israelite merchants were few then, but now? they have increased in this city beyond any comparison. I speak of them as a nation, not as a religion. There are 80.000 Israelites in the city, and it is the high standard of excellence of the old Israelite merchants of 1800 that has made the race occupy the proud position it does now in this city and nation.

Towering aloft among the magnates of the city of the last and present century is Bernard Hart.

In 1795 he resided and did business at No. 100 Water street. That was the year the yellow fever raged so fearfully ; 732 died. Although 2,086 died in 1798 — yet it was not so horribly fearful to the citizens as in 1795, for then they had got used to it. It was not a new pestilence. Mr. Hart and Mr. Pell, of the firm of Pell & Ferris, who kept store at 108 Water street, a few doors from Mr. Hart, were unceasing in their exertion — night and day, hardly giving themselves time to sleep and eat ; they were among the sick and dying, and relieving their wants, and were angels of mercy in those awful days of the first great pestilence.

Two years before, in 1792, Mr. Hart had become a member of the St. George's Society, re-established in 1786, and he was a constant watcher on the health of the few members of that society in the sickly season of 1795.

In these days, too, they were famed for their sociability. There were all sorts of societies and clubs. There were in 1797 the " Harmonica society," the " Urania Musical society," the " Columbian Anacreonic society," the " St. Cecelia society," and the " Friary." Bernard Hart was " Father " of the " Friary," Charles Buxton was Chancellor, Baltus P. Melick was Secretary. This B. P. Melick was founder of the great com-

mercial house of Melick & Burger. They kept at 76
Washington street, and did a heavy St. Croix business.
They owned the ship " Chase " in the trade. She was
commanded by David Rogers, and I think that in after
years David Rogers founded the great sugar house of
David Rogers & Son. Thirty years ago I visited his
sugar plantation in Santa Cruz, an island belonging to
Denmark.

Dr. Buxton was a physician, and lived at 216 Broadway. John Marschalk was treasurer. He lived at 3
Wall street, and was an old-fashioned book-keeper.

Of this " Friary " Walter Bowne, Jacob Bradford,
and John Motley were " Priors." Walter Bowne was
a merchant in Pearl street. We knew all about him in
after years.

Bradford was a merchant, and lived with his sister,
Catherine, at 38 Courtlandt street. John Motley was a
merchant, too, and lived at 30 Beekman street, and his
store was 188 Front.

The " Friary " men had a standing committee of such
names as William Hartshorn. He was a large merchant, of the firm of Hartshorn & Lindley. Andrew
Smyth lived at 53 Beekman street, and was of the firm
of Smyth & Moore, iron merchants. Robert Murray
was of the firm of John Murray & Son, in Burling slip,
that I have written much about. He lived at 31 Warren street. Anthony Pell was an insurance broker, and
so was Bernard Hart. In 1798 he lived at 12 Broad
street. Nicholas G. Carmer kept a hat store in Pearl
street, and was of the firm of N. G. & H. Carmer.
William Parker was a grocer up in Augusta street (now
City Hall place.)

John Banks had been a merchant, but from some
cause, did not succeed. He was personally acquainted

with General Washington, and the latter ordered the
Collector to appoint him in the Custom House.

Isaac L. Kip was a notary public and a clerk in the
Chancery Court.   He lived at 4 Nassau street.

These gay gents met every first and third Sunday in
the month, at No. 56 Pine street.

Mr. Bernard Hart was also a great military man in
his early years.   In 1797, although New York was exceedingly small, she could sport a brigade of militia, of
which James M. Hughes was brigadier general.   Jacob Morton was lieutenant colonel commandant of the
third regiment.   Isaac Heyer, Henry J. Wyckoff,
John Elting, Nathaniel Bloodgood and John Graham
were captains.   William Hosack, Edward W. Laight,
Henry Sands, Peter A. Jay, Henry Cruger Jr., and
such old names were lieutenants.   Bernard Hart was
quartermaster, and John Neilson was surgeon mate.
What a party !   The last was the celebrated Dr. Neilson, who for many years was one of the most prominent
physicians in this city !   His house at the northwest corner of Greenwich street and Liberty is still standing, as
also a magnificent palace that he built in Chambers street
near Greenwich, that was afterwards purchased and is
now occupied by the famous Madam Restell.

I am not positive, but I think Bernard Hart was a
mason, and belonged to Holland Lodge No. 8, of which
John Jacob Astor was Master in 1798, and they met at
66 Liberty street.

In 1802, Mr. Hart formed a partnership with Leonard Lispenard, under the firm of Lispenard & Hart.
At this time or from 1790 there were two prominent
Lispenards.   They owned breweries on what was then
called the Greenwich road.   One was named Anthony,
the other Leonard.   There were the founders of the cel-

ebrated Lispenard estates. Lispenard & Hart first started in business at 89 Water street. At one time, they did a large auctioneer business, but always did a general commission business. In 1806, they moved to 141 Pearl street, and continued there as late as 1812.

During this time Mr. Hart had made another partnership. In 1806 he married Miss Rebecca Seixas, a daughter of Benjamin Seixas, all of whose daughters were famous for their wonderful beauty and exceeding loveliness, both in person and character. Mrs. Hart was not an exception.

Mr. Benjamin Seixas was a merchant, and did a large business in Hanover square as early as 1780. In 1792 he moved to Broad street, No. 76. He bought the ground and built a large double house on it in 1791. At that time he had a country seat up in Greenwich village. It was adjoining that of Isaac Moses. The house at No. 76 Broad street was for many years the residence of Harmon Hendricks, also Mrs. Gilles. After the great fire in 1835, that swept Delmonico off, he opened 76, as Delmonico's Hotel.

Benjamin Hendricks was a wonderful old man. He was born in this city in 1746. In 1779, he married Ziproah Levy, daughter of old Hayman Levy. The latter was once in the fur business, and in his account books are many records of money paid John Jacob Astor for day's work in beating furs, at the rate of one dollar a day. Miss Levy was a beautiful girl, and was born in 1760 ; she lived until 1832 ; and when she died, fifteen children were present, and she left seventy granchildren. His relative, the old clergyman, the Rev. Gershon Seixas, lived at 11 Mill street. Mr. B. Seixas in 1800 moved to 321 Greenwich street. He had several sons as well as daughters ; and when he died, in

1816, he left sixteen children living, eight sons and eight daughters. I have already alluded to their extraordinary beauty. Men talked of it half a century afterward.

Their destiny is worth noting. Rebecca, as I have said, married Mr. Bernard Hart. She was born in 1782 and is still alive, 79 years of age.

Leah is yet living, having never married. Hester married Napthali Phillips. They are both living — both blind. He is over eighty-five years old. I remember him well, many years ago, when Gen. Jackson was President. He was then in the Custom House. They have a numerous family of children and grandchildren. I have before me writing of his when he was a boy.

Grace married Jacob I. Cohen, of Charleston, S. C. She is, I think, the mother of Gershon Cohen, a successful politician of the Eighth Ward. She is living.

Rachel married Dr. D. M. L. Peixotto, once President of the Medical College of this city. He is dead, but she is still living.

Sarah married Seixas Nathan. She is dead, and so is Abigail, who married Benjamin Phillips, of Philadelphia. Miriam married David Moses of Charleston, S. C.

The sons that I remember are Daniel, who is in business in Wall street, and has been many years.

The eldest son was named Moses. He married Miss Levy, a daughter of Jacob Levy of this city. He is dead, but his children are doing business in this city.

Isaac was minister of the Congregation Shearith Israel, in Crosby street. He is dead, but his widow is alive, and his sons are in business in this city.

Hayman L. Seixas, named after his grandfather, H.

Levy, is married, has a family, and is, I believe, in a department of the custom house.

Aaron died in 1852. I knew him well, and a better hearted man never lived than he was.

Solomon is dead. He was a colonel in the war of 1812. His widow is alive, and so are two sons.

Abraham died in Charleston, where he had married Rachel Cardoza.

Madison is in New Orleans, and a partner of the large house of Gladden & Seixas.

I now return to Mr. Bernard Hart.

There was another famous society to which Mr. Hart belonged, and I do not think any one of the members of it can be alive. They called themselves the " House of Lords," and also " Under the Rose."

The society held their meetings at Baker's city tavern, No. 4 Wall street, corner of New.

Joseph Baker was originally a brass founder, at No. 4 Wall street, and he pursued his work from 1800 up to 1804, when it was put into his head that he could do better by adding a porter-house to his business. In 1805, the public house became so profitable that he dropped the brass business, and became a publican. His place became famous as the old city tavern, and it was frequented by the best men in the city. William Niblo, or " Billy," as the merchants called him then was with old Joe some time.

Joe Baker kept that city tavern as late as 1822, when he moved to No. 1 Nassau street, and started a boarding-house. He continued there as late as 1831. Then he moved off, and I have lost his track. There was a Joe, Jr.

In the days of the great glory of Baker's city tavern, the "House of Lords" met at his house every week-day

night. Bernard Hart was president. It met at half-
past seven, and adjourned at ten o'clock. Each member was allowed a limited quantity of liquor, and no
more. The merchants discussed business, and important commercial negotiations were made. In these
days, all the prominent men lived down town. Among
the members most prominent were Robert Maitland,
Thomas H. Smith, Preserved Fish, Captain Thomas Carberry, who lived at No. 79 Greenwich street, old Gulian
Verplanck, Peter Harmony, Robert Lenox, William
Bayard, Thaddeus Phelps, Samuel Gouverneur, Solomon Saltus, and Jarvis, the painter.

This was a lively crowd of our prominent citizens of
the olden time.

In 1813, Bernard Hart left the Lispenard, and went
into business under his own name, at No. 86 Water
street, and lived at No. 24 Cedar street. In 1818, he
went into Wall street. I think about this time the
Board of Brokers must have been founded, for Mr.
Hart was elected its secretary, without salary, and he
continued its secretary until he died in 1855.

The title was " Brokers of the New York Exchange
Board." In 1817 there were only twenty-eight members ; and, as it is in curious contrast to the legion in
1861, I give the list :

Leonard Bleecker,	Gurdon S. Mumford,
Benjamin Butler,	R. H. Nevins,
Leonard A. Bleecker,	Seixas, Nathan,
Wm. G. Bucknor,	Isaac G. Ogden & Co.,
Jas. W. & J. Bleecker,	Prime, Ward & Sands,
Bleecker & Lefferts,	Andrew Stockholm,
Samuel J. Beebe,	John Roe,
Davenport & Tracy,	Fred. A Tracy,
A. N. Gifford & Co.,	John G. Warren,
Bernard Hart,	W. H. Robinson,

Benjamin Huntington,	W. I. Robinson,
Israel Foote,	Smith & Lawton,
Philip Kearney,	H. Post, Jr.,
A. H. Lawrence & Co.,	Henry Ward.

Bernard Hart was much respected, and was one of those men that ought not to perish from the records. When he died, his was the peaceful death of the just man. He was 91 years of age. What an eventful life was his!

He left several children, and he lived long enough to see them occupy positions of uusefulness and high honor.

Emanuel B. Hart was one of the sons of this old merchant. He has been a merchant and a broker, following in the footsteps of his father. This son was alderman of the Fifth Ward in 1845 and 1846. He represented the city in Congress from December, 1851, to March, 1853. He was appointed Surveyor of the Port in 1859, and left it in 1861.

Another son, Benjamin I. Hart, is also a broker, and married Miss Hendricks, a daughter of old Mr. Hendricks, of whom I gave a lengthy sketch a year ago.

David Hart is another son. He was and is a teller in the Pacific Bank — went to the war, and fought gallantly at Bull Run, but was badly wounded.

Another son, Theodore, is in business in this city. So also is Daniel Hart, another son.

6*

CHAPTER XIII.

Besides the large merchant who figures extensively in all sorts of commercial transactions, either on his own account or doing business on commission, there are other very large merchants who devote themselves to a special business — as, for instance, an iron merchant. There is the large dealer of this class who sells iron in bars, bolts, pigs, etc., of all sizes — wholesales it — and there is the "hardware" merchant.

In the early years of the city, there was a class of merchants called "ironmongers." They were not exactly "iron" merchants, but they were the class of traders now known as "hardware" merchants. They used to signify their business with such signs as "tea kettles," "anvil and sledge," "a vice," and other emblematic indications. The name "ironmonger" and the signs were both derived from the old English custom, in the iron manufacturing districts of Birmingham, Sheffield, and such towns. I am inclined to think that the early iron merchant of the city also included the hardware business of the present day. The regular iron trade was a limited one until within a hundred years. In 1749, the city only contained 9,000 inhabitants. It was nothing but a good large village, and a modern hardware store would have supplied it with a

stock that woul l have lasted ten years. It was well
known to the authorities that governed this province,
that there were immense quantities of iron ore in this
region. A year later, in 1750, the Parliament of England passsed an act to encourage the exportation of pig
and bar iron from New York, and added heavy penalties for any one who endeavored to manufacture it or
to erect a mill for rolling iron, slitting it, or forge to
work with a hammer. But one such establishment was
suppressed in New York. Sam. Scraley, a blacksmith,
owned a plating forge, then worked with a tilt-hammer.
Of course he had to give it up. Between that date, 1750,
and 1756, Robert Livingston had the only iron works
in the New York province.

In 1771, William Hawkshurst procured a grant for
the sole making of anchors and anvils in this city and
province, for the term of thirty years. It expired May 21,
1801. I am not certain that he lived to enjoy it
the full term. He or his son went into business as late
as 1795, under the firm of Hawkshurst & Franklin,
ironmongers, 309 Pearl street. They moved to Water
street, and did not dissolve until 1809. He left many
descendants.

In 1767, there was a little foundry started to make
iron pots, by a few persons who had money. It lasted
until the Revolution of 1776.

Governor Cosby as early as 1732 informed the London board of trade, that he understood Great Britain
paid in ready money to Sweden for all the iron used.
He thought that as there was plenty of iron mines both
of the bog, and of the mountain ore in New York, that
if England would encourage " iron work," immense
quantities in " piggs and barrs," if free of duty would
be sent to London, that could be paid for in the manufactures of Great Britain.

Iron in all shapes became a different kind of business after the Revolution. One of the most prominent merchants in it was Joseph Blackwell, who kept his store and resided in Hanover square in 1780. Old Joseph was a son of Jacob Blackwell, who was a grandson of Robert Blackwell, who was a merchant and came out from England in 1661, two hundred years ago. He first did business at Elizabethtown, New Jersey. He moved from there in 1776, and came to New York being a widower with several children. He married a second wife.

She happened to be Miss Mary Manning, of "Manning's Island," East River, where he took up his residence, and gave it his name — Blackwell's Island. It originally was called " *Verken*," or Hog Island. It was granted to a Dutch officer in 1651, named Fyn. In 1665, when the English conquered this country, it was confiscated. In 1668, it was given to Captain John Manning, whose sword was broken over his head for surrendering the city of New York to the " Dutch " in 1673. After marrying the daughter and heiress of Manning, Robert Blackwell became proprietor, and it remained in the family until about thirty years ago, when it was sold to the Corporation. His youngest son Jacob, succeeded to old Robert's property when he died, in 1717. In size, Jacob was the greatest man in the country. He stood six feet two inches high, and weighed 429 pounds. The door-jamb had to be removed to get his coffin out of the house when he died, in December, 1744. His son Jacob was born the very year old Robert died, 1717. He was a whig in the war, and fled when the British took New York ; his estate was seized and confiscated by the British. The losses he sustained hastened his death. He died in 1780, aged sixty-three years. Col. Jacob was one of the deputies in the New York Provincial Congress.

I presume that it was owing to pecuniary embarrassments of this sufferer in the war, that led his sons, Joseph, Josiah and Jacob, all to embark in trade again, as the former of the house, old Robert, had done in 1670. Joseph started after the war, as I have said, in Hanover square, and here I must mention, in order to avoid confusion, that his son Joseph was also in commercial business in this city, and of the firm of Blackwell & Ayres. Old Joseph married Miss Mary Hazard, a daughter of N. Hazard ; and besides Joseph, there was a son named William Drayton, and a daughter named Harriet. Joseph married William Bayard's daughter, Justina. He was of the firm of Le Roy, Bayard & Co., and gave his son-in-law $20,000. In after years, when Le Roy, Bayard & Co. where embarrassed, Mr. William Bayard asked his son-in-law to indorse for him. He declined. Said he never indorsed, but would give him back the $20,000 that he had received with his daughter. Never was there such a kind-hearted, loving father to his children, as Mr. Blackwell.

In 1792, one Joseph kept at 45 Great Dock, and the young one corner Coenties slip and Little Dock street (Water.) The next year it was kept at 8 Coenties slip and corner Water street, for many years after. Josiah, another brother, kept his iron store at 31 South street. In 1796, Joseph made a partnership with Henry Mc Farlane, under the firm of " Blackwell & Mc Farlane." Mr. Mc Farlane had been in the iron business for some time, and I think was connected with John Mc Farlane, who had charge of the " air furnace " out on the Greenwich road, at the close of the last century.

In 1801, there were two Blackwells in the concern, and it was Blackwells & McFarlane. I think the other Blackwell was his nephew Jacob, who succeeded afterwards to the business of Josiah. Josiah never married. Josiah, the brother of Joseph, was in the iron business at 31 South street, as late as 1805, when I think he died. He was succeeded by Jacob, who kept up the firm until 1810, when he moved round into Cherry street, and went into business afterwards under the firm of Blackwell & Smith. He was a son of Samuel Blackwell, who was son of Col. Jacob Blackwell and father of Joseph. He had a brother named Samuel; one named Robert M., another Henry F., another John. There were several daughters.

Jacob, above alluded to, married a daughter of Thomas Lawrence, of the firm of Thomas & John F. Lawrence. Thomas was a son-in-law of George Ireland, who is still living in this city.

Jacob was a boy in the counting room of his uncle Josiah. When he died in 1805, Jacob succeeded him. He was only eighteen years old when he married. His fate was singular. Many will remember a large fire that occurred a few years ago, at the corner of Burling slip and Front street, in the day time. Jacob was in the store. He walked to the front window of the second floor, and put out one leg. He was told by hundreds to jump. He deliberately pulled of his spectacles, wiped them, and turned to descend the stairs. He was never seen alive, but his bones were found at the foot of the stairs. His brother Robert M., is of the firm of R. M. Blackwell & Co. Mr. Zophar Mills, Jr., so well known in the fire department, is the partner. They still do a large commission and naval store business, and keep up the old merchant stock.

Joseph continued in business under the same firm of
Blackwell & McFarlane until he died, 1827. The firm
was kept up as B. & McF., until 1830, when it changed
to McFarlanes & Ayers, Mr. Henry McFarlane senior, having formed a partnership with Daniel Ayers,
and his son Henry Mc Farlane, Junior.

Joseph Blackwell left several children — one son and
several daughters. The son was named Drayton. Jo-
sephine married Alfred Livingston, of Trenton. She
died. He afterwards married her sister Eliza. One
daughter married a Mr. Bleecker. Another married
Mr. Forbes.

The widow of Joseph lived in the old house, No. 16
State street, as late as 1836, when the family moved up
town. Joseph lived in State street many years, having
gone there before the war of 1812. He was always a
First Warder, living many years at 55 Broadway. For
over thirty years Blackwell & McFarlane was one of
the heaviest houses in the iron trade. They did an immense business. They bought out entire cargoes of
iron without hesitating. When such houses as Boorman & Johnston received a cargo of Swedish iron,
James Boorman would walk into the store of B. & M.
and say, " Well, I have just got my invoice for a cargo
of iron. I give you, as usual, the first chance. Do
you wish to buy it, Mr. McFarlane ? "

" What do you ask ? "

Mr. Boorman would name his prices.

" Very well : we will look around, see what we can
do, and let you know by Saturday."

Blackwell & McFarlane would then write to their
correspondents at Albany — Erastus Corning, Isaac &
John Townsend — and state the facts. They would
also see J. G. Pierson, and other leading iron houses in

this city, and then divided up among them one or ten cargoes of iron. Sometimes, they would tell old Boorman
" We can't take your cargo." He would reply;
" Well, I must sell it; if you will not buy it, gentlemen, I will start an iron store myself." He did carry
out his threat in after years, much to the annoyance
of the great iron dealers. He took in a Mr. Clark,
whose father had been in the iron business largely in
New York, but failed. Another house that used to co-
operate with Blackwell & McFarlane, in buying cargoes of iron, was David Watkinson & Co., of Hartford
Conn. He died a short time ago, worth a million of
dollars. He left a large portion to public charities.

After the death of Mr. Blackwell, McFarlanes, &
Ayres went into manufacturing. They actually bought
the land and started the town of Dover, New Jersey.
They started a bank, forges, founderies and everything
else. Dover is a beautiful place, about ten miles from
Morristown, and you reach it by the Morris and Essex
railroad, in about an hour's ride from New York city.
It is up among the iron mountains of New Jersey,
and mines are as thick in the region as tombstones in
Trinity churchyard.

The Morris canal company owed McFarlanes & Ayres
$80,000 to $90,000. Young McFarlane had been sick.
He went into the office of the canal company, although
the firm continued on the same. That was the time
when the Morris company built inclined planes, and
other improvements. McFarlanes & Ayres imported
iron for their use — drums, chains for pulling up the
boats, and accumulated an enormous debt, which the
Morris canal could not, and did not pay. There was
no written contract, and I think about this time old
Henry McFarlane died. At any rate, the house dis-

solved about this time. He had been very much esteemed in this city. When he first commenced business he resided at No. 20 Garden street. In 1806 he
moved to Vesey street, No. 4, where the Astor House
now is. In 1816 he moved to No 12, same street, and
lived there until until 1833, when the Astor House was
being built and the neighboring houses were all torn
down. Henry McFarlane was a vestryman of Trinity
church from 1815 to 1831. That fact shows what kind
of a man he was.

He must have been a prince of a man. He married
a Miss Carmer. So did Robert Lennox. So did Robert Maitland. So did one or more of our first men, who
thus became his brothers-in-law. In those days, of
course, business was mixed. Nicholas Carmer was a
vestryman of Trinity church from 1787 to 1805. Immediately after the war — 1782 — he had a cabinet-
maker's store at 34 Maiden Lane. A few years after
he added to it "ironmonger;" that is, he sold hardware as well as wooden chairs, bureaus, &c., in the same
old store. He had a son, of whom I have written,
Nicholas G. Carmer. He was an "ironmonger" at
230 Queen (Pearl), in 1792; afterwards got into the
hat business with his brother; but I do not think that
things went well with the Carmer males, although the
girls had married well. How many admirers among
the youths they must have had seventy years ago!
How many youths attended devoutly every Sunday at
Trinity to see the Miss Carmers? Old Nicholas gave up
business, and became an inspector of lumber, and was so
until 1808, when he died. His son, Nicholas G., also
seems not to have succeeded in trade, for he became a
weighmaster at the Phœnix Coffee House ; and died, I
think in 1806.

All the sons-in-law were rich, of course.

After the dissolution of McFarlanes & Ayres, Daniel Ayres went with James Boorman in 1834. The previous year he had separated his business and carried out his plan of starting an iron yard. He took the store No. 119 Greenwich street and its large yard. In 1835, when Mr. Ayres joined him, he carried on the business of Boorman, Johnston, Ayres & Co. at this place, and the regular business of Boorman, Johnston, & Co., was down at the old place, No. 57 South street. Boorman, Johnston, Ayres & Co. continued in existence until 1844, when Mr. Ayres retired from it. He is still alive and very wealthy. I should think he was not far from 70 years of age.

Young H. McFarlane kept the Dover works all going. He has had a concern in New York since 1834. His private residence, when he first started house-keeping, in 1828, was at No. 79 Dey street. A long time he lived at No. 54 Varick street, but of late years, twenty-three or more, he has resided at Dover, where he has a superb establishment. When he comes into town he stops at the St. Nicholas. His house was at one time McFarlane & Cotheal, up at No. 385 Water street, in 1838.

I mentioned William Drayton Blackwell, who was a brother of Joseph. He has been dead many years. He was rich and eccentric. He prided himself on being indifferent as to dress. He certainly was extremely slovenly in his habits. He speculated in stocks heavily, and his brokers were Dykers & Alstyne. A sister of the above brother, Harriet, married William Howell. I think he was a captain in the navy. After his death she resided at No. 365 Broadway, corner of Franklin street. She lived there as late as 1838, when Charles

A. Davis, of the firm of Davis & Brooks, took it. Mr. Davis married the only daughter of Mrs. Howell. Those who frequent Taylor's immense establishment, if they sit on the south side, occupy the same ground as Mrs. Howell did in her days of glory. They all moved in the highest strata of society, as any lady has a right to do, whose history is recorded in the Old Merchants for 200 years back.

Blackwell & McFarlane brought up many young men as clerks, during the thirty-five years that old strong iron house existed. Among the number was Daniel A. Gallaway. After leaving his old employers, he went with William Scott, who was a great iron manufacturer up at Parville, New Jersey, and who was a brother of Colonel John Scott, so long the president of the Dover bank. Scott & Gallaway occupied the store, corner of Water and Coenties slip, occupied by Blackwell & McFarlane from 1800, and that had been occupied by McFarlane & Ayres, when they dissolved in 1833.

Next door to Mr. Scott was D. M. Wilson, who had been a grocer under the firm of Wilson & Chamberlain ; but seeing how money was coined in the iron trade, determined to embark in it. The concern No. 41 Water street was a large double store, and Wilson joined Scott, under the firm of Scott & Wilson. The fire of 1835 burned them out, and the concern dissolved. The firm of D. M. Wilson was then formed, and William Bruen, a brother-in-law of D. M. Wilson, and a clerk named George T. Cobb, were taken into the firm. Mr. Cobb is now vice president of the Importers Bank.

Mr. Gallaway left them and formed a partnership with Frederick A. Gay, under the firm of Gay & Gallaway. They kept at 73 Water, corner of Old slip. They kept hollow hardware, iron kettles, and all sorts of i on. They had a curious italic lettered sign on a green ground. That store, No. 73, was owned by Jacob Southard, a rich coal dealer in the Fifth Ward. After a few years Mr. Gallaway sold out to Gay, and they dissolved, and he went with William Scott again, under the firm of Scott & Gallaway. They kept a large iron store on the corner of Dey and Washington streets. After a few months, one hot day Mr. Scott fell dead in front of the store. He owned an immense quantity of property at Powersville, near Dover. He owns the Hibernia, Boonton, Durham, Parnill and other forges, besides a vast quantity of real estate. Every year he burned hundreds of charcoal pits. After the death of Mr. Scott, Francis McFarlane, a son of old Henry, of Blackwell & McFarlane, was taken into the firm, and it was Gallaway & McFarlane. Finally the latter sold out, and Gallaway went back to his old store, 73 Water street, corner of Old slip, and those monster iron kettles graced the front of his store up to within a few months. No worthier or more enterprising mortal ever lived than that same Mr. Gallaway. As he did an enormous Southern business, I suppose the rebellion finished him, for I do not recollect seeing a kettle in the vicinity of his Old slip store for a year past.

D. M. Wilson, who kept the old Coenties slip stand, was bought out by T. B. Coddington, who had previously been in the tin, copper and sheet iron business. Thos. B. was a nephew of old Sam. Coddington, who kept a drinking place in Coenties slip near Water. T. B. C. was a clerk of John A. Moore, of whom I wrote much a year ago in one of the first chapters. I believe Mr. Coddington is still in business.

John A. Moore was brought up by Harman Hendricks.

CHAPTER XIV.

John A. Moore after he left Mr. Hendricks, bought out Troup & Goelet, iron merchants, corner of Old slip and Water street. They did an enormous business. The partner was Robert R. Goelet, of whom I have already written. John A. Moore was rather an ordinary looking person, but as smart as a steel trap. His store — the one above alluded to — was a very large one, and he added to the old iron business of Troup & Goelet, copper, sheathing and nails. He had thoroughly learned that business with old Mr. Hendricks, and he determined to make money by it. Mr. Moore was a regular gambler in merchandize. He had his regular business, but was not satisfied with that. One day he would take it into his head that a rise would occur in a particular kind of iron. He would go to a large capitalist and commission house, and by agreeing to pay a certain amount of interest and commission, would raise $100 to 250,000 to buy up all that particular kind of iron in the market. Now and then he would make money by such a bold operation, but it was not strict " business," and did not add to his mercantile credit.

At another time he would buy up all the coffee in the market. Sometimes it would be French brandy. Those who wish to see an interesting account of Mr. Moore

should read chapter eighth in this book. Mr. Moore
was an energetic man, and added to the wealth of the
city ; his gambling mercantile operations, however, as a
general thing, were personally very disastrous to himself.

Nicholas G. Carmer, to whom I have alluded, was
secretary, to the Hand in Hand fire company. It was
instituted in this city in November, 1780, for the purpose of averting as much as possible, the ruinous conse-
quences which occasionally happen by fire. It continued, certainly as late as 1798, for that year Carmer was
Secretary and John Murray, the merchant, was president. The company consisted of fifty members, who were
provided with *bags* for the removal of effects at a fire.

Sir N. G. was standard bearer of the Knights Tem-
plar encampment. He was master of Howard Lodge
No. 9, for some years.

Mr. Carmer and his father were both " ironmongers,"
or hardware men ; and I alluded to him as a monk of
the " Friary " in my article about Bernard Hart.

He was also in the militia, and, in fact there was
hardly any good or sociable work that did not find in
Mr. Carmer a ready assistant.

I notice among the list of officers who have gone in
the naval expedition that sailed on Wednesday, the name
of John A. Tardy, Jr. He is a lieutenant in the army,
having graduated from West Point in 1860. The
youth — not over twenty-two — and yet his name is
one that years ago was heard on 'change. He is a
grandson of John G. Tardy, an extensive merchant in
this city before 1800.

He entered at West Point when sixteen years of age,
and remained there five years. He graduated with the
highest honors, and was appointed brevet second lieu-

tenant in the engineer corps. He refused to take his three months' leave of absence, and was appointed Assistant Professor of Practical Engineering at that post. He was ordered to Washington with his company of sappers and miners to defend the Government, and they were the only regulars who were present at the inauguration of Mr. Lincoln. After the " Sumter " affair, young Tardy was ordered to Fort Pickens, in the first expedition. There he remained six months fortifying the place, and was then ordered North, where he arrived just in time to be ordered South with the great naval expedition, as the second engineer officer in it.

His grandfather, John G. Tardy, was born in Switzerland, but went to France to learn business in a French counting room.

He was brought up in the office of Burral Carnes, who was American consul at Nantes, in France, appointed by General Washington in 1792. Mr. Tardy left Nantes to go to Hayti, or St. Domingo, to establish a commercial house, intending to do the American business. He landed in Boston, came to New York, and called on president Washington, to whom he had a letter of introduction. He sailed for Hayti, and settled there. He received a large share of the American business, and coined money. Then came the terrible insurrection. He sent his wife and two children, and five negro servants, with nothing on but their night-clothes, on board an American schooner lying off the " Cape." They had no time to take anything else. He returned to the city to fight the negroes, remained the whole night, and only when the town was in flames did he come on board, and the vessel sailed for New York. He, however, knew many persons in this city — merchants whom he had done business with — and they

took him by the hand. Among them was Gurdon
S. Mumford, who then lived at 37 William street. This
was about 1797. Mr. Mumford went on board the
vessel when she arrived in the harbor, and took the Tardy party on shore, and procured for them a house at 41
Beaver street.

John G. Tardy soon got into active and profitable
business, and took a store and house at 53 Gold street.
He was a mason, and was made master of the Lodge
" L'Union Francaise No. 14."

His business became very extensive. He sold on
commission ; all his vessels were running blockades at
Bordeaux and other ports in Enrope, in 1812, when he
formed a partnership under the firm of Majastre & Tardy. In the war of 1813 this house loaned the Government $10,000. They did a heavy business as the
agents of French merchants, in Philadelphia, who did
their business of importing, by way of New York. At
that time Bordeaux was the great port of France.
Havre was nothing forty-eight years ago. It started
up after the peace, in 1815, took place. Mr. Majastre
died during the war. He was from Marseilles, but was
only here a short time. Mr. Tardy had several sons.
Two went to sea in their father's ships. One was in
the Dartmoor prison ; another died at Plymouth, England, of fever. One of his vessels was the " Dart,"
clipper. She was taken by a British frigate. Mr. Tardy became embarrassed by indorsing custom house
bonds for his friends. It ruined him. He died in 1831,
aged 72 ; would have been 102 had he lived until now.
The latter years of his life were made comfortable by
holding an office in the Marine Court. He was appointed clerk of that court by his political friends, and
he held it until he died. He was politically and per-

sonally friendly with all those great men who originated
the old Republican party — now called the Democratic.
Among them was Edward Livingston, Aaron Burr,
Captain Thomas Darling, and others. He was a great
man in Tammany Hall, and spent money like water.
At that time, the capitalists and merchants were all
Federalists, as a general thing. He was an intimate
acquaintance of Governor Tompkins, until the latter ·
died. So also he was of Albert Gallatin, whose principles and talents he admired. They were born in the
same Canton of Switzerland, and Mr. Gallatin only
preceded him to this country one year.

He had one son named John A. Tardy, who was educated at Columbia College. He wished to make a
merchant of him, and for that purpose placed him in
the counting-room of his friend, Joseph Bouchaud.

He was there some years, and became the principal
clerk of the firm of Bouchaud & Thebaud, and only
left them when he went into partnership with Mr. Voisin, who was also a clerk with Bouchaud. They did a
very heavy French importing businesss for some years,
and then dissolved. Meanwhile, Mr. Tardy married
Miss Eustaphieve, one of the belles of the city. She
is the mother of the young warrior, Tardy, Jr. She
died early. Her father was the Russian consul general fifty-two years in this city. He died in 1857. There
are very few persons who do not remember old Alexander Eustaphieve. He was a splendid specimen of a
man, and was much beloved. He was warmly attached
to the two children of Mr. Tardy and his daughter, for
there was a grand-daughter as well as son. She married Captain Charles Seaforth Stewart, of the United
States engineer corps. He is now the chief engineer at
Fortress Monroe. In the class in which he graduated at

7

West Point, he stood number one, and General M'Clel-
lan number two.

He married Miss Tardy at Buffalo. The old consul
was present, but died within a month of the time.

After Voisin & Tardy dissolved, Mr. Tardy went
with Eugene Grousset to manage his business. Who
don't remember that little, short, dashing French wine
merchant?

Eugene Grousset will be well remembered here by
many of the present generation. I do not know when
he made his first appearance in this city, but think it
must have been about the year 1827. He was celebrated as being the brother of Grousset de Granier, a wine
merchant of Marseilles, who, at one time, did an enormous business with this country and other parts of the
world. He owed the Bank of France at one time three
millions of francs. He failed in 1839, or thereabouts,
and then Eugene's agency on this side was closed. He
went to New Orleans, where he died.

This wine made by Grousset de Granier was sold in
all parts of the country. It was called *Marseilles Madeira*, and was a very good imitation of the real Madeira. It was manufactured at a cost not exceeding $6
for a quarter cask of 31 gallons. It sold readily in this
market for 50 or 60 cents a gallon — say $15 to $18
per cask. The profit was enormous. Grousset ought
to have made two millions of dollars, if he had managed
his business properly. Unfortunately he was forever
financiering — selling cargoes at low prices to raise cash
for immediate necessities. He had three clerks, well
known. One was Goodman. Another named Brady,
now clerk in a bank in Broadway; and a third, named
John Mitchell, still a resident of this city.

Mr. Grousset was a great wag. At that time the

old City Hotel was in its glory. It boasted of as fine
a lot of wines as could be had in any part of the world.
It was at this hotel that the dinners were given by societies and parties. On one occasion (I think it was
after the upsetting of Charles X, of France, and the
success of Louis Phillipe,) a great dinner was given
to celebrate the event at the City Hotel. The finest
wines that the City Hotel could furnish were placed
upon the table. In addition, private individuals who
possessed rare wines had contributed a bottle. One celebrated individual had wine bottled in Madeira in 1786.

This brought out Grousset. He had sent to his store
in Broad street for four bottles of wine that he pur-
posely had carefully dusted to make them look old. It
was really his trash Marseilles Madeira. Mr. Grousset
stated that nearly all present knew that he was in the
wine business. He professed to be a judge of wine
and his father before him was a judge of wine, and they
possessed a few bottles of wine that they never offered
for sale because it was priceless. It was old Madeira,
and if it was not two hundred years old he did not know
how old it was. Of course only a few drops, at most,
could be tasted by any one ; it was too precious. He
hoped that the company would appreciate his patriotism,
which was as pure as his old wine. He was cheered to
the clouds. The wine was served in cordial glasses, and
pronounced to be something beyond any wine that had
ever been brought to this country. There were men
of unquestioned veracity, and also good judges of wine,
who so pronounced this trash that was selling in the
market at about ten cents the bottle ! The awful sell
was confined to the knowledge of a few French gentlemen who were friends of Eugene Grousset. Mr. Tardy was for a long time an active politician in the Whig

ranks, and his influence was very considerable. Of late years I do not think he has meddled with commerce or with politics. His face is seen occasionally in the streets or reading the daily journals at some of the quiet hotels. His health is poor, and I do not think the world has many attractions left for one who has seen about all that was going on. His hopes in his two children are his life-blood just now — the one daughter who is Mrs. Stewart, and this son who bears his name. For his sake I hope the expedition will be a success, and if he falls he will die a soldier's death.

Since the above was written, young Tardy has been promoted to a higher rank.

CHAPTER XV.

Within a short time, three persons of some distinction — mercantile and quite celebrities — among the fast and dashing portions of the city have died, and have already been mentioned among the " Old Merchants," during the past two years. I allude to Charles Davis, Theodore Dehon, William D. Kennedy, Edward Vincent, J. Sherman Brownell, and Henry P. Gardner.

The last named died October 4, 1861, aged thirty-seven. It is nearly twenty-two years ago, when he entered mercantile life, under the mercantile auspices of Fernando Wood. He was a boy in the store of Fernando Wood, at No. 133 Washington street. He was his clerk at the time Mr. Wood had $1500 placed to his credit wrongfully, and which Mr. Wood with prudent foresight drew out of the clutches of the " Merchants' Exchange Bank."

That year Mr. F. Wood went before the people as their candidate for representative to Congress. The real facts of the case were laid before the people, and honest men like W. B. Astor, and leading merchants, indignant at the swindle attempted to be put upon Wood by the " Merchants' Exchange Bank," took his part, and elected him to Congress.

Henry P. Gardner was a most excéllent young man.

He knew the real facts of this case, but being young he was taken care of by Charles A. Secor, and went into his employ. It is a curious fact, that the devil does protect and take care of those he loves. There never has been a good and true man who has stood up and fought Fernando Wood, with naked name, and naked facts. I say there has been no such man who did not die out before he had succeeded. Lorenzo B. Shepard was a glorious fellow. The battle with Wood killed him. Had he lived, most probably Mr. Wood would not have been in Congress at this time.

Another man who believed Fernando Wood capable of any wickedness, was William D. Kennedy. He was a merchant. He knew New York, and I have a sketch of him that will appear, and be one of the deepest interest. He despised Wood, because he knew him to be treacherous. He admired his sublime impudence, his church membership, his sending his carriage to Irish funerals; but if the colonel's gallant spirit could have been present at the funeral of his own body, and seen Wood weep crocodile tears, and heard his voice say, " Poor Bill," while he would probably have begged some friend to kick the audacious man out of the precincts of the church, he would have added : " Wood is right. He acts out his part to the life, to the death, and to the last. He hates me. He comes to my funeral with his feelings crawling with gratification. He says to himself, ' I want to see that Kennedy in his coffin, cold, and ready to be food for worms. See it with my own eyes — then I can gloat over what I know to be an undisputed fact. He has crossed my path day and night, in season and out of season.' Wood is right." So William D. would have said, and he was a good judge of human motives.

Others who do not know Wood, think he went to the funeral of Kennedy to make political capital. That is not so. A shrewd man told me : " Wood went there as I once went to see an infernal scoundrel who had wronged me individually, who had also wronged the State, and was sent to Sing Sing for ten years. I wanted to see with my own eyes that he had met his fate I wanted to feel that he who had opposed, thwarted, exposed, and tried to blast my prospects, was a degraded, hapless criminal."

I am not aware how long Mr. Gardner was with Wood. In 1834, Wood himself had left making cigars, and had been hired as a clerk with Francis Secor & Co., at 103 Washington street. To that family, and the combinations they were enabled to make, Wood owes his political start. The old Francis is still alive, has a farm out in Westchester county. He was foreman to Henry Eckford, when the first steamboats were built. Eckford's ship yard was in Water street, up near Clinton street, in 1810. He had several sons, Thorne, Zeno, Henry, Charles A. and James. They all were connected with the establishment in which Wood was a clerk. Then there was Joseph Sherman Brownell, at 100 Washington, where he had commenced business in 1830. He had hosts of friends. There was John S. Gilbert, the ship joiner, at 118 Washington street, James Munson, the block-maker, at 108. Thomas Shortland, the cooper, was at 101, and lived at 111 Washington street. All these men had great primary influence, employed many men, and could carry political meetings in several of the wards. They were excellent materials to build up any man. While Wood was a clerk with Secor & Co., he became personally known to these men. Toward the close of 1836, Wood proposed to start the liquor store (the lowest three cent shop is dignified with the name of "ship stores,") at 99 corner of Rector. At that time there was no West street, Washington faced the North river. The numbers were continued on the same side; 99 was Wood's store; 100 next, was Brownell's; 101 Shortland's; Secor, 103. Shortland owned the property on the corner, and he leased it to Wood, without any security, believing him to be an enterprising young business man. The business was a shocking one. It was to sell bad liquor at three cents a glass to the hundreds of workmen that worked in the stevedore gangs on board ships lying at the docks on that side of the town. These men, of course, would have no money during the week, and it would have been a losing business but for the extraordinary mercantile sagacity and commercial foresight of Mr. F. Wood. There were several prominent stevedores at that time. Mr. Seeley was one. Everleigh was another, and Smith one. Wood arranged with all these stevedores that their men should be paid off in his groggery. Wood kept an alphabet book of charges, so that when Saturday night came, when "Jo Smith," "Bully Bob," or "Jack Duff" was called up to be paid, Wood was asked, "What have you got against him, Fernando?" Wood would turn to his alphabet, and reply, $3, $4,50, $1,25, or 75 cents, as the case might be. The sum would then be deducted from the wages due of $9, or $7, and the poor fellow would have two or three dollars to take home to his family, while the rest went to the till of the future great statesman of New York!

It was a common occurrence that the men would say: "Wood, you have charged me with three dollars' worth of your stuff, and I know I have not had it. Mr.

Wood would try on his irresistible amiability, offer to treat, and it would pass over to be renewed again week after week for three years. On one occasion, a worthy fellow, named Ferguson, said to several of his cronies: " Last week, my wages were docked two dollars and fifty cents for Wood's charge. I had no such sum, but to satisfy myself whether he is a rascal or not, I have not drank a drop this week and will not." Saturday night came. Ned Ferguson, called the stevedore, " How much have you, Wood ? "

" Seventy-five cents," said Fernando Wood. Furguson replied : " I have not drank a drop here or anywhere else this past week, and by the help of God I never will again, and thus rescue myself from the clutches of such a man as you are. All the men know that I have not drank, for they heard me say I would not, and have watched me." Wood insisted, and got the seventy-five cents he had charged.

When his first year was up, Thomas Shortland, the landlord, said : " If you can give me security, you can have that place for another year, not without."

" But Tom, you let me have it when I was poor ; you know that I have made money while I have had it, and yet you now want security ? "

" Yes, Wood, that is it ; when I let to you first, I knew you poor, but I believed you would pay me. Now I know you have made money, but I believe you to be anxious to make money, and lawless how you make it. It shall not be out of me. I know that you can give security. I know it will be Charles A. Secor."

That Thomas Shortland was one of those who added to the wealth of New York, though merely a cooper. His two sons, Thomas Jr., and Stephen, are carrying on the same business in the old locality, and under

Henry P. Gardner's recent store, 50 West street, and the old gentleman has the Atlantic Docks, Brooklyn, and is very wealthy. One of Thomas Shortland's sons married a daughter of John S. Gilbert alluded to. Gilbert was the inventor of the celebrated Balance Dock. It has been adopted by the Government and by several foreign governments. He is worth half a million of dollars.

J. Sherman Brownell at 100 Washington street did a large business, and I believe he went into politics after Wood's first success. He was led into it by the force of example, as have been many others, who have said, "If Fernando Wood can be elected to Congress, there is no office I can not aspire to." I don't think Sherman Brownell would ever have aspired to any civic dignities had he not kept a store next door to Fernando Wood.

Henry P. Gardner, after leaving Wood, became a junior clerk with Secor & Co., afterwards Secor & Livingston. After being some years with the Secors, Henry was taken into partnership under the firm of Secor & Co., his partner being Charles F. Secor, son of Charles, Joseph Morton and H. P. Gardner. Young Charles married a daughter of James B. Nicholson, now one of the Commissioners of Charities and Corrections.

After the firm had existed some time and coined money, it was dissolved. Henry P. Gardner then became a partner in the large house of William A. Freeborne & Co., ship chandlers, at No. 254 South and No. 501 Water, and brass founder at No. 498 Water. About a year ago he left that house, and started the ship chandlery business on the North river side, at No. 50 West — a new street, but fronting the Water, as Washington

street did when he first went with the Secors. Henry
was very much beloved by all who knew him. He was
married, had four children, and had every prospect of
happiness and a successful mercantile career before him.
He was a member of the Masonic order. His death
was very sudden. I met him a short time previous,
and he asked me to drop in and see him at his new store.
I never was more shocked than when I heard of his
death.

Edward Vincent died suddenly. He was formerly a
merchant in this city. Curious enough, in Chapter 26
of this work, I alluded to him pleasantly in this way:
" Captain Edward Vincent, James B. Glentworth, and
George L. Pride, used to go out to Cato's in the early
summer morning, and drink mint juleps together, previous to the late war with England in 1812." The
next day, Mr. H—, a broker went to Captain Vincent,
and asked him if he would sell him a land warrant,
granted to soldiers of the 1812 war. Of course, the
captain had none. The visitor expressed surprise, as he,
Captain Vincent, was out in that war. He took the
joke at once — said he should have to challenge W. B.
for making him nearly seventy years old.

I do not think he was far from sixty years old. Thirty years ago he was a merchant, under the firm of Vincent & Butterworth, in Pearl, near Old Slip, about No.
86. At that time Vincent was a splendid fellow of
very agreeable manners, plenty of customers and plenty
of cash, lived at Mrs. Mann's, or one of those ostenta-
tious boarding houses in Broadway, below the old Grace
Church, (Rector street.) He was a Virginian, and
was welcomed wherever he went. He was a military
man and popular. He was a regular attendant upon
the old City Hall assembly balls. He could have

picked a wife any where. Vincent & Butterworth did
a very extensive business, until the cold night in December, 1835, when the lower part of New York, on the
East river side, was laid in ashes. They were insured,
but no insurance company paid their losses. I think
the concern was staggered and a new order of things
was started, for he opened again at No. 45 Broad street,
under the firm of Brett & Vincent. That firm continued some years, at least as late as the election of General Harrison in 1840. From Tyler, his successor, I
think, Captain Vincent received an appointment in the
Custom House, and if my memory serves me, he was
not removed from it until within a few weeks of his
death. He was a man with many friends. He enjoyed society. He had his share of the good things of this
world, and he knew how to make the most of them.
I am not aware when he ceased to command the " Light
Guard," or when that brilliant company was disbanded.
Certainly it has not been heard of since the war commenced. Of course, Captain Vincent, being a Virginian by birth, could not have been expected to command
against his own State, although General Scott took a
different view of it. George L. Pride has since died.

Charles Davis and Theodore Dehon were at one time
both partners of the house of Davis & Brooks. I have
written fully about the house and its partners in previous chapters. When they died, they were not of the
firm. Davis had retired from business altogether, and
Mr. Dehon was in business on his own account. He
died in London. Davis died in this city.

Twenty-five years ago, no fashionable person could
have gone to two or four aristocratic parties a week in
this city without meeting one or both of these men.
They were welcome everywhere. Such is life, and such

is death. To the list I might have added another old merchant's name. I had much to say of Peter Embury, and mentioned his son, Daniel Embury, president of the Brooklyn Bank. On the 2d of November, a son of the latter was killed by an unknown assassin, while proceeding to the residence of W. S. Verplanck, about two miles from Fishkill Landing. Phillip Augustus Embury was a young· man of much promise. He was a clerk of an insurance company in this city, and betrothed to Miss Verplanck. He left the city at 5 o'clock P. M., November 2, in the great storm that raged. It was a fearfully dark night ; when he left the cars he had proceeded but a few rods when he was stabbed in the back by some unknown assassin. His body was not discovered until the next day. His age was twenty-five. His mother was the celebrated authoress, Emma C. Embury, the most popular poetess and magazine writer of the day, from 1840 to 1850. She is dead.

CHAPTER XVI.

I have frequently alluded to hereditary commercial houses. These are much more common in Europe than here. There a firm continues from the founder down two hundred and more years. The same name and style being retained through this long period, and long after any one bearing the name of the founder is connected with it, and none of the old name in it. This, however, cannot occur here. A law passed by the State Legislature, in 1833, prevents it. Now, to continue the style of a house, parties of that name must be connected with it. This makes not only a hereditary commercial firm in name, but in fact. It is more difficult now to keep even the same firm and same name any number of years, but yet there are many firms that do it. None, however, are more remarkable, than the firm of N. L. & G. Griswold. It exists to-day in 1861, and it existed in 1796, at 169 Front street, where the house at that time kept a flour store. George Griswold came to this city about two years previous to his brother Nathaniel. At that period many well-known houses of merchants did not find it necessary to put the number of the street in which they lived. The city was small, and in offering merchandize for sale, they made it, adding, apply to N. L. & G. Griswold. Every-

body of any consequence knew where such a heavy concern lived. It was so in 1803, when this house moved
from their Front street store to their new store, No. 86
South street, near Burling Slip. I think they lived in
that spot a third of a century or more, when they moved to a new, rough, granite, double store, Nos. 71 and
72 South, north corner of De Peyster street. There is
a fitness in things, and the solid stone was just the
building for two such men as Nathaniel and George
Griswold. They were grand old fellows. I can see
them in my mind's eye now as they used to look — tall,
imposing — both brothers men that you would take a
second look at.

A bold signature was that of the firm, as written by
old Nathaniel. I have it now before me as, in 1804,
he dashed off " Nath'l L. & Geo. Griswold," with a
good old-fashioned flourish under it. These Griswolds,
too, sprang from a grand old race. They were Connecticut born, and came here from old Lyme, on the
Connecticut River. Their ancestor, a six-footer, too,
named Edward Griswold, came over from Kenilworth,
England, in 1635, and settled at Windsor. He had a
son named Matthew, born in 1653, who went afterwards
and settled at Lyme, where he was a great man, and
"represented" that town many years. He died in
1699. He left behind him a son named George, who
was born the 13th August, 1692. That man was the
ancestor of the two Griswold boys who, in 1794 — 102
years later — left Lyme for a larger port, at which they
were destined in after years to become eminent merchants.

I think it hardly necessary for me to say, that if the
founders of the house were both living, George would
be about eighty-five years old, and Nathaniel about
ninety.

When George arrived in this city he was only just of age, and his brother Nat. a few years older. They were very stout, fine looking young men, six feet high each, and well proportioned. They were "six feet" men in all their business operations in after years, when they did an enormous business. They shipped flour heavily to the West Indies, and in 1804 they had become large importers of rum and sugar, receiving cargoes of these articles.

The merchants in 1861 who do a business of $30,000,000, are not regarded as doing as large a business as the merchant who, in 1800, did a business of $30,000 a year.

I do not know what year this house went into the "China trade." They did an immense business in it for years, and made a *specialite* of it at last. They owned the ship "Panama," and I do not suppose there is a country store however insignificant, in the whole of the United States, that has not seen a large or small package of tea, marked "Ship Panama," and N. L. & G. G. upon it. Millions of millions of packages must have been imported from the first to last. In fact, they owned in succession three ships named the "Panama." The first was 465 tons. When she became nearly worn out, the firm of N. & G. Griswold built a second ship of 650 tons burden, named her the "Panama," as she succeeded to No. 1 in the China trade. When the No. 2 "Panama" got old, the Griswolds built a third ship of 1170 tons burden, and named her the "Panama." The three ships in the successive periods that they flourished, must have made an uncommon number of Canton voyages.

Many men who were afterwards prominent went out to Canton as supercargo of the "Panama." One was

a son named John N. A. Griswold, who resided out
there some years. Another was John C. Greene, who
afterwards became a partner in the great Canton house
of Russell & Co. When he retired from business and
returned to this country, he married a daughter of Mr.
George Griswold.

Another daughter married George Winthrop Gray,
who has been identified with the house of N. L. & G.
Griswold, as a partner, over a quarter of a century, and
is well known to all New Yorkers. I believe Mr. Gray
is from Salem or Boston, where the name of William
Gray is as noted as Astor in New York, or Girard in
Philadelphia.

This house, like many other houses from the Eastern
States and ports, did an immense business by merely
selling, chartering or freighting new ships. A ship-
builder East would build a large ship — sixty years ago,
a ship of 350 tons would be the very largest kind of a
vessel. He would send on, for instance, such a ship as
I have now an account sale of before me. It was the
ship " Windsor." She was new, built of the best materials; her upper works were all of live oak, locust
and cedar, fastened with wrought copper; duck and cord-
age of the first quality; completely found in sails, rig-
ging and furniture, and needed nothing whatever.
They built ships strong and good in those days. There
was less fancy work; but all was solid and substantial,
as many merchants and ship owners were their own in-
surers. The fact is, fifty or sixty years ago, there was
not much capital in the city of New York; ships and
cargoes were generally found in Eastern ports — Salem,
Boston, New Bedford, and other places. There were
few houses that like N. L. & G. Griswold, were able
to own ships, and make up long voyages, requiring
great outlay on their own account.

In their day, or after the war, the duty on tea was enormous. Green tea paid as high as sixty-eight cents per pound. Black tea as high as thirty-four cents, from Canton. In all cases the duty was twice or three times the cost of the teas in Canton. The credit given by the United States Government was twelve and eighteen months. This, of itself, became an immense capital to any house engaged in the China trade. They could raise say $200,000 and send it in specie or merchandise in their ships. These ships left in May. In a year they would be back loaded with teas. Merely supposing the duty double the cost in China, (it was four times on low-priced black teas,) the teas would be worth at least double, being $400,000. Add freight at a fair profit, would make the cargo worth $500,000 at least. These teas would be sold, on arrival, to grocers at four and six months credit. These notes would be discounted easily, while the Griswolds had to pay duty, $200,000, half in a year and half in eighteen months! Thus really having of the United States an independent capital to do an enormous business.

However, the house of Griswolds did a safe but heavy business. That concern needed no capital but its own. Still many houses did go into this kind of business merely to get capital for other operations, as for instance, many imported brandy that had an enormous duty, forty years ago — about eighty cents a gallon. Government gave a credit of six, nine, and twelve months. Many, however, imported largely, sold to grocers, got their paper discounted, and had two thirds of their money to use nine and twelve months!

Singular as it may seem, both George and Nathaniel made a great deal more money outside of the business than in it. " Old Nat " got up a dredging machine.

He went up to Albany and made a contract to clean out the Albany basin, and also the overslaugh. He must have cleared over $100,000 by the contract. He also used it in New York at various slips. Then he built machines here and sent them South to work. There was an Albany man named Williams who used to be very thick with him, and had an interest in some of the city jobs. Mr. Griswold would hire docks from the Corporation at so much a year — generally a low figure, and then re-hire them and collect the wharfage himself. Nathaniel Griswold lived in Cliff street many years, afterwards at No. 3 Robinson (3 Park place.) Formerly Robinson street ran from Broadway to the College Green, and then continued from it on the western side to the North river ; but in 1813, the name was retained west of the college, while east it was changed to Park place. In 1819, old Nathaniel moved to 78 Chambers street, where he resided until he died in 1847. That year his widow and the family, as well as Nathaniel L., Jr., moved up to No. 136 Tenth street.

Old Nathaniel had several sons and daughters. At the time of his father's death, Nathaniel L. Jr., was in business at 92 South, under the firm of " I. L. & N. L. Griswold," and had been for some years, I believe. I. L. is another son. Nathaniel L. Griswold still carries on business at 102 Broad street.

The oldest daughter of Nathaniel Griswold married Charles C. Havens. She has been dead many years. Another daughter married Peter Lorillard. Another married Alfred H. P. Edwards, who was consul at Manilla, in the East Indies, many years, and did a very heavy business out there. These young ladies were all very handsome. Mr. Griswold built the house in Chambers street, No. 78. It stood near where the " Shoe

and Leather Bank" now stands, within twenty-five feet
of the rear of that splendid edifice, that now graces the
south-west corner of Broadway and Chambers street.

Old Nathaniel Griswold was very quiet, and retiring.
He cared nothing about being a bank director, or having
anything to do with any one's business but his own.
He differed from George in that respect. As early as
1807, George was made a director in the Columbia Insurance Company. From that time until he died he
was honored with being a director in almost every
society or monopoly of any importance. He was a man
to be trusted, and he liked activity. I have already alluded in a previous chapter, to the manner in which the
Bank of America, with its immense capital, was started
in 1812, to take the place of the then defunct United
States bank. Mr. George Griswold was, at that early
period elected a director, and he continued to be one
for scores of years.

George Griswold was of a very speculating turn of
mind. He operates heavily in land speculations. He
was in 1836 and 1837 extensively engaged in Brooklyn
purchases. He was an enterprising man and a thorough
merchant. He was in 1814 a director in the " Humane
Society," of which Matthew Clarkson was president.
I do not know how long that lasted. George Griswold too,
was connected with Swartwout's gold mine operation in
1836. Gold was to be coined in North Carolina faster
than it was afterwards in California. That speculation
also smashed up. He was greatly respected, and the
house of N. & G. Griswold has given wealth to the
city.

George Griswold died in 1859, at his house No. 9
Washington square. He had a large and interesting
family. Two of his sons succeeded him in the house

that he established — viz. : John N. Alsop Griswold and George Griswold, Jr. Two daughters married Gray and Greene, another married J. W. Haven, formerly of Haven & Co., 24 Broad street, twenty-five years ago, and of whom I have written. Another married Mr. Frelinghuysen, of New Jersey. He was recently Attorney General of that State.

Mr. George Griswold made an excellent presiding officer at political meetings, or at popular meetings for any other purpose. He was always ready to do his part in promoting the interests of the city. He loved it. He felt the degradation of the New York merchants. He felt that here, in this great city, the merchants were what Nick Biddle once designated them —" wealthy white slaves." Now and then a scheming lawyer would rouse up a few of the class to take an interest in politics for some specific purpose. George Griswold mourned the degeneracy of the race of merchants in his latter days. At the commencement of his career, the glorious conduct of the merchants of 1776 was fresh. Those noble old merchants were alive. He himself had met John Hancock, of Boston, and Francis Lewis, of our own city, both merchants — both singers of the immortal Declaration of Independence. When George Griswold arrived in New York in 1794, he could not turn a corner without meeting honored merchants of the city, who had been the " Liberty boys " of the Revolution.

In those years, none but the merchants ruled the city. There were seven wards. Of the fourteen Aldermen and Assistants, twelve were merchants. George Griswold felt that so it ought to be to the end of time. That merchants should rule — should command, and not be mere tools, as they had been. Merchants should

rule the city, and represent it in the State Legislature
and in Congress. He was ready with his money at any
time to spend it freely to give the merchants political
power. It seemed to him at times that there were no
merchants with brain power, or of an intellect equal to
other classes of society.

It not unfrequently happened that a few merchants
would spend, in some abortive political effort, more money than it would cost to elect six intelligent merchants
to Congress, if properly spent. As an instance. In
the spring of 1852, a few lawyers, such as Hiram Ketch-
um, Wm. M. Evarts, George Wood, and others, wished to get up a great city demonstration for Daniel Webster. The Whig National Convention was shortly to
come off in Baltimore, and these scheming lawyers
thought that if an immense sensation meeting was got
up, they would be able to elect Webster delegates from
all the districts in the city. The merchants of New
York, although they never initiate any great political
scheme, are always ready to be the tools of any lawyer,
and, as a general rule, they regard lawyers as several
degrees higher in the social thermometer, higher intel-
lectually, and they bend and bow to them. The men I
have named, set George Griswold, Moses H. Grinnell,
P. Perit, all bell-wether merchants, to get up this meeting in favor of Webster at Tripler Hall. It was accomplished, and cost directly $5,370. The advertising bills
paid newspapers was $1,200. George Griswold presid-
ed, and it cost him a large check. It had no more effect
upon Webster's prospects than a snow flake. Not a
delegate was friendly to Webster from New York, and
the Convention nominated Gen. Scott.

George Griswold had some noble traits. There are
very few persons in this city who do not know George

S. Robbins. George started the dry goods business in Pearl street, at No. 211, on his own account, in 1822. The next year he moved to 148 Pearl street, and there he kept until the great fire of 1835. His firm for a few years had been Robbins & Painter. The fire fixed George S. Robbins. Insurance companies were ruined and did not pay their losses. George Robbins, like George Griswold, came from the banks of the Connecticut, and they were good friends. After 1837 his affairs were at a very low ebb. He scratched his head often and vigorously, without producing any new commercial idea. At that time, 1837, he was back at a new store, at the old number, and in 1838, he moved to 114 Water — Robbins, Painter & Co.— there they kept until 1840, when Mr. Robbins moved to 54 William street, above. In these years, and long after, there were no regular note-brokers, as now. A few large broker houses, such as Prime, Ward & King, and John Ward & Co., did this kind of business to a limited extent. George Robbins paid George Griswold a visit, to take his advice. He got advice, and he also got $30,000 as a loan at 6 per cent. interest per annum, without any security being asked. With this capital George S. Robbins commenced business at the corner of Pine and William, where once Wm. Niblo had his "Bank Coffee House," and in latter years the great auction house of Haggerty, Draper & Jones flourished. In this locality the banking house of George S. Robbins & Son still exists, as it has in the same place for twenty years, enjoying uninterrupted prosperity, and discounting more notes than any bank. The foundation of this prosperity was owing to George Griswold.

The two Griswolds are in their graves, but they will

long be remembered, and certainly they added greatly to the prosperity of their adopted city.

A sketch of Duncan Pearsall Campbell, who died recently, and was buried at Trinity, will appear in the next chapter. He was 80 years old. He was once of the firm of Le Roy, Bayard & Co., and a son-in-law of William Bayard.

CHAPTER XVII.

I had prepared a sketch of Mr. Duncan P. Campbell, about six months ago. It was very imperfect, and knowing him personally, I thought I would some day or other fall in with him — show what I had written, and get some points from himself. I took time to accomplish my purpose, for I thought that I had noticed that Mr. Campbell had been shy of me, since he ascertained that I was the author of these recollections. The last time I ever saw him was in Chamber, near Centre street. He complimented me on one of the chapters that he had recently read. I remarked :

" Seme day when you are at leisure I want to talk over old matters."

" Any time," was his reply, as he passed on.

" Any time ! " don't hold good with a man who is eighty years old, and shortly after I read to my amazement and also deep regret :

DIED—On Saturday, Nov. 9th, 1861. DUNCAN PEARSALL CAMPBELL, in the 80th year of his age.

Very few of the people in the present city of New York, will recognize this name, or know anything about Mr. Campbell. Yet he was a great man in this city in his day. Of late years he had hardly been known to take an active part in public affairs. For twenty years

8

he had frequented a place called " The Grotto," at 114
Cedar street, kept either by Barnard or by Patrick Reilly
since 1840.   I dare say he has spent two or three hours
every fair day in the place, and drank one or perhaps
two " mugs " of the unrivalled old beer kept in the establishment.   At about mid-day in fine weather, any
one on Broadway could see a pale-faced man turn into
Liberty street from Broadway, treading carefully — a
shadow of the past — eyeing suspiciously any face in a
town where once, but more than half a century ago, he
knew everybody.   When he got safe into Liberty street
he passed down by Temple street into Trinity place,
turned the corner, and kept on until he reached Cedar
street, when he looked anxiously at the place where
stood the little two-story building kept by Reilly, as if
fearful that that too, like a thousand other things he
had seen, might have passed away or been moved up
town.   So methodical was this old New Yorker, that I
do not think, in going to or from his favorite spot to his
home, he ever varied a hair from one route.   He was
aged, and yet dignified in his bearing until the last hour
of his existence, although of late years he was very
feeble.   Many will recollect his old residence at No.
51 Broadway, part way between Morris and Rector
streets.   His door-plate had his name upon it in heavy
commercial letters, " Duncan P. Campbell."   He
had lived in that house from 1810 to to 1850, when he
moved up town to 138 Second avenue.   In early life
Mr. Campbell married a daughter of William Bayard,
and was himself a partner of the house of Le Roy,
Bayard & Co., in the days of its greatest glory.   He
also married a second daughter of Mr. Bayard.   He
was in business on his own account in Water street,
in 1809.

He was honored during the active part of his life with being director in banks, insurance companies, and many beneficial institutions. He was also one of the most amiable of men. He was one of the directors of the city Dispensary in 1815, when old Matthew Clarkson was its president, and his colleagues were such men as John Watts and Jonathan Goodhue. Peter S. Townsend was the Secretary. He was in after years Assistant Editor, with Major Noah, in *The Evening Star*; and Bennett, of *The Herald*, crucified him under the name of Peter *Simple* Townsend. He was a physician.

Mr. Campbell was one of the most active of those citizens who founded the savings bank in 1819, and of which his relation, William Bayard, was president many years. He commenced in 1819, and died in office in 1826. Mr. Campbell was treasurer from 1819 to 1823.

Mr. Campbell, in 1826, was elected one of the trustees of the College of Physicians and Surgeons of New York. I may as well note that this College, established by an act of the Legislature of the State in 1791, has had among its trustees, since it commenced operations in 1807, some of the best merchants in New York. For my knowledge of this last fact I am indebted to Doctor George H. Tucker, who has composed a work of great value, being no less than a " Catalogue of its Alumni Officers and Fellows from 1807 to 1859." Among many names are George Griswold in 1836, George W. Bruen in 1826.

If Mr. Campbell had died in 1815, he would have had one of those most extraordinary Knickerbocker funerals, such as had Wynant Van Zandt, Sr., who died in 1814, and was buried from his old residence, No. 35 William street — a fact I forgot to mention in my sketch of him.

Mr. Campbell used to narrate many pleasing matters relative to New York city — not the least interesting was one relative to the shooting of Alexander Hamilton, and the taking of his body to the house of William Bayard, the father-in-law of Mr. Campbell. The latter was twenty-five years old at the time, and the sad event made an impression upon his mind that was never forgotten.

He was a man of wealth, and held real estate in the city that was valued at over $400,000.

Mr. Campbell felt a just pride in being connected with the great house of Le Roy, Bayard & Co. People in these days cannot comprehend the feeling. There are so many large houses that we cannot now even imagine the profound respect inspired by LeRoy & Bayard. They founded the grand old house in 1790. It had rolled on for thirty-five years, its partners changing its style sometimes. Le Roy & Bayard, then Le Roy Bayard & Co.— afterward Le Roy, Bayard & McEvers, and last it was Le Roy, Bayard & Co., in 1824. All its partners up to this time had been kings, princes, and dukes among the merchants. Socially, no families stood higher; commercially, none stood so high. I presume there was less capital in the concern in 1825, than at any period of its existence since 1790. Its reputation, however, was sound, and its credit undisputed. In 1826, an event occurred that made the name of Le Roy, Bayard & Co. ring through the whole world. For a long time they were the lion house in New York. The event was of this character.

The government of Greece was struggling to free itself from the tyranny of the sultan of Turkey. It was persuaded that there could be no salvation, unless a navy could be obtained. This led to a decree of the

Greek government, dated August 24, 1824, authorizing the Greek deputies in London to purchase or build as speedily as possible eight frigates of fifteen guns each side.

At that time there was a strong feeling for Greece in New York. A committee had been appointed, of which the worthy father-in-law of Duncan P. Campbell was the chairman. The Greek deputies in London thought they could not do better than to send this order for eight frigates to be executed in New York, where they had so many friends, among whom was the " Greek committee," of which William Bayard was chairman. He was then the head of the house of Le Roy, Bayard & Co., and his sons — William Jr., and Robert — were partners and managers. At that time no Le Roy was actually in the house, although the name was used. The Greek deputies selected this house in preference to any other, for information as to the cost of the frigates. Le Roy, Bayard & Co., on the 7th of December, 1824, sent to London an estimate of a 50 gun frigate, and stated that the entire cost of such a frigate, equal to those built for the United States, of live oak, with her armament, should not cost over $247,500. They agreed by letter to do it for that sum, if they had the order in hand. They stated that they had a favorite builder ; that they needed a London credit on Baring Brothers or N. M. Rothschild ; that 8 to 10 per cent. premium would be obtained, that the deputies would have no financial trouble, and that they would attend to the interests of the government of Greece with their usual zeal towards their business friends — augmented, if possible, by the sentiments that united them to the cause of that unhappy country. Here is the estimate

sent out. It is a curiosity in these days of government
ship building :

Frame, 20,000 feet live oak at $1,50 per foot. .	$30,000
Other wooden materials.	30,000
Labor.	60,000
Smith's work.	20,000
Copper bolts.	8,000
Sheathing copper and nails.	12,000
Joiner's bill.	7,000
Carver's do	1,200
Painter's do	3,000
Plumber's do	1,600
Turner's do	700
Rigger's do	1,500
Blockmaker's bill.	1,000
Ship Chandler's bill including pitch and oakum .	4,000
Hull and spars complete.	180,000
Rigging, one suit of sails, anchors and cables. .	42,000
Guns and carriages and other expenses. .	25,000
Fifteen hundred tons at $165 per ton. . .	$247,500

No sooner did the deputies get such a fair, square
statement, than they agreed to order two such frigates
in March, 1825, and sent out General Lallemand at a
salary of $600 per month. The orders to build were
addressed to him, Le Roy, Bayard & Co., and G. G. &
S. Howland, in case of accident. The agent reached
New York in April, 1825. He bought a credit of
£25,000 from Samuel Williams, (a celebrated American banker in London,) and a promise of a credit from
I. & S. Ricardo, the great London bankers, to whom the
loan of £2,000,000 sterling contracted for the Greek
government had been entrusted. On the 15th of April,
Le Roy, Bayard & Co. acknowledged receipts of cred-
its for £50,000 sterling, $250,000. G. G. & S How-
land also signed this letter. They had got their name
in the business through the friendship of Mr. Williams.

It was hoped the frigates would be built by October, and be in a Grecian port by the month of December. In August, the firm of Le Roy, Bayard & Co. stated that they could not give the exact cost until the frigates were completed; but on that very day Commissioner Chauncey, who was employed to superintend the work, had given an estimate that each would probably cost $500,000. The deputies in London were kept in ignorance of this enormous expenditure and ruinous misapplication of their sacred funds. Had the first estimate been correct, or adhered to, many vessels could have been built, dispatched, and Missolonghi would not have fallen. Instead of which, one frigate alone cost $550,000. The two frigates were named one the Hope, and the other the Liberator. The Hope was built by C. Bergh & Co., directed by Le Roy, Bayard & Co. The Liberator was built by Smith & Demon, superintended by G. G. & S. Howland.

I presume, in the history of commerce, there never was a more barefaced grab game practised than these New York merchants pursued toward the unfortunate Greeks. The *placer* was a rich one, and worth digging. The credit on London was undoubted. The temptation to acquire a large amount of money was irresistible, and both houses, utterly regardless of their business reputation, went in. In addition to an extravagance that was unheard of before in ship-building, three houses charged about $80,000 for their commission. Instead of completing the vessels in six months, they overran double that time. They drew over $750,000 at the first start, before half the hull was completed, $200,000 more than Le Roy, Bayard & Co., had stated both frigates would cost, and neither was launched.

In addition to this, they sold the sterling bills at nine

per cent. premium, crediting the Greeks only at $4,44, thus pocketing $76,500 — which, added to the commission, gave the agents the nice sum, for their own pockets, of $156,500. On the 18th November, the Liberator was launched; a few days later the Hope was launched. About this time old Samuel Williams, of London, failed, and many drafts came back. However, the statements were ready;

The Hope cost . .	$438,793 68
The Liberator cost .	449,130 15
	$887,923 83

The commission charged by Le Roy, Bayard & Co., was ten per cent.

On the Hope it was . . .	$39,811 82
On the Liberator	40,770 37
	$80,615 19

Which was divided equally between Le Roy, Bayard & Co., and G. G. & S. Howland.

The ships were ready for sea, but there was a balance due of $137,000, and Le Roy, Bayard & Co., would not listen to any proposition. The " money " — " the balance," — was what was wanted by the patriotic house where its head was chairman of the Greek committee of New York, and who had scorned about charging commission! The Greeks sent out an agent, Mr. Contostavlos. He came here, went on his knees to the Bayards and Howlands — begged in the name of a merciful God — a heroic people — that they would keep one frigate for security, but allow the other to depart, and perhaps avert the awful tragedy that a few months later filled the world with horror, I mean the massacre at Missolonghi. In vain. " Pay up," said Bayards and Howlands.

Still worse than all — on every bill of exchange

drawn, Le Roy, Bayard & Co., and Howlands, deduct-
ed a commission at brokerage of about 4 per cent., or
$36,000 ! This, added to $156,000, makes $192,500
— nearly $200,000, that these two firms received.

Greek patriotism pays well. So matters went on until the 5th of June, 1826, the frigates being kept here,
and Le Roy, Bayard & Co. trying to sell one to the
United States. These gentlemen stated that if they sold
the frigate to the government, they should also charge
their usual commission of *ten* per cent. for the sale.
There were a few friends of Greece in this city, and the
idea that the last resources of the unfortunate Greeks
were in the possession of such insatiable merchants, fill
them with absolute horror.

Finally it was agreed to leave the arrangement and
settlement to arbitrators, who should sell the frigates, or
resort to any other mode to arrange with the eminent
merchants, Le Roy, Bayard & Co., and G. G. & S.
Howland. These were the arbitrators : Henry C. De
Rham, Abraham Ogden, and Jonas Platt. About this
time matters were made more complicated, by its becoming known that Le Roy, Bayard & Co. were in a
very delicate situation, and supposed to be insolvent.
It was of course, unsafe to have so much property involved in their desperate fortunes.

Both ships were now conveyed to the arbitrators on
the 24th of June, 1826, in trust.

They were obliged to make the award within twenty
days.

CHAPTER XVIII.

It was also agreed that the Greek agents should have thirty days to sell one of the frigates, in order to redeem the other from the clutches of the American merchants.

It was also agreed that the arbiters should be paid for their services as arbitrators, cost, charges, commission, &c.

It was also stipulated that the arbitrators should sell within ten days, one of the frigates of the Greek government, if the Greek agent did not, out of which was to be paid the balance due Le Roy, Bayard & Co. and G. G. & S. Howland.

The arbitrators met for the first time on the 27th of June, 1826.

Among the items passed as correct was a charge for the use of the two ship yards, $50,000! One was that of old Bergh, up near Grand street and East river. The ground of both could have been bought for that sum! This was sympathy for the Greeks. Christían Bergh was a venerable looking man in his later years. He was six feet two inches high, and his hair was as white as snow. He has been dead some years.

I have not stated all the claims made by Le Roy, Bayard & Co. I have stated that

They charged 10 per cent commission on .	.	$80,000
They made on the premium of exchange	.	76,000
They charged a broker on sterling bills	.	36,000

$192,000

In addition, they claimed damages on sterling bills returned from London amounting to £55,000, although the bills were paid. Their damages were allowed, viz. . . . $60,000

$252,500

Here is more than the estimate of the cost of a frigate ($248,000) drawn by the two houses, and received by them in one shape or another. This amount was actually taken, for it was awarded by the arbitrators, as a proof of their approbation of brother merchants in managing the resources sole and sacred of one million of Greek Christians, struggling at that time not only against famine, but against Turkish despotism.

The $80,000 commission is what was allowed. The original charge made was for drafts on London, $1,200,000 at 2½ per cent, $30,000. Commission on their disbursements of $1,200,000 at 10 per cent., $120,000 — $150,000.

That was the rate of commission charged by prominent merchants who were friends of Greece. It almost suggests a question, viz : What would the enemies of Greece have charged ?

Facts were brought before the arbitrators to show that the frigate Brandywine, the largest and finest frigate in the service of the United States, only cost $272,000. This was proved by a certificate, signed by the Secretary of the Navy. The Brandywine also was

built of seasoned live oak, while the Greek frigates
were built of unseasoned white oak.

It is not true that Mr. Henry Eckford had anything
to do with building these frigates.   He had built several for South American governments.

There was only one way to get out of the hands of
the merchants.   The Liberator had cost $450,000.

The Greek agents sold her to the United States
for half price, viz: $226,000 less than she cost Greece!

The best joke is that Le Roy, Bayard & Co., and G.
G. & S. Howland immediately claimed $22,500 com-
mission for the sale!   It was not allowed.

The arbitration lasted thirty days.   As I have stated, the arbitrators were Henry C. De Rham, Abraham
Ogden and Judge Jonas Platt.   The latter acted as
chairman.   They gave their award the 27th day of
July 1826.   They decided that $75,933,81 was yet due,
and should be paid to William Bayard, Robert Bayard,
and William Bayard, Jr.   They decided that a balance
of $89,921,52 was due to Gardner G. Howland and
Samuel S. Howland.

They awarded to themselves, for one month's services,
$4,500, or $1,500 each.   They ordered the *one* ship
left to be delivered to the Greek agent, after he had
paid the above amounts from the proceeds of the sale of
the other one.

At this distance of time we can look back upon these
transactions, nearly forty years ago, without prejudice.
It strikes us as incredibly monstrous and horrible.   No
wonder the friends of Greece in New York swore and
raved.

Commodore Chauncey got out of this Greek plunder
about $14,000, and yet he was a captain in the United
States Navy all that time.

The most cruel part of the whole proceeding was to make the Greeks pay the whole of the $4,500, arbitrators' fees. How a lot of merchants of high character could unite to swindle those people — pluck every hair from their heads, skin them alive, when all Europe and America was alive in reference to that nation — when subscriptions of every kind, and under a thousand modes, were being collected in every nation of Europe in order to promote a sacred cause, and assist the unequal and exterminating contest between a handful of Christians and the whole Turkish Empire — at a time when the charity before given to the orphan, the blind, and the invalid, was taken from their mouths for the purpose of sending some little bread to the inhabitants of Greece— once the pride of the world, but then oppressed and persecuted — and that two prominent commercial houses of New York should perpetrate an enormous swindle upon this sacred capital, and that other men, Christians and citizens of New York, should award it as all right!

The facts are plain. The frigate Liberator cost $449,606,41, without arbitrators' fees, and was shortly after approved by these gentlemen of the highest rank, at $233,570,97, and paid for accordingly by the United States, less $7,500 expense and commission.

This made the remaining frigate Hope actually amount to £155,000 sterling, or $775,000; and this, too, would have been lost to Greece but for the Greek agent. On the 30th of August he placed her in the hands of Capt. F. H. Gregory (still alive, and a gallant captain in the U. S. Navy.) The great lawyer, Henry D. Sedgwick, was the law counsel of the Greek deputies.

When the arbitration was made, Mr. Sedgwick sent a note, stating that he considered it both unjust and illegal.

To this letter, the following cool reply was sent:

NEW YORK, *August* 3, 1826.
" SIR — We have received your letter of the 1st instant. Upon reflection, we feel it to be our duty to proceed to sell the frigates Liberator and Hope with their appurtenances, and with the extra property assigned to us, according to the terms of the submission and assignments.

JONAS PLATT,
H. C. DE RHAM,
ABRAHAM OGDEN."

That same day Mr. Sedgwick got an injunction from the court, forbidding the arbitrators to dispose of the ships. But for this, both ships would have been sold and sacrificed, and the swindle been complete.

But the most horrible part of the transaction was this. When the Greek deputies commissioned the building of the two frigates, they wrote to Le Roy, Bayard & Co., and Howlands, not to undertake the building of them in case the laws of the United States should be opposed to their construction and departure. Messrs. Bayards & Howlands answered that there was no law to prevent it, and, without any further trouble, commenced building the two frigates.

After they were built it was ascertained that the transaction was illegal, and that the frigates were subject to seizure and confiscation at any moment. The arbitrators, after paying Le Roy, Bayard & Co. and G. G. & S. S. Howland their enormous claims, threw upon the agent the whole responsiblity of evading the law, and also of getting out of New York this last resource to his country. It was necessary to give a bond for $600,000 to the government before the frigate, costing $775,000, could leave. She never would have left

but for those glorious lawyers, Henry D. and Robert
Sedgwick. They went to work soliciting persons to
sign this bond. John Duer and Beverly Robinson aided them. Some capitalists became responsible, and the
frigate was allowed to depart for Greece.

Le Roy, Bayard & Co. refused to execute a bond,
and had the collector insisted upon such a bond from
them the frigate would have rotted at a New York dock.
They had been the particular friends of Greece.
They had professed a zeal in their letters unequalled in
any cause. They took out a register in their own individual names for the frigate Hope. Here is a copy of
the affidavit as it now stands on the files of the custom
house in this city:

" PORT OF NEW YORK, ss.
I, Robert Bayard, of the City, County, and State of
New York, merchant, do solemnly swear, according to
the best of my knowledge and belief, that the ship or
vessel called the Hope, of New York, of the burden of
1,778 $\frac{31}{95}$ tons, built at the city aforesaid in the year
1825, as per certificate of C. Bergh & Co., the master
carpenter under whose direction she was built, that my
present place of abode is New York aforesaid, and that
myself together with William Bayard, William Bayard,
Jr., of said city of New York, merchants, citizens of
the United States, are the true and only owners of the
said ship or vessel, that there is no subject, nor citizen
of any foreign power or State, directly or indirectly, by
way of trust, confidence, or otherwise interested therein, or in the profits or issues thereof, and that —— is
the present master or commander of the said ship.
   Signed,   ROBERT BAYARD.
" Sworn this 12th day of April, 1826."

That was an awful oath to take. In these days, if a
merchant was to take such an oath under the circumstances, it would be called perjury. However, Robert

Bayard took that oath, and the register stood in the name of himself and partners. Being thus owners, and they not having transfered her, it became necessary to sign a bond (merely nominal) which simply binds the obligators, that " the owner and owners of the ship " should not employ her in contravention of an act of Congress of 1818. In violation of this act, Le Roy, Bayard & Co. had obtained and placed in jeopardy the enormous funds belonging to the Greeks. They refused to execute this bond, and consequently the frigate Hope was forced to traverse the Atlantic Ocean and Mediterranean Sea, without a register or any document to manifest her national character.

The arbitrators received the cash from James K. Paulding (who was then the Navy Agent) for the ship Liberator $233,570,97. They paid it out to satisfy the awards and the sales.

David D. Field is a witness to one of these documents. He was then a young man, studying law in the office of the Sedgwicks.

The arbitrators issued an address, in which they say : " We rejoice that the gallant ship ' Hellas ' has at last sailed, according to her original destination, and we cherish the fond hope that she will be a minister of vengeance to the oppressors of the heroic Greeks."

Considering the fact that they had done all in their power to have the Greeks swindled out of both ships, the above sentence is particularly cool.

The father of Duncan P. Campbell was an officer in the British Army that was sent out in the Revolution. He belonged to a Highland regiment, and was billeted in the house of an old Quaker, Thomas Pearsall, at No. 203 Queen street (above Franklin Square, in Pearl street.) There he became acquainted with the beauti

ful and demure Quakeress, Miss Pearsall. Old Thomas
would have as soon consented to the marriage of his
daughter with a Calmuck Tartar as with a Highlander,
or a British officer. The result was a runaway match.
Of course the parties were forgiven, but neither husband or wife lived long after she gave birth to a son,
who was Duncan Pearsall Campbell. Old Thomas
adopted the son and brought him up as his own.

Old Thomas Pearsall's son, Thomas, married Fanny
Buchanan, of whom I have spoken. Young Tom was
the companion of Duncan P., and they were like brothers. He went to Europe and traveled some years, and
among other exploits got a party of six high on cham-
pagne in the dome of St. Peter's. He was a fine young
fellow — died many years ago.

Mrs. Pearsall is still living in Waverley Place. One
of his daughters married Samuel Bradhurst, the eldest
son of John M. Bradhurst. What a biography can be
made of old John M. Bradhurst. I will do it some
day. In the latter years of his life he lived out beyond Manhattanville. He had three sons, Samuel, William, and Henry. Samuel died. I never knew what
became of William, or whether he is dead or alive. I
have not seen him for eighteen years.

I now return to Duncan P. Campbell. After reading my first chapter, I find that I have given an account of the Greek frigate in a way that would lead the
reader to suppose he had something to do with it. I
did not so intend it. I do not believe a purer man ever
lived in this city than Mr. Campbell. His connection
with Mr. William Bayard, Senior, led me to speak of
that house. Mr. Campbell was not a partner. Old Mr.
Bayard's name was used, but I do not think he had
much to do with the management of the affairs of Le

Roy, Bayard & Co. On the contrary, when the final award was agreed to, the name of old William Bayard, Sept 9, 1826, was signed " by his attorney, Robert Bayard." It must have worried his mind very much. He died a few weeks after the award was made.

I have alluded to the Bayards in former chapters. There was an old family of that name, that came out to the city before 1647. They were Huguenots. Old Governor Stuyvesant married Miss Judith Bayard. She was the daughter of Balthazar Bayard, a French protestant, who had taken refuge in Holland. She died in 1687. At that time there resided in this city Colonel Nicholas Bayard, a leading politician. I believe he was brother to Balthazar and Peter Bayard. The two latter were married and resided on Broadway. Both were Aldermen of the city for many years. Nicholas married Judith Verletti. They lived on the High street. He was Mayor of the city in 1685.

This Nicholas was a grand old fellow. He had but one eye ; he was the ancestor of the present Bayard race in this town. How he got in with Queen Anne, I don't know, but that he was a favorite with her is a fact. In 1709, the Queen, at his recommendation, took steps to settle the interior of New York. She issued a proclamation in Germany offering land *free* and an exemption from all taxes, to those who would come out. Under her auspices many Germans emigrated to New York and settled upon Schoharie creek. Later, others settled along the Mohawk, and as far up as *German* flats. The first party of Germans left England in January, 1710, and reached New York in June. They became rich, up in Schoharie. In 1713 the Queen thought her settlers might be settled in comfort, and she sent out her agent, Nicholas Bayard, with power to give to any settler a deed for his land in use and possession.

The stupid Germans, mistaking her motives, surrounded the house where Mr. Bayard was stopping in Schoharie, and accused him of a design to enslave them. The men had guns and pitchforks, and the women hoes and clubs, and determined to have Mr. Bayard any how. They fired sixty balls into the house. Mr. Bayard had his pistols, and wanted to fight; but his friends would not permit it, and got him safe off in the night to Albany. He sent word from thence, that if any of them would come to him, acknowledge him as the crown agent, bring the gift of one ear of corn, they should have a free deed of all they possessed. Not one would do it. Mr. Bayard got angry, and sold the whole of the land to seven persons, who afterwards went by the name of the " Seven partners of Schoharie." Among them were Lewis Morris Myndert Schuyler, Rut Van Dam, and Peter Vanbrugh Livingston.

The son of Nicholas Bayard afterwards married into the Livingston family. They published queer notices in those days. Here is one from *The New York Mercury*, published by Hugh Gaines, under marriages :

" On Tuesday night last (April 26, 1762,) Mr. Nicholas Bayard Jr., to Miss Livingston, daughter of Peter Vanbrugh Livingston, of this place, merchant ; a very agreeable young lady, endowed with all the good qualities necessary for rendering the connubial state perfectly agreeable."

I do not know that William Bayard was the son of this marriage. That Nicholas Bayard was assistant alderman when he got married. He was alderman as late as 1778. Two years afterwards, William Bayard was assistant alderman of the Second Ward. Old Nicholas lived in Bayard's lane.

Queen Anne's old Nick must have lived to a good old age, for in May, 1762, he has an advertisement:

" To MONEY DIGGERS.— Nicholas Bayard offers a reward of £4 to be informed who it is that comes by night to *his farm*, near the city, and digs great holes in the land, to the damage of his people and cattle. If they be money diggers, he will allow them the indulgence of a search, if they come to him personally, and dig by daylight, and fill up again. I will also give them two spades and one pick-axe, left behind in their supposed fright."

Bayard's mount was a small cone-shaped mount, on which was erected a small fort, or what is now corner of Mott and Grand streets. It looked down upon the distant city, having the *Kolch* between. (That is the great lake of fresh water from Reed to Grand.) The house and farm of Nicholas Bayard were on the north side of the *Kolch*, and not far from the said *mount*. To the west were swamps and woods, and to the north-east orchards and woods.

In 1785, property near New York went down greatly : few or none had money to buy it with. In 1786, William Bayard wished to raise cash by selling his farm of 150 acres on the western side of Broadway. He devised the scheme of offering them in lots of 25 by 100 ; only $24 was bid, and but few of them were sold. It was well for him, for very soon after feelings and opinions changed ; and those who had bought for $25 sold out for $100. Since then the progressive rise has had no end. Some of those lots have brought within five years $20,000 each.

When that farm was in existence Dutch was partly spoken in our city — to 1795. *Paus* and *Pinkster* were of universal observance. All made it an idle day ; boys and negroes might be seen all day standing in the market laughing and joking and cracking eggs. In the afternoon the grown up apprentices and servant girls used to dance on the green in Bayard's farm.

Rip Van Dam, a son of one of the seven purchasers of land of Mr. Nic. Bayard, kept an iron store in Duke street.

CHAPTER XIX.

I am not aware that there ever lived in New York city a more respectable commercial house — one that bore a mercantile credit unstained, and never tainted — than the firm of Coster Brothers & Co., before 1786 and " Brothers Coster & Co.," for ten years after — as I have their signature before me in 1796 — and " Henry A. and John G. Coster," as they signed after 1801, until Henry A. died in 1821.

What a splendid pair of old merchants? They did honor to New York. That house added greatly to its wealth. They were Hollanders — modern Dutch — the right sort of stuff to make good old merchants of in the New World. Of the two brothers, Henry A. Coster was the oldest. Both were born in Haarlem, Holland, the city where the great organ is. Probably Henry received his commercial education in an Amsterdam counting house. He came out to this city previous to the Revolution — I believe he was sent out as agent by an Amsterdam house. His brother John G., who had been educated for a physician, did not come out until a few years later. No better merchants ever lived in this city than these two. When these two honest, guileless merchants formed a partnership in the town, for it was a small one, their place of business was at 20

Dock — now Pearl — street, south side, ten doors from Broad. Eight years after, they moved to No. 35 Little Dock street. That store, when the names of the streets were changed in 1793, became No. 59 Water street. In 1799, they moved to 26 William street, and there they lived and did business until 1821. John G. kept store at that place three years longer, until 1825. He lived over the store until 1805, when he removed his residence to 110 Broadway. He afterwards bought the lot 227 Broadway, corner of Barclay, and built upon it, moving into that house in 1810. Henry A., in 1801, lived at No. 28 William street, next door to the store, No. 26 William — that was on the west side of the street, near Garden (Exchange street now.) The great success of these two excellent men was in the store No. 26 William street. They dealt in all sorts of Holland goods — one article in particular, called "krollenvogel," a species of tape, made of flax. They imported all kinds of oil cloths. Not only did they import, but they were constantly buying and shipping to Europe all kinds of produce. They had strong connections in the old Dutch cities, for they had heavy orders, and they traded also in their own ships, sending out supercargoes.

One of the supercargoes was Daniel Holsman. He was brother-in-law to John G. Coster. Mr. Holsman was a long time a clerk in the counting-house of the Coster Brothers. His signature is before me, signed in 1804. If I had no other evidence I should know from that signature, that he was a Hollander. While out in Holland, supercargo of one of the ships belonging to Coster Brothers, he was applied to by the celebrated Aaron Burr, who wished to get passage to the United States, from Amsterdam. Mr. Holsman refused to have anything to do with him, and would not let

him return to America in the ship. Bonaparte's brother Louis ruled in Holland at that time, and it was not
exactly safe. I presume, however, the true reason was
that Daniel Holsman was in New York city when Burr
shot Hamilton, and consequently had all the prejudices
a New Yorker would have from that event. After he
retired from business, Mr. Holsman settled in the State
of New Jersey. He died in 1840 ; he left several children — among them a son named Daniel Holsman, who
was Speaker of the New Jersey Legislature a few sessions since. I believe Mr. Holsman went to the East
Indies as supercargo of one of the ships of Coster
Brothers. At any rate, they owned several Indiamen,
and were largely in that trade.

They also did a heavy importing business from the
West Indies, in rum, coffee, and sugar. Over the
door was a sign (1803) " Henry A. & John G. Coster."
They received more consignments of Holland gin than
any other house in New York. They were excessively
prudent and economical. Both partners worked with a
good will, and they employed no clerks more than was
actually necessary. One of the firm, Henry A., stood
up at a little pine desk in the back part of the store ;
that desk was the plainest ever seen ; the boards were
planed off and fastened together ; it was not even painted. John G. sat down at a table standing near the
older brother's desk. The store was on the first floor
of No. 26 William street. Both partners spoke good
English. Everything about their business went on like
clock work. Their word was as good as gold ; yet they
were very clever men, and they looked after the pen-
nies ; everybody, however, respected them. Sometimes
they would buy an entire cargo of West India goods.
On one occasion, Henry A. was on the dock when a

cargo of coffee, that his firm had purchased, was unloading from the vessel. From some of the bags coffee was running out of the little holes. Henry went along, carefully picked up the scattered grains, and placed them back in the coffee bags, and then set a man sewing up the bags. Some of our modern merchants would call that a small business. It was not so. Mr. Coster exhibited the true mercantile spirit of the olden time. He could not bear to see anything wasted. Another trait of the old school merchants like the Coster Brothers, was that they were thorough-bred merchants, and attended to the details of their business. They understood every part. Nothing was beneath their notice. If goods were consigned to them from abroad, they examined their value, and sold them at the highest price in the markets, doing with them as if they were their own. When they made out an " account sales," they made the charges precisely what they paid, and did not seek to make money out of the " charges," as is now the case. The modern merchant, if tried by the severe standard of honesty of old school merchants like the Brothers Coster, would be deemed little better than a swindler. A merchant abroad in these days sends a consignment to a merchant in New York. He does not examine the goods, but passes them for sale to a broker, who gets some sort of a price, but the consignee merchant knows nothing about it, and cares less. There is a regular commission to be charged, but the modern merchant is not satisfied with this. He has his tariff of charges, and they are charged regardless of the truth. Storage, labor, cartage, fire insurance, brokerage, guarantee commission, even if sold for cash, and the sale is made out as a time sale. How little do merchants abroad dream of the horrible imposition

9

practised upon them. If they were wise they would get back to the old custom ; and if they sent an invoice of valuable goods, or a cargo, to New York, would send a supercargo along with them, instead of trusting any " commission house ; " for the larger the business of a modern house, the less attention do they give to consignments from abroad.

The Costers were model merchants. The costume of the oldest one was short breeches, white stockings, and shoes with large buckles. Of course there were no boots in those days. He did not wear a cocked hat, although many persons did wear them in 1800, and long after. Both wore that sign of an old-fashioned gentleman — the *queue*. It required care. The only relic of the queue race now in New York is ex-senator Westcott, of Florida.

Henry A. and John G. were both Masons. They belonged to the " Holland Lodge, No. 8," of which John Jacob Astor was master. The members of the lodge met on the first and third Fridays in every month, at No. 66 Liberty street.

As I have before said, the house hired few clerks, as both gentlemen were not afraid of work. Besides, Daniel Holsman, already named, there were John Inness and Francis Barretto.

As early as 1801, Henry A. was elected a director of the Manhattan Bank. He withdrew from the directory in 1806, and connected himself with the Merchants' Bank. He was a director in that twelve years. John G. was first elected a director of the Manhattan Bank in 1813. Thirteen years later, in 1826, he was elected president in place of Henry Remsen, and so continued until 1830. Both brothers were engaged in many of the money corporations. John G. was a director of the

Phœnix Insurance Company for twelve years. Henry was a director in the Globe Insurance Company from 1815. It was a famous company in its day, in 1817. Henry A. Coster moved from No. 28 William to a new house in 85 Chambers street. He had a country seat in what is now First avenue, between Thirtieth and Thirty-first streets. It was sold to Anson G. Phelps in 1835. To-day it is for rent. He died in that house in 1821. His widow lived there until 1824. She afterward married the celebrated Dr. Alexander Hosack. She was immensely rich. Henry A. Coster left two sons. One was named Henry A.— the other Washington Coster. It is impossible for any one but an old New Yorker to conceive of the intense interest that was thrown around these two young men.

There are many among us who well remember young Harry Coster, as he was familiarly called. He was the eldest son of Henry A. Coster. It would have been far better for poor Harry had he had a dozen brothers. He was a noble-hearted young fellow, and possessed many noble qualities, but his wealth spoiled all. It called around him a lot of worthless hangers on, who induced him to commit all sorts of follies and extravagances, in order that they might share in them. Young Harry was *rather* wild before his excellent father died, but he did not fairly break loose from all restraint until his governor was no more. Then he " *went it.*" There was nothing at all criminal in his actions. He spent his money like a prince. " A short life and a merry one," seemed to be his object, and he obtained it. His property was immense ; he did his best to spend it, but he did not live long enough. He left considerable when he died.

Harry Coster was an amiable young fellow. His

brother Washington married Miss Depau, one of the
loveliest girls that ever trod Broadway. I do not know
what induced Washington to go into business. He certainly was in business as a banker in Wall street.
Charles Christmas was one of the best brokers and
bankers in this city. He is now a partner of the great
banking house of A. Belmont & Co. Fortunate as Mr.
Belmont seems to be in everything, he never was more
fortunate than when he secured the brains, financial experience, and the integrity of Charles Christmas. He
was for many years the chief manager of Prime, Ward
& King, whose fame was world wide. Their banking
house was at 42 Wall street. Mr. Christmas left that
house in order to go into the same business at 44 Wall
street, with Robert I. Livingston, in 1834, under the
firm of Christmas & Livingston.

The next year the firm was changed to Christmas,
Livingston, Prime & Coster, brokers and bankers.
Washington Coster was a partner. He lived at No. 15
Laight street at that time. Rufus Prime was another
partner. He was a son of old Nathaniel Prime. I do
not know how long Washington Coster continued in
business, but this I know, he died in 1846, suddenly. At
that time he was stopping at Blançard's old Globe hotel,
still standing in Broadway, below Wall street. The
fate of both of the sons of Henry A. Coster was melancholy. Washington left several children. Henry A.
Coster had several daughters ; the eldest married Francis Barretto, already alluded to, who had been a clerk
with Coster Brothers. I think they live out in Westchester, and are both alive.

Another daughter married Mr. Hamilton Wilkes, a
son of old Charles Wilkes, so long president of the
Bank of New York. He died in Europe, leaving a

lovely daughter, who afterwards married Count Quelke-chow, a member of the body guard of the Pope.

Another daughter of Henry A. Coster married William Laight, a son of Henry Laight, who was president of the Eagle Insurance Company. She died about two years ago, leaving a large family of children. Young Laight never did any kind of business in his life. Shortly after he graduated from Columbia College, he married Miss Coster. John G. Coster left several children. He died about 1846. When John Jacob Astor wished to build the Astor house, he bought the house and lot belonging to Mr. Coster, at No. 227 Broadway. The latter moved up to a splendid granite double residence he had built in 1833, up at 589 Broadway, where he died. That was a palace in its day. It is yet standing, and known as the Chinese building. The occasion of its being so named, was from the fact that a Canton merchant brought an immense quantity of Chinese articles, and exhibited them in that mansion. It was one of the most attractive exhibitions ever got up in the city.

One of the sons of Mr. John G. Coster, John H., married Miss Boardman. She was one of twin sisters, very beautiful, and daughter of Daniel Boardman. Both were deemed the prettiest girls in New York. Mr. Boardman lived in Broadway 214, next block above the residence of John G. Coster, at No. 227. He was a very rich man, and the younger members of the two families were very intimate. John H., at one time, owned Washington hall, that stood where A. T. Stewart's great dry goods store now stands. I believe he sold that property for the trifling sum of $65,000. It is worth twenty times that, now. John H. died only a few days ago.

Gerard H. Coster was another son, and remarkably handsome. He married Miss Prime, a daughter of Nat. Prime. At one time he was a partner in the banking house of Coster & Carpenter. Carpenter is still alive, somewhere up on the Lakes. Mr. G. H. Coster I meet occasionally, on Broadway.

Daniel J. Coster was another son. He was in the auction business for some years, under the firm of Hone & Coster. He married the accomplished Miss Delancey, descended from one of the oldest families in the State. I believe she was a daughter of Oliver Delancy.

Another son was Henry A. Coster, named after the uncle. He died about a year ago.

George Washington Coster was another son of John G. Coster. He married Miss Oakey, a daughter of Daniel Oakey, who was a cotemporary of the Costers as early as 1800, when Daniel Oakey went into business at 80 Pearl street. In 1803 he formed a partnership with Henry Watkins, and they did business under the firm of Oakey & Watkins, at 51 William street, then a great business street. After a few years he dissolved with Watkins, and kept on under his own name at the same place, 51 William. Meanwhile he had married, and lived at 41 Pine street. He kept in that same store in William until 1826, when he moved his store to where his house had been in Pine street, and removed his residence to Art street. (It was a street that crossed Broadway, and led into the Bowery, about Eighth street now.) He was a thorough merchant, and very much respected. Charles Robert Coster was the youngest of all John G.'s sons. He died quite recently, making three deaths of sons within a year.

The eldest daughter of Mr. John G. Coster was a beautiful woman.

She married a Mr. Berryman. He was a Kentuckian, and a fine looking man. He was called the handsome Berryman. I believe he was at one time in business with Henry H. Coster, under the firm of Coster &
Berryman. His wife died suddenly on the night of the
great fire in 1835. She left three daughters and two
boys. He has been dead some years.

The eldest daughter of Mr. Coster never married.
Another daughter married Charles A. Heckscher. At
that time he was of the firm of Charles A. & Edward
Heckscher. They were very large merchants thirty
years ago. Charles A. came out from Bremen in 1830,
and started business at 44 Exchange place. The next
year he took in his brother under the above style.
Later they moved to 45 South street. Charles A. was
appointed " Mechlenberg " Consul. After he married
Miss Coster, his brother-in-law, Gerard H. (already
mentioned) became a partner, under the firm of Heckscher, Coster & Matfield. They retired from business
some years later, but I believe Charles A. Heckscher is
a large proprietor of coal mines, and manages them
himself.

CHAPTER XX

There are many honored mercantile names among the citizens of different periods, but none stand higher than that of " Ogden." I have in one chapter given a sketch of James De Peyster Ogden, once an extensive merchant, and ever a most useful citizen. I will now give another merchant of the name of Samuel G. Ogden.

He was one of the New Jersey Ogdens. His father was a clergyman at Newark. Samuel G. Ogden was one of several sons; one went to China. Samuel served the usual apprenticeship, or rather clerkship, in order to thoroughly learn mercantile business, with the then (1795) great commercial firm of Gouverneur & Kemble, No. 94 Front street. Joseph and Isaac Gouverneur were both partners at that time; although Joseph was absent in Europe, and he died shortly after his return, about 1798. Isaac lived a few doors from the store, at No. 98 Front street.

The house did an enormous trade, and young Ogden was in a good school to learn business. As one item of the business they did a commission business. The ship " Cleopatra " came consigned to them from the Isle of France; she was commanded by Captain Beare. G. & K. sold one invoice of sundry goods, and the net proceeds were £54,195—or $135,488. G. & K.'s commission, and they only charged 2½ per cent, in those days, was $3,387 20.

That was seventy-six years ago, when New York was small ; but, even now, there are not many commission merchants who carry $3,387 20 to the credit of the " commission account" in one line on one day. Besides Samuel G. Ogden, Gouverneur & Kemble had other clerks. There were John Wilkes, Nic Ogden, and A. Carroll. Five years later, in 1800, Samuel G. Ogden went into business under his own name at No. 119 Pearl street. For some years he did an extensive shipping business, and owned several vessels. Their names were the " Empire," the " Indostan," the " Diana," and the " Leander."

About that time he married Miss Lewis, a daughter of Francis Lewis, and grand-daughter of the celebrated Francis Lewis, the worthy old merchant who signed the Declaration of Independence.

Most of the vessels belonging to Samuel G. Ogden were armed, as the custom was in those days. When the oldest son of Mr. Ogden was born, Samuel G. Jr., he was saluted with sixty guns, fired from the ships owned by his father.

In 1806, Mr. Ogden was so unfortunate as to make the acquaintance of the celebrated General Miranda. At that time the Surveyor of this port was a high-spirited gentleman, known as Colonel William Steuben Smith. He had received his appointment from President Washington. He was a son-in-law of one of the presidents of the United States. I think he owned a cottage, that he built the year Washington died, 1799 ; it is located at Sixty-first street, East river. Col. Smith became acquainted with General Miranda. The latter was born in Caraccas, South America, and was for

9*

many years in the service of old Spain. He left in
1785, and then entered his brain an idea of freeing that
section of South America from Spain. He came to the
United States for this purpose. He went to Europe on
the same business, and pursued his project for many
years, applying successively to France, Great Britian
and the United States for aid. In 1805 he came to
New York, and commenced getting up a military expedition against the province of Caraccas. He knew the
surveyor of the port, Col. Smith, and he explained to
him all his views.

Colonel Smith promised to aid him, and pointed out
to him one excellent vessel that could be obtained for
the expedition. It was the ship " Leander," belonging
to Samuel G. Ogden, whose place of business, as well
as residence at that time, was at 102 Greenwich street.
The surveyor was a shrewd man. He met Mr. Ogden
in the street.

" Sam, have you heard of Miranda ? '

" Yes, I have."

" Well, how would you like to make his acquaintance? He has been a very great traveller — he is a
man of science — has extended views of matters and
things in general, and I dare say he might open up new
commercial fields to you."

" I should like very much to make his acquaintance,"
was the reply of the merchant.

That same evening General Miranda spent at the residence of Samuel G. Ogden, and, with the aid of a few
bottles of old Madeira, such as could be procured only
by old New York merchants in those days, the two
talked upon various subjects.

They spent a pleasant evening, and agreed to meet
the next morning upon the battery. This was not an

uncommon thing for the first people in New York, to
make appointments and walk upon the battery in winter
as well as summer mornings. At this interview General Miranda explained to Mr. Ogden that he had recently returned from Washington, where he had met President Jefferson, and had talked freely with Mr. Madison,
the Secretary of State, who thought the freedom of
South America generally a very desirable and praise-
worthy object ; and proposed to Mr. Ogden to go into
it, and aid him with vessels and means to fit out an expedition to free the province of Caraccas.

I may as well add, that at this time, no one dreamed
that President Jefferson would be openly hostile to such an
expedition. General Francis Miranda, when at Washington, was received in the most cordial manner by all
the high officials of the Federal Government. This introduction by Surveyor Smith of General Miranda to
Mr. Ogden, cost Colonel Smith his Surveyorship. He
was removed a few days later. He was so confident of
the success of the " Miranda " expedition, that he allowed his own son, William S. Smith, to go out as supercargo of the ship " Leander " belonging to Mr. Ogden.

The result of several interviews between General
Miranda and Samuel G. Ogden, in December, 1805,
was that in January, 1806, the latter went to work
heart and soul to fit out his ship, and load her for the
rebel service. He bought cargo, shipped 150 men, cannons, gunpowder, muskets, stores, etc., to a very large
amount. The captain of the ship " Leander " was
named Thomas Lewis. While the expedition was fitting out, General Miranda boarded at the Widow
Avery's, No. 7 State street, until the ship " Leander,"
was ready to sail, and then he went on board of her.

She had on board all told, eighty persons, and mounted seventeen cannons, as the complement of the ship.

The cargo fitted out by Mr. Ogden was a very valuable one. William Armstrong was the principal agent of Mr. Ogden in shipping the men and cannon. When the "Leander" cleared at the Custom House, it was for Jaquemel, in the West Indies. Mr. Ogden was, however, too shrewd a merchant to fit out such an expedition upon the mere word or promises of General Miranda. The latter had a much more substantial basis. When he reached here he brought a letter of credit for £700 sterling on Daniel Ludlow & Co., merchants at No. 19 South street. Daniel Ludlow lived at that time at No. 56 Broadway. This sum Ludlow & Co. paid over to Samuel G. Ogden for General Miranda. Miranda gave Mr. Ogden his bill on Nicholas Van Sittart, London, for £2,000; others for £5,000 on Joseph Lambert and Wm. Brown, of Trinidad. I do not know whether the last was ever paid. The "Leander" was to clear for Jaquemel, but on her way, near the Province of Caraccas, she was to land what she had on board, and then and there Mr. Ogden's captain or agent was to receive, in cash, the cost of cargo — which was $40,000 — the amount of outfit, and 200 per cent. advance on the amount of the cargo and outfits. (Outfits included, of course, money advanced to the soldiers of the expedition.) The whole sum, adding 200 per cent., estimated to be paid for by General Miranda, was $217,000. In conversation, Miranda stated that the "Leander" would land her cargo near the town of Caraccas, probably at La Guayra. He did not believe that La Guayra had a force of but few men.

I think there was some lack of knowledge in reference to landing a cargo near Caraccas. I have myself been from La Guayra to Caraccas, but it is over a mountain several thousand feet high, and which only mules can travel. Caraccas is up in the mountain. It was nearly destroyed by an earthquake in 1812, a few years after the celebrated Miranda expedition.

Mr. Ogden bought the cargo partly for cash, but the greater part was on time. The ship sailed in January, and her owners expected that she would be back in the month of March. After landing General Miranda, his men and ammunition, the "Leander" was to proceed to Jaquemel, and there load with a return cargo of coffee, to be bought with a part of the money received from General Miranda, according to agreement. All the leading men of New York city at the time, and among them was Rufus King, were perfectly familiar with the expedition and its object. Mr. Ogden took a great risk, and if it succeeded he meant to get a proportionably large share of profit.

Some of the sons and relatives of many of the first people of the State were in the expedition. The "Leander" sailed about the 1st of February, 1806. On board were Thomas Lewis; William Steuben Smith, alluded to, who ranked as aid of General Miranda; there were Henry Sands, Barent Roorbach, William Hosack, Edward Gates, Elisha King, James B. Gardner, Alexander Buchanan, John Moor, David Burnett, Dr. Samuel Scofield (surgeon to the army,) Henry Perry, John T. O'Sullivan, and such like names. That Henry Perry was an uncle of mine. Here is one of the commissions of Miranda:

"DON FRANCISCO DE MIRANDA,
Commander-in-Chief of the Columbian Army.

By virtue of power and authority invested in me, I hereby constitute and appoint William Hosack a first

Lieutenant of Artillery in the army of Columbia, under my command ; and all officers, his superiors and in-
feriors, non-commissioned officers and others, are hereby
required to respect and obey him as such, agreeable to
the articles of War.

    Signed,   FRAN. DE MIRANDA.
THOMAS MOLINI, *Sec'y Reg't* ——."

The " Leander " went straight to Jaquemel, reaching
that harbor on the 19th of February.

There they expected to be joined by the " Emperor,"
another ship belonging to Mr. Ogden. She did not
come, and the schooner " Bacchus " was hired to ac-
company the " Leander." She did not leave Jaquemel
until the 28th of March. The " Leander " was accompanied by the schooners " Bee " and " Bacchus." All
the men to conquer Caraccas did not exceed 200 on
board the three vessels. These were to drive the King
of Spain out of South America. After being twelve
days at sea, they landed at Aruba, seventy miles to the
leeward of where the expedition really wished to go.
The troops went ashore, and staid until the 16th of
. April, when they embarked again. For several days
more they were cruising about, and came near the
Dutch island of Curaçoa. They fought on board ; all
was confusion from day to day. Captain Lewis, who
had been appointed a colonel in Miranda's service, now
said he would have no more to do with Miranda or his
enterprise, except as captain of the " Leander," to se-
·cure the interest of Mr. Ogden. I believe he was his
brother-in-law. April 24th the vessel reached Curaçoa.
Two days after they reached the Spanish main, and
were ready to land, when they were attacked by the
Spaniards, and nearly all captured. Two Spanish
Guarda Costas first attacked and captured the two

schooners, with sixty men and officers. This was off
Puerto Cabello. The " Leander " stood off for sea.
The cause of the capture of the schooners was the captains of those vessels not obeying orders and keeping
near the " Leander."

The battle was fought April 20th, 1806. May 6th
the " Leander " was at sea with but six gallons of water
on board. She went to Bonair. She put to sea again
after getting water, and wandered about, Miranda
quarrelling with his men, until May 28th, when the
ship reached the Island of Granada. From that island
she went Barbadoes, where the celebrated Lord Cochran
had a British fleet. She continued there until June
28th, when Capt. Lewis had a serious quarrel with Miranda, and left for New York. She was now the reputed property of General Miranda. July 14th the " Leander " reached Port of Spain, Trinidad. August 1st,
the " Leander " got to sea again, and on the 3d troops
were landed on the Spanish main, and the Columbia
flag hoisted in place of the royal standard of Spain.
General Miranda fooled about the interior for a short
time, but finally went on board ship. He left the " Leander " on the 27th of September. A Capt. Atkins
now took command of the " Leander," but having no
ability he was succeeded by a lieutenant of the British
navy. Nov. 26th the " Leander " was lying in Trini- ·
dad, the agent trying to get a settlement with Miranda,
who was lying at the Government House. I will now
give the final of the ship " Leander." She lay in the
harbor of Trinidad until Feb. 24th, 1807, when the
sailors belonging to her went in a body to the Governor
and told him that they were hungry and naked, that
the ship had no stores, and they wanted their wages.
He tried to get their wages from Miranda, and failing

in that, tried the ship's agent. Finally 33 out of 266
shipped from America, addressed the governor a petition. He promised pay, and they waited. Day by day
the little band became less. They were pressed on
board of British ships of war. At last the ship " Leander " was sold in September, 1807. Some of the money was paid to the few sailors who adhered to the ship.
Mr. Ogden, her owner, never received a dollar. Most
of the young men who joined Miranda in New York,
were liberally educated. Such as Hosack, Sands, Scofield, Loudon, Burnett and others.

Of the prisoners taken from this expedition by the
Spaniards, near Puerto Cabello, ten were hanged on
the 24th of July, 1806; ten were sentenced to labor at
Omoa ; fourteen were sent to Porto Rico to labor ten
years ; nineteen were sentenced to labor at Bocca Chica,
near Carthagena, for eight years. Among them was
Henry Perry. He was never heard of again from that
day to this.

All that Mr. Ogden ever got out of the concern was
the £800 sterling I have alluded to, and one of the
drafts for £2,000 was paid. He never received a penny from the proceeds of the " Leander." All the property of his that Miranda took out of New York was
spent, dissipated or lost. General Miranda was at last
captured by the Spaniards, and died in a Spanish prison.
His son came to this city some years ago. When Columbia became free, in later years, President Bolivar
always expressed a deep sympathy for that expedition,
and if ever Samuel G. Ogden had gone to Caraccas before Bolivar died (about 1828,) a portion of his losses
would have been refunded to him.

CHAPTER XXI.

It would seem hardly creditable were I to state that while his commercial adventures in this direction were so unprosperous, and culminating so unhappily not only to his prospects but to human life, and that Samuel G. Ogden was suffering quite sufficiently for any mistake he had made, that the United States Government should take a part in the proceedings. Yet so it was. The ship "Leander" had barely time to get outside of Sandy Hook, when Nathan Sanford, the United States District Attorney, commenced legal proceedings against Mr. Ogden. He and his friend, Colonel W. S. Smith, were both indicted by the Grand Jury, April 1, 1806. He was held to bail in the sum of $20,000. Samuel Gouverneur was one of the sureties, and Mr. Ogden himself was one. Mr. Gouverneur was a son-in-law of James Munroe. Mr. Ogden employed as his counsel Thomas A. Emmett, Cadwallader Colden, and Josiah Ogden Hoffman. Mr. Smith was first tried. The trial commenced before Judge Talmadge — July, 1806. The following jurors were sworn. There is a lot of my old merchant names among them : John Sullivan, John A. Fort, John Rathbone, Jr., Lewis C. Hammersley, Courland Babcock, John P. Haff, Goold Hoyt, James Masterton, Schuyler Livingston, Henry Panton,

Gabriel Furman, Augustus Wynkoop. This jury acquitted Mr. Smith. A few days after, the trial of Mr. Ogden came on. A new jury was drawn up, viz.: Joseph Strong, Benjamin Butler, William Coit, James McConell, David A. Cunningham, James Palmer, Jr., John Bachellor, Ezra Weeks, John P. Groshon, John McPhie, William Dunstan, and Andrew S. Norwood.

Those jurors' names are some of them well known. At that time Ezra Weeks was an object of curiosity. Only a few years previous he and his brother Levi lived at the corner of Greenwich and Harrison streets. The last was an architect, and the former a builder. On the 5th of March, 1800, Levi was tried for the murder of the beautiful Gulielma Sands. It made quite a noise. Ezra was the principal witness.

The jury chosen in the case of Mr. Ogden found him " Not Guilty."

I am not certain of the fact, but I think that of those two celebrated juries there is not now living one man. Of many of them long sketches have been published in the " Old Merchants," in the first series. John Rathbone, Jr., was one. He was of the firm of John Rathbone & Co. So too was Lewis C. Hammersley, in a former chapter. Goold Hoyt, also, has appeared in the " Old Merchants." He was one of the great East India firm of Hoyt & Tom. They owned the ship " Sabina," that brought in tea cargoes from Canton for many years. Old Goold Hoyt lived at the corner of Park place and Church street; his coach house was in the rear, and faced on Murray street. That ground is now occupied by a large store of Wilmerding & Mount, auctioneers of old standing and great wealth.

Mr. Samuel Ogden does not seem to have been at all discouraged by his ill-luck with General Miranda. It is quite evident his credit was not injured among the other merchants of New York when he went into the business, for nearly all the merchandise, ammunition, etc., that he purchased, was on time. Among those who sold him goods was John McLane, who was at the time commissary of military stores, at No. 27 Oliver street. He had been in the habit of arming all the vessels belonging to Mr. Ogden. He supplied a large amount on time.

Ebenezer Stevens also sold him six iron nine pounders on time. That Mr. Stevens was afterwards a merchant in South street, and had a firm of Ebenezer Stevens & Sons. Those sons are now old men, but leading merchants. John A. Stevens is one of them.

John Jacob Astor sold Mr. Ogden all the swords required for the expedition.

Bernard Hart, of whom I have written, sold fourteen cannon to Mr. Ogden on time, and took his note for the amount.

Abraham Vannest, an old saddler, sold 250 saddles for Mr. Ogden. He was a very wealthy man in after years in this city. He formerly did business in Hanover square, and owned a cottage with an acre of ground corner of Bleecker and Charles streets, where he lives now.

Jonathan Ogden — no relation, I believe, of our Mr. Ogden — sold him a large quantity of gunpowder. It was delivered from the powder house of Martin Boerum, at Brooklyn. The people of that great city would not stand a powder magazine, in these days, in the heart of their city. Old John Murray, of whom I have written, sold a large amount of swords and cutlasses to Mr. Ogden for this expedition. At that time Augustus Fleming was a clerk with Mr. Murray. Mr. F. became in after years a very noted citizen. There was another

great firm at that time — " Corp, Ellis & Shaw." Sam
uel Corp was at the head of it, and he lived over the
store at 171 Pearl, corner of Pine, in those years.
This concern sold a large quantity of cannon to Mr.
Ogden for his notes.

Mr. Ogden continued on in his business in the city of
New York for some years. He lived at No. 9 Hudson
street, until 1815, when he went to France and established himself in commercial business at Bordeaux.
There he did a very large business for several years,
forming many valuable mercantile connections. He
left Bordeaux for New York in 1825, and became agent
for several large houses in France. One was the house
of Lafitte & Co., merchants, Havre. He was a brother
of the great banker Lafitte of Paris, once so celebrated
in history. Another house there Mr. Ogden represented, was Vassner & Co., of Havre, and sent to his friends
large consignments of cotton and other American produce. He advanced heavily to shippers, and drew bills
on the credit furnished him by the French house for
whom he was acting. His counting house, when he
held these agencies, was at No. 49 Wall street. His
private residence was at No. 41 Warren street, a large
house, where he entertained in the most magnificent
style. His dinner parties were unequalled, and there
met the first merchants in the city. I have mentioned
that his first wife was a grand-daughter of old Francis
Lewis, one of the signers of the Declaration of Independence. Of course she was a niece of Governor
Morgan Lewis, a famous man in this city in the olden
times.

The second wife of Mr. Ogden was Miss Fairlie, a
daughter of Major Fairlie, a celebrated man in his day.
He was alderman for many years. He was clerk of

the Supreme Court of this State a great many years, and had several daughters. One married Thomas Cooper, a popular actor. His daughter married Robert Tyler, a son of John Tyler, president once of the United States. The old Major James Fairlie lived at No. 41 Courtlandt street. His home was a favorite resort of the citizens. He had one daughter named Louisa, that was very pretty and very witty. She never married. All the young men were afraid of her. Slidell, who is now at Fort Warren, will remember her very well. His father was a highly respectable tallow chandler in early life, and president of Mechanics' Bank in after years. Young John had travelled extensively in Europe. After his return, he met Louisa Fairlie, upon whom he was rather sweet. He told her of many places he had visited. " Did you go to Greece ? " she asked. " No, why do you ask ? " replied Slidell. " Oh, nothing — only it would have been so *very* natural that you should have visited *Greece*, to renew *early* associations." He had no more to say.

Cora A., daughter of Mr. Ogden, married Mr. Mowatt. He was very rich when Miss Ogden married him, but in 1837 he became largely involved in land speculations, ruined himself, and became poor. This was the cause of her going upon the stage. He died after a few years, and she married a second time, Mr. Ritchie, a son of old " Father Ritchie," of Richmond, Virginia. Mrs. Ritchie is now in Paris, and a great favorite.

Another daughter of Mr. Ogden married a Frenchman of the name of Guillet. He lived in this city, and afterwards moved to Richmond, where he became a clerk in the great tobacco house of Rogers, Harrison & Gray. She was an artist and painted very well. She died many years ago, leaving several children.

A son of Samuel G. Ogden of the same name is auditor in the Custom House in New York, and has been for many years. I think Mr. Ogden succeeded " old Shultz " as he was called, during the time of Sam Swartwout. Mr. Shultz was an old Dutchman, and I think was appointed about the commencement of the Government, under President Washington. He was celebrated for two things. One was for the enormous quantity of tobacco that he chewed, and the other was the extraordinary correctness of his accounts. It used to be told of him, that on one occasion when his accounts were made up and sent on to the Treasury department, an error of one cent was found, and the account was returned to Shultz. He re-examined them, and ascertained that the error was not his, but in the Treasury department. That was conceded finally, but Shultz was requested to alter the New York Custom house books, so as to make them agree with the Washington treasury accounts. He refused to do it, saying, " They made the mistake, let them correct it."

When an auditor understands his business, it is not safe to remove him. A valuable and experienced accountant is not picked up every day."

Mr. Samuel G. Ogden, Sen., had several other children beside those I have named. Mr. Ogden had a brother who was a leading merchant in Canton, China, and very extensively mixed up in business transactions with the late John Jacob Astor.

He had been sent out to China by Mr. Astor, and was a partner in business with him. He had been abroad many years, and had acquired, as every one supposed, a very large fortune. His letters to his brother Sam, and other relatives, had conveyed that idea, and it was probably so. At any rate the Canton Ogden had determined to retire from business, and go to New York. He embarked at Whampoa on board of one of the ships belonging to John Jacob Astor, that was bound to New York. He had with him in the ship all his books and papers. On the passage he died. All his papers went into the possession of Mr. Astor. His relatives applied to Mr. Astor for a settlement, but they could get no satisfaction. I believe Samuel G. Ogden bought up all the claims of other relatives, and then commenced a suit against John Jacob Astor. This suit lasted many years, and was going on when Mr. Astor died. After that event, Mr. W. B. Astor took the matter in his own hand, and made an offer for a settlement. I believe the amount was over $200,000. This was a handsome sum, and made the latter years of Mr. Ogden very comfortable. He died in 1860.

Some time ago a friend sent me a printed handbill, without date, headed, " Funeral of our murdered countryman, John Pierce." The document states that a public funeral will be given to the deceased under the direction of Aldermen Fairlie, Mott, and John D. Miller ; that "the corse is now in the Council chamber, and will be interred to-morrow at 12 o'clock, in St. Paul's churchyard." It adds : " The Mayor has transmitted intelligence to the president, in order that measures may be taken to obtain satisfaction to our injured and insulted nation." I am asked to explain that document, which I shall keep as a curiosity. It should have been dated April 27, 1806. It is signed, " T. Wortman, city clerk."

I give it now, as it is likely the British Government will give us a few years of the " same sorts." For years before we declared war against England in 1812, the English were insulting us on our own coast :

April 26, 1806.

The British ship " Leander," of fifty guns, the " Cambriam " of forty-four, and the " Drain " sloop of war, were off Sandy Hook yesterday. They brought to and boarded every vessel that left this port, and pressed several seamen from them. They also captured the ship " Amour " from Havana, the brig " Ceres " from Martinique, and the ship " Nimrod," Curocoa. The sloop " Richard," a coaster coming from the Brandywine, while entering the harbor, was fired at by the " Leander," and brought to ; although the sloop lay to upon the first shot, another was fired that struck John Pierce, the helmsman, and killed him on the spot.

This John Pierce lived at No. 55 Mulberry street, and was respected. His body was brought up to Burling slip, and there lay exposed all day to thousands of spectators. Our people were crazy at the sight. They became mad with rage. Four schooners were fitted up to go and retake the prizes. The purser of the " Leander " had been up in town, and purchased three boatloads of all kind of provisions ; two of the boats were stopped at the wharf, the other was overtaken near the Hook by a pilot-boat, and brought back ; the provisions were put into carts, and paraded through the streets with drum, fifes, etc., and were afterwards left at the poor house.

Next day the Grand Jury indicted Henry Whitbay, captain of the " Leander," for the murder of John Pierce.

CHAPTER XXII.

There have been some illustrious merchants in this city — men who have added to its wealth by their extended business operations — to its fame by their individual efforts, standing out in bold relief above all others. Those who in the last century have done most, have been rewarded least, and names that would adorn any city or nation, are now almost obscured or forgotten. I looked to-day at a Directory for 1862. I found there:

" Pintard, Phœbe, widow John, h. 30 Canal."
" Pintard, Samuel, seaman, h. 3 Birmingham."

I know these are neither kith or kin of the proud old mercantile race of Pintards, that have flourished in this city almost 200 years, and that I am going to write about to-day.

All the males of that great merchant race lie in a vault in the church of St. Clement in Amity street, between Sullivan and MacDougal streets. John Pintard, of whom I shall have much to say, and to whom the word illustrious applies, as much as to any man that ever lived, was an only son of John Pintard, and the younger left no males of the race. He had two daughters.

How few of the hundreds of thousands that live in this city now can answer this question : " Who was
10

John Pintard?" Yet no man did more or as much to raise the character of this city. He was in everything. He was born in it, when it contained but a few thousands. Yet nearly sixty years ago he foresaw its future grandeur, and I have before me as he wrote it at the time, the very paper left by him. Here it is :

Statistical.— By the numeration of the inhabitants of this city recently published, the progress of population for the last 5 years appears to be at the rate of 25 per cent. Should our city continue to increase in the same proportion during the present century, the aggregate number, at its close, will far exceed that of any other city in the old world, Pekin not excepted, as will appear from the following table. Progress of population in the city of New York computed at the rate of 25 per cent. every 5 years.

1805	. .	75,770	1855	. .	705,650
1810	. .	95,715	1860	. .	882,062
1815	. .	110,390	1865	. .	1,102,577
1820	. .	147,987	1870	. .	1,378,221
1825	. .	184,923	1875	. .	1,722,776
1830	. .	231,228	1880	. .	2,153,470
1835	. .	289,035	1885	.	2,691,837
1840	. .	361,293	1890	. .	3,364,796
1845	. .	451,616	1895	. .	4,205,995
1850	. .	564,520	1900	. .	5,257,493

From this table it appears, that the population of this city, fifty years hence, will considerably exceed the reputed population of the cities of Paris and London. Cities and nations, however, like individuals, experience their rise, progress, and decline. It is hardly probable that New York will be so highly favored as to prove an exception. Wars, pestilence, and political convulsions, must be our lot, and be taken into calculation. With every allowance, however, for the " numerous ills which life is heir to," from our advantageous maritime situation, and the increase of agriculture and commerce, our numbers will in all probability, at the end of this century, exceed those of any other city in the world, Pekin alone excepted.

From the data here furnished, the politician, financier, and above all the speculator in town-lots (a subject to our shame be it spoken, which absorbs every generous passion,) may draw various and interesting inferences.

Is not that wonderful ? How can we reconcile it that a man possessing such wonderful sagacity — convinced, too, in his own mind that he was right,— that the city would be a mine of gold to speculation,— that he should not have availed himself of his knowledge, but should have died comparatively poor, having lost a great deal in the fire of 1835 — about nine years previous to his death. Yet so it was. He left the speculation in town lots — " which absorbs every generous passion," as he expresses it — to others. And men roll in wealth, and are surrounded by every luxury, because they did buy town lots, and from no other cause.

Few knew that John Pintard was a merchant. Yet he was so, and a most able merchant. He was one of the most famed in his day, and would have been one of the most wealthy but for his confidence in others. I hardly know how to begin with John Pintard, and with such a sketch as will render him even one part in a hundred of his just dues. The Pintard family was Huguenot, original immigrant being Anthony Pintard, who settled at Shrewsbury, Monmouth Co., N. J.

Our John Pintard was born in New York, May 18, 1759. Three weeks later his mother died, and the next year, in 1760, his father, John Pintard, sen., died leaving the little human boat to navigate alone before he was a year old. The father, John Pintard, was a merchant of the old school. He owned vessels — he com-

manded, and was supercargo of his own vessel, and was
on a voyage to the West Indies when he died at Port-au-
Prince. Another John Pintard, who was grandfather
of our John Pintard, was Alderman and Assistant of
the Dock Ward in this city for ten years — viz., from
1738 to 1747. The Dock Ward was a little fellow.
It was bounded by Broad to what is now Water street,
(the water came up to it in those days) — Wall from
Broad to William, and William down to the Water at
the Old Slip. Besides the streets I have named it had
but these, viz., Garden (now Exchange,) Prince (Beaver,) Duke (South William,) Mill, and Dock (Pearl)
streets. I fancy in that district, not many people sleep
at night even now. In 1757 John Pintard, son of the
alderman, married the lovely Miss Cannon. She died
shortly after giving birth to John Pintard, Jun. She
was the daughter of John Cannon — a great merchant
of the city about those days. The family was Huguenot also; and John C. was brother to the famous *Le
Grand Cannon*, of Canada notoriety.

After the death of his parents, the child John Pintard, in 1760, was taken by his uncle, Louis Pintard, to
bring up. As soon as he was old enough he was sent
to the famous grammar school of the Rev. Leonard Cutting, at Hempstead, Long Island. Mr. Cutting was a
remarkable man, and a great disciplinarian. He was
the grandfather of the present Francis B. Cutting, one
of our most eminent lawyers. Mr. Cutting said that
John Pintard was the best Latin scholar in his school.
He was there three years. From the celebrated school
of Mr. Cutting, John went to the college at Princeton,
and was nearly prepared to graduate, when the war of
1776 broke out. He was ready to take his degree.
At this time the entire college was ready to enlist.

The professors became captains, and enlisted companies of soldiers. The professor of mathematics raised a company, and it was immediately started for New York city. He forbid John Pintard joining it; but he did, notwithstanding, and smuggled himself off with it to New York. Before he left Princeton, he drilled soldiers every day. He went back with his company to Princeton, and received his degree, notwithstanding his disobedience in going to New York. After he left college, he went to the residence of Louis Pintard, at New Rochelle, where he had a country residence, as well as a counting-room in New York city. When the troops came in the vicinity, he went to Norwalk, Connecticut, where he had relatives. After being there a short time he was sent for by his uncle, Louis Pintard, who had been appointed by General Washington as commissary for the prisoners in New York city. He gave his nephew, John Pintard, the appointment of deputy, and for years he did the entire duties of the office held by his uncle. Dr. Boudinot, a brother-in-law, was commissary general of the American army.

It was the duty of young John Pintard to procure articles for the prisoners, and to relieve them as much as possible. It was known that 11,500 prisoners died on board the British prison-ships. How many died in the prisons in this city never will be known. The sugar house in Liberty street, torn down a few years ago, was one. The provost prison (the Quaker church in Pearl street, between Franklin square and Oak street, erected in 1775, of brick, and torn down in 1824) was used as a hospital. In that gloomy and terrific abode many of the principal citizens were confined. In December, 1777, the state of the prisoners became so horrible that the prison doors were opened in order to disgorge their wretched contents. The poor prisoners started to go to Jersey and the country for relief, but they were so weak from disease and famine, that many fell dead in the streets before they could get to the boats on the river side.

When John Pintard was released from his duties, and from witnessing horrid outrages upon prisoners, in 1780, he went to Paramus, N. J., where resided Col. Abraham Brasher, a great "Liberty boy" in his day, and also a distant connection of Mr. Pintard.

That Abraham Brasher was a member of the first Provincial Convention that assembled in the Exchange in New York, April 20, 1775, for the purpose of choosing delegates to represent the colony of New York in the continental Congress. Old Philip Livingston presided. Col. Brasher was also a member of the second and third New York Provincial Congress, as well as the first. He was also a member of the Convention of the State of New York, held in 1776 to 1777.

At the residence of Col. Brasher, Mr. Pintard met Eliza Brasher, a daughter of the patriotic colonel. They became engaged, and in 1785 they were married. A more splendid couple never approached the marriage altar. He was a very handsome man, and she was the very loveliest girl in the land. Her hair was black and massive, and done up on the cushions of that day, made her look magnificent — this, too, combined with the most lovely face, made her,— as she was for many years — a charming woman. He, too, looked well, with his powdered hair, blue coat, standing collar, and handsome person. If our girls in 1863, would adopt the style and mode of dressing the hair one hundred years ago, they would look a thousand times more lovely than now. Pity the girls "don't see it!"

After 1782, John had gone to clerking it again with his uncle Lewis, who was doing a heavy East India business, and was among the first to go into that trade largely after the war closed in 1782. Before that, in 1685, King James issued an order prohibiting all trade from New York colony with the East Indies.

Lewis Pintard continued business during the war, although on a limited scale. He was one of the original incorporators of the Chamber of Commerce of this city, granted by George III, in 1770, and incorporated by the New York legislature in 1784. John Pintard remained with his uncle, Lewis, until after he married ; then he started upon his own account, at No. 12 Wall street. He went into the East India trade, and bought or built the ship " Belgiosa." He owned the ship " Jay," and she was among the first vessels that brought cargoes from China. In 1789, he was so popular that he was elected assistant alderman of the East Ward, and was re-elected until 1792. The East Ward took in Wall street, below William ; and in 1788 John moved from 57 King (Pine) street to 43 Wall. The East Ward was next to the Dock Ward, and ran up William street as far as Golden Hill (John,) and down to the water. He gave up the aldermanship when he was elected to the legislature, in 1790. It held its session in New York city in those days (as they should do now,) and began in January and ended in March. John Watts was speaker of the fourteenth session, when Mr. Pintard was a member. But a calamity was coming upon him at that time, that was to end all political as well as commercial success for a few years. He was a happy man in the year 1786 to 1791. His eldest daughter (Eliza. Noel) was born in 1787. In after years she married Doctor Davidson, of

New Orleans; went there and died. A second daughter (Louisa) married Mr. Thomas L. Servoss, an eminent merchant of New York city.

In 1792 John Pintard, who did not owe a dollar in the world — who was rich by property inherited from his grandfather Cannon — who was doing a heavy and successful business, put his name on the back of notes drawn by his friend William Duer, for over a million of dollars. Mr. Duer lived at that time at 12 Partition street, (Fulton street now from Broadway to the North river.) He had married the Lady Kitty, daughter of the celebrated Earl of Sterling. Mr. Duer was the bosom friend, and the agent and manager of Alexander Hamilton, who then lived at 57 Wall street, only a few doors below Mr. Pintard. It was about the time the debts of the United States were funded according to a scheme of Hamilton. Everybody had confidence in Duer, for he was supposed to be a great financier. He was operating enormously in these stock operations. But he failed, and poor John Pintard was the great sufferer. He gave up all he had to pay these indorsements — ships, houses, cargoes, furniture, library, everything, but it was not a drop in the bucket. Then he moved from this city and went to Newark to live. In 1791 he had been appointed one of the commissioners for erecting bridges over the Hackensack and Passaic rivers, and also to survey the country between Powel's Hook (Jersey city now) and Newark. I have the map and report he made, before me now. That work was done in February, 1791.

That year he was doing another work. Who that passes the American Museum of Barnum, with a thousand flags, etc., ever dreams that John Pintard planted the acorn that grew up to be *the* oak? Barnum has no idea of the history of it. What connection can there be between Tammany Hall and Barnum's museum? Yet, Tammany Hall started *that* museum! I have before me a document, dated May 1, 1791. It is headed " AMERICAN MUSEUM, under the patronage of the Tammany Society, or Columbian order." The Corporation granted a room in the City Hall for its use, to be open every Friday and Friday afternoon. " Any article sent on those days, or to Mr. John Pintard, No. 57 King street, will be thankfully accepted."

John Pintard was the secretary of that " American museum," and Gardner Baker was keeper. It went along very successfully for some years. In 1808, it was the sole property of Gardner Baker, and was called Baker's American museum ; then he sold it to Doctor Scudder, and he kept it ; the building then used to be at the back of the City Hall, up in the third story, and it was Scudder's American museum. Then the immortal Barnum bought it. Once John Pintard loaned Scudder a large square block of crystal ; Scudder sold it with the " other things " as if it was his own. I have watched that block (it used to stand in the corner) for about thirty years. I believe Mr. B. took it up to Iranistan, when he had that place.

I will go back to the Pintard indorsements of William Duer's notes. The creditors were unmerciful. They followed Mr. Pintard into New Jersey, and they incarcerated him in the Newark jail for fourteen months, for debts not his own. He read immensely while in jail, and when forty years old concluded to study law. He passed his examination, but found that he could not make a public speaker, and gave it up. His powers of conversation were very great, but he was excessively modest, and could not speak in public. In 1797 he

10*

took the benefit of the act in Jersey, but found that it would do him no good, and he came to New York and afterwards took the benefit of the general bankrupt law of the United States, in 1800.

The exasperated creditors never let up the drawer of the notes. Mr. William Duer was put into jail in the city, and finally died on the jail limits. He was the father of William Duer, president of Columbia college, and also of Judge John Duer, both of whom have died within a few years.

William Duer was a prominent man in the Revolution. He was in the first Provincial Congress, and was one of the committee to draft a constitution for the "State of New York." He hailed from "Charlotte county " in New York.

Old William Duer would have succeeded in all his great financial operations, but for an accident and an unjust charge. When Alexander Hamilton was Secretary of the Treasury, in 1791, he frequently used Government money for secret purposes, known of course by president Washington. This money was given to William Duer to buy up Government debts, or other purposes as the agent of Hamilton, and was charged to Mr. Duer. When Oliver Wolcott succeeded Hamilton, a large sum was found charged to William Duer. The clerk who made the discovery at once announced that William Duer was a defaulter to the government. The news went to New York. Mr. Hamilton made the matter straight in a few days, but not before the credit of Mr. Duer was damaged, and he became a ruined man.

About 1800, Mr. John Pintard came back to this city from New Jersey, and went into business. Not being a Sachem of Tammany Hall, I have no right to

look at their sacred records, but I am aware that John
Pintard was a brother of high standing. He was the
first Sagamore of the Society. On the evening of the
last Monday in April, 1791, at the annual election of
officers of the Tammany Society, held at their Great
Wigwam, in Broad street, the following brothers were
duly elected, viz: Sachems — John Pintard, Cortland
Van Buren, John Campbell, Gabriel Furman, Thomas
Greenleaf, Josiah Ogden Hoffman, William Mooney,
John Onderdonk, Anthony Post, Jonathan Post, William Pitt Smith, Melancthon Smith, Ebenezer Stevens
and James Tylee. Treasurer — Thomas Ash. Secretary — John Swartwout. At the annual meeting of
the Council of Sachems of said society, the following
brothers were duly elected, viz: May 21, 1791, Josiah
O. Hoffman, Grand Sachem ; James Tylee, Father of
the Council ; DeWitt Clinton, scribe of the Council.
John Pintard has been a Grand Sachem.

The following also was written by John Pintard,
" On Thursday last (May, 1791) was celebrated by
the sons of Tammany, the anniversary of the Tammany society or Columbian order. The day was ush-
ered in by a Federal salute from the battery, and welcomed by a discharge of thirteen guns from the brig
' Grand Sachem,' lying in the stream. The society assembled at the Great Wigwam in Broad street, five
hours after the rising of the sun, and was conducted
from there in an elegant procession to the brick meeting
house in Beekman street. Before them was borne the
cap of Liberty ; after following seven hunters in the
Tammanial dress, then the great standard of the society, in the rear of which was the Grand Sachem and
other officers. On either side of these were formed the
members in tribes, each headed by its standard bearers

and Sachem in full dress. At the brick meeting house an oration was delivered by their brother, Josiah Ogden Hoffman, to the society, and to a most respectable and crowded audience. In the most brilliant and pathetic language, he traced the progress of the liberty we enjoy, and thence elegantly deduced the origin of the Columbian order, and the society of the Cincinnati. From the meeting house the procession proceeded (as before) to Campbell's grounds, where upwards of two hundred people partook of a handsome and plentiful repast. The dinner was honored by His Excellency the Governor (old George Clinton,) and many of the most respectable citizens."

No wonder old Tammany prospered in those days. Why were those ceremonies dropped? Where are all those worthies now? The old Wigwam in Broad street is gone. The "brick church" is no more, " Campbell's grounds " are covered with lofty buildings, and — Well, well, it does us good to wake up those pleasant memories. That brig " Grand Sachem ? " I have an idea that she was owned by John Pintard, and was sold to pay his unfortunate indorsements for William Duer, who left *his* family well off, if he did die " on the jail limits."

In the above procession Mr. Pintard was a prominent object. He was dressed in the full tog of old Tammany, but not an article was upon his person that was not *American*. The very buttons of his coat were made of American conk shell, set in buttons of American silver.

When our splendid old Sachem and merchant got back into the United States again from New Jersey, where he was locked up in jail fourteen months, he went into the book trade and auction business — that is, he sold books at auction. He was a born book-dealer ; he was fond of them ; liked to handle them, overhaul the contents, and make them useful. I have an idea that those who know David T. Valentine in these years, know such a man as John Pintard was in his palmy days. No one seemed to have thought John Pintard a wonderful man in his day, yet now what think those who know who and what he was ? So, too, it will be with Uncle David, when he has passed from among us, and other generations look on what he has done to preserve the past : he will be honored and appreciated, though I hope his children will not be allowed to almost starve in their old age. It is a sin and a shame, and a disgrace, that in this city of wealth, the children of those who have been its greatest benefactors should have to worry and struggle for a home.

But to return to John Pintard, whose name and what he has done shall be better known before I have finished this chapter. In 1801 he was at work in the city once more, and had his family at No. 31 Dey street. I think he had tried brokerage a year or two, but not with much success.

After his return his uncle, Lewis Pintard, bought *The Daily Advertiser*, and gave John one quarter interest in it, and his son-in-law, Samuel Bayard, another quarter. Old Lewis eventually died at Princeton, leaving his only daughter. From some cause or other Mr. John Pintard did not long continue an editor. About 1802 he went to New Orleans, then just annexed to this country, and regarded as a wonderful place. Mr. Pintard went there determined to try a new career. He remained out there several months, and gathered very valuable statistics ; but he did not like the place, and returned to his favorite city.

CHAPTER XXIII.

After the return of John Pintard from Newark, in
the winter of 1804—05, he was appointed Clerk to the
Corporation of New York, and City Inspector. His
office was in the City Hall, then at the corner of Nassau and Wall street, where the Custom House now
stands, and he lived at upper Reed street, No. 11, (upper Reed, upper Chambers, or upper Duane, meant
those streets on the east side of Broadway.)

I think that the City Inspector office must have been
created about that time, as I have seen no mention of it
previously.

Dr. Francis made an address to the Historical Society in November, 1857, and he says : " Our enlightened founder, John Pintard, was personally known, during a long life, to a majority of our citizens." The doctor then goes on to say : " Examine for yourself the record of the office of the City Inspector, and learn the
obstacles he encountered to establish the department
of the city institution for the registry of births and
deaths."

While Mr. Pintard was " Clerk " and City Inspector,
he was the fast friend of the firemen of the city, and
all the laws most conducive to their advantage were
drafted and recommended by him.

In 1812, when there was a scarcity of change, the Corporation appointed John Pintard to sign all the paper notes of a small denomination that were issued at that time and during the war. I give here a fac simile of those small bills of 4, 6, 9 and 12½ cents.

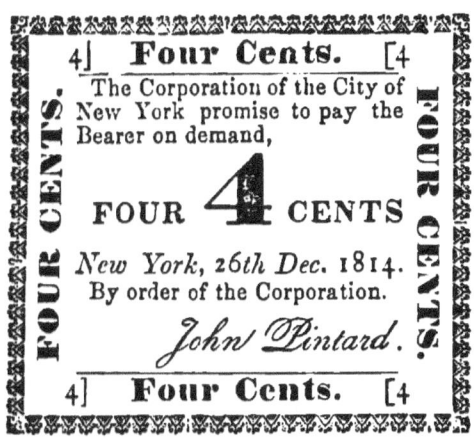

FOUR CENTS.

The Corporation of the City of New York promise to pay the Bearer on demand,

FOUR **4** CENTS

New York, 26th Dec. 1814. By order of the Corporation.

John Pintard.

The above has the following cut on the back:

MOBILITATE VIGET.

The above has the following cut on the back:

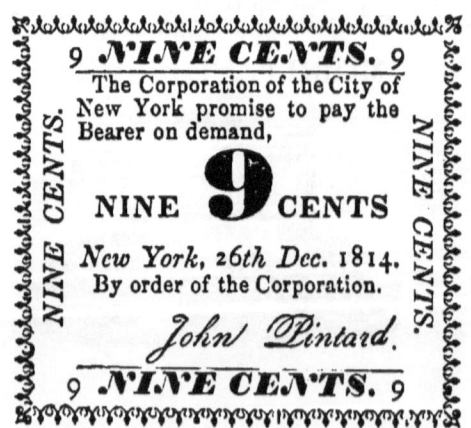

The preceding has the following cut on the back.

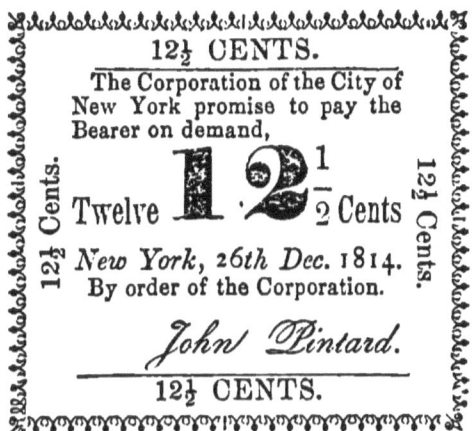

The above has the following cut on the back.

It is a singular coincidence that we are now approaching an era when "shinplasters" (as those sort of issues were denominated in 1837) will be in vogue again.

I do not know why Mr. Pintard left the office of city inspector, but he did leave it in 1809, and was succeeded by General Jacob Morton, who was both clerk of the Corporation and city inspector in 1810, as Mr. Pintard had previously been. Mr. Pintard was appointed secretary of the Mutual Insurance Company in 1809, at No. 52 Wall street. This company was the oldest in the city of New York. It was established in 1787, was chartered in 1798, and re-chartered in March, 1809. When Mr. Pintard became its secretary, Robert Lenox was president of it at the time, and Mr. Pintard's old friend, Gabriel Furman, (who was afterwards its president) was a director. It was a fire insurance company, upon the mutual plan, although not so at the present. He was secretary of this company for twenty years, or until 1829. Afterwards George Ireland was president, and A. B. McDonald, the successor of Mr. Pintard, was secretary, and kept at 52 Wall street, until 1845, where it had been from 1807, when it was in Pine street, opposite the old French church. I believe it suffered a great loss in the terrible fire of 1835. In 1846, the name was changed to the "Knickerbocker" Fire Insurance Company, but Mr. Ireland and Mr. McDonald remained; and, in fact, the company was the same. Mr. Pintard had died two years before, or it would have added one grief more to his many, for he fondly loved old names as well as old faces. It is creditable to that old company that they continued Mr. Pintard a director, after he ceased to be capable of performing the duties of secretary, (he was seventy years old when he resigned the office in 1829,) and he had a desk in the office as long as he lived, though in the last years of his life he was almost blind—quite deaf, and his world was inside of himself — the old world of the past. His deafness arose from having been blown up by gunpowder, while celebrating the 4th of July, when young, and when Independence day was young also. The old Mutual, under the name of Knickerbocker, still flourishes. Mr. Ireland had been succeeded by Mr. Tucker, a much esteemed citizen, and once alderman of the Eighth Ward.

When the Mechanics' Bank was chartered in 1810, the leaders in it were Gabriel Furman, George Ireland, Stephen Allen, Matthew L. Davis, John Slidell, and other friends of Mr. Pintard, and they insisted he should be cashier. For reasons that I am not aware of, he would not take the position. John Slidell, father of the rebel in Fort Warren, was made president, and W. Fish was cashier.

The Historical Society, now one of the most valuable literary institutions in the world, and one that the city may well be proud of, owes its existence mainly to John Pintard. Dr. Francis calls him " our enlightened founder." It was organized in 1804, and was chartered by the Legislature in 1809. Dr. Francis, as well as Mr. Pintard, was one of its most efficient members. A list of its officers in 1810 is worth looking at just fifty-one years later ; Egbert Benson, President ; Governeur Morris, first Vice President ; De Witt Clinton, second Vice President ; Samuel Miller, Corresponding Secretary ; Charles Wilkes, Treasurer ; John Pintard, Recording Secretary and Librarian. The standing committee were William Johnson, Samuel L. Mitchell, John Mason, David Hosack, John McKesson, Anthony Bleecker, and Gulian C. Verplanck. All dead, I believe, but the last. In 1807, the officers were the same, except that Benjamin Moore was first Vice President, and Brockholst Livingston, second Vice President, and Daniel D. Tompkins was one of the committee, and John Foster was Librarian. They have a portrait of Mr. Pintard at the Historical Society rooms.

Mr. Pintard was also a trustee of the New York Society Library — another very old concern, having been established in 1772. Most of the books were destroyed during the Revolution, but in after years it was replenished, and is now as splendid a library as we have in the city.

On the 19th of February, 1805, twelve persons assembled, at the request of two or three individuals, who desired to extend the benefits of education to poor children. Thus commenced the " Free School System " that is bearing such glorious fruit. John Pintard was among the first in this humble movement, which has had such magnificent results in the present public schools of New York city. There were subscribers from $5 to $10,000. Standing on the list is John Pintard; but this is a small matter compared with the valbe of his active personal services in perfecting the early movement.

Mr. Pintard in 1807, took a very active part in the preliminary steps that led the Legislature of the State to pass an act, April 3, 1807, appointing Governeur Morris, Simeon De Witt, and John Ruthford, as Commissioners of streets and roads in this city.

Those commissioners did their work faithfully and well. They reported on the 22d of March, 1811, and that splendid plan of avenues and streets was started.

I have mentioned that Lewis Pintard was one of the incorporators of the Chamber of Commerce. John

Pintard was one of its early members. In fact, after the Revolutionary War, it lay dormant. It was Mr. Pintard who went to work and revived it, giving it a new vitality, for it was almost dead.

In 1817 he was elected secretary, and continued to perform those duties until 1827, when he was sixty-eight. He was succeeded by John A. Stevens.

He was a prominent member of the American Bible Society; was one of its founders in 1816. He was at one time secretary, and afterwards vice-president for many years.

He was secretary for a long time to the Brooklyn Steamboat Company, of which William Cutting (father of Francis B.) was the principal stockholder.

There never lived that man in the city who could start great measures as John Pintard could do. He could indite a handbill that would inflame the minds of the people for any good work. He could call a meeting with the pen of a poet, and before the people met, he would have arranged the doings for a perfect success. He knew the weak point of every man, and he would gratify the vanity of men and get their money, and accomplish his good purpose, without any of them suspecting that they were merely the respectable names and moneyed tools that Mr. Pintard required. Here is an instance. I will here mention that he was the friend, from first to last, of De Witt Clinton, and he could always get the latter to preside at a meeting, or give his name for any purpose. He had faith in John Pintard. He was the propeller of the first meeting to establish a Savings' Bank in New York. It was called at the old City Hotel in Broadway, Nov. 29, 1816. All his men were fixed, and it was

Resolved, That it is expedient to establish a savings' bank in New York city.

So far so good. Then Zach Lewis submitted a constitution — prepared by John Pintard.

Then a list of twenty-eight directors and officers was proposed and carried. (Prepared by John Pintard.) The list of directors was headed by De Witt Clinton and ended with John Pintard.

It did not commence operations until the 3d of July, 1819, and then John Pintard headed the " Attending Committee " for the month. When the savings' bank got fairly under way, John Pintard withdrew, as was his usual custom when he had achieved a great success. He kept away from it for some years, but in 1828 the bank elected him its president, and he continued to be so until 1841. When eighty-two years old, his frame began to give away and he became blind. It was in 1842, when he ceased to be the bank president, that he made his will, leaving his few earthly valuables to his only surviving daughter, Mrs. Louisa H. Servoss, with whom he had made his home for many years. He died in 1844, aged eighty-six years, and his body was buried in the family vault in St. Clement's Church, in Amity street. That church was built in 1830. Mr. Louis Bayard was its rector for many years. To that same vault, John Pintard, with pious and reverential hands, had removed the bones of his parents, uncle, and grandparents from the old French graveyard that stood between Pine and Cedar streets, near Nassau (opposite the post-office.) They were all members of that church, and John Pintard, who was a good French scholar, made the translation of the English Common Prayer Book, into French, precisely as it is now used in the French Episcopal Church in this city.

In 1811, the plan had been mooted for connecting the waters of Lake Erie with the Hudson river by means of a canal. A bill in favor of it passed the Legislature in 1811 ; between that and 1815 applications were made for aid from the general government. During the war nothing could be done. The whole affair hung heavily, when John Pîntard went to work to get up one of his great meetings of citizens. This was near the close of the year 1815. The meeting was a great success, for immediately after, a law was passed, appointing a board of commissioners to lay out the track of the Erie Canal, and DeWitt Clinton was made its president. On the 4th of July, 1817, the first plough that opened a furrow was used. In 1825, the canal was completed, New York then containing 160,000 people. On the 7th of September, 1825, the merchants and citizens of New York had a great meeting in the chamber of commerce, in the Tontine coffee house, to make arrangements for celebrating the completion of the great western canal. John Pintard was appointed Secretary, and the following resolutions were submitted by W. W. Woolsey. Of course, the whole programme was written by John Pintard — the whole arrangement was his. The Resolutions are his style. The last one says :

Resolved, That a committee, consisting of the following gentlemen be appointed to make inquiry, and to give public notice of the day on which the great event will occur, and where the celebration should take place, and that it be the duty of the committee to confer with the Corporation on this subject, and take such measures as may be deemed necessary to call out a full expression of public feeling, in relation to an event so important to the interests of the community. .

Resolved, That the committee consist of fifteen members : William Bayard, John Pintard, Thomas R. Mer-

cien, William W. Woolsey, M. M. Noah, John Rathbone, Jr., Eldad Holmes, George Griswold, Joseph G.
Swift, Campbell P. White, Jonathan Goodhue, Cadwal-
lader D. Colden, Isaac Carow, Silas Richards and Lock-
wood Deforest.

JOHN PINTARD, *Secretary.*

The meeting then adjourned.

I believe of all those name, not one is now alive. I
have written sketches of nearly all of them who were
merchants.

On the 28th of Sept., 1825, the merchants delegated
John Pintard and Thomas R. Mercien to go to Albany
and meet the committee from all parts of the state in
reference to the celebration.

The arrangements were all made, and the plan published was drafted by Pintard.

Mr. Pintard carried the bottle that contained the
Lake Erie water that was emptied into the Atlantic, as
an emblem of the union of the great inland water of
the West, and the still greater outside Ocean.

I need not add any details of what occurred. I alluded to it, to show more of the character of John Pintard. De Witt Clinton never forgot him. He was
mayor when Mr. Pintard was city inspector. The at-
tachment only ended when De Witt Clinton died, and
the last letter he ever wrote was in reply to our friend,
Mr. Pintard. In the letter he used this remarkable
sentence : " I do not know that I have a hostile feeling against any human being." The next day, in a fit
of apoplexy, he died.

I could allude to many others of our best institutions
that John Pintard aided materially in founding. One
was the House of Refuge, and another the Merchants'
and the Mercantile Library.

The wife of John Pintard was a fit companion for him. She was a sharer in his prosperity, as well as adversity.

I have not space to enumerate all the performances of John Pintard for the good of this city, any contemplated institution found a friend in him. He was ever ready to aid it. He regarded money as water, except when it would benefit the city. He pleasantly said to his friends, " I will be my own executor," meaning that he would spend all he had for useful purposes while alive.

As an instance, he felt a deep interest in the general Theological Seminary of the Episcopal church, founded in this city. He did everything for it, laid out his plans, imported writings of the Fathers, and valuable works at his own expense, and he went to everybody that he knew that had money. Among others, he applied by letter, to a very rich man named Jacob Sherrard, who was a painter and glazier at No. 37 Broad. Jacob lived next door at No. 35. Jacob had no children nor near relatives. He belonged to the Dutch Reformed church. On the 18th day of a month he wrote him a letter commencing with : " Lord, let me know the end of my days." John Pintard in this most charming letter stated the claims of his favorite society, told him much good could be done if it had money. He did not stop there. He talked it all over with the wife of Jacob, and so convinced her that she agreed to it, and what was the result ? When Jacob died in 1820, the seminary was his " residuary legatee," and benefited some $60,000. At his funeral, John Pintard was one of the pall bearers.

He was not less successful with George Lorrillard. Previous to making a dead set at George, he wrote a

11

letter to both Jacob and Peter Lorrillard, asking them
if they had any objection to his getting as much money
as he could out of their brother George, for the benefit
of the Theological Seminary. They replied in the
most prompt manner, " No." Then he went at George
with a letter that was so convincing that George Lorrillard gave the institution $25,000.

He was not so successful with Dennis Mc Carthy.
Most of us remember when Dennis lived at 352 Broadway, second door from Leonard street, in the Sixth
Ward. His house was torn down to build up the Carl-
ton house, that has also gone down in its turn to make
way for great stores. Dennis had stores in Chambers,
Chatham, and Market streets. He was a wholesale as
well as retail grocer. He was a Catholic. To him Mr.
Pintard went, and stated the claims the Roman Catholic Orphan Asylum had upon him. He appeared to be
convinced. He had a wife, but no children, and no
near relations. " Leave her well off," wrote the active
Pintard, " and leave the rest to the Catholic Asylum,
and your memory will be blessed." Mr. Mc Carthy
thought so, too. He had been the father of a beautiful
daughter, but she had died. Dennis Mc Carthy lacked
the moral courage to make a will, and he died without
one. His property was in litigation for years. Distant
relations made claim to it.

" Do all the good you can, young man," was his advice
to every friend who was younger than himself.

He was very active in old matters of the city. For
instance, the Bank of New York, though it was started
in 1784, had no charter from the state. It did business
upon its own hook. After the war was over, the Legislature doubted their power to charter a bank. How-

ever, after the constitution was adopted in 1787 by the " United States," and after Congress had chartered a United States Bank, our State Legislature concluded to charter two banks. It did so. One was the Bank of New York, and the other the Bank of Albany. The person most active in getting this matter arranged satisfactorily, was John Pintard.

When New Year's day arrived in 1790, General Washington had a house in this city at No. 1 Cherry street. He was well aware that the receiving and making of calls on New Year's day was an old Dutch custom. He liked it, and he determined to add the power of his name as an example of the observance of the time honored custom. Everybody in New York on that day called upon the general and his lady. In the evening there was a grand levee, and both the general and his lady were present. He told John Pintard, who was present: " I am delighted. I have experienced the most intense gratification in observing this good old Dutch custom. I am apprehensive that in time it will be laid aside and rooted out, owing to the immense number of persons who will come to New York on account of its favorable situation, but who will have no sympathy with this time-honored Dutch custom and ceremony."

John Pintard was the man who went to work and had the names of all streets bearing foreign names changed — such as King, Queen, Duke, Princess and Crown — to good republican names.

He was one of the most active Sailors' Retreat friends.

He wanted to die in harness as an officer of the Bible Society, and the president of the Savings' Bank. The last was not his happiness, although his own fault.

We shall find in our city few such men as John Pintard, the last of his race.

Since writing the above the private papers of Mr. Pintard have been placed in my possession. I am compiling a work, to be called " The Life of John Pintard." It will be issued by Mr. G. W. Carleton, the Publisher, in 1863.

CHAPTER XXIV.

There are many things that I forget at the moment I am writing a sketch about a particular person, firm, or matter, and that properly belong to it. For instance, when I was writing about Mr. Samuel G. Ogden and the expedition of General Miranda in the " Leander," to the Spanish main, I ought to have mentioned the fate of two of those New Yorkers who went out in it. I knew both personally. John M. Elliott and Thomas Gill were sentenced to ten years' labor at Omoa. They were imprisoned at Carthagena. I do not know how they made their escape, or whether they served out the ten years to which they were sentenced. Thomas Gill, after his return, was connected with the *Evening Post.* He managed the business of that concern, and he was considered to be quite as important a personage as the editor. That was thirty years ago, when the *Evening Post* office was in William street, No. 49. Mr. Coleman, the editor, was lame. At precisely 3 o'clock he would come out and get in a carriage, and drive off to 61 Hudson street, where he lived. Mr. Gill was regarded as so important a part of a well regulated newspaper establishment, he being a methodical business man, that Major Noah, when he started the *Daily Evening Star*, secured the services of Mr. Gill, by giving him a half

interest in the new enterprise, and it was owned by
" Noah & Gill."

Mr. Elliott, after his return from campaigning in
South America, went back to the printing business again.
I think it must be as early as 1817.   In 1827, he formed
a partnership with John W. Palmer, another printer,
and the firm was Elliott & Palmer, at No 7 Wall street,
corner of New.   Afterward they moved to No. 20
William street, where they opened a moderate sized
"stationery store," and kept all kinds of books and
blanks, such as are used by merchants.   Mr. Palmer
used to attend in the store, and Mr. Elliott on the
upper floor, where the printing office and presses were
stationed.   In that store I used to meet Samuel Wood-
worth, the poet, author of the " Old Oaken Bucket."
There was nothing poetical about the looks of Mr. W.
Elliott & Palmer were getting out a book of poems for
the poet.   I was presented with a copy, and kept it
many years.   The firm published many books and
pamphlets for some years.   In their time, the pamphlet
was a common resort.   "Effects of establishing a recip-
rocal exchange with Europe, by Publican ; " " Dissertation on Political Equality, by J. C. ; " " Vindication
of Andrew Jackson, by Grotius ; " " Dissertation on
the French claims, by Lucius Junius Brutus," and such
sort of stuff.   Some of these bear the imprint of " Elliott & Palmer, 20 William street, New York. ·

" What ever become of Nick Palmer ? " I asked the
other day, of a person who knew both of us a third of
a century ago.

" Nick ? — why he is cashier of the Leather Manu-
facturers' Bank," was the reply.

I missed Mr. Elliott many years, and naturally supposed he had gone to a better world, until last week,

when I was told that an old printer named Elliott, the oldest printer in New York, could probably set up the fac simile of the old Corporation money (published in last chapter) in the same quaint style. I went to Old Slip, No. 12, and there found out that the old printer was still living, now eighty years old, in Jersey city, but did not attend to business any more, having resigned it to John M. Davis.

Abraham Vannest is yet alive, and I should think must be among the oldest of the Old Merchants now alive. His father, William Vannest, was in the same business at 47 Hanover square (111 Pearl,) soon after the peace of 1782. He died about 1794, and then his widow Deborah continued the business for a short time. About 1796, Abraham put up his own sign, and he kept it up many years. As he was in business sixty-six years ago, and did not publicly engage in it until he saw twenty-one, he must be eighty-six or eighty-seven years of age now. The house has continued down to this day, and is now Abraham R. Vannest & Co., "Saddlery, Hardware and Carriage goods," at No. 50 Warren and 150 Chamber streets, store extending through the block. John Haggerty is still alive, and a very aged man, but he did not go into business under his own name until 1800. George B. Rapelje is an old merchant, is still alive, but he did not go into business until after 1802. I have his bold signature before me, signed December. 1804. John Robbins is yet hale and hearty, as when I wrote about him in last edition. He commenced about 1800 to do business on his own account.

The first ship ever sent to Canton from this city was sent by the old firm of Franklin, Robinson & Co. Their counting-house was at No. 279 Pearl street. The partners were Abraham and Samuel Franklin, and

William T. Robinson. They did a heavy East India
business. I think the founder of the house was Walter
Franklin, who died in 1780. He lived at No. 1 Cherry
street. Gen. Washington occupied his house afterwards.
His daughter married De Witt Clinton. The ship that
was sent by the house of Franklin, Robinson & Co.,
was one of the largest that had then been built in the
city. The supercargo was William Bell. During the
later years of his life, any one passing down Wall street
would see him, in the middle of the day, sitting upon
the stoop of Mr. McCormick, No. 57 Wall street. Mr.
Bell was a Scotchman, and a tall, fine-looking man.
He was often seen in company with Captain Frederick
Phillips. The latter was a half pay British officer,
who lived in the splendid mansion corner of Pine and
William streets. After his death, Niblo took it as his
Bank Coffee House. His only child, a daughter, married Samuel Gouverneur. His son Samuel L. Gouverneur yet lives in this city, and he married Miss Monroe, a daughter of James Monroe, who was President
of the United States.

This Captain Phillips was one of the most popular
men of the town. He remained here after the war, and
I think died about 1813. He was tall, stood as straight
as an arrow; he carried under his arm a short cane, and
when he appeared in Wall street, with his head flung
back, any one could discover that he had received a military education. He was a thorough Englishmen. He
joined the St. George's Society in this city in 1788; he
was a long time vice-president of it. This daughter I
have alluded to, who married Samuel Gouverneur, was a
favored belle in her day, said to have been a most
charming as well as beautiful girl. The Gouverneur family was then in its prime, and Sam was a great match.

He was one of the firm of Gouverneur & Kemble. The eldest son of this marriage took the name of the superb old Captain " Frederick Phillips," his grandfather, and dropped that of Gouverneur. The captain was a very rich man when he died.

What talking times those old jokers (young once) used to have on stoop No. 57 Wall street. The house stood below the present Merchants' Exchange, on, the south side, three doors this side of Pearl street, until the great fire. It was forty feet wide. It was built of brick — plastered over to represent stone, and was painted blue. Daniel McCormick bought the property about 1790, built that house, and moved into it about 1792. He was a bachelor. I am not aware that he had any near connection, but one. That one came out from Ireland, and it was the intention of his uncle to make him his heir, but, they did not agree. One was raw and uncouth, and the other (old Daniel) was one of the most polished gentleman in the city. The raw one went back to the old country, and strange to say, rose to high rank in the legal profession. I think he became " Lord Advocate," or something of the sort. Before the war Daniel had been in the auction business I think. He was an Irishman by birth, came to this country poor, but amassed a large fortune and retired. He was president of the St. Patrick Society for many years, and I believe a member all his life. It is curious to look back and see who were the leading Irishmen in this city, and officers of the St. Patrick Society, from 1790 to 1804. John Charleton was one. He was physician at No. 110 Broadway as early as 1786. Thomas Roach (president in 1792) was a wine merchant in Water street. William Edgar, was vice president. He was the founder of the Edgar family, in this city.

11*

The white marble palace of Mr. Edgar is still standing at 7 Greenwich street. In 1797 he lived at No. 7 Wall street. He was treasurer of the first insurance company started in 1793, " Mutual." He was director in the Bank of New York. He was a merchant, and prominent in everything that was going on for many years. John Shaw was a merchant in Water street. Carlisle Pollock was a merchant, and lived in Whitehall street, but had his store on Gouverneur wharf. James Constable, who was one of St. Patrick's " Council," was a merchant, and one of the firm of William and James Constable. They lived corner of Wall and William streets. John McVicker was a merchant, and had his store and dwelling house at 27 Queen (would be about half way betwen Pine and Wall in Pearl.) He was an Irishman, and head of the great McVicker family of the city. He was father of Professor McVicker of Columbia College. A grandson of his, Bard McVicker, was one of the cleverest young man that ever gradu- ated at Columbia College. He died, I believe, of consumption about twenty-five years ago. William Wade was a grocer in Water street, only a few doors from Whitehall. " Hugh Gaine " was the treasurer of the St. Patrick's Society. He was a printer, and a wonder- ful person. In 1752, 110 years ago, he started the *New York Mercury*, a weekly. During the Revolution, he was regarded as rather unsound upon the " goose question " of that day, but after the war was over, he became all right and was a great favorite. In 1787 he got out a Universal Register, and in it he gives the popu- lation of New York at 30,000 inhabitants and 4,200 houses. About that time he was a bookseller and sta- tioner, at 25 Hanover square. What is also very cu- rious, he was a vestryman of Trinity church from 1792

to 1808. So, too, was John McVickar, from 1801 to
1812. So, too, was William Hill from 1812 to 1818.
He was a merchant in Broad and lived in Courtlandt
street. He was treasurer of the society for some years.

Dominick Lynch was for a long time a counsellor of
St. Patrick. He was of the firm of Lynch & Stoughton,
merchants at 41 and 42 Little Dock street (Water
street, from Whitehall to Old slip.) Mr. Lynch lived
at No. 16 Broadway. Don Thomas Stoughton, his
partner, was the Spanish Consul General. I have a
chapter written about this firm, and it will be one of
the most interesting of any that I have written, when
published. So that I will say no more about it now.
These Irish families are the cream of the cream of the
old families here. George Barnewell was an importing
merchant, and had his counting-room at No. 21 Wall,
in the rear of No. 19, with such vice presidents and
other officers as William W. Wallace, Robert R. Wad-
dell, William Hill, Hugh Gaine, George Barnewall,
John Caldwell, Cornelius Heeney, and they were all
leading Irishmen seventy-five years ago. Irishmen used
to be aldermen in those days, too, for Daniel McCormick
was alderman of the East Ward in 1789 and 1790. It
is curious, too, that John Pintard, of whom I wrote,
should have been his assistant. In those two years
James Duane and Richard Varick were mayors.

When the Bank of New York was started, Daniel
McCormick was among the first directors; Samuel
Franklin, of the firm of Franklin, Robinson & Co., was
another. Isaac Roosevelt was the president. Mr. Mc-
Cormick continued in the board of directors twenty
years. His house as I have said before, was the resort
of several of the leading men. On his stoop, in the
middle of the day, could be seen Captain Phillips, who

was the acknowledged authority in war matters, as was
Supercargo Bell about Chinese matters, he having been
the first supercargo out there.   In another chair could
be seen Colonel William Steuben Smith, surveyor of
the port, that President Jefferson afterward removed for
supposed complicity with the General Miranda expedition.   Two doors above Mr. McCormick, at No. 53, lived
Mrs. Mary Daubeny, the wife of Captain Daubeny.
At 43 lived Thomas Pearsall, and at 41, Thomas Buchanan.   Next door below Mr. McCormick, at 59, was
the Eagle Insurance Company.   He himself was a director in the United Insurance Company, at 49 Wall,
and so were his neighbors, Buchanan and Pearsall.   At
the time Mr. McCormick left the board of directors of
the Bank of New York, his friend, Nicholas Gouverneur,
was president of it.

Mr. McCormick was a glorious sample of the old
New Yorker.   He stuck to Wall street to the last.
Death alone could get him out of it.   He died in 1834,
and from 1792 until that date he never budged an inch
out of the honored old street.   He witnessed the removal of his neighbors one by one, year after year, until all had gone.   He saw offices and business crowding
into the cellar and floors and garrets of the vacated
buildings ; he saw new buildings put up for offices ; but
he was firm, and finally was left alone, the only gentleman who continued to reside in his own house, in the
good old fashioned style.   He never changed his habits.
He stuck to short breeches and white stockings and
buckles to the last.   He wore hair-powder as long as he
lived, and believed in curls.   He was without a stain
upon his character.   He was fond of his friends, and
they loved him, although he saw nearly all of them enter the grave.   He gave good dinner parties, and had .

choice old wines upon the table. In his invitations for
dinner he invited three, or five, or seven persons to dine
with him, but never an *even* number; and he was always anxious to have those come that he invited, so
that ill-luck might not chance by one not coming, thus
giving the unlucky *even* number of persons to entertain.
After dinner came a good old game of whist for one or
two tables, according as he invited more or less. He
was fond of the game, and his friends also were good
whist player. He owned a large landed property, and
when he died was very rich. On those days, and for
years, the great topic of conversation was Bonaparte.

In a former chapter, I alluded to that great old firm
of Gouverneur & Kemble. He was the one that gave
the name to Gouverneur's lane, back or near his house.
That house was quite a remarkable one in its day. It
was destroyed in the great fire in 1835. Many people
used to visit it to see the paper hangings on the walls, paper imported from Canton, having been used by Mr.
Gouverneur. The counting house of Gouverneur &
Kemble was up on Gonverneur's wharf, which was at
the bottom of Gouverneur alley, at the second wharf
east of Old Slip. About 1798, Isaac commenced building his grand house on the corner of Sloate lane (now
the end of Hanover) and Hanover square; it was No.
121 Pearl street. That house was a great affair, and
what added to its wonder was that it had a drain
to Old Slip, independent of any other drain. He
could not have enjoyed his new house very long, for he
died about the commencement of the century. His
widow resided in it until 1803. It was afterwards rented to the celebrated General Moreau, of whom I have
spoken in former chapters. Here Moreau lived in grand
style, entertaining like a Prince, until he went back to

254 THE OLD MERCHANTS

Europe to join the allies against Napoleon, and lose his life at Dresden.

The firm had an immense law suit with a Frenchman, involving over a hundred thousand dollars. It was taken up to Albany. Aaron Burr and Alexander Hamilton were counsel for the Frenchman Le Guin, and all the celebrated lawyers of the state were engaged upon it. It was decided against Gouverneur & Kemble, and it killed Isaac Gouverneur. He died at Albany shortly after the result of this suit was known. His brother Nicholas married a Miss Kortwright. They lived at 23 Beaver street for many years. He died in that house in 1807. Samuel L. Gouverneur who was postmaster, was a son of this Nicholas. A daughter of Nicholas married Johnson Verplanck, who was a son of Gulian Verplanck, an eminent citizen, who was as early as 1790 and for many years after, president of the Bank of New York, and who is uncle to our Gulian C. Verplanck. Johnson Verplanck at one time was the editor of the celebrated *New York American*, with which Mr. Charles King was so long connected. It was the organ of the Federalists in its day, as the *Evening Post* was of the Republican.

CHAPTER XXV.

In the last I spoke of Gulian Verplanck, the second president of the Bank of New York in 1790, and who was a man of extraordinary ability. He was born in this city, and received an education in Amsterdam. He came over to this city to act as the agent of an old established Dutch house in Amsterdam. Although extremely young for such a great responsibility, yet he conducted their business to the perfect satisfaction of his former employers. In after years he did a very heavy business with Holland. About 1792, he bought of Alexander Hamilton a house and lot in Wall street. He tore down the house and erected a splendid mansion upon it, where the Merchant's Bank now is. In his day it was No. 12 Wall street, (now 33.) He was an accomplished man and a good speaker, and was much esteemed. As early as 1788, when the Legislature met at Poughkeepsie, and we sent such men as Richard Varick, Evert Banker, Nicholas Bayard, Nicholas Low, Comfort Sands, to represent this city, Gulian Verplanck was among them. He continued to represent this city until 1790. That year he was speaker of the assembly. He was sent to the Legislature again in 1796, and was elected speaker again—He died about 1800. His widow continued to reside in the old mansion until 1803.

The name of Gulian has been before this city for eighty years. The first was Gulian who was speaker at Albany in 1796. He died in 1800. He left a worthy and even more distinguished representative of the name in the person of his nephew (who was named after him,) Gulian C. Verplanck. A few years later, in 1808, he took his place among the citizens as an attorney-at-law, 50 Wall street, and residing in Partition (Fulton) street. This Gulian C. was in the Legislature for some years, commencing in the Assembly in 1821, and ending in 1823. Ten years later he was elected to the twenty-second Congress from this city, and held it from 1831 to 1833. He was in the Senate of this State from 1838 to 1841. He is now and has been for many years one of the commissioners of emigration. He is a most remarkable man. It would require a volume, instead of a part of one of my chapters to give any idea of the varied occupations of Mr. Gulian C. Verplanck. They have been almost as numerous as those of John Pintard. In former years, when New York was younger, hardly any institution, Literary, Scientific, Benevolent, Political or Religious, could get along without his name. I have been forced to allude to him, in this sketch, in order to draw a line between my good old merchant, Gulian Verplanck, and the one who is yet living, and who I hope will live many more years to be an honored " landmark " in the progress of the city.

I mentioned as clerks of Gouverneur & Kemble, Samuel G. Ogden, and John Wilkes, and Nic Ogden. I might have mentioned Staats Lawrence, W. H. Jepson, N. G. Rutgers and George A. Bibby, who were clerks ten years later (in 1804) than the former ones. John Wilkes, I think, was in the counting room, but did not continue in commercial business. There were two brothers came out to this country after the Revolutionary War,— Charles and John. They were nephews of the celebrated Wilkes, who made such a figure in English politics for a long period. He was the (North Briton) Wilkes, member of Parliament — locked up in the tower, and a great public favorite.

Charles Wilkes had been a banker's clerk, I think in London. When the Bank of New York was started in 1784, he went into it as principal teller. He must have been somewhat experienced, for in 1794, he was made cashier. He had among the directors who voted for him, Nicholas Gouverneur, Daniel McCormick, and Gulian Verplanck, who was president of the bank that year. John Wilkes, the brother of Charles, was a public notary in 1792. He lived at No. 13 Wall street. He was the father of several sons : John, Edward, Henry, and Charles. The last married Miss Renwick, a sister of Professor Renwick. He is the celebrated "Commander" Wilkes, the hero of the capture of Mason and Slidell. Here I must mention one of those curious coincidences that are really laughable.

There was another John Slidell, a tailor, at No. 21 Duke (South William.) His brother was a shoemaker, at No. 21 Broadway. Yet another brother, Joshua, was a measurer of grain, and lived in Dutch street. These last were distant relatives of the John Slidell of whom I shall speak. In 1794 he had his factory at No. 50 Broadway.

In 1795, the old man continued to live at the old soap factory, No. 50 Broadway ; but he gave up the business to John Jr. (who had served an apprenticeship to it,) and he became a soap and candle maker at the old stand. He lived at that time at 60 Broadway, where John Slidell, the future ex-senator, Rebel Minister, and so forth, was born. The son of one neighbor and First Warder, became the capturer of the son of another. These boys, *old* boys they are now, both being over sixty-five, have played together in their early years, neither dreaming of their future destiny, or how they would afterwards meet. When John Slidell went on board the " San Jacinto " and met Commodore Wilkes, what curious sensations they must both have felt ! The old First Ward times, when as boys they called each other " Jack " and " Charley " — went to school together, played tag together, snowballed each other ; and when a little later, they became older, and experienced puppy love for the first time, it was for a First Ward little girl !

If a London paper were to make such a statement as this. it would be called " romancing." It would not be believed. New York journals would call it a fabrication. Here it is different. There are a hundred, perhaps a thousand people who will see this article, who will know that what is stated is true. There are persons who have known them as boys.

In 1798, John Slidell Jr., took his brother Thomas into partnership, and the business was then continued under the firm of " John Slidell, Jr., & Co." The old John moved up into Winne (Mott) street, where he died in 1804, and after that the firm was John Slidell & Co., and so it was continued at the same old stand and manufactory, No. 50 Broadway, until 1817.

In 1804 there was a " General Society of Mechanics and Tradesmen " in the city of New York. This society had its President John Slidell ; its first and second vice-presidents, its secretary, its collector, its poor overseer, and loaning committee. Jacob Sherred, William G. Miller, Andrew Morrill, Jonathan Weedover,

Anthony Steenback, and such other good names among them. Mr. John Slidell, Jr., had belonged to it in other years, as early as 1798, when James Tylee was president; Thomas Timpson, vice-president; Cornelius Crygier, second vice-president; John Striker, treasurer; William Whitehead, Abraham Labagh, Daniel Hitchcock and Samuel Delamater, were the "Poor Masters."

What possible connection there could have been between a benevolent society and a bank, passes my comprehension, yet so it was. In 1810, the Mechanics' Bank was chartered, and John Slidell, Jr., Anthony Steenback, Mr. Miller, Jacob Sherred, and other names of the old society, "Poor Overseers" were made directors of the new Bank of Mechanics, and John Slidell was made the first president of the Mechanics' Bank. He kept that place as president until 1817. Meantime his soap and tallow candle manufactory was moved up to No. 189 Elizabeth street, near the cathedral, and the old gentleman moved his residence to Bloomingdale. About 1825, he moved back into town, and his house was at No. 624 Broadway. That year 1825, the Traders' Fire Insurance Company was chartered, and Mr. John Slidell, Sr., was president. Previous to this, however, in 1817, John Slidell, Jr. (Rebel now) had gone into mercantile business at No. 52 South street, with James McCrea. The firm was "McCrea & Slidell." This firm continued in busine ss as late as 1820. The store was at No. 41 South street in 1818, and afterwards John Slidell Jr., (Rebel) lived at No. 50 Broadway, and so did James McCrea. It was about this time the concern failed. James McCrea married a daughter of Augustine H. Lawrence. It was about this time that John Slidell, Jr. had a duel with Stephen

Price, the manager of the Park Theatre. They fought in the morning, and Slidell shot his antagonist, giving him a bad wound. It was the failure of his firm and the scandal of this duel that determined John Slidell, Jr., to go to a new State when there was an opening. He pitched upon New Orleans.

The old John lived up at No. 174 Grand street, where he died of the cholera in 1832. He limped for many years, having had a leg amputated. One of his daughters married Commander M. C. Perry, a brother of Oliver H. Perry, of Lake Erie fame. M. C. was famed for his great Japan expedition, and was a most excellent man. A daughter of Commander Perry married Augustus Belmont, the celebrated banker — a most excellent man, now in Europe.

Thomas Slidell, the brother of John (Rebel,) died a bachelor.

Another brother, Alexander Slidell, was placed in the Navy. He rose to be a commander, but put to death two persons on board the U. S. brig " Somers." One of the men happened to be a son of the Hon. John C. Spencer, who was then the Secretary of War. A nice time was made in consequence. Previous to this sad affair, Alexander Slidell had had his name changed by act of the Legislature, to Mackenzie. An old Scotch relative had left him a large sum of money, on the condition that he would do so. He died many years ago. I think he married a daughter of Morris Robinson, who was the celebrated cashier of the United States Branch Bank in this city, until its affairs were wound up in the days of General Jackson. Mr. Robinson left several sons.

In a former chapter I had a sketch of N. L. & G. Griswold, the extensive East India merchants and ship owners. There were other Griswolds, who were also ship owners. One was John Griswold, *Junior*, when he came to this city in 1812.

I presume the father of this family was named John Griswold. Young John opened at 68 South street, and lived at 52 Broadway. In 1815, about the close of the war, John took into partnership Charles C. Griswold. He was a brother. That firm lasted until 1818, when I think, Charles died. At any rate the house was dissolved, but John still continued the business under his own name at 68 South street. He kept in that store until 1827, when he moved next door to 69, corner of Pine street. About fifteen years later he moved to 70 South street.

The history of packet ships, and of those who started them, is very attractive. Up to 1815 there were nothing but transient ships. Then was first commenced that regular line of packets, such as the world had never before seen. The merchants of the city of New York led off in this undertaking. In 1815 a line of Liverpool packets was established. The ships were to leave New York and Liverpool on the first day of every month. Isaac Wright & Son and Francis Thompson were the proprietors of that line, and they ran it with such success, that after seven years' trial they determined to run a second line, starting from Liverpool and New York simultaneously on the 16th of each month. Additional ships were added, and they were all of the first class, in mercantile observation.

The great success of the Liverpool line led John Griswold to start a London line of packets about 1823. At first they sailed on the 1st of each month from London and from New York, touching at Cowes. Fish & Grinnell became interested, and a second line was start-

ed, the ships to leave New York, on the 16th of each
month. They had eight of the finest ships that sailed
out of port. John Griswold's ships were the "Sover-
eign," "Cambria," "President," and "Hudson."
Those belonging to Fish & Grinnell were the "Columbia," "Hannibal," "Corinthian," and "Ontario."

A few years later when the packet ships were in the
height of their glory (1837, just before steamer ships
superseded them in part,) the London line was increased
to twelve magnificent ships, leaving New York on the
1st, 10th, and 20th of each month. With the exception of two of the former list, all the rest were new, viz.:
"St. James," "Montreal," "Gladiator," "Mediator,"
"Quebec," "Wellington," "Philadelphia," "Samson,"
"Toronto," "Westminster," "President," and "Ontario." Such was the rivalry, and so great was the
fear of being outdone, the owner would not keep these
fine ships in the line for but three or four years. The
London line touched at Portsmouth, instead of Cowes
as at first.

What popular fellows their captains were! Where
now are the Delanos, Champlins, Hebards, Morris,
Morgans, Chadwicks, Sebors, Brittons, Griffins, Griswolds, Sturges, and a host of the old fashioned packet
ship captains of this line?

For fifteen years after the London line was started, our
packet ships went everywhere. There was Havre, Belfast, Greenock, Hull, Carthagena, Havana, Vera Cruz;
and as for domestic packet lines, they ran all over —
New Orleans, Mobile, Charleston, Savannah. Old and
new lines to each, in most cases.

Mr. John Griswold, the founder of the London line,
died within a very few years. The line of packet ships
continues still in existence.

As I have said much about the rise of the house of Goodhue & Co. in former numbers, giving a full account of its commencement as Goodhue & Swett in 1808, and its changes to Goodhue & Co., and its partners, good old Jonathan Goodhue, Pelatiah Perit, C. Durand, and others, I ought now to give its closing chapter. The following appeared in the journals on the first day of this year.

The co-partnership heretofore existing under the firm of Goodhue & Co. is this day dissolved by mutual consent.

The outstanding concerns of this house will be adjusted by either of the partners, who will use the signature of the firm in liquidation.

ROBERT C. GOODHUE,
CHARLES C. GOODHUE,
PELATIAH PERIT,
RICHARD WARREN WESTON,
HORACE GRAY.

New York, December 1, 1861.

The undersigned have this day formed a co-partnership under the firm of Weston & Gray, and will continue the business heretofore conducted by Goodhue & Co.

RICHARD WARREN WESTON,
HORACE GRAY.

New York, January 1, 1862.

For this country, a continued existence of one house fifty-four years, is a long time. The above Robert and Charles Goodhue are sons of the old gentleman who founded the house.

CHAPTER XXVI.

In one of the previous chapters when speaking of the celebrated house No. 57 Wall street, occupied by Daniel McCormick, I said :

"What talking times these old jokers (young ones) used to have on stoop No. 57 Wall street. The house stood below the present Merchant's Exchange, on the south side, three doors this side of Pearl street until the great fire. It was forty feet wide. It was built of brick—plastered over to represent stone, and was painted blue. Daniel McCormick bought the property about 1790, built that house, and moved into it about 1792."

I was in error when I said he built that house. It was an old house before the Revolution broke out, in 1776. In 1779, William Backhouse lived there, and kept boarders of a high class. He charged rather high, viz., eight dollars a week, and a dollar extra for washing. John J. Glover boarded there, and so did dozens of our first merchants. Wm. Backhouse himself was a very successful merchant in after years. In 1790 he was a partner with William Laight, and they did business at No. 200 Queen street. I think William Backhouse died in 1792. About that time there was another William Backhouse in this city. He was Captain Backhouse, a celebrated sea captain in his day.

That grand old fellow, Daniel McCormick, had so many good points, that I forget some of them. He was a Mason, and as early as 1786 was Grand Treasurer of the Grand Lodge of Free and accepted Masons of New York. I wish those who have read this, and who have read the former chapters, and who are in possession of facts about Mr. McCormick, would send them to me. I will make good use of them.

Some of the firms in which the Suydams were members, were great mercantile houses in their day, and three existed previous to the commencement of this century.

There was a house of R. & J. Suydam as early as 1791. They kept at No. 10 Albany pier (where Coenties slip now is.) Rynier Suydam, of that firm, lived at No. 4 State street. In 1794, two new firms were started. One was Suydam & Wyckoff, at Nos. 11 and 13 Coenties slip, the same John Suydam that was with Rynier. John lived over the store, at No. 11, in the slip. Henry J. Wyckoff was of this firm, and lived at No. 42 Stone street.

Mr. Wyckoff was one of those men who ought not soon to be forgotten in New York. He died in 1839. He was one of those good old-fashioned Aldermen, such as New York used to have in the olden time. He was Alderman of the First Ward from 1821 to 1825. Early in life he married Phebe Suydam, a cousin of his partner. They had but one daughter ; she married Francis Olmstead, a partner in the house of Peter Remsen & Co. The only daughter of Mr. Olmstead married Henry W. Sargent. Henry J. Wyckoff was one of the Directors of the Merchant's Bank, when it applied for a charter in 1805, and he was one of its leading men for many years.

The Eagle Fire Insurance Company was started in
12

1807 ; W. W. Woolsey was its first President, and John
Meyer, Secretary, No 59 Wall street.   I have before me
now one of its handbills, dated March 11, 1807, printed
in the clear type of those days.   Mr. Wyckoff was a
Director at the start ; in 1809 he was chosen President
of it, and held it until 1815.   I believe the company (Eagle and Albion) is still in existence, at No. 44 Wall
street.   Mr. Wyckoff was elected a Governor of the New
York Hospital in 1802, and he held the same position
until he died, in 1839.   Just before Alderman Wyckoff
died, his son Henry failed, and the old gentleman altered
his will, and made Henry W. Sargent, his grandson-in-
law trustee for the portion of his son Henry, and Mr. Sargent paid off all young Wyckoff's debts.   The house of
Suydam & Wyckoff did a very heavy business for thirty
years.   Mr. John H. Bailey was a clerk for them in
1797.   He was afterwards of the firm of Bailey & Voor-
hees.   The house of Suydam & Wyckoff dealt largely
in teas, wines, and groceries generally.   John Suydam,
who was of this firm, was called " Boss John."   He
was son of Hendrick Sudyam, of Long Island, who died
in 1818, aged eighty-one.   John, of the firm of Suydam
& Wyckoff, was born in 1763.   He had a brother Samuel, who was of the firm of Suydam & Heyer.   Isaac
Heyer was of that firm.   He married Jane Suydam, the
sister of his partner.   Suydam & Heyer commenced business in 1794, at No. 67 Front street.   The firm lasted
until Samuel Suydam died, in 1797.   Isaac Heyer continued the business for many years, and was one of our
most respected merchants.   He was brother-in-law to
Stephen Whitney, who married Harriet Suydam, his
wife's sister.

Another brother, Henry, went into business in 1800,
under the firm of H. Suydam & Co.   They did business

at No. 45 Front street. He lived at No. 23 Whitehall. In 1804 he formed a partnership with John Wilson, a Scotchman, who came to this country about 1790. He was a clerk with Isaac Heyer for some years. In 1801 he was an accountant, and lived in Beaver lane No. 1. He was then Junior. I think he was son of an old baker, John Wilson, who had a bakery at No. 93 Fair street, from 1795 to 1808. Whether he was a son or connection I do not know. In 1803 this one, while yet an accountant, embarked all his capital to aid his brother Alexander, under the firm of J. & A. Wilson, at 60 John street. That baking establishment continued for years and years at that locality. In 1815 it was changed to No. 34 Fulton and No. 45 Front, where the firm of Suydam & Wilson was kept. That last firm continued in business in the same street, at No. 45 Front, until 1834, when the firm was dissolved, old Mr. John Wilson retiring from business. His son, James B. Wilson, who was a junior partner in the house, united with Sanford Cobb, Jr. (of Herriman, Nash & Co.) and formed the house of Wilson & Cobb. That was dissolved in 1854, young Mr. Wilson then retiring from active mercantile business. Mr. Cobb still continues on the business in the same place, under the firm of Cobb, March & Gross.

A half century ago business was not done " with a rush," or on the railroad plan, as in the present " fast times." Business men in those days had more leisure to converse on business matters and the topics of the day. On entering a merchant's office you were not admonished, by the peremptory and positive command, in flaming letters on a large placard, warning the visitor not to open his mouth on any subject but that of business, and that, too, within the limits of certain hours ;

and when through to "go about his business." This is
one of the improvements of the age and the two-forty
system. They had time to " drop in " and see their
neighbors, and the store of Suỳdam & Wilson was the
favorite meeting place of the merchants in the vicinity,
among whom were Samuel Gilford, Edward H. Nicoll,
Peter Remsen, Henry J. Wyckoff, Gabriel Wisner,
James Bailey, Francis Saltus, Stephen Whitney, and
others, all now deceased. Robert Lenox, Samuel Craig,
and John Laurie, among other prominent rich Scotch
merchants, were frequent visitors.

Mr. Wilson was widely known among the business
men of that day, and highly esteemed for his high-toned
purity of character as a merchant and a citizen. He
lived and died an humble Christian : peculiarly domestic in his habits, he found his greatest enjoyments in the
society of his immediate family. He often told the following incident on his arrival in this country, on landing
from the vessel at one of the wharves in the City of
Philadelphia. He was accosted by a fine looking, el-
derly Quaker gentleman, with, " Well, my lad, in which
part of the States do you intend to settle ? " He replied,
" I have not yet made up my mind, sir, whether to go
to the North or to the South." " Well," said the Quaker gentleman, " if thee wants to retain thy morals and
thy health, thee must go to the North ; if thee wants to
lose them both, thee must go to the South."

Just before the declaration of war in 1812, the Hon.
John Smith, of the United States Senate (by the way,
a very extraordinary man ; he was elected to Congress
as a representative from Suffolk in 1799, kept in until
1804, when he was made a Senator to fill a vacancy,
and re-appointed, and was senator until 1813,) wrote to
his step-son, Edward H. Nicoll (Smith & Nicoll that I

have wrote much about) that war was inevitable, and suggested the purchase of such goods as would be affected in value by the war. This letter was submitted to Suydam & Wilson, and joint purchase was proposed ; but the conservative, patriotic character of the house forbade the idea of speculating under such circumstances. Neither of these great houses availed themselves of the information of the senator, and missed a glorious opportunity of making an immense fortune. Edward A. Whitlock, of the house of B. M. & E. A. Whitlock & Co., was a clerk with the firm of Suydam & Wilson for some time, and left it to go West. Mr. Wilson left his family (besides his estate) the rich legacy of a pure and unsullied name.

I mentioned in a previous chapter that Moses Taylor married a daughter of Mr. Wilson, the ship-bread baker. He is the one I have been writing about as of the firm of Suydam & Wilson. The ship bakery is still carried on by John T. Wilson, a grandson of the old one, at 73 Fulton street, same locality.

Edward Holland Nicoll, of Smith & Nicoll, married Miss Mary Townsend, a daughter of Captain Solomon Townsend. I have already mentioned old Thomas Buchanan, who died in November, 1815, aged 71 — a royalist merchant of the city. During the war, he resided at Oyster Bay. He married Almy, a daughter of Jacob Townsend.

He left her a widow. They had issue eight children. 1. Jane Buchanan, died unmarried. 2. Almy, married Peter P. Goelet. 3. Martha, married Thomas Hicks. 4. Margaret, married Robert R. Goelet. 5. Eliza, who married Samuel Gilford. 6. George Buchanan, born September 7th, 1775. 7. Frances, who married Thomas C. Pearsall. 8. Fanny Buchanan, who died unmarried. The only survivor is Mrs. Frances Pearsall. She was born the 4th of June, 1799, and is one of the few survivors of the nominees for the Tontine stock. Her father took up two shares, and nominated two lives. Her own, and her brother George.

Mr. Buchanan owned the ship "Glasgow." Solomon Townsend above was the master. The vessel traded to and from London about the time of the Revolution. She was in London when the war broke out, and her owner, Mr. Buchanan, ordered her not to come home. Captain Townsend went to Paris, took the oath of allegiance to the United States before Ben. Franklin, who commissioned him a midshipman in the American navy. He got home in 1778. He married his cousin, Ann Townsend. His daughter Mary married Edward H. Nicoll, as I have above stated. Henry Nicoll, formerly an M. C., and Solomon Townsend Nicoll, are sons of this marriage. These last were great grandsons of Benjamin Nicoll, who settled in New York about 1745, where he married Mary Magdalen, the daughter of Edward Holland, an eminent merchant. One of Benjamin's sons named Henry, married Elizabeth Woodhull, the only daughter of General Nathaniel Woodhull, who was president of the first Continental Congress. Their eldest son was Edward Holland Nicoll, who married Captain Townsend's daughter Mary. Mrs. Henry Nicoll, after her husband's death, married the above John Smith, who was "General." He was a member of our State Legislature from 1784 to 1800. In 1788 he was a member of the convention that adopted the constitution of the United States; in 1800 he was in Congress, as above stated; In 1814, James Madison appointed him U. S. Marshal for this district, and he held the office when he died in 1816.

Henry Suydam, of the firm of Suydam & Wyckoff, is still alive — a hale, hearty specimen of the old school merchant and gentleman. He was also brother-in-law of Isaac Lawrence. He married a half-sister of Mr. Lawrence, president of the United States Bank, of whom I recently wrote a lengthy sketch.

The continuation of the Suydam merchants and their firms, as well as that of the Heyers,— Isaac, Walter and Cornelius, — will be in next chapter.

CHAPTER XXVII.

Another brother of the Suydams was Ferdinand Suydam, who was born in 1786. He started business in New York on his own account at No. 37 Front street, in 1808. Previously he had been a clerk with Suydam & Wyckoff for some years. I have his signature before me now, as signed in 1805, when he was at his brother's learning business. The next year he became a partner of William Boyd, and the firm was Boyd & Suydam, at No 21 South street. He lived in the house No. 9 Bridge street, with his brother Henry. Ferdinand married a daughter of Anthony Lispenard Underhill, who kept at No. 172 Front street. Old Andrew in 1790 lived in 167 Queen street, and his store was at No. 20 Peck slip ; his firm was Underhill and Bulckly. His brother David commenced business in 1793, at No. 78 Water street. Old Andrew, I think, died about 1794, for the next year Anthony L. started business as a grocer at No. 170 Water street ; and the same year David took his son into partnership, under the firm of David Underhill & Son, at No. 234 Water street ; they were iron mongers or hardware merchants. Old David lived at No. 337 Pearl, near Beekman street. Andrew L., in 1797, while he was living at No. 31 Dey street, took into partnership Mr. Benjamin Hustace, and the firm was for

some years Underhill & Hustace, at No. 172 Front street.
I believe it dissolved in 1802. Hustace lived next door
to Mr. Underhill, at No. 33 Dey street. When they
dissolved, Benjamin Hustace started next door to his old
partner, at No. 170 Front street. Anthony L. moved
his residence to No. 42 Dey street, and lived there a
great many years. It was in that house Ferdinand Suydam married Eliza Underhill.

David Underhill & Son kept steadily in the hardware
business from 1795 to 1810, when they moved to No.
112 Maiden Lane. The old gent lived at No. 13 Oliver
street. The house went under about 1813.

In 1811, Richard Suydam, another brother, com-
menced business in New York at No. 140 Pearl street.
In the same year he married a young lady named Miss
Henderson, of Pennsylvania, a very accomplished girl.
He resided at No. 6 Stone street.

Anthony L. kept on his house at 42 Dey until 1817,
when he moved next door, to 44. He retained the old
store No. 175 Fulton until 1819. In April 2, that year,
the Fulton Fire Insurance Co., was incorporated. Anthony L. Underhill was elected President, and O. H.
Hicks was Secretary. He continued President of it until the great fire in December, 1835, when the losses
made that company go into liquidation. Still Mr. Underhill continued to reside at 44 Dey street until 1835, when
he moved to 28 Courtlandt street, but kept his office at
the Insurance Company No. 8 Wall street. In 1837,
he had his place of business in Broad street, and following the up-town track, moved into Fourth street. From
that time he passed from a business life. I believe he
died in 1847 at Saratoga Springs. From 1811 to 1847,
a period of 36 years, he was a vestryman of Trinity
Church. This mere fact is an unwritten story of a long
12*

Christian life.   He was Assistant Alderman of the Third
Ward from 1814 to 1816, and Alderman in 1817—18.

Suydam & Wyckoff, 31 South street, of which John
Suydam who lived at No. 4 Broadway, was a partner,
continued until 1821, and then it dissolved — 40 years
ago, but John kept on the business in the same street
until 1835 and the fire, when he was burned out.   He
had a large family of sons.   There was Henry, John R.
and Peter M.— all in business.   About 1840, old John
moved up town to Waverly Place.   These Suydams
were great people for sticking in one place and were not
eternally moving.   Frederick, who married Miss Underhill, was of the firm of Suydam & Boyd.   That firm
kept their store in South street, No. 21, from 1809 up to
1834, when the house of Suydam, Sage & Co. was started.   Ferdinand Suydam resided in these early years in
Bridge street, No. 5, near Whitehall, more than a quarter of a century.   When he died, he left three sons —
Henry L, Ferdinand, and Charles.   Young Ferdinand
married Miss Whitney, a daughter of Stephen Whitney.
Suydam, Sage & Co. did an enormous business in South
street until about 1850 and '51.   I do not know but
they failed.   I have heard they did, but failing is no
crime.   It is evidence of doing an open, generous, and
grand business — of carrying on commercial operations
on a most magnificent scale — of adding wealth to our
city, giving employment to thousands.   These are the
merchants who fail.   Merchants of minor minds, who
can calculate closely, and know to a fraction that twice
one are two, and that two times two are four, never fail.
On the contrary, they make princely fortunes, but they
do not add to the city wealth.   The city adds to theirs
by its growth.   It is the merchants who fail that add to
the wealth of the city, though they may die in the grand

charitable institutions their bold operations have helped to erect. The merchants who like Suydam, Sage & Co. throw millions into the West to advance on great grain crops and bring them forward to this city, that sometimes fail when times are against them, they only are the sufferers, not the city. In that firm when it failed were the three sons I have named, of the old founder, Ferdinand. I believe he lived up in Broadway, corner of Seventeeth street, until a year or two after 1850, and then I think he died in Buffalo, being there on business.

Richard Suydam, too, another brother, was one of the unmovable Suydams. I have already alluded to him as having started in 1811 at 140 Pearl street. He never moved his store from that number until 1830, and then only moved a few doors away. In 1824 or '25, he founded the house of Suydam, Jackson & Peck. His partners were Daniel Jackson and Allen Peck. The latter lived in Courtlandt street. He was in the firm only one year, and then it became the great house known to all New Yorkers in the days of General Jackson, as " Suydam & Jackson." Not that Dan was any relation of the President, but he was a worshipper of Old Hickory, and down upon the Old United States Bank, and somehow or other, his house of Suydam & Jackson had all the great Indian contracts, sold blankets by the million, and got Government pay. That was all right.

What Tammany man does not remember old Dan Jackson, with his hard features, great and expressive, and a very determined man he was. He married Miss Dunham, a daughter of David Dunham, who was a large auctioneer about the commencement of this century. He lived in Moore street. The auctioneer's store at the time was 144 Pearl, under the firm of " Dunham & Davis." The last named was the celebrated Mat-

thew L. Davis, the friend and biographer of Aaron Burr.
The latter was at the wedding of Miss Dunham. Her
father, old David, was killed by being knocked overboard from a sloop while coming from Albany to New
York.

In 1830, the above firm of Suydam & Jackson was
changed to Suydam, Jackson & Co., and so continued
until 1841. Richard, too, was a down town man, living at No. 6 Stone street, until 1820, and after that at
65 Pearl street, " close by the store," in the good, old
fashioned style of our ancestors, until 1835, when he,
too, moved up town to No. 6 Carrol Place, not near so
cosy and so nice as it was at No. 6 Stone street, with
the young Pennsylvanian wife in 1811. I do not think
there were any sons. There were five daughters — Mary, Caroline, Adeline, Jane and Louisa. Suydam,
Jackson & Co., was kept up until 1840. Another firm
was in the same buiiding, No. 78 Pearl — Suydam &
Kevan. Mr. Alexander Kevan and that partnership
ceased about 1844 and 1845, and then Richard Suydam
closed a concern in Pearl street he had started more than
a third of a century previously. He left business, but
he resided at No. 6 Carroll Place until 1858, when he
moved to Bleecker street. I think he died that year.

I did not finish what I had to say about Suydam &
Heyer. Samuel, who was of that firm, was a splendid,
gay fellow ; he went into business with his brother-in-law,
Isaac Heyer, in 1794, when he was twenty-one years
old ; he died in the autumn of 1797, only twenty-four
years old. Had he lived, he would have been a splendid merchant. The firm was kept up for a few years,
for not at that time, nor until 1833, was there any law
against doing business under any style or firm. If a
partner died, his partner continued on the firm as long

as he pleased. So in 1796. Isaac Heyer kept up the name until 1803, at the old store No. 67 Front street. He did a very heavy business for many years at that same place. George B. Rapelje was a clerk with him in 1804. There were three distinguished brothers of the Heyers — Isaac, Cornelius and Walter. They were sons of William Heyer, who, as late as 1793, was an iron monger (hardware) in Smith street ; four years later, " Walter & Isaac Heyer," in 1797, started the iron-monger business at No. 234 Pearl street, and they kept at the same old stand far into the next century, at least, twenty years. The Isaac of the hardware firm was our Isaac. In those days the name of one brother was used to give credit and standing to another younger fellow. Yet I do not believe that Isaac shared in the profits of the hardware concern in which his name appeared.

In 1815 Isaac Heyer went into partnership with Henry Rankin, at the same old stand Suydam & Heyer had in 1795, No. 67 Front street. Isaac then lived at No. 24 Beaver. It was a large double house, south side. His brother Cornelius lived upon the opposite side, at No. 29, a high stoop three story house. He dissolved with Mr. Rankin about 1824. In 1825 the firm was Heyer & Black. He took W. H. Black into partnership, and so it continued until Mr. Heyer died. Then I think his only son, John S. Heyer, continued the business.

He closed his life of distinguished usefulness on the 6th of April, 1827. He left a large family. He was an officer of the Collegiate Dutch Reformed Church, now the Post Office. He was a pillar and an ornament of it. He was among the first in every work of mercy and munificence. His mind, means, and labors, were devoted with unsparing liberality to the promotion of good. He was one of the soundest and most valuable citizens. There were few such as him to lose. There were more splendid men in his day than he, but none more pure and blameless. He had an active, busy life, in the years we have mentioned, and he went to his grave unsullied by a spot.

Just as he was about to die, he said, " I find much neglected that might have been accomplished."

He was an efficient member of the Board of Conference of the Grand Synod. He was Treasurer of it. He was a Director of Rutger's College. When he died he gave $2,500 to the Dutch Theological College, $1,000 to the Mission Society, and $1,000 to the American Bible Society.

It was a melancholy sight for many to see his large family of daughters, dressed in deep black, leaving Beaver street on their way up to the old Dutch Church, where their father so long worshipped.

There was a sister who married Richard Duryee. He became a partner with Cornelius Heyer, under the firm of Duryee & Heyer. They kept a hardware store at 47 and 48 Walter street. This C. Heyer was for many years Cashier and President of the Bank of New York.

Gulian C. Verplanck was a son of Daniel Crommeline Verplanck, a very distinguished man in his day. He married Miss Johnson, a daughter of President Johnson of Columbia College. Gulian C. resembled his father very much in his personal appearance. The father also represented this State in Congress.

Gulian, of whom I have written, also married a Miss Johnson, a daughter of Daniel Johnson, a farmer in Dutchess county. After the death of Mr. Gulian Verplanck, she married George Caines, May 27, 1802, a reporter in the Supreme Court.

Our readers will recollect the long notice of John W. Mulligan, in the first volume. He died January 17, 1862, aged 88 years. After the volume appeared, he called once or twice at the office to see the author. I add a few lines from an obituary notice published in the *Commercial*. Those who wish to see a more complete biography can look back for the chapters that contained the sketches to which I allude.

" The subject of the above notice was born in New York while New York was under British rule, but he well remembered and frequently related how he stood as a little boy on a hill where Grand street now crosses Broadway, and saw the last British sentinel file off, on the memorable 25th November. He graduated in Columbia College, and afterwards practised law. Gov. King was a student in his office. At one time he was a member of Baron Steuben's family, and assisted at his interment. He was acquainted with Jay and Hamilton as well as with other distinguished men of those times, and partook of their strong federal views. In religion he was an Episcopalian — a churchman. Some years since he had the pleasure of visiting Athens and seeing the fruits of labors for the cause of Christ in the school founded by his daughters, Mrs. Hills and Frederica Mulligan. His manners were urbane, and his conversation remarkably interesting — his memory being good to the last. We shall never see his like again."

I will add a few words correcting my statement in regard to the Slidells. Thomas Slidell married Miss Callender of this city, and has two children — one, Lieutenant William Slidell, in the Federal army, and one younger. Thomas and John were law preceptors in New Orleans 1844 to 1848. Tom was on the Supreme Bench of Louisania in 1847, and was Chief Justice. That year John went to Mexico. When Daniel Lord

made his fiery speech in the Sumner (Broadway Taber-
nacle) indignation meeting, 1856, and gave John Slidell
a rhetorical milling, Tom challenged Daniel Lord to
fight. Then Daniel, a second time went to judgment,
and issued execution against Thomas. Shortly afterward, at an election in New Orleans, Tom was so badly
(not accidentally) injured, by a blow on the head, that
he has become insane, and is a patient in a Rhode Island
lunatic asylum. The Sumner abolitionists said this
was a judgment for his justification of the "Sumner
head beating," and that he would soon follow Brooks
and Butler to the tomb.

CHAPTER XXVIII.

Among other of the olden time merchants, is one to whom I have often alluded, and who is the founder of a family, whose name is interwoven with the prosperity of the city — John McVickar. He was a merchant of the last as well as present century. The manner in which he came to this country is as curious as his subsequent successful mercantile career. He was Irish born. John and Nathan were sons of an Irish gentleman of moderate estate, and he lost his first wife — their mother. He afterwards married a second time, to give a mother to his boys. She was not different from the general run of step-mothers, and the home ceased to be a home to them. Under those painful circumstances, John, the eldest brother, determined to abandon it and try his fortune in the Western hemisphere. He told his younger brother that if he succeeded in New York, whither he was bound, he would send for him.

He came to New York at about the age of seventeen years. He had an uncle already established in this city, and he was under the special guardianship of Daniel McCormick, of whom I have written so much. The familiar address to him of " John," in after life by the old merchant, often awakened the surprise of strangers. John was fortunate. He did succeed, and he sent for

Nathan, who came out, and they established themselves in the city. I have already alluded to him as being among the founders of the St. Patrick's Society, when such men as William Edgar, Hugh Gaines, and Daniel McCormick belonged to it, in 1792. At that time Mr. McVickar was established and doing a leading business under his own name at 27 Queen street (Pearl.) He commenced in this city in Maiden lane, No. 39, before 1786. In 1793 he was elected a director in the Bank of New York, and continued to be re-elected annually until 1810. In 1795 he was made a director of the Mutual Insurance Company. At the same time he was a director in the United Insurance Company, of which his friend Nic. Low was president, and so was until 1809. At that time he lived in 228 Pearl street, his old place, and kept his place of business at 2 Burling slip. He was vice-president of the St. Patrick's Society in 1797. In 1798 Nathan got here, and the firm was John & Nathan McVickar. In 1801, the style was changed to John McVickar & Co. John moved from 228 Pearl street to 231 Broadway, and Nathan went to house-keeping in the house John left. In all this time John had continued a director in the Bank of New York. In that year he was elected a vestryman of Trinity Church, and held it until he died in 1812.

McVicar & Co., in 1803, and for some years afterwards, had among their clerks Hubert Van Wagenen, Jr., who afterwards became very celebrated in this city. Hubert, Jr., was a son of Hubert Van Wagenen, of the firm of G. & H. Van Wagenen, ironmongers. For years they kept their store in Beekman Slip. The " G," of the firm was Garritt H. Van Wagenen.

Hubert, Jr., was placed with Messrs. McVickar & Co.,

to learn business thoroughly, but he afterwards joined his father Hubert, and they carried on business at 241 Pearl street, under the firm of H. Van Wagenen & Son. The old Hubert lived to be a very aged man. Hubert Jr., was a very religous man, and for years attended at St. George's church in Beekman street, with his interesting family. Few men were more universally respected than the Van Wagenens.

I now return to John McVickar. He married a Miss Ann Moore. She was a daughter of John Moore, of Long Island. She was born 1761, and was sister to Patience, who was Lady Dongan, having married John Carleton Dongan.

They had nine children — seven sons and two daughters.

James was the oldest. He was a merchant and a partner in the house of J. McVickar, Stewart & Co. He married Euretta a daughter of William Constable, and his son John A. McVickar, M. D., is still a resident of this city, and has a large practice.

Archibald McVickar the second son of merchant John McVickar was a lawyer in the city. He married Catherine, a daughter of Judge Brockholst Livingston. Archibald, after he graduated at Columbia College, New York, went to England and finished his education at Peterhouse College, Cambridge.

John, the third son, was a professor and clergyman. He married Eliza, daughter of the celebrated Dr. Bard who was president of the first Medical College. He is still alive and has several children. One is a much esteemed clergyman, William McVickar.

One son named Bard, I have alluded to in the first series of Old Merchants.

The fourth son of old merchant John McVickar was

named Henry. He was a merchant and was lost overboard coming from Europe. He was one of the finest young men in New York, very handsome and a great favorite.

Edward, the fifth son, married Matilda, a daughter of William Constable. He has chiefly resided in northern New York, but spends his winter in the city.

Nathan was a merchant and in business with his father. He died unmarried. He was a young man of great promise and brilliant talent.

Benjamin, the seventh son, was a physician. He married Isaphene Lawrence, a daughter of Isaac Lawrence, the president of the U. S. Bank in this city. He was very well off, but became mixed up in some way wish the speculations of his brother-in-law, William Beach Lawrence, and lost a large amount of property. I think he moved out West. He was a very clever (English clever) man. In fact, so were all the McVickars that came from the old John and Nathan stock.

Doctor McVickar is still living, and has a large practice in this city.

Eliza McVikar married William Constable, a son of old merchant William, and settled at Constableville, Lewis County, New York.

Augusta, married William Jay (Judge Jay), the youngest son of Governor Jay, the friend of Washington.

Eliza, Edward, John and Benjamin are the children living of the elder John McVickar. His grand children are very numerous, and are intermarried with the first families in the United States.

In 1798 to 1802 John was a Governor of the New York Hospital.

John McVickar, in 1805, became one of the Directors

of the Western and Northern Coal Company. About this time, 1806, the first ladies of New York city began to discover that there was a great field open for their aid in relieving suffering and misery, and they commenced to band together in organizing societies. The first was the Orphan Asylum. It was founded in March, 1806. Mrs. McVicar was one of the trustees, and associated with her were Mrs. Bethune, (Divie Bethune's wife,) Mrs. Fairlie (wife of the Major), and other leading ladies. They appealed to the public, and started off with the bold declaration, that no institution so much merited the aid of the well-inclined as this,— to feed and clothe the infant bereft of father and mother. They said : " We believe charity in this country consists more in finding employment for the needy, than in supporting them in idleness."

> " Pity, I own, to the distrest is due ;
> But when the afflicted may themselves relieve,
> The fault 's their own if they will suffer on."

The next year a Society was started for the " Relief of poor Widows," of which also Mrs. McVickar was a first manager, and so such female good works have gone on almost sixty years in our midst.

In 1809 John took into partnership his son James and a Mr. Stewart, and the firm was " John McVickar, Son & Stewart," at the old stand, No. 2 Burling slip. But both son and John, the father, lived at 231 Broadway, while the old Nathan lived at 20 Dey street. In 1810 Mr. John McVickar moved to No. 6 Vesey street. I think he gave up business in 1811, to his brother Nathan, and the firm was McVickar & Stewart, until 1812. In that year John McVickar died. His widow removed from No. 6 Vesey street back to the old No. 231 Broadway. The firm dissolved, and Nathan resided at 24 White street.

Among the leading traits of the character of John McVickar may be noted that nice sense of commercial honor which gives to the merchant his highest dignity and leads to the noblest use of wealth. He was marked accordingly by generous aid to deserving young merchants in trouble so much so that it became a common speech on Change in disastrous times "Well! who is McVickar going to help to day? In building churches and aiding the clergy, he was always prominent—on the " Dongan Domain" Staten Island, he both gave the land and built the church.

Of this large Domain coming down from Dongan, the first Governor of the Province, one legal claim still remain to the heirs of McVickar, viz: the original reservation to the Lord of the Manor, of " all Ponds, water courses and mines.' Such reservation being expressly named and provided for in all the early deeds.

At his late seat at Bloomingdale, he was one of the original founders of St. Michael's church, and during the occurrence of the yellow fever in the city, he provided for the family of Rev. Dr. Hobart his clergyman, a safe country retreat.

As a merchant he was marked by sound judgment and large views. In addition to his regular business of importation, he was a large ship owner, and one of the earliest in the direct trade with China from the port of New York. His favorite ship " Betsy," Captain Carberry, was familiarly known.

Though himself without classical education, he highly valued it for his sons, and prized and patronized the best schools. Columbia College received the next son. One, Archibald, enjoyed the farther advantage of an English

University training, and all in turn had the benefit of a European visit for health or pleasure.

In 1804, he revisited for the second and last time, his native land, accompanied by his son John, born in America — a circumstance which in these days of alien laws, in England led to a singular controversy with government — the office refusing to regard the father as lien, and McVickar insisting that as an American citizen he was an alien, and demanding that he should be included in all the penalties and restrictions that rested on such, — a proof of patriotism, we may add more unquestionable than many that now pass for such.

In his visit to Ireland, so familiar was his name and reputation in commmercial circles, that it was jokingly proposed that the Lord Lieutenant should confer on him the dignity of knighthood, as a benefactor to Ireland.

The two brothers John and Philip Hone, afterwards so prominent in the city were trained from boyhood in his counting-house, and then established in business. John Hone in after life often acknowledging that he owed all his success to the unlimited credit opened for him in London by John McVickar, with his correspondents, more especially with the great house of Phyn, Ellice & English.

In 1814 Henry McVickar started in business at No. 55 Pine street, and the next year took in a partner, and the firm was H. McVickar & Co.

Archibald McVickar, of whom I have written, was a lawyer in Wall street, having married the daughter of Hon. B. Livingston, Judge of the supreme court of U. S., until 1816.

Old John McVickar had a country seat out at

Bloomingdale, where he used to spend a great deal of his time in summer, after he retired from business, and while he lived at No. 6 Vesey street. That was a large mansion.

The old merchant John was one of the most sterling men in the city. His firm did a general commission business — receiving vessels and cargoes from all parts of the West Indies as well as from Europe. In addition, his house dealt heavily in Irish goods. John Mc-Vickar & Co. were the heaviest importers of Irish linen into the New York market. Every vessel from Belfast brought them heavy invoices. They never sold less than a case of their linens. The store of old John, where he did business so many years, was on the right hand side of Burling Slip as you go from Pearl to Water. It was about in the rear of where a bank is now located. In these times, we can form no idea of the vastness of the Irish linen trade sixty years ago. It was all old fashioned made, spun and wove by hand in Ireland, and of course, there was no machinery as now. It was the great article of trade. Here we had no such goods. The highest of our manufactures then was old " tow cloth." We had no cotton, or woolen goods made here. No sattinets, and the numerous fabrics of American manufacture were made in a thousand factories. So for this small village in the olden times, Irish linen was a great article of trade.

All the buyers used to go to old John himself, or if not in, to the brother Nathan. Clerks were not deemed the right persons to buy of. The buyer thought, of course, he could get better bargains of the principals ; and their say, too, as to prices was final, while with the clerks it was not. Old John was not above his business. Sometimes, he would take out his watch and look at it.

" I am to meet the board of directors at the bank, won't brother Nathan do?" If brother Nathan would not do, although such an answer was rare, then brother John would do the selling until the customer was satis- fied, for he regarded good sales as one great element of success in the career of a leading merchant, and he was always the salesman when at home. He was rather tall, somewhat sharp featured, and looked like a for- eigner. An early portrait of him supposed to be by Copley, gives the impression of a fine and resolute will, yet gentle heart.

In those days, the great merchants like John McVick- ar & Co., always sent the goods home to the store of their customers, free of expense. Only goods bought at " vendue " were carted home at the expense of the buyer.

Nathan, as I have stated, kept up the firm of McVick- ar & Stewart at the old store, No. 5 Burling slip, until 1813, when the house dissolved.

Mr. Nathan McVickar had acquired a large property, and was much respected. After retiring from an active and successful business, though a bachelor all that while, he concluded to marry. His choice was directed to Miss Catherine Bucknor, the daughter of a West India gentleman, who came out here before the Revolutionary War on a visit, and while here married Miss Goelet, a daughter of old Peter Goelet, of whom I have written so much. By this marriage Nathan connected himself with some of the oldest and best families in the country. The Goelets were Huguenot refugees, and were by mar- riage allied to many of the titled exiles who at that pe- riod made this country their home. Mrs. Nathan Mc- Vickar was a sister of one of the most remarkable men of the day. I allude to William Goelet Bucknor. He

was a dashing, go-ahead, clever man, worth a thousand
old fogies in a gay city. He made things fly. I remember him as well as if I had only seen him yesterday.
He was a prince of a man. He was slim in size, but as
wiry as a cat. He was an uncommon man. He commenced business at No. 54 Wall street, just after the
late war. In 1816, old Nathan McVickar lived at No.
52 Walker street, and William G. Bucknor lived next
door to him, at No. 50. These numbers were about
half way between Broadway and Church street. At
that time that range was the most fashionable part of the
town. I think William G. Bucknor did business in
New York nearly twenty years. I alluded to him some
time ago, when I published his name among the list of
those who founded the Board of Brokers about 1816. I
think he continued in business at No. 44 Wall street
until 1836. If I am not mistaken, he then went West.
He married a Charleston lady, and had sons and daughters. One of the latter I believe married Mr. Hurry, a
broker in Wall street. Wm. G. Bucknor has been dead
some years. He died in this city. His widow lives
with her daughter.

The sister that married Nathan McVickar is alive yet.
Nathan lived at No. 52 Walker street until 1827, when
he died in that house. His widow resided there some
years after.

Nathan left several children. One was named Nathan, but I believe only one of them is now living,
William H. McVickar. He married a daughter of
Thaddeus Phelps, an eminent merchant in the city.
Miss Phelps was one of the most beautiful girls in the
city. William H. McVickar, of the old Nathan stock,
is an active, energetic business man, and has acquired
a large fortune in business, and is very much respected
and esteemed.

I have many Old Merchants that I have partly written sketches of, and, sooner or later, they will be printed. Among them is old Thaddeus Phelps, the father
of Mrs. McVickar above mentioned. He was a splendid merchant. He was one of the founders of the early packet lines, and was a great shipper of cotton and
other produce to Europe. He had one of the best
heads that ever sat on a man's shoulders. His smile
was perfectly fascinating. To see him halt on those
crutches, and hear some of his pleasant words, was
worth remembering. He was a man of extraordinary
ability, and a merchant of a sagacity such as we do not
see in these days often. I do not know that my sketch
of him, when it appears, will do him justice; but if
it does, even in part, it will be worth reading.

CHAPTER XXIX.

The race of magnificent old East India merchants of the early part of this century, and a later period, are passing away — in fact, have nearly all gone. There is something grand in the title of an East India merchant. It conveys the idea of large ships, long voyages occupying a year and more to the distant Oriental climes, whose commerce is still a mystery. East India merchant ! — we at once think of " India's coral strand," " the golden Ind," " palmy plains," " the breezes of the Spice Islands," and a thousand other things that Columbus started to discover when he blundered upon this great continent.

We are all accustomed to accord the highest mark of mercantile greatness to the merchant who owns his own ship, loads her with silver, ginseng, lead, and sterling bills, and starts her off on a voyage of a year, with or without a gentlemanly supercargo, and to come back a wooden island of spicy perfumes, equal to any from Araby the blessed, as she lies at anchor in the North or East river, loaded with teas of all classes, with silks, nankeens, cassia, and a thousand other things that come from China. To us, the real East India merchant is the one who sends his ships to China. We do not have as much trade with British India, and the Calcutta merchant of the olden time ranks second to those houses who have in former years, before other ports were opened to the world, done a large trade with Canton. Among those eminent houses in this city, well known to us of this generation, were the Franklins, Minturns, and Champlins. Archibald Gracie & Sons, Thomas H. Smith & Son, John Jacob Astor, Hoyt & Tom, N. L. & G. Griswold, Talbot, Olyphant & Co., Alsop & Co., Russell & Co., Edward Carrington & Co., Goodhue & Co., Howland & Aspinwall, and Wetmore & Co. The founder of the latter house was William S. Wetmore, who was of a more recent generation of East India merchants. When the East India houses I have named were in their glory, about the commencement of this century, he was born in a little Vermont town in the early part of the year 1801. He received the ordinary district school education of a New England boy, and when about fourteen started out into the great world, as so many of the sons of New England do. At the age of twenty-three, he was shipwrecked near Valparaiso, to which port he had gone as supercargo of one of the ships of Edward Carrington & Co., of Providence. Samuel Wetmore, an uncle of young William, was the partner of Mr. Carrington. The latter was the largest ship owner and East India merchant in the United States. The chief clerk in the house for many years was Thomas P. Bucklin, now of the firm of Bucklin & Crane of this city, in the East India trade. The agent in Canton of Mr. Carrington was Isaac M. Bull, now of the firm of Bull, Purdon & Co., in China. At present, Mr. Bull resides in this country.

The sending of young W. S Wetmore to South America, as supercargo of one of his ships, by Mr. Car-

rington, was the stepping stone to his getting into the house
of Alsop & Co., and this accident led to the formation in
1824, of the great house of Alsop, Wetmore & Cryder
in that city. That Alsop was named Richard. He
was great grandson of Jno. Alsop, a freeman in this
city, who died in 1761. He left two sons, John and
Richard. They were brought up as merchants in the
city, and did a heavy business in the cloth and dry
good line. John also engaged in politics, and represented New York city in the Colonial Legislature, and
was a delegate to the first Continental Congress, in 1774.
He was a vestryman of Trinity church. He died in
1794. He left one child, Mary, who married Rufus
King, father of Gov. John A. King, and president
Charles King. The Ex-governor was named John Alsop. The other brother and partner of John, the cloth
merchant and legislator, was named Richard. He
served his time with the extensive merchant, Philip
Livingston. After he retired from business he removed
to Middletown, Conn. He had a son Richard who was
born in 1761, and was bred up a merchant, but devoted
himself chiefly to literature, for which he had an unusual
fondness. He became very familiar not only with our
literature but with that of Europe. He loved poetry,
and was himself a poet. He wrote a book, the " National and Civil History of Chili," in two volumes 8vo.
In 1800 he wrote a monody, in heroic verse, on the
death of Washington. He died in 1815, leaving one
son, who was the celebrated Richard Alsop, who founded the house of Alsop & Co., in Valparaiso, Chili, and
Lima, Peru. He was partner of W. S. Wetmore. I
may as well mention that this, the most celebrated of
the commercial Alsops, died in 1842, without issue.
He had a relative named Joseph W. Alsop, who died

in 1844, and whose daughter Lucy married Henry Chauncey, of the firm of Alsop & Chauncey, of this city, and a son named Joseph W., of the same firm, at 42 South street.

Richard Alsop, when he died, left by will his one-third interest in the house of Alsop & Co., to his relative, Joseph W. Alsop. This was a fortune of itself, for it was notorious for many years, that Alsop & Co., every five years, made a profit of over a million of dollars.

The widow of Richard is still alive. These Alsops are a roving race. They are scattered all over the world. Their arms are on a field sable, three doves agate, wings expanded, and beak gules. Crest, a dove argent, wings expanded, holding in his beak an ear of wheat.

There are Alsops in every grade of society. They trace back to Richard Alsop, who was Lord Mayor of London in 1597. His descendant, Richard, was a major in Cromwell's army, but having had a flare up with the Protector, was obliged to fly for safety to New York.

I now return to Alsop, Wetmore & Cryder, of Valparaiso. The house did all the English and American business of the old Chilian city. Their common fame was world wide. Mr. John Cryder was born in the United States. He had married a daughter of Mr. Samuel Wetmore, uncle of W. S. Wetmore, and of the house of Wetmore, Hoppin & Co., in this city, for many years.

W. S. Wetmore also married Miss Esther Wetmore in 1837, a daughter of Samuel Wetmore, his cousin, for his first wife. W. S. left the house of Alsop & Co. in 1831, retiring from it with a large fortune. He came back to the United States. Not long after he went to Canton, China, and in connection with Joseph Archer of Philadelphia, established the house of Wetmore & Co., and succeeded to the large and profitable business of Nathan Dunn & Co. There has always been a great number of Philadelphia merchants engaged in the China trade. Such men as Dunn, W. R. Thompson, Israel, Samuel Comly, Henry Tolland, Richard Alsop, Bevan & Humphreys, John McCrea, Eyne, Massey and others.

Mr. Wetmore in 1841 married Miss Rogers, of Salem, for his second wife. She was a daughter of the celebrated merchant Rogers of that place. He was largely engaged in the East India trade, and also to the domains of the Sultan of Muscat. He had an agent who constantly resided at Zanzibar.

W. S. Wetmore remained in Canton, personally superintending his large business, until his return in 1839. He arrived in New York in February, 1840, and established himself in this city.

His principal clerk and business manager from the time of his arrival was Fletcher Westray, who had been previously with the house of Wetmore, Hoppin & Co., for some years.

The father of Mr. Westray was in business in New York for a long time. He died in 1832. His widow is still living in this city. After W. S. Wetmore retired from active business, Mr. Westray continued the East India trade on his own account. He is now at the head of the house of Westray, Gibbes & Hardcastle, largely engaged in the East India trade. His partners are English, and were brought up to business in old-fashioned English counting-rooms. Mr. Westray has a brother John J. in his establishment.

Before W. S. Wetmore established himself in New York city, in 1840, Richard Alsop had been the principal agent in America of Wetmore & Co. of Canton. This connection continued until an unfortunate quarrel broke off all intimacy between the two old friends and partners. After that quarrel, Mr. Wetmore acted as the agent of his Canton house, and established in the city the house of Wetmore & Cryder.

I ought here to mention that previous to this time John Cryder had resided several years in London, where he had formed a partnership with the celebrated John Morrison, under the firm of Morrison, Cryder & Co., bankers. About 1836 or '37, in those bad times, the house lost immensely. This absorbed all of the capital of Mr. Cryder, but was nothing to Morrison. James Morrison had made an immense sum in the dry goods business, under the firm of Morrison, Dillon & Co. It still exists now, although Mr. Morrison, senior, is dead. After the retirement of Mr. Cryder, the banking firm became Morrison, Sons, & Co. This house afterwards purchased all the assets of the Bank of the United States, and it turned out a splendid purchase for them.

The history of the elder Morrison is singular. He started poor. When he died, a few years ago, his affairs were alluded to as follows in the London papers:

" The will of James Morrison, of Upper Harley street, London, and of Basilton Park, Berks, dated 3d July, 1852, with three codicils attached, has been administered to in Doctors Commons. It is the longest document upon record. Upon its production were engaged conveyancers and barristers of eminence, and during its progress to completion the testator evinced much anxiety. The estate exceeds four millions of pounds sterling (twenty millions of dollars.) The last codicil

13*

was dated in 1856. He left to the widow an annuity
of £10,000 — a legacy of £5,000, the residences in
Upper Harley street and Basilton Park. The last cost
£126,000, and the furniture there alone has been valued at £90,000. To his eldest son, Charles, £1,000,000
including the estate of Basilton, the Islay estate in
Scotland, and estates in Middlesex, London, and at Go-
ring. To his son Alfred, £750,000, including estates
in Wiltshire, Hampshire, and Glamorganshire, and all
other articles of vertu and art, and other effects at Font-
hill. To his son Frank £300,000, including estates in
Kent, Surrey and Sussex. To his son Walter £300,000
including estates in the West Riding, Yorkshire. To
his son George £300,000, including estates in Bucking-
hamshire and Oxfordshire. To his son Allan £300,000
including estates in Suffolk and Essex. To his three
daughters, £50,000 each. His business he transferred
to his son Charles Morrison for £350,000. Mr. Morrison owned £80,000 in the Victoria Docks, and vast ac-
quisitions in America."

Mr. Cryder came to this country after leaving Mr.
Morrison, and joined Mr. W. S. Wetmore under the
firm of Wetmore & Cryder. Afterward Mr. Wetmore
retired from that firm, and from all active business, in
June 20, 1847, and removed his residence to Newport,
where he had purchased a magnificent property, and
erected an elegant stone villa known as the *chateau sur
mer*, at which he resided until his death, that has occurred there June, 1862.

He commenced his career with no capital, save his
education, honesty, and a determined will to succeed.
He did succeed in becoming one of the most eminent
and extensive merchants in the world. He left the
South American house with a large fortune. When he
retired from the China house, he had acquired an additional fortune. He was a man of splendid personal ap-

pearance. He was large, stood six feet high, was well proportioned. He was a perfect philosopher. When he married his second wife in 1837, he settled a large income upon her. The whole country was shocked at her indiscretion a few years after with the coachman of Mr. Wetmore. It was a terrible calamity for a high-spirited man like Mr. Wetmore. He bore the trial like a hero. Instead of making a town talk, he quietly flung over it the veil of charity and silence. No one ever heard what become of his wife or his coachman.

Mr. Wetmore was a fortunate man in all his financial operations. In the China war of 1841 and 1842, when the Chinese refused to do business with English houses, the American houses did all the trade, and Wetmore & Co. got the lion's share.

His property is very large. He has in this vicinity property valued at over a million of dollars. At Massillon, Ohio, he has 10,000 acres of the finest farm lands. In Tennessee he named a town after himself (Wetmore,) and there he owns 70,000 acres.

His firm in Canton and Shanghai, is still kept up as Wetmore, Cryder & Co. The partners are W. S. Wetmore (same name as his own, but a nephew,) and Mr. Wetmore Cryder, also a nephew and son of John Cryder, who is yet living, though retired from business, and managing the estate of his late brother-in-law. The house of Wetmore, Cryder & Co. is still in existence in this city, at No. 77 William street.

When George Peabody, of London, came out to this country, in 1857, Mr. Wetmore gave at Newport a *fete champetre* upon the most magnificent scale. Nothing approaching it was ever before seen in this country. Peabody was a life-long friend of Mr. Wetmore. He named one of his sons after him. A son died a few

years ago. There are other children by the second
wife. The first wife died in child-bed, and the child
died also.

Mr. Carrington who first sent Mr. Wetmore to sea
in one of his ships, died some years ago. He has a son
yet living in Providence, R. I.

James Webber Lent was a large merchant in this
city. His father, John, was a master builder, and died
in North Carolina in 1768. He married Ann, a daughter of Adrian Hoogland, of this city. He was a captain in Braddock's expedition during the old French
war. He was also present when General Wolf fell at
Quebec. He was a fierce old fellow, full of fight and
full of fun. He left several children, and two of them
went into business in New York,— James Webber and
John. John was a gold and silver smith at No. 18
Nassau street, after peace was proclaimed. James W.
fought all through the Revolutionary war. After that,
in 1790, he opened a grocery, corner of Little Water
and Broad streets. In 1784 he married Miss Macomb,
a daughter of Nathan Macomb. In 1798, he had
moved into South street, where he kept a flour store in
addition to groceries. In 1802 he was appointed inspector of pot and pearl ashes. His office was at No.
92 Broad, and house at No. 97 Stone streets. He held
that office for several years. James W. Lent was elected register about thirty-two years ago, and held the
office several years. His son George W. Lent went
into business on his own account at No. 82½ Pearl
street in 1828, but lived with his father down in the
First Ward, at No. 31 Water street. James W. died in
1739. The son is yet living.

There was another James Lent, who was a merchant in this city for some years. He married a Miss

Bull, of Connecticut. He went to reside on Long Island, and was elected to Congress from King's County in 1813, and died at Washington in 1833. He had a sister who married Anthony Barclay. He died in 1805. He was the son of Henry Barclay, who became rector of Trinity church in 1746.. He was called Dr. Barclay. He married Mary, the daughter of Anthony Rutgers. His eldest son, Thomas, the brother of Henry, was British Consul General for the United States many years. He left several children ; — Anthony, who married Miss Lent ; one daughter married Colonel Beverly Robinson ; another married Colonel Stephen De Lancy, the father of Miss De Lancy, who married Daniel I. Coster.

CHAPTER XXX.

There have been many merchants in this city, during the past one hundred years, of the name of Hicks. Some were very eminent, and became very rich. Probably they all came from the same stock.

Oliver H. Hicks, who was of note here for some years, was a son of Stephen, and came from Rockaway, Long Island. He had a brother Stephen.

Another family of the Hicks name was that of Isaac, Samuel and Valentine, that afterwards became the great house of Samuel Hicks & Son, of which the principal was Samuel Hicks, Jr. All were sons of Samuel Hicks, who was a clever tailor at Westbury, L. I. He went about doing small jobs. Isaac started the house in 1796, at 14 Crane wharf (South street.) He did a very exten sive commission business ; and if he had done nothing but bringing up Jacob Barker, that would have been sufficient to immortalize his name. The celebrated Jacob was in the counting-house of Mr. Hicks until 1800, a period of three years. In 1802, Samuel and Valentine Hicks (brothers to Isaac) opened a store at 345 Pearl. The next year, Sylvanus Jenkins was taken into partnership, and the firm was changed to Hicks, Jenkins & Co. In 1805, the concern moved to 67 South street.

About this time, or in 1806, Isaac retired from busi-

ness with a very large fortune, and gave his business to
the firm of his two brothers. He lived at 272 Pearl.
I believe he died about 1811. Samuel moved to 215
Broadway, opposite the Park, in 1814, and there he
lived a great many years. His firm, Hicks, Jenkins
& Co., continued in business as late as 1818. They
had moved up to 154 South street, above Peck
slip. About that time Sylvanus Jenkins died. He
was a splendid merchant. A Liverpool packet ship
was named after him. In 1819, Samuel Hicks continued on the business under his own name. In
1825 he took into partnership two of his sons, John
and Henry, and the firm became Samuel Hicks & Sons.
They moved down to 80 South street, where the firm
did an enormous business until 1837, when old Samuel
died at his house No. 245 Broadway. The concern was
then changed to Hicks & Co., and the sons carried on
the business for a great many years after. John Hicks
died about six years ago. Both of the sons had families. Old Samuel Hicks was very much respected. I
could write a lengthy article about him and his house,
but I did not commence to do it. I have digressed.
. The Hicks merchants of whom I intended to write,
are another family. I have alluded to the above houses
in order to make the distinction. Whitehead Hicks was
a celebrated merchant, who came to this city in 1796.
He was descended from Thomas Hicks, who married
Deborah, a daughter of Daniel Whitehead, a great
land owner in Flushing, about 1723. He had a son
Whitehead, who was born in 1728, and who was the
last British mayor. He was a lawyer, and I have
nothing to say about him, except that he married, in
1757, Charlotte, the only child of John Bennett, and
their son, Thomas, married Martha Buchanan, a daugh-

ter of Thomas Buchanan, spoken of in the last chapter.
He had three daughters, and he died in 1815. Mayor
Whitehead Hicks had a brother Gilbert, who married
Mary Allen. The latter had a son that he named
Whitehead, after his grandfather Whitehead ; he married in 1795, and the next year started as a lumber
merchant in Lumber street (changed in 1805 to Lom-
bardy street, and yet later to Monroe street.) About
the year 1801 he moved to No. 1 East Rutgers street.
He was one of the founders of the Seventh Ward, and
bought the first foot of land that old Henry Rutgers
ever sold in Market street. That old Henry Rutgers,
had he lived until now, could not have done what he did
do for many years, from 1800 to 1820, viz : to every New
York boy that would call upon him on New Year's he
gave a cake and a book. Thousands of boys would go
and see him on these conditions. Whitehead Hicks
made a large fortune in the lumber business. He built
blocks of houses, and got the famous Georges street
broken up. It is now Market street. It began in Division street, and ended in Cherry street. It was the
devil's own hole. It was worse than the Five Points
was in 1830.

The Quakers clubbed together and bought a block
of ground to build upon, and tried to improve this fearful neighborhood, where all kinds of debauchery was
carried on. In 1814, the Quakers and respectable
people in the vicinity, who did not wish their property
depreciated in consequence of the bad name of the street
and its well known vile character, petitioned to the
Corporation that it might be changed from Georges to
Market street. At the same time, all the bad women
got up a petition and presented it to the Corporation.
They, too, wished Georges street to be changed, and to

have it named after Commodore Rodgers, a popular
naval commander, who had just been winning a great
victory over the English. The quakers carried the
day against the frail women, and the street was named
Market street. It is now one of the best streets in the
city. In 1811 he took into partnership Michael M. Titus, and the firm was Hicks & Titus. Both parties are
now dead. Mr. Titus left a son, who is now in the
Seventh Ward Savings Bank. Mr. Whitehead Hicks
died in 1830. He had two sons. One was named Gilbert, after his grandfather, and the other was Robert T.
Hicks Jr. In 1819, the latter went into the ship chandlery business, under his own name, at 107 South street.
That property was owned by the old house of Bogert
& Kneeland (still in existence.) At that time, 1820,
the water had just been filled in with dirt. Those stores
were just put one story, and then allowed to stand one
year. It was called Crane's wharf. I have already alluded to it in this chapter. The store, No. 107, was three
doors above the Fulton market. That same store stands
now. Mr. Hicks bought it. In 1825, Robert took in
his brother Gilbert, and the firm became G. & R. T.
Hicks. The house did a very heavy business in supply-
ing ship chandlery to numerous vessels. It also owned
a great many vessels, that traded to the West Indies
and South America.

Gilbert Hicks married Miss Embury, a daughter of
Effingham Embury. His health was very poor, and his
friends advised that if he wished to save his life, or to
prolong it, he should go to the West Indies. He selected St. Thomas, and there opened a house in connection with the New York house. He received vessels and consignments of goods from all parts of the
United States, and he shipped goods from St. Thomas

on his own account. St. Thomas, with its splendid cli-
mate and mild government, is a paradise. It is wonderful to me that thousands do not go thither every
winter. It belongs to Denmark, and so does Santa
Cruz, a lovely island only a few hours' sail from St.
Thomas. Mr. Gilbert Hicks was a very hopitable man,
and no American visited that island that he did not in-
vite to his house — and it made no difference whether he
did business with him or not. I dined with him frequently in 1833, being in that port with a brig and cargo that I afterwards took down the Spanish main. Although I consigned to W. B. Furniss & Co., yet at no
house was I so kindly received as by Mr. Hicks. Of
course he spoke Danish freely, and the best Danish society on the island could be found at his dinners.
They have a good old fashioned custom after dinner of
all kissing each other, and saying in Danish something
like this : " May God bless what you have eaten and
drunken to your future good, and may you always be
very happy." At any rate it is very pleasant. Mr.
Hicks found that at home or abroad consumption had
fastened upon his vitals, and he returned home to die.
I think he lived until June of 1834 — the next year after I met him.

Robert T. Hicks kept the same business for a number of years, under the firm of Robert T. Hicks & Co.
He married in 1822 a daughter of Thomas Everitt, a
heavy leather dealer in the Swamp, but who resided in
Brooklyn. This fact made the son-in-law go over there
and buy ground to build a house on for himself. Land
was cheap, and he bought largely, resulting in making
him the owner of a large property in after years. Old
Mr. Everitt was a fine man, and an extensive merchant.
He did business many years. His house at one time

was Thomas Everitt & Sons. He had several sons. There were Henry, Richard and Valentine. I believe the house is still continued in the business, under the firm of Hyde & Everitt, at No. 32 Ferry street.

Robert T. Hicks kept in business in the old stand in South street until about 1848, when he retired rich. About 1859, he moved up to Poughkeepsie, where he had built him a splendid country seat. No man has worked harder than he to acquire a competency, and he has proved himself a sagacious merchant. He had two sons. One was named Gilbert. He married Miss Gibbs. Archibald Gracie Jr., a son of our much esteemed New Yorker, Robert Gracie, married another sister. Another son is Robert. After old Robert T. Hicks retired from business it was carried on by Hicks & Bailey, at 36 South street, for four or five years later. The partner was Gilbert E. Hicks.

Oliver H. Hicks, to whom I alluded, was a very eminent and a very extensive merchant in the early part of this century. He did a large commission business, and sold more pipes of imported Holland gin than any other merchant of his day. He went into business as early as 1800. His counting house was at 83 South street, and he lived at 87 Maiden lane. He continued to do a very large business as late as 1819. In that year, the Fulton Fire Insurance Company was incorporated with a capital of $500,000, and he became its secretary. Anthony L. Underhill, of whom I have written, was its president. Mr. Hicks was secretary of that company until 1828. In 1831, he was elected president of the Farmers' Fire Insurance and Loan Company, and he continued to be its president until 1832, when he died of the cholera. He was a man universally respected.

CHAPTER XXXI.

I have had occasion in former chapters to mention at
some length two large commercial firms that once existed in this city of the name of Rogers.   One was
the firm of David Rogers & Son, large sugar merchants
forty years ago.   The other was Rogers & Co., a heavy
shipping house, largely interested in forwarding tobacco
under French government contracts for several years.
Both of these houses have been long since extinct.
The business of the latter is still continued by the
founder, John T. Farish, who was a nephew of the
founder Lewis Rogers, of Richmond, Va.

The Rogers' commercial house that I shall write
about in this chapter, existed soon after the Revolutionary war.   In 1784, Rogers & Lyde did business at 209
Queen street.   The founder of that house was Henry
Rogers, who resided at 28 Beekman street.   His partner
was Edward Lyde.   That house did an immense iron
business, and were called iron importers.   It kept in the
same store (229) Pearl, as late as 1821 — thirty-seven
years.   I will give a history of it and of its eminent
partners, before I finish this sketch.

Another brother of Henry was named Moses Rogers.
He certainly was in business immediately after the Revolution, if not before it.   He married, about 1773, a Miss

Woolsey. In 1785 he did business at No. 26 Queen street. Afterwards, he founded Moses Rogers & Co. ; after that it was Rogers & Woolsey in 1793 — at 206 Queen — (235 Pearl,) and there it was kept for nearly forty years afterwards. I will give a sketch of him and his partner before I finish.

The oldest brother was Fitch Rogers. He settled at Stamford, Conn. He lived in New York in 1803 and 1804, and was a partner with one of his brothers. He lived in Connecticut and died there.

Nehemiah was the youngest brother; in 1792 he came here from St. Johns, New Brunswick, and founded the house of Rogers & Aspinwall at 45 Queen. He lived at 48 Beekman. His partner was Gilbert Aspinwall. It was dissolved in 1793, and Gilbert started business at 186 Queen (207 Pearl) with his brother John, under the firm of Gilbert & John Aspinwall. Nehemiah Rogers kept his store at 272 Pearl, until 1796, when he took the store 232 Pearl, and founded the house of N. Rogers & Co. His partner was David R. Lambert. In 1799 the firm was changed to Rogers & Lambert, still at 232 Pearl, where it was kept 28 years later. These were all great firms. Before Nehemiah came to this city from the British Provinces, where he had established himself, he was the first mayor of St. John, N. B., and entertained the Duke of Kent, father of Queen Victoria. He married a daughter of James Bell of Frederickton, N. B., who was father of Isaac Bell — captain they call him, though he never was a captain but had been supercargo to the East Indies several times. Captain Isaac Bell was one of the finest men that ever drew breath. He was for many years connected with Francis Depau and his line of Havre packets. His son is the present Isaac Bell —

one of our most prominent city officials. Nehemiah
Rogers was probably married about 1786 to Miss Bell.
He was born in 1754. He died in 1849 — aged 95, almost the last of the great race of old merchants who
were in active business in the last century. His venerable form could have been frequently seen in Greenwich street until within twelve years. His was one
of the finest of human faces.

These brothers had a sister, Esther Rogers. She
founded a family, or a race of merchants. She married
the celebrated Archibald Gracie. He came out to this
country from Scotland as supercargo of a small vessel,
directly after the Revolutionary war was finished. He
became one of the heaviest merchants New York had
seen up to his time. When he was in his prime, he was
doing business with all parts of the world. He owned
many ships. There was the " Eliza Gracie," the
" Braganza," the " Mary," and many whose names I
do not recollect. Mr. Gracie suffered severely from the
Berlin and Milan decrees. He could not get any redress during his life. After his death, which occurred
in 1829, General Jackson forced the French Government to pay this as well as other claims. Between the
British and French governments he had suffered losses
to an incredible extent. Over a million dollars was his
loss. As many of the readers have heard about French
claims, I will give a statement made by Mr. Gracie
himself. He had waited and waited until he was heart
sick for redress. None came. Finally he sent the following eloquent petition to Congress before he died :

*To the Honorable the Senate and House of Represent-
atives of the United States of America in Congress
assembled :*

THE MEMORIAL OF ARCHIBALD GRACIE,
Of New York, a citizen of the United States,
RESPECTFULLY SHEWETH,

That your memorialist, in the year 1806, loaded the
brig " Perseverance," and in 1807 the ship " Mary ; "
that they were cleared directly for Antwerp — sailed —
were captured by British cruisers, and after a forcible
detention of a few days in England, arrived at Antwerp,
one in March, the other in July, 1807. At the time
of their arrival, the only extraordinary decree in existence which affected the navigation of neutrals was the
Berlin, of the 21st of November, 1806, which, among
other provisions, declared that English property, or manufactures, or her colonial produce, were good prize ;
that no vessel coming directly from England, or going
to England or her colonies, should be permitted to enter a French port ; and that every vessel contravening
the decree, by a false declaration, should be seized and
her cargo confiscated. In consequence of an applica-
tion to obtain the property in question, the French
Government gave orders to admit and land the cargoes
in Entrepôt. This decision evinced that the government
did not consider the *relache forcee* in England as sufficient to justify the *non-admission* of the vessels and cargoes ; subsequently an inquiry was directed to be held,
to ascertain if there were any English property on board.
This inquiry was scrupulously carried into effect by the
agents of the government, and a report was made that
no English property was on board. The ship's papers
are acknowledged to have been regular, and no ground
was ever set up that there was a false declaration ; nor
could it have been set up ; for the fact of having been
forced into England was stated by the captains on arrival. Thus none of the provisions of the Berlin decree
of 1806 having been contravened, all opposition to the
property passing into the hands of the consignees was
expected to cease ; but, though the vessels were suffered

to depart, upon bonds being given to abide the issue of such decision as should be made, the cargoes were still retained in Entrepôt ; nor was it until their perishing condition was represented, that orders were issued to sell them under the joint inspection of the government officers and the consignees, and to place the proceeds *provisionally* in the Caisse d'amortissement.   At length, by a financial decree of Bonaparte, without trial, adjudication, or any civil process whatever, the proceeds of all sequestered property were directed to be taken out of the Caisse d'amortissement, and placed in the public treasury.   Part of the cargoes of the " Mary " and the " Perseverance " being ashes, had been previously, in 1809, delivered over to the department of war, according to a decree, by which the value thereof was directed to be paid into the Caissé d'amortissement (though such payment was the condition of the delivery, yet it never has been made,) there was a process verbal drawn up at the time by the committee appointed by government, detailing the transaction by which the weights are given, and the value, notwithstanding heavy deductions, stated to be about fr. 450,000 ; the remainder of the " Mary's " cargo produced about fr. 627,711, and that of the " Perseverance " about 193,212, making the claim amount to in all, fr. 1,270,000, without including interest, which, as the French nation has had the use of the money, is as fairly due as the principal ; more especially as no claim is made for the depreciation of the goods by damage during the illegal detention in Entrepôt, which depreciation was great, in general, and upon the ashes amounted to twenty per cent.   No possible ground exists for withholding this property.

Enough seems to have been said of the undeniable justice of this claim ; and of the duty incumbent upon the French Government (having in several instances admitted American claims and paid them separately) no longer to withhold the same measure of justice from your memorialist.   Under this statement of his case, your memorialist submits with confidence to the wisdom of Congress to such steps in relation thereto as to them shall seem fit.

Few in the present day know how much many of the Old Merchants suffered by war. The descendants of Archibald Gracie and Esther Rogers have married into most of the principal families. The firm was Archibald Gracie & Sons. William, the eldest son, and afterwards partner of his father, married a daughter of Oliver Wolcott for his first wife. His second was Miss Fleming. Archibald Gracie, his second son, is yet living at Elizabethtown, New Jersey. He married Miss Bethune, of Charleston, S. C. Robert I shall speak of fully before I finish this sketch. A daughter, Sally, married James G. King. Eliza married Charles King, the president of Columbia College, who was of the firm of A. Gracie & Sons. Another daughter, Hetty, married William Beach Lawrence. Another sister of the celebrated Rogers brothers married David Lambert. His son was David Rogers Lambert, who was a partner of Nehemiah Rogers, under the firm of Rogers, Lambert & Co. until 1811, at 232 Pearl. That year two of the younger Lamberts started a store at No. 231 Pearl, opposite. David R. Lambert was killed many years ago up by the Sailor's Snug Harbor (near where Tenth street now is.) He was coming home from a party at Edward Lyde's house. They met a gang of rowdies; one of them struck him a blow that killed him instantly. The parties were tried for murder, convicted of manslaughter, and sentenced to ten years in the State prison. D. Lyde was a partner of Lyde, Rogers & Co. in 1792. At the time of his death, Mr. Lambert was living in Bond street, and owned two others besides the marble house he lived in.

Another sister of Nehemiah Rogers never married. Her name was Elizabeth.

Nehemiah Rogers lived at No. 4 Greenwich street

14

from 1810 to 1849, when he died. He moved there
from No. 19 Robinson (now Park place), where he had
lived from 1801. While he was living at No. 19 Robinson street, in his own house, old Colonel George Turnbull, an English gentleman of wealth, who lived many
years at 43 Broadway, had a country seat, *out of town*
(where Waverley place is now.) It was a pretty cottage, with twenty or twenty-two acres of land attached.
One afternoon the Colonel met Mr. Rogers, and said:

"Rogers, I like that house of your's very much indeed. How will you trade for my country seat and
land?"

"How will you trade?" asked Mr. Rogers.

"I will make an even exchange with you."

"That is about fair; but I will not exchange for one
reason. It is too far out of town," replied Mr. Rogers.

"Nonsense, you keep a carriage, and can ride into
town every day," urged Colonel Turnbull.

At that time (1806) there were only fifteen persons
that kept a carriage in New York. Among them were
Archibald Gracie, Moses Rogers, Colonel Turnbull, Nehemiah Rogers, Herman Le Roy, Mr. Bayard, and a
few others.

The house, 19 Robinson — it ran through to Murray
street — was worth $15,000. He sold it for $17,000,
when he moved to Greenwich street — 1810. The
twenty acres out of town (Waverley Place neighborhood) would now be worth millions. Either Henry or
Edward Wilkes married a daughter of the Colonel
Turnbull, who lived upon his income. Nehemiah Rogers in 1807 took in his son Samuel as a partner, and the
firm was Rogers, Lambert & Co. When Mr. Lambert
retired, it was changed in 1811 to N. Rogers, Son & Co.
They did a very heavy business. The firm was largely

engaged in importing for many years, from all parts of
Europe. It received consignments from all parts of the
South — cotton, turpentine, tar, and provisions. Mr.
Rogers was largely engaged in the East India trade,
helping to make up cargoes for the East India ships
owned by his brother-in-law, Archibald Gracie. Mr.
Rogers also owned interests in some vessels. He was
much esteemed in every relation of life. He was a
courteous merchant of the old school. He was truly a
Christian, and did everything that he could do to pro-
mote the good of his fellow men. In 1807, he was
elected a vestryman of Trinity Church, and so continued until 1816, when he became a warden, and kept the
honorable office until 1842 — a period of over thirty-
five years. He was in several of our moneyed corporations as director. In 1816, he was a Director of the
Bank of New York, and was chosen several years. He
had several sons. Samuel, Edward M., Henry, who
married Miss Livingston, a daughter of John S. Livingston ; George I., Archibald Gracie, named after the old
merchant, his uncle. I believe all are living, except
Edward and Henry. The mother died this year (1863)
aged 93 years.

When Mr. Rogers moved into Greenwich street, all
the wealth and fashion of the city was in that quarter.
The old Custom House was in front of the Bowling
Green Row. When he died, in 1849, the character of
Greenwich street had completely changed. Up to
1825, there were remaining twenty or more of his old
cronies. Colonel Robinson, father of Beverly Robinson, Isaac Bell, Varick, William Bayard, Robert Lenox, Joshua Waddington, Cornelius Ray, Mr. Lewis, Jacob Stout, and others. These used to meet and dine
together occasionally, at each other's house, and talk

over old New York. Old Captain Jacob would tell me with great glee about bringing over in the ship he commanded, John Jacob Astor as a steerage passenger, and recite the regulations, that no steerage passenger should be allowed to go on the quarter deck among the cabin passengers; and was ready to take oath that Astor had a few things such as are used in making umbrellas, and that they were not worth $90; and these facts, that even now can be proved, but which have been most terribly falsified, would be commented upon by these old New Yorkers, whose early career had made New York the great commercial city that she is. One by one these old diners were carried to their graves; and, after a long delay, Mr. Rogers followed to the tomb, with none of his old companions to follow him. Had he lived until now, he would have been 108 years old. He was executor of the estate of Archibald Gracie.

CHAPTER XXXII.

Moses Rogers was a grand old merchant. He was in business as early as 1785. His place was at 26 Queen street. In 1792, he formed the house of Moses Rogers & Co., at No. 206 Queen street. His partner was William Walter Woolsey, his brother-in-law. In 1793, the firm was changed to Rogers & Woolsey. When Queen street was changed, it became 245 Pearl. Meanwhile Moses Rogers lived at 272 Pearl as late as 1795.

Moses Rogers married Sarah Woolsey about 1780, daughter of Benjamin Woolsey, who was father of W. W. Woolsey — a famous New York merchant, and brother-in-law of Mr. Rogers. They had several children. One was Benjamin Woolsey Rogers, who was born the 18th May, 1775. Another, Archibald Rogers, and a daughter, Julia Ann, who married F. B. Winthrop, a brother of John Stille Winthrop. F. B. Winthrop was of the house of Winthrop, Rogers & Williams, about 1820. Moses Rogers was early a member of the Marine Society, in 1780. In 1793, he was a member of the Society to relieve Distressed Prisoners. It is difficult to understand at this time, how there should be a regular society to relieve prisoners in old New York. Yet, so there was, and it was a humane society, that numbered the first merchants of New York among its members.   It lasted many years, and the venerable and reverend Dr. John Rodgers was president of it.

In those years we had a jail, and our fellow-citizens who could not pay their debts outside were locked up in the debtor's prison in the Park.   This society mitigated the hardship by giving the prisoners decent food and fuel : about 150 persons were constantly locked up.   The jail, I believe, allowed no fire, and only bread and water.   The humane society furnished wood and soup to the extent of 16,000 quarts annually.

Two years later Moses Rogers was one of the jury on the trial of John Young, an actor, who had killed the sheriff's officer in the Park.   The latter was going to arrest Mr. Young, and take him to the old jail that stood where the Hall of Records now is.   Young shot him.   He was then arrested in good earnest, and locked up in the Bridewell, that stood on the Broadway side of the present City Hall.   He was tried, and the jury found him guilty.   He was hung on the high hill east of where the Tombs now is, and on the ground now bounded by Broadway, Benson and Leonard streets. The military and all the citizens turned out to see the fun.

In 1793, Moses Rogers was one of the most active members of the Society for the Manumission of Slaves. So was his brother-in-law, William Dunlap, the celebrated historian, who had married a Miss Woolsey.   W. W. Woolsey, his wife's brother, was the secretary of this society.   Moses Rogers was a director of the United States Branch Bank in this city, in 1793.   At that time he lived at No. 272 Pearl street : it was near Beekman street, a large house, with a hanging garden extending over the yard and stable.   He was a governor of the New York Hospital from 1792 to 1799.   In 1797 he

was one of the principal managers of the City Dispensary. He was treasurer. That same year he was elected a director of the Mutual Insurance Company, and
he continued to be so until 1807. In 1798, the firm at
No. 235 Pearl was changed to Woolsey & Rogers. I
think that year old Moses Rogers went out of the concern, and that his son, B. Woolsey Rogers, took his
place. The old gentleman then went into the sugar refining business. He took for that purpose the old sugar
house in Liberty street, No. 42. It was used as a prison in the war. It stood, until within a few years, adjoining the Dutch church, now used by the Post-Office.
The firm was Moses Rogers & Co. He kept in the sugar refinery until 1806. At that time he lived at No.
7 State street. That grand house with pillars stood as
late as yesterday, and Valentine's Manual of 1859 has
a capital engraving of it. It was built by Moses Rogers.
He occupied it as late as 1826. His son, B. W., lived
next door at No. 5, in 1826, and after his father died he
moved to No. 7 and lived there until 1830, when the
house was taken by G. G. Howland. The family still
own it.

In 1804, Mr. W. W. Woolsey retired, and the business was carried on under the firm of B. W. Rogers &
Co., at 235 Pearl street, until 1826, when it was
changed to Rogers, Taylor & Williams. Mr. Taylor
was Jeremiah H., a brother of Knowles Taylor. He
had been a clerk with B. W. Rogers for some years.
The other partner was Timothy Dwight Williams.
This house lasted only until 1830, when B. W. Rogers
continued it in his own name, as he had commenced it
in 1804, for one year, and then he moved his place of
business to No. 4 Fletcher street, where Jeremiah H.
Taylor had commenced business on his own account.

This house, conducted by father and son, existed over forty-six years, and for forty-two of those years it was in the same store. So it has been with the three great mercantile houses founded by the brothers Moses, Henry and Nehemiah. They believed in the proverb, that a "rolling stone gathers no moss." Old Moses was a vestryman of Trinity church from 1787 to 1811, and his son, B. Woolsey, was the same from 1821 to 1826. I have already mentioned that old Moses was a governor of the New York hospital for seven years. His son was governor from 1818 to 1855, and some portion of that time was assistant treasurer.

The first wife of B. Woolsey Rogers was a daughter of William Bayard. His second wife was a Miss Elwyn. Her mother was a daughter of the famous Governor Langdon, of New Hampshire. She married Mr. Elwyn, of an old wealthy English family. Each of the daughters of B. W. Rogers, Eliza and Sarah, became the wife of W. P. Van Rensselaer. His brother, Archibald Rogers, married Miss Pendleton, a daughter of old Judge Pendleton, and sister of the Judge Pendleton who died a few days ago. One daughter of Moses Rogers married Francis B. Winthrop. Archibald Rogers died about ten years ago. He left several children.

One daughter married a Mr. Livingston, who is concerned in the Havana line of steamers. B. Woolsey Rogers had three sons. Elwyn died many years ago. The second son was Woolsey, who married Miss Hoffman. He is dead. The eldest son, William Bayard Rogers, is still living. The heaviest importers in the hardware trade fifty years ago, were B. W. Rogers and W. W. Woolsey. When Moses Rogers and his son B. W. Rogers resided in State street, their neighbors were

John B. Coles, Wm. Neilson, Henry Overing, Jonathan Ogden, William Bayard, General Jacob Morton, and Corrié's public garden.

B. Woolsey Rogers died in 1859 or 1860, in this city. I have already alluded to the house founded by Henry Rogers in 1785, of Rogers & Lyde. In 1793 it was changed to Lyde & Rogers, and their store was at No. 209 Queen street. The partner was old Edward Lyde, who was very rich. He married a daughter of Governor Belcher, of Massachusetts. He was every inch a gentleman. He was in business as early as 1777. He occupied No. 200 Queen street for a store, and paid for it $240 per annum. Same store now rents for $1400. When Queen was changed to Pearl, the numbering was changed, and it became No. 229 Pearl street, same building though. In 1797 the firm became Lyde, Rogers & Co. I think Edward Lyde, Jr., was taken into the house that year. In 1807, Edward Lyde, Jr., went out of the concern, and started business at No. 230 Pearl street, opposite the old store. The old house was continued on under the style of Rogers, Son & Co. At that time Francis B. Winthrop was taken into partnership.

The son was Henry F. Rogers. Old Henry Rogers lived at No. 42 Courtlandt street for a great many years. In 1811 the firm became Rogers & Winthrop, at the same old store, No. 229 Pearl street. A sister of Henry F. married Daniel Remsen, of the firm of Peter Remsen & Co. Henry F. married for his first wife a daughter of Fitch Rogers, of Stamford. So did John S. Winthrop, and there were two sons, John S. Jr., and Henry. In 1818 the firm became Rogers, Winthrop & Co. I think J. Smyth Rogers, a son of old Henry, became a partner. He married Miss Winthrop, a daugh-

14*

ter of Gov. Winthrop, of Boston. The firm kept in the same old store until 1821, when they moved to No 56 South street, and went into the commission business. In that year Henry F. Rogers became a partner of Robert Gracie at No. 56 South street, under the firm of Rogers & Gracie. Robert was the youngest son of old Archibald Gracie, the great New York merchant, who died in 1829. He married Miss Neilson, a daughter of Wm. Neilson, a great merchant half a century ago, and afterwards a leading man in marine insurance companies. Robert Gracie, who probably commenced business on his own account in 1821 with Mr. Rogers, is a very remarkable man. He is yet alive, and has for forty odd years plodded on steadily, working like a beaver, industrious as a bee. Faithful to every duty, never tiring, of an unquestioned integrity, he ought, if wealth is any reward for a faithful service, to be worth many millions. He had one son by his first wife, named Archibald Gracie; I saw him when he was a baby, some thirty years or more ago, and have not seen him since. I have alluded to him in a previous chapter as having married a Miss Dashwood, her mother was a Ludlow, and his second wife was a Miss Gibbs. Robert Gracie, for his second wife, married the accomplished and beautiful daughter of John B. Fleming, an old merchant. A quarter of a century ago, she and her sister, Mrs. William Gracie, were two of the most beautiful girls in the city of New York.

Robert Gracie was once a great church goer, and a leading man in the St. Thomas church, where the bones of his father lie in one of the vaults close to Broadway. His was the first funeral I ever attended in my life. Rogers & Gracie continued in business until 1826, at 64 Pine street. The firm was then changed to Gracie & Co., but Henry F. Rogers I think continued the company for many years after. In 1820, Gracie & Co. moved to 20 Broad street. It was the third or fourth store that was erected in Broad street. The entire street was filled with dwelling houses, and occupied by our principal people up to twenty-five years ago. A store was a rarity. Now, a dwelling house is the novelty in the street. Gracie & Co. did a very heavy business in choice wines and English beer and porter for many years. In his time he educated many clerks. Among them was John S. Winthrop, Jun., a son of the old member of the firm of Rogers, Winthrop & Co. John, Jun., was afterwards a clerk with Prime, Ward & King. He afterwards married in North Carolina, and resided South. Richard K. Anthony was another clerk of Mr. Gracie. He was one of the old Dutch Anthony family. Their names are among the early Dutch records in 1644. The father of Richard Anthony was one of the principal tellers in the United States Branch Mint in this city for a great many years. I think Richard Anthony became a partner of Gracie & Co. in the wine business, but I am not certain. He still carries on the business in Liberty street.

Mr. Henry F. Rogers married, for his second wife, Miss Maxwell, a sister of Mrs. George Douglass. He died in 1862.

There was in this city, after the Revolution, a John Rogers, who was a merchant of extensive business, and highly respectable. His residence was at 7 Beaver street, and his store was in Hanover square. He had two sons. One named John Rogers, Jun., who was born 19th June, 1787. Another son was George Pixton Rogers, who was born 15th December, 1789. The latter is yet alive, and lives at 17 Washington square. Old John Rogers was an eminent merchant in his day, and very much respected. He was a member of the Marine Society in 1784.

John Rogers died at 7 Beaver street about 1800. His widow continued to reside there as late as 1809. George Pixton Rogers eight years ago paid taxes on real estate, $329,000. His chances are good for being one of the seven to whom the Tontine property will fall. He was one of the nominees. I have been frequently asked, who, out of the 203 names nominated, are alive. As near as I now recollect, George P. Rogers, born 1789; Gulian C. Verplanck, born 1786; his sister, Mary Ann Verplanck, born 1793; William Bayard, born 1791. His sister Maria, born 1788; Miss Frances Buchanan (Mrs. Thomas Pearsall), born 1779; John A. King, born 1788; Charles King, born 1789. There are others yet alive; I think about thirty-five of the nominees.

In one of my chapters I alluded to unfortunate merchants of a high class, and their desperate fortunes. Frequently, after having assigned every dollar to creditors, they, perhaps at an advanced age, are exposed to the evils of the worst species of poverty. True, the city provides for such, at the almshouse on Blackwell's Island. I heard of one of them there to-day, who, but a few years ago, was one of the largest houses in the city, and his partner was a descendant of one of the old Dutch Governors. This merchant did a large business, and added to the wealth of the city. The city will not let him starve, but will feed and home him for a few months, and then find him, free of cost, a pauper's coffin and a grave.

There are many in the same situation at this hour. I personally know of such.

It is a black shame to merchants that it is so. The Chamber of Commerce of this city is a remarkable body of men. It is getting quite democratic, and they are extending their admission to everybody who buys or sells, whether it be ships, tea cargoes, old rags, or clams. The members offer *resolutions* upon every subject. At one meeting, they pass a resolution, thanking the Arctic Ocean for something that it has done. At the next, they " Resolve to do honor to " John Bright, or Bill Jones, or Jack Ericsson, or Commodore Wilkes, or somebody else. The chamber is eternally recommending somebody, or something to somebody, or " gratefully recognizing," or " placing on record. " The last effort of this kind was on Wednesday last, when they pitched into the " Monitor " as follows :

Resolved, That the floating battery " Monitor " deserves to, and will be forever mentioned with gratitude and admiration.

If the " Monitor " after surviving the hard whacks of the " Merrimac " can survive the soft soap of the Chamber of Commerce, it will stand up against any thing. Certainly, the coolest thing that was ever done by any outside corporation, was passing such resolutions as the following :

Resolved, That the Chamber of Commerce, expect that the Government of the United States will make to Captain Ericsson such suitable return for his services as will evince the gratitude of a great nation.

Resolved, That a copy of these resolutions, duly certified, be forwarded to Captain Ericsson and to the President of the United States.

" The Chamber *expects* that the President &c., " *is good*.

There is a report in town that the private Secretary

of the President was ordered to telegraph to the Chamber of Commerce to mind its own business. If John Smith, who was made a member of the Chamber of Commerce last week, pleases, I would suggest, that the next time the body meets, he should offer the following resolutions :

Resolved, That the Chamber of Commerce of the State of New York gratefully recognize, and desire to place on record, their profound sense of the obligations under which they rest to former merchants in this city, and who are now in the Alms House at Blackwell's Island, or in more desperate fortunes and worse off than if they were there.

Resolved further, That the five principal stereotyped speakers of this Chamber be appointed a Committee to seek out such cases — to buy old clothes for them — to provide cheap but respectable lodging for the said Old Merchants at the Globe Hotel, price seven shillings per week, or one shilling per night, and that arrangements be made for a free lunch in Chatham street for old broken down merchants generally ; and that the President of the United States be requested to appropriate some part of the $150,000,000 raised to " carry on the war," to the support of some of these Old Merchants, who have contributed in former years to make New York City so imperial, so great, and so wealthy, that she is now able to bear the burden of these millions while they are without a cent in their pockets.

Resolved further, That a permanent fund be established for the support of Old Merchants, by this Chamber of Commerce, we individually bearing in mind that by the Providence of God, some of us, in our old age, may be reapers in the field that we now benevolently sow for others.

Merchants of other years since that Chamber was established, in 1770, have seen most striking changes.

Misfortunes may come to all. It is possible for the richest to become poor. Astor may fill a plain pine box, if God so wills it. Neither Mr. Astor, nor any other rich man, would feel the loss of a few dollars appropriated to the relief of unfortunate, but honest, deserving merchants, who may become poor, helpless, and — beggars, in this great mart of commerce, where they once were princes. Sailors have their " Sailor's Retreats," or " Snug Harbors. " There are " Blind Asylums," there are " Deaf and Dumb Institutions," there are " Orphan Asylums," there are " Mad Houses," — " Asylums for Lying-in Women, " " Associations for the Relief of Aged and Indigent Females," for " Colored Orphans," " Homes for Indigent Christian Females," etc. There are hospitals for men and for women. There is a " Society for the Relief of Destitute Children of Seamen," and there is a home for the broken-down prostitute in the Magdalen societies, but no home provided for the once worthy but now poverty-stricken old merchant, and his loved ones.

If the Chamber of Commerce should build a palace for its broken-down ones, God will bless it. Dying old merchants and their families will bless it. It will be a practical deed. It will be caring for its own glorious list. It will be a deed worth recording by men and by angels in 1862.

The Chamber of Commerce of the city of New York ought to be respected throughout the world. The way it goes on now, makes its proceedings as tasteless as dishwater, and its " thanks " and receptions as common as at cheap eating houses.

I glory in the probable fact, that when " Walter Barrett, Clerk," goes to his grave, the newspapers that publish his obituary may speak of him as one of the exceptions to Chamber of Commerce lions, and say " Mr. Barrett was never ' honored,' ' noticed,' ' forever mentioned,' ' resolutionized,' or ' received,' by the Chamber of Commerce among the promiscuous mass of 1862 who were, and consequently passed through the world without being rendered supremely ridiculous. "

CHAPTER XXXIII.

It would be a very difficult matter to find a name more famed in mercantile annals in this city for the last one hundred years, than that of Aspinwall. Old John Aspinwall — father of Gilbert & John Aspinwall, a famous mercantile house in this city in 1790, was a sea captain. He commanded vessels out of this port long before the Revolutionary War. He was made a member of the Marine Society, April 13, 1772, but he had been a master of a vessel long before that. He was also in mercantile business, and he owned considerable real estate. In 1761, the Colonial Legislature that then met in this city, passed a law that all buildings to be erected after 1766 in New York, south of the Fresh Water (below Duane street,) should be of stone or brick, covered with slates or tiles. Such materials could not be had in sufficient quantities, and so the time was extended to 1768, when it was finally extended to 1774. After that date, no wooden buildings were to be erected, nor any houses to be covered with shingles, in what is now First, Second, Third, and part of the Fourth and Sixth Wards. The law was beheld with such horror, that the citizens applied to the Legislature to have it suspended. It was not granted. Three thousand then signed a petition to the Governor, May 2, 1774.

The list of names is headed by John Aspinwall.   It was
the most funny petition ever got up.   They had never
had any very large fires in the city, but two years later
a fire broke out that destroyed 500 buildings, including
Trinity Church, of which this same John Aspinwall
was vestryman from 1756 to 1760.   The petitioners
stated in the most affecting terms, that if no wooden
buildings were allowed to be put up, and nothing but
brick or stone, with slate or tiles on the roof, there
would be fearful times in the city.   " Useful members
of society will be unable to pay their just debts, the
wives and families of many will become burdensome to
the city, and jails will be filled with objects of the
greatest compassion, viz : men willing to extricate themselves by their daily labor from which they are prevented by this grievous law."   It seems incredible that sensible men would have so thought not quite a hundred
years ago.

Captain John Aspinwall married late in life, then settled down, and became the father of six children.   He
bought a country seat and mansion at Flushing, L. I.,
and there he assisted mainly to erect a church.   His
sons were Gilbert, William and John.   He had three
daughters.   He died about 1779.   His youngest son,
John, was born about a month after his father died.

One daughter married Abijah Hammond, a great
man in this city, in the Revolution, and afterward.   He
owned a large quantity of land on this island, and ought
to have been worth more than Astor.   Taxes and assess-
ments were high, and his tracts were unproductive.   He
owned nearly all of that part of the city called Greenwich.   He sold a large portion of his real estate at auction to pay taxes, and Astor bought it.   He has a son
living in this city, I believe.

Another daughter married Colonel Platt, a revolutionary officer.

There was a third daughter, but I do not know who she married.

Gilbert Aspinwall lived at 29 William street in 1790, and next year formed a partnership with Nehemiah Rogers, under the firm of Rogers & Aspinwall. Gilbert, at that time was ensign of a military company in town. In 1794, Gilbert took into partnership his brother, John, and they did business at No. 186 Queen street, under the firm of Gilbert & John Aspinwall. They were heavy importers as well as wholesale jobbers of dry goods, and all importers in early New York had to be, for even the importer could not sell over a case of goods at a time, and more frequently had to sell by the piece. They also did a large general commission business, and received consignments of goods from foreign ports, as well as domestic merchandise. They were large purchasers of domestic produce for foreign account, and the old house shipped abroad largely on their own account. They owned several ships ; also after the brothers parted, each owned vessels. Gilbert owned the ship " Aristomines," about 350 tons burthen. She traded direct to St. Petersburg. Gilbert and John did the business for some years of a large house in St. Petersburg, sold Russian goods to the extent of $100,000 per annum, and never made a bad debt for the foreign house. In those days, and down to 1814, the great merchants of New York, never kept a guarantee account. They sold the goods for the owner, and they ran the risk, not the sellers. They did the best possible. The losses finally became so severe to the foreign houses who consigned merchandise to this port, that they proposed that the seller should guarantee all such sales and charge therefor

a guarantee commission of 2½ per cent. The old system developed great integrity in the commission merchant. John Aspinwall also owned vessels. He was
for making money rapidly. One of his vessels was the
brig " Blooming Rose. " In the war, she went into
the French business, and cleared $20,000 in one trip.
Gilbert was plain, methodical, and extremely prudent.
John was more venturesome, and a very generous man.

In 1795, when Queen was changed to Pearl, the
number was 207. Until 1800 the brother Gilbert lived
over his store. That year he moved to No. 80 Greenwich street, and the store to 216 Pearl street. In 1803,
Gilbert lived at 2 Beaver street, corner of Broadway,
and there he remained until he died in 1819. Gilbert
was in many of the leading financial corporations as a
director, and among others he was in the Eagle Fire
Insurance Company, and also he was a director in 1805,
of the Northern and Western Canal Company. He
was in the Ocean Insurance Company. He was a Governor of the New York Hospital in 1799, and in 1819,
when he died in that office.

In 1812, the two brothers dissolved partnership.
John kept the old store, and Gilbert a year or two afterwards took his son John M. into partnership, under
the firm of G. Aspinwall & Son. His place of business
was at 3 Coenties slip, and afterwards at 98 Pearl street.
When Gilbert died, John M. continued the business at
the same place, but resided at 26 Whitehall street. In
those days, Whitehall street was the residence of some
of the most noted merchants. Jonathan Goodhue resided on the corner of Pearl and Whitehall for many
years. Many suppose that this Whitehall name was
derived from the English Whitehall. It is not so. In
old times, say in 1661, before the capture of the city by

the British, the best house in town was the Governor's. It stood in Water, between Whitehall and Moore streets. It was built by Governor Stuyvesant, of stone, and called the " Governor's House." The water came up to it. It was called the " White Hall " by the people, and this gave the name to the street in after years. John M. only continued business a year or two, and then he died in 1829. He married a Miss Winthrop, a daughter of Francis B. Winthrop. The second son was named Thomas Sowers, after his old grandfather the captain — his mother's father. He was a young man of uncommon promise. After he graduated from college, he went to study law with the eminent Slosson, at 48 Pine street. He continued there until he died in 1813, aged twenty-one.

Another son was named James Scott Aspinwall, after old James Scott, who had married the sister of Mr. Gilbert Aspinwall. He was a Scotchman, did a large business in Washington street, and lived at 102 Greenwich street. He was a great friend of Robert Lenox. He was a son of James Scott who did business in this city as early as 1784, under the firm of James Scott & Co. All of these Scotts belonged to the St. Andrew's Society. Old James joined in 1784, and young James in 1801. James S. married one of the accomplished and beautiful Miss Maxwells. There were three sisters. Their father, Dr. Maxwell, was a celebrated physician in Scotland when he died. His widow, an accomplished lady, came out to New York city. One daughter married George Douglass, who died a short time ago, a man of large property. Another daughter married Mr. Rogers. Mrs. Maxwell is still living, but a very aged lady.

The son, James S. Aspinwall, was regularly bred in

a South street counting-room, but in 1830 went into the drug business with Wm. L. Rushton, who had started in 1828, at No. 81 William street, between Liberty and Maiden Lane. The new house was Rushton & Aspinwall. For years the concern did an immense business, both wholesale and retail. The largest wholesale store was in William street. At one time there was a retail branch at No. 110 Broadway, and another under the Astor House. I think the partnership between Rushton & Aspinwall was not dissolved until 1843, and Mr. Aspinwall, old Gilbert's son, kept the wholesale store No. 86 William street, which had been built for the firm by old Mr. Post, the owner of the property. There the wholesale store has been kept until now. He was in that thirty-one or thirty-two years. A more methodical man or merchant never existed. I do not think he was ever sick or absent a day from his business from that cause since he commenced it. William Hegeman, who has founded several drug stores, was brought up by the old house.

G. & J. Aspinwall received consignments of cotton from every part of the South. James Scott was in the same business. He had a country seat on Long Island. He had no children. Rufus King had a place in his vicinity. Miss Aspinwall (Mrs. Scott) had an immense cat that she was very fond of, and exhibited it to visitors. She only died a short time ago, aged eighty-six years.

The concerns of G. & J. Aspinwall were as methodical as a clock. All the Old Merchants of the time used to have what they called *files*. They were made of thick pasteboard, neatly covered, and about the size of a half-sheet of foolscap. A little brass wire ran through this pasteboard, and had a sharp point with a hook.

These hung up on nails ; and were very neatly labelled " Bills Paid," " Memorandums," " Bills of Lading Inward," " Bills of Lading Outward." These were neatly backed by the head clerk or partner. The stationers kept them of every variety and pattern. It is many years since I have seen a genuine one, the same seen sixty or eighty years ago. I suppose there are families who possess these relics, but they must be very rare.

At the time Gilbert lived over his store, at No. 207 Pearl, in 1796 — '7, he was a prominent member of a Society, called " The Friendly Club." In those days there was not the promiscuous dissipation that there is now. There were no frightfully bad liquors either. Men of standing — young or old — drank freely, and thought no harm of it : but they drank at each other's houses, or at some famous resort, like Baker's Tavern in Wall street.

Now, this Friendly Club to which I have alluded, met in rotation at the house of the members every Tuesday evening. If it was in winter, refreshments were served, or could be had from the side-board — wines, metheglin, cider, cakes, hickory nuts and apples. They were an intellectual sort of people in those days. The member who received his friends at his house, had to read a passage from some author, in order to lead conversation into a particular channel. All form was rejected. As soon as the host for the evening had read a passage, every one took turns in talking about it. It kept up for some years until after Washington's death, when the members of the Friendly Club began to take sides with the Republican and Federal parties, headed by the elder Adams and Jefferson, and they got wrangling, and eventually broke up. Among the members of the Friendly Club was William Dunlap, the historian, who then managed the new theatre (Park). There was James Kent the Recorder, Charles Brockden Brown, the author of " Wieland," W. W. Woolsey, his brother George Muirnson Woolsey, Dr. Samuel M. Mitchell, William Johnson, Anthony Bleeker, Dr. Edward Miller, John McVickar, Dr. Elihu H. Smith. He died during the yellow fever of 1798, and was carried to the grave by a few of the club, when the pestilence had become so fearful that everybody who could quit New York had done so, and no persons were seen in the streets except such as were engaged in burying dead people. Gilbert Aspinwall did not leave his business or his house. He had the fever in 1795, and consequently, in after years, when the fever prevailed in 1798, 1803 and 1805, he never feared it. Gilbert Aspinwall in 1768 married Ann, a daughter of Captain Thomas Sowers, one of the New York sea captains of the olden time. Besides the sons I have named,— John M., Thomas Sowers, and James Scott, he had three daughters. Elizabeth S. married John Van Buren, a large merchant in Washington street, thirty-five years ago. He was in the flour trade, and also owned a distillery. He resided in the old Beaver street mansion owned by Gilbert Aspinwall, and where he had lived so long.

The Van Burens moved out to Ohio some years ago, and have quite a numerous family. She is still alive. Rebecca, the second daughter, married the celebrated Dr. Francis E. Berger, the celebrated French physician in this city from 1825. He and his family are now in Paris.

Sarah, a younger daughter, married Thomas Irving, of the well known house of Thomas Irving & Co.

The second son of old Captain John Aspinwall, William, died early in life. He left but one child, a daughter. She married the well known David Hadden, an

eminent merchant before 1810, and many years afterwards. His descendants keep up the firm of Hadden & Co.
yet. David Hadden was one of the most respected men
in this city. He was president of the St. Andrew's Society many years, and a great favorite with the Scotch
people in the town. He was a prudent, careful man.

John Aspinwall, the youngest brother of Gilbert
married Miss Howland, a sister of Gardner G. & S. S.
Howland. They had several children. One was William H. Aspinwall, the founder of Aspinwall city.
Another son was G. Woolsey, another, John Lloyd As-
pinwall. William H. married Anna Breck of Bristol,
Delaware. Her father was a member of Congress from
Pennsylvania, and she was adopted by a Mrs. Lloyd,
from whom she received a fortune of $70,000. Her
money was invested in the building No. 57 Wall street.
William H. has one son named J. Lloyd Aspinwall, who
is at the present moment one of the firm of Howland &
Aspinwall, the great house founded by his father.
Another son is at present in Gambier College, Ohio.
His name is John A. He is studying for the ministry.
The oldest daughter of W. H. married Renwick, the
architect — a son of Professor Renwick of this city.
He has others.

George Woolsey Aspinwall, another son of old merchant John, was bought up by G. G. & S. Howland.
He went to Philadelphia, and formed the house of Pope
& Aspinwall. He married Miss Hare, the daughter of
the celebrated Dr. Hare, and a great belle in her day.
He is dead. John Lloyd Aspinwall, another brother,
was once a partner in the house of Howland & Aspinwall. He married Miss Breck, a sister of Mrs. W. H. Aspinwall. He retired from business, and lives in a magnificent country seat upon the banks of the North river,

15

and his brother William II. also has a superb seat near
Tarrytown. Mr. Read of Charleston, S. C., married
another Miss Breck.

Beside these sons, John Aspinwall had three daughters — Margaret, who married Doctor Hodge, of Philadelphia ; Emily Phillip, who married Edward John
Woolsey, a son of George Muirison Woolsey ; and
Mary Rebecca, who married a son of James Roosevelt,
of the Isaac Roosevelt family.

W. H. Aspinwall had been brought up in the house
of G. G. & S. S. Howland, his uncles. They gave him
an interest in the business, and he signed the name of
the firm as early as 1830 or 1831. He received twenty
per cent. of the commission account. He became an
open partner, under the name of Howland & Aspinwall,
about 1837. At that time the two old Howlands went
out, leaving about $150,000 each in cash as special part-
ners. William Edgar Howland, a son of G. G., was
one of the general partners, W. H. Aspinwall the other.
William H. was the engineer of the house. When he
went out of the house, his brother John Lloyd became
a partner, with Mr. Comstock. It would require a volume to give any idea of the mercantile career of W. H.
Aspinwall, and yet he is, comparatively speaking, quite
a young man. His father lived until 1848 or 1849, at
60 Bleecker street. The latter years of his life he was
a broker in Wall street. His wife died a few years ago.
He never did much business as a broker, though he was
greatly respected.

A large drug house, like that of Rushton & Aspinwall, with their wholesale store at one point and their
retail stores in the most prominent parts of the city, must
have had a great many young men with them. I think
the only one with the old house soon after it first start-

ed was William Hegeman. I can recollect when he was a smart, active boy in William street, not over twelve years of age. After Rushton & Aspinwall dissolved, I think Mr. Aspinwall kept on the wholesale store in William street, and Rushton the retail drug store on Broadway, under the firm of Rushton & Co. Mr. Rushton took in a Mr. Clarke who had formerly been a partner in the firm of Clarke & Saxton, in Broadway. Shortly after, Rushton died. I think at that time Mr. Hegeman, who was the man of the business, was a partner of Rushton & Co., and afterwards Rushton, Clarke & Co. The stores were at 110 and 273 Broadway, and 10 Astor House, in 1850. Clarke was no druggist. Then the firm was Clarke, Hegeman & Co. Then Clarke left, and his son came in under the firm of Hegeman, Clarke & Co., with stores at 165, 273, 511 and 756 Broadway. Later it became Hegeman & Co., occupying the above stores, except changing 273 to 399 Broadway. I believe the company consists of Henry King, who has charge at 399 Broadway, corner of Walker, and of Ray B. Easterbrook, who is at 511, under the St. Nicholas. They have an establishment for making soda water, that supplies the whole city.

Mr. Hegeman himself is not only the best druggist in the city, but he is a man of great wealth and refinement. He has his house filled with pictures of great merit, and what is more meritorious, he painted them himself.

In this chapter I have commenced at the fountain head —when New York had but its 12,000 inhabitants— with old Captain Aspinwall, of 1762, down to the present day. Certainly but for the old captain, there would have been no Howland & Aspinwall, with their ships and trade all over the world, or the drug house of As-

pinwall, and the half dozen well kept drug stores on
Broadway, of Hegeman & Co.

The family of Moses, and the other brothers Rogers,
were originally from Connecticut, where they resided
before the war, but some of them taking part in the favor of the Crown and against the rebellion of 1776,
went away to the British Provinces.

There was a Moses Rogers who was a captain of a
ship out of this port, and was the commander of the
steamship "Savannah" that sailed from this city in
March, 1819. She went to Savannah, Ga. She left
Savannah on the 25th of May, and arrived at Liverpool
on the 20th June. She left there 23d July for St. Pe-
tersburgh, moored off Cronstadt the 5th of September,
left there the 10th October and arrived back at Savannah on the 30th November. She did not meet with a
single accident. This was really the commencement of
Atlantic steam navigation. In April 22d and 23d, 1838,
British steamers the "Sirius" and the "Great Western"
arrived in this city. This was not the *first* successful
experiment, although the British officers were loaded
with honors. A New Yorker, Moses Rogers, is entitled
to the real fame. He stopped five days with his steamship "Savannah" at Copenhagen, and four days at Ar-
undel, in Norway. She was visited by the Emperor of
Russia, Alexander the First, and also by Bernadotte,
King of Sweden. Each made Captain Moses Rogers a
present, as a token of their approbation of his skill and
enterprise. The "Savannah" afterwards went to Con-
stantinople, where Captain Moses Rogers also received
a present from the Sultan. The present from the Emperor of Russia was a silver tea-kettle — the first noticed
generator and condensor of steam.

I regret to hear of the death of Philip Dater, Esq.,

of the house of Daters & Co., in this city. Mr. Dater had been connected with the grocery trade for some forty years, formerly as one of the firm of Lee, Dater & Miller, and at the time of his death at the head of the firm of Daters & Co. Long in business, he was always noted for his nicety in all business relations. He was a man full of charity to the poor, as many now living can testify, and peculiarly genial in his social relations. We gave a lengthy sketch of him in the first series.

CHAPTER XXXIV.

Thomas Eddy was one of the commissioners appointed March 26, 1796, to build one of the State prisons in New York. His associates were John Watts, Matthew Clarkson, Col. Isaac Stoutenburgh and John Murray. They went to work soon after their appointment, and November 27, 1797, they had completed, ready to receive prisoners, the New York prison, known as Newgate. Eddy and his associates surrendered their powers to the Inspector, February 15, 1799. A portion of the old prison is still standing. It was found totally inadequate to the purpose for which it was erected, the reform *of* offenders, and for which Thomas Eddy — his heart overflowing with humanity — was anxious. It was crowded. In 1816, a new prison was commenced at Auburn. It worked so well, that on the 9th of March, 1825, a new set of commissioners — Stephen Allen, George Tibbits and Samuel M. Hopkins — were appointed to build a new prison at Sing Sing, and sell the old one in New York, to defray the expenses of the new one.

Mr. Eddy commenced business as a merchant about 1780. His parents were Irish. His father was largely engaged in the shipping business until 1766, when he died. Young Eddy was born in Philadelphia in 1728.

Four years after the death of his father, his mother apprenticed him to the tanning business at Burlington, N. J. He only remained there a couple of years, and then went back to Philadelphia. When the British evacuated the city, he came to New York, 1779, whence his brother Charles had just sailed for London. He was then twenty-one years old, and had $96 capital in his pocket.

Mr. Eddy when he reached this city, boarded at the house No. 57 Wall street, that I have described as the residence of Daniel McCormick, in the chapter where I spoke of that celebrated merchant. Mr. Eddy commenced business in this city in a funny way; he had not the first rudiments of a mercantile education; he knew nothing about it. However, with his little capital, he used to go down into Coffee House Slip, where most of the auction sales were conducted. There he would buy a small lot and resell it; or first get a sample of the goods the day previous to a sale, and with this sample he would go to merchants and dealers and ascertain what they would give him for such an article. If the offer was more than the goods sold for at the auction, he would become the purchaser. Where there is a will, there is a way. He used to advise, too, with the shrewd old fellows who boarded where he did. He made the most of his ninety-six dollars' capital. Money never produced such an interest before. It was living by mercantile wit and many thousands of persons have got on the same way. It is about as genteel a mode of getting a living as collecting advertisements from merchants for a newspaper.

He had not been many months in New York, doing the business of buying at auction and selling again, before he fell in with another smart young man named

Benjamin Sykes. His brother, Charles, returned from Ireland in 1780, where he had made many business connections, and large consignments of provisions, linens, etc., were sent over with him by merchants in Cork and Belfast. The three then formed a house under the firm of Eddy, Sykes & Co. Sykes was an Englishman ; and although he was not very active, yet he brought to the new house many valuable connections, and the concern did a large business. The two brothers Eddy belonging to this house, had another brother in Philadelphia whose name was George.

They made a splendid thing after Lord Cornwallis surrendered at Yorktown, by agreeing to supply him and the British and other foreign troops who had been captured, with money. This was done with the consent and approbation of General Washington. It was a sort of *kiteing* business. George Eddy, in Philadelphia, drew drafts on Eddy, Sykes & Co. in New York. These drafts he got cashed, and paid the proceeds over to the paymaster of the British forces for use among the British prisoners at Lancaster, Pa. He put drafts on the British paymaster in New York into the hands of George Eddy, who remitted the same to Eddy, Sykes & Co. On these transactions, amounting to millions of dollars, Sir Henry Clinton, the British commander, paid them six per cent. commission. This was so good a start in one partnership, that Thomas Eddy determined to try another partner. He had loved a pretty girl named Hannah Hartshorne. In 1782 he married her. The ceremony was performed in the old Quaker meeting house that stood in Crown street, north side, half way between Broadway and the little alley back of Nassau street. Grant Thornburn used it afterwards as a seed store. He bought it, and the deed for the premises speaks of it as being " outside the wall of the city," meaning of course, Wall street. Many will remember that when the Manhattan Company's pipes were laid, and the men were digging in Broadway, at the junction of Wall, they dug up the posts of the city gate. It was built in 1696 was this old Quaker meeting house. Mr. Eddy was a Quaker. So was his father, the Irishman, who came over, being the first Irish Quaker I ever heard of.

The result of this marriage with the pretty Quakeress, Hannah Hartshorne, was a son, who was born on the 14th of March, 1783. He was named John Hartshorne Eddy, after the father of his mother. Another son was Thomas Eddy, Jr.

Previous to 1783, and before the Americans got possession in November of that year, Mr. Eddy went to Philadelphia, and went into business with his brother George. Charles had gone to Europe and settled in London, where he did a very heavy business, until Thomas & George Eddy bought tobacco largely, and ruined themselves and their brother in London. It was a general smash up.

In 1790 he came on to New York, and opened business as an insurance broker, being about the first of that kind that started. He made money rapidly. In 1791, when the public debt of the United States was funded, he speculated heavily and coined money. At that time he lived at 184 Queen street (277 Pearl.) He left off operating as an insurance broker, but he took risks as an underwriter, and was very successful. In 1792, he was elected a director in the Mutual Insurance Company, of which I have said so much. Many of our principal men were in it. I am inclined to think it was the first time he ever had his name figuring in the papers as an

15*

officer of a corporation. It was seen often enough afterwards, and for many years, until he died in September, 1827, lacking one year of threescore and ten. Wherever Mr. Eddy could do any good, he went to work with all his heart and soul. In 1793, he was one of the members to receive donations for " The Society for the Relief of Distressed Prisoners." That year, too, he was elected one of the Governors of the New York Hospital. In 1794, he was made Secretary to the Board of Governors ; he held it eleven years. He was treasurer of the same from 1808 to 1818 — ten years. He was vice-president to 1822 — four years; and he was president of the Board of Governors until he died in 1827 — five years more. He was thirty-four years in harness, and died in the harness. But for him the Hospital would have been dead broke a dozen times. He could out-lobby at Albany any other man alive. Members respected him, and what he proposed was listened to and acted upon.

Of course, he was one of the very first to form the " Society for Promoting the Manumission of Slaves, and for protecting such as have been or may be liberated," and of which John Jay was president in 1786. In 1797, Mr. Eddy became chairman of the corresponding committee of that society.

He was one of the directors of the Western Inland Navigation Company, a corporation that broke down.

He was very active in the great work of the Erie Canal. He was also one of the originators of the savings banks of this city. Few of the old school merchants were more useful. He died in 1827.

This is the first opportunity that I have had to correct a few items in reference to an article about the Waltons that appeared in the first series. The family came from Norfolk, in England, and settled at first on Long Island. I spoke of Robert Walton, who was a mayor. I got it from Goodrich's Pictures of New York, generally a very reliable book. He so states it, page 48. He meant Robert Walters. The first of the Walton name of note was William Walton. He married Mary Santford, in 1698, and died in 1747, aged 82. His wife died in 1768, in the ninetieth year of her age. It was this William Walton who purchased the property in Pearl street, running to the water, and established the ship yard. His name appears in the subscription list for finishing the steeple of Trinity Church, in 1711, and for enlarging the church in 1736. He had two sons, Jacob and William. Jacob married Mary Beekman, and had a large family. One of the daughters married David Johnston, of Annandale, Dutchess Co., N. Y. Another married Lewis Morris, Jr., of Morrisania. Jacob died in 1749, aged 46 years. His wife died in 1782.

William Walton, the old New Yorker, called *Boss Walton*, was not a bachelor. He married Cornelia Beekman, a sister of Mary, but had no children. He died in 1768, at the age of 62. His wife survived him several years, and died about 1780. The number of his house was 328, and not 326. He devised it to his nephew, William, for life, with remainder to his eldest son in fee.

The printer made me say that the ship yards existed in 1796. I wrote 1696. They could not have existed in 1796, because the land from Water to Front streets was filled up long before that. The old store at 243 Front street was built about the commencement of the present century. William Walton (3) died in the family mansion in 1796, in the sixty-fifth year of his age.

His nephew William succeeded in the possession under the will of his great uncle. He never married, and died in 1806, in his forty-seventh year. He was social and hospitable, and much regretted by his many relatives and friends. His father founded the Marine Society.

James DeLancy Walton, his brother, was very far from morose. He was genial with those who knew him, and liked to talk of old times. He had a large circle of relatives and old friends, by whom he was much esteemed, and, not being in business, he confined himself to them. He was a vestryman and churchwarden for many years of St. George's Church, and a warm friend of its rector, the late Dr. Milnor. He died in November, 1834, in the seventy-third year of his age.

Gerard Walton was never in the British Navy. He lived at No. 328 Pearl street, and died in 1821, in his eightieth year. He was a bachelor.

The family vault was in Trinity churchyard, and the interments have generally been made there. Mrs. Roosevelt was the daughter of Abraham Walton, the brother of William, Jacob and Gerard.

Jacob Walton was the youngest of the children of William Walton. He entered the British navy when twelve years old, and saw some hard fighting in the West Indies, in 1780, as a midshipman in the " Intrepid," 64. In his subsequent services he saw every quarter of the world. He attained the rank of Rear Admiral of the Red, and died in this city (where he had resided for upwards of twenty years) in April, 1844, having very nearly completed his seventy-seventh year. He had a numerous family. The Rev. Dr. William Walton, who married a daughter of Dr. Seabury, is a son. One daughter married Sylvester L. L. Ward, and another is married to John G. Storm.

I mentioned John S. Winthrop, Jr., as a clerk with Prime, Ward & King, and as having married a lady in North Carolina. I should have mentioned that he was dead. James and Edward N. Strong, who are aids to General Foster, with the Burnside expedition, mention in their letters home that they saw Mr. Winthrop's house in Newbern, N. C.

Philip Dater, one of our old, respected merchants, and of whom I gave a lengthy sketch, died about two weeks ago, of congestion of the lungs. He was well and attended to his business on Thursday, but was taken sick on Friday, and never left his room after that day. Mr. Dater was one of the oldest merchants of New York, having been in the wholesale grocery trade upwards of thirty-five years. He was esteemed as an honorable and upright man. His benevolent and charitable disposition will cause his loss to be severely felt by many who were recipients of his bounty.

I have received this following letter :

NEW YORK, *April* 2, 1862.
WALTER BARRETT : In reading your " Old Merchants " in the Leader of Saturday last, I was much struck by your story of the decayed merchant, now enjoying the hospitalities of the alms-house. On inquiry I find that I know the man, and that it is even so.

You argue justly, I think, in this matter : the soldier, the sailor, the shipmaster, the mechanic, all have a harbor, a home, a rest, for their days of poverty — and provided, too, by their class ; but the *poor* merchant must find his bread among the very scum of society — the depraved, the debauched, the vagabondized. This

should not be ; he is intelligent, educated, refined ; in
fact, has all the attributes that drive the sting of poverty
deeper into his heart of hearts, and makes his existence
a daily death compared with the suffering of the hungry hod carrier, who eateth and is satisfied.

The merchant has made this city great, and more
than any other, our country strong. Though he may
be in the alms house, he has done his work, and it re-
maineth to our benefit. The work he failed in, he suggested, started, and it is being carried out by other
hands. Surely, the debris of the " man on change,"
the " merchant prince " we talk of, may in his reverse of
fortune have something better than city charity and a
pauper's grave.

We have unquestionably in this large city a great
many most excellent men who are anxious to do good,
and to spend a portion of their gifts in the amelioration
of the sufferings of their fellow creatures ; these men
only need to know, to do. I think, Mr. Barrett, I can
point my finger to at least a dozen such, whom, some
third of a century ago, in the days of down-townism,
were the active, now the retired, merchants of our city
— and its glory, too, let me tell you — for the article
has, I fear, depreciated in the market.

A Merchant's Home — it sounds well. A few thousands would start it ; a yearly contribution (with right
of access) keep it alive. The hard times I consider no
bar ; the liberal are more so in times of adversity. I
would suggest a plan, but think it best to hear what
others think first ; and perhaps you may elicit information from them by printing this ; if otherwise, consign
it to your waste paper basket. Yours &c.,

The name of the above merchant has been left with
me. He is one of the most respectable in the city.

CHAPTER XXXV.

In the chapter relating to the Tardy family, I stated that John A. Tardy was for a long time a clerk with the late Joseph Bouchaud, who was a great merchant in his day, and did an immense amount of business with France, Mexico, Campeachy, and South America. He came to this country about 1805, having been sent for when quite a lad by Joseph Thebaud. He formerly resided at Nantes. Joseph Thebaud wrote to his correspondent in France to send him a competent and reliable young man to take charge of the interior department of his counting-house. Joseph Bouchaud was the young gentleman selected, and possessing testimonials of the highest character in his native country, arrived in this city in 1805, being then twenty-two years of age.

Joseph Thebaud, his patron, came to the United States near 1793. He was the agent of the French East India Company, and representative of several French capitalists and merchants. He first settled in Boston, remained there a short time, then changed his residence to New Haven, where he became acquainted with and married Miss Le Breton, a daughter of a highly respectable Martinique gentleman of that place, and from thence came to the city of New York, where he permanently established himself in mercantile affairs, and up to his death remained one of the leading merchants of this city. He resided at No. 12 Beckman street, and had his counting-room opposite, at No. 11. He possessed what in those days was esteemed a magnificent country place, situate where Orchard street now runs. The old family mansion, built of brick, situate on the westerly side of that street, near Rivington, still stands, although somewhat modernized. Could it speak, what glorious tales it could tell of the hospitality, the festive scenes, and the old French regime style its four walls have witnessed! Old Joseph Thebaud was a great botanist and passionately fond of flowers. He possessed magnificent green-houses, at that time the wonder of the town. He took great pride in showing his flowers, and was the intimate friend of old Dr. Hosack, whose taste in this respect was similar. His neighbors were David Dunham, Cornelius Dubois, and the Stuyvesants. He spent a great deal of his time in his green-houses, to which is ascribed his early death, which occurred in the year 1811, aged 45. He was a very benevolent, kind-hearted man, and was the originator of the French Benevolent Society of this city, and was a leading director and friend to the old Mechanics' Bank.

At the time of his death the newspapers of this city teemed with flattering and highly eulogistic obituary notices of him.

Previous to his death he recommended his wife and children to the constant care and watchfulness of Mr. Bouchaud, entrusting them to his protection, and to that counsel and support which he knew he could rely upon their receiving from him.

He left a very large estate, and appointed Joseph Bouchaud, his clerk, together with Mr. John S. Roulet, his executors. His children at the time of his death, being all minors, Bouchaud immediately took charge of the estate, continued the business of his late employer, and married his widow. In the meantime, two of Joseph Thebaud's sons, John and Edward, returned to New York, having completed their education at the Moravian school at Bethlehem, Penn, (which still exists), and found handsome fortunes awaiting them. Edward Thebaud, of industrial habits, entered the house of Gardner G. Howland, principally to acquire a knowledge of business, where after remaining some years, Joseph Bouchaud, wishing to increase his capital, made propositions to him as well as to his brother John J., which were accepted, and in 1820, the house of Bouchaud & Thebaud was formed. Mr. Bouchaud became acquainted with a gentleman named John L. McGregor, of Charleston, S. C., and he introduced Mr. Bouchaud to the South American trade. McGregor settled at Campeachy and Yucatan, and the house and he did a joint business together, purchasing and sending goods from this market, receiving in return specie, log wood, sisal-hemp, goat skins and hides. He also did a large business with Bordeaux, Havre and Marseilles. Up to 1824 the house of Bouchaud & Thebaud was the largest importer of French brandies in the city of New York. They were constant and heavy shippers of goods. In size, Mr. Bouchaud was a very small man, but in bold mercantile operations he was a very large one. He moved his store to No. 37 South street, a great business part of the town for foreign merchants, and at this period his residence was at No. 109 Fulton street, a favorite street for Frenchmen. Edward Thebaud married in 1823 Miss Boisaubin, a daughter of a distinguished French noble exile in this country, a victim to the French Revolution. In 1824, the house was obliged to suspend

payment, having been involved to a large amount by the
failure of Le Seigneur, Alexandre, Frères & Co., of
Havre. After having honorably settled the affairs of
the concern, the partnership of Bouchaud & Thebauds
was dissolved, at which time Mr. Tardy's connection
with the house ceased.

Edward Thebaud, retiring into the country, near his
father-in-law, lived the life of a country gentleman upon
a beautiful estate at Morristown, New Jersey, and
John J. went to Mexico, engaged in some financial
scheme, where he was overtaken with a prevalent disease of that country, and died.

In a short while after, Joseph Bouchaud resumed business on his own account upon a capital of $5,000, loaned
him by his mother-in-law, Madame Le Breton, together
with consignments which were made him to a large
amount by his old and steadfast friend, McGregor, of
Campeachy. By his frugal management, together with
his indomitable perseverance, he again became successful, and with the first fruits of his returning fortune,
paid with interest the loan so kindly made him by his
mother-in-law. At this period, his store was at No. 64
Exchange place, corner of New street. From this time
forward, his business became one of considerable lucra-
tiveness. He afterwards purchased the property 171
Duane street, where he resided until he removed, a few
years before his death, to 258 Fourth street, opposite
Washington Parade Ground. Meanwhile, matters had
remained in *statu quo* with Edward Thebaud, who in
the beginning of the year 1835, wrote to his old partner
and father-in-law, Mr. Bouchaud, representing that from
the increase of his family and the accumulating de-
mands appertaining thereto, he thought of abandoning
his rural life among the blue hills of Jeresy, and once

more embarking in mercantile pursuits. Mr. Bouchaud invited him to an interview, which resulted in his generously tendering him a partnership on an equal footing, which being accepted, led to the re-establishment of the house of Bouchaud & Thebaud, the latter contributing to the capital about $15,000. The new firm continued the business at 64 Exchange place, and afterwards removed to 35 New street.

In about the year 1850 the firm was changed to Bouchaud, Thebaud & Company, having admitted into their firm the eldest son of Edward Thebaud. In 1851, at his new residence in Fourth street, Joseph Bouchaud died. He was an honest, upright man, and endeavored to emulate the virtues and high-toned principles of his benefactor and patron, Joseph Thebaud. He was an active member of the French Benevolent Society, and connected with many of the leading banks of this city, more especially with the National Bank, which was regarded and generally called the Frenchman's Bank.

Mr. Bouchaud had three children, a son and two daughters. The son died of the croup about the time his business troubles commenced. His youngest daughter Celeste married Joseph A. Voisin, a French importing merchant. She has left one son, Joseph A. Voisin, Jr., a student of medicine.

The other sister, Estelle N. Bouchaud, married Victor Arnaud, a French gentleman of Paris.

The other partner, Edward Thebaud, retired from active business shortly after the death of his old partner, and now lives in quiet elegance near the homestead of his wife, in Madison, New Jersey. His old house, under the name of Edward Thebaud's Sons, was continued by two of his sons for some years, when each forming alliances with other mercantile houses in this city, dissol-

ved this old mercantile house which had been in existence since 1796. It is the boast of this establishment,
that since the day of its formation to the day of its dissolution, from old Joseph Thebaud down to Edward
Thebaud's Sons, their word was as good as their bond.

CHAPTER XXXVI.

I have frequently alluded to the old iron mongers, as the hardware merchants were designated until about a half century ago. I mentioned that they frequently had over their doors, on the front of their stores, peculiar signs. One would have an old scythe snath, painted handsomely, and perhaps gilded. Another would have a golden padlock of immense size. That denoted everything for sale, because it locks up everything. Another was a handsaw. The scythe indicated that all sorts of farmers' utensils were kept, as it is only within the recollection of many when agricultural stores have become a specialty in this city. Another sign, and one that many will remember, was a hardware store in Greenwich street. It was an immense long plane, nearly half a foot square, that extended from the third down to the second story. That indicated all sorts of carpenters' tools kept in that particular hardware store. Other signs were equally significant — the " golden tea kettle," " the anvil," as large as life, but made of wood, and painted iron color. About the first of the hardware merchants that had the boldness to move up town, or go above Canal street, were the Delevans.

Forty-two years ago the house of Edward C. Delevan was at 121 Pearl street, and Mr. D. lived at 396

Broadway.   In 1827, Robert J. Delevan opened a hardware store up at 489 Broadway, near Broome street.
The next year, Daniel E. Delevan opened the same
store under his own name.   That was thirty-four years
ago.   Daniel E. had been brought up to the business
by E. C. Delevan, the celebrated temperance benefactor at Albany, who built, and I believe owns the Delevan
House.   He was here several years.   He once did a very
large business.   He had a commercial house in this city,
and one in Birmingham, England.   He did a large business, and was a capital merchant.

When Daniel E. Delevan commenced up town, you
had to pass only a few streets above to find, not a wil-
derness, but a very few houses.   Niblo's garden, with a
boarding house in the centre, occupied the whole of the
block where the Metropolitan Hotel now stands.   Opposite the block there were no buildings.   Collect street
(now Centre) ran up to Grand street, where it connected with Rynders (now Marion) street.   Rynders and
Cross streets had large sluices in the middle, instead of
being elevated, and when there was a freshet the water
rushed down like a small river, and poured over a wall
at the junction of what is now Howard and Centre
streets, forming a complete water-fall.   There were no
buildings above North (Houston) street, on the East
river side.   Thirty-three years ago, too, the city had
not advanced so far in civilization.   In it was the old
Bridewell, the terror of every one who gazed upon it.
In the rear of the City Hall stood Scudder's Museum —
a long building.   The museum that now belongs to
Barnum was kept there, and was only open on Tues-
days and Fridays.

The old debtor's prison cupola loomed up in the Park,
and contained on an average about two hundred un-

fortunate debtors. In these days, if such a barbarous law existed, it would be the few who don't owe money that would have to be locked up — there would not be room for the hundreds of thousands who do owe money. However, locking up was not so close as it might have been. There were jail limits, and these were easily known, because they were lettered on boards, and these were nailed up in all parts of the city on the corners.

There were but seven public school buildings, and the only one down town was at No. 1 Tryon row, corner of Chatham street. That was the time when the solid Fine Arts flourished here. Old honest John Trumbull was alive, and was president of the American Academy of Fine Arts, and Gulian C. Verplanck was vice president. May he live a thousand years longer ! Col. William Gracie was alive then, and next to John Trumbull was John Vanderlyn. The colonel had bought the " Ariadne," and he introduced me then to the artist, and I knew him years after — met him twenty years later, night after night, at the old French coffee house kept by the famous Blin, at No. 9 Warren street. Blin has wilted down to keeping a small cigar store in Hudson near Vandam street, and he who has known and served the cleverest intellects in the country, now sells two cent cigars to the roughs of the Eighth Ward.

I now return to my hardware merchant, Daniel E. Delevan. The merchants are the legitimate monarchs of New York city. They should rule here undisputed, and when I see one of the class step out of the usual beaten, two and two make four tracks, of nearly all of them, and take a position in city affairs, it does me good. I love New York city with all my heart and soul, and I despise the pretentious suburbs in proportion. New

York city has a population to-day of nearly 1,500,000, if she exercised her just rights. Greenpoint, Brooklyn, Williamsburg, Astoria, Flushing, Fort Hamilton, and Long Island generally, are really parts of New York; so is Staten Island; so is Jersey City, Newark, Rahway, Elizabethtown, Saltersville, Hudson City, Bergen, Hoboken, Weehawken, and New York city should stand upon its rights. If these suburbs are not willing to be called New York, and be annexed to New York, then pass a few such laws as these: "Any person living outside of New York, and doing business therein, shall pay $10,000 annually to the said city for the privilege; and any person failing to do so, shall be confined in the state prison. Any person living in any place, city, or town in New Jersey, and coming in the city daily, shall be charged $500 annually for the privilege."

This is the idea. It could be carried out in a thousand shapes, so as to prevent anybody being allowed to live anywhere within twenty miles of New York, unless they were willing to be classed as " New-Yorkers," and give her what is justly her due in the census table. Every true New-Yorker feels keenly upon this subject. I despise all those outside places. I would not live in Brooklyn, Saltersville, or any of those illegitimate suckers upon the teats of New York, if I was presented with a house and barn in either of them. Any place in this region that does not add to the glory of New York, I will have nothing to do with.

After this digression I once more return to Mr. Delevan. For several years Daniel E., did business under his own name. Then he had his brothers Charles H., and Christian S. In 1837, I think the firm was Delevan Brothers, Christian being the partner.

Charles H. was at one time in the Broadway store,

and thereafter he was in a similar business on his own account in Maiden Lane. Probably Charles was one of the most active men in the Whig campaign of 1840, for " Tippecanoe and Tyler too." As a reward for such devotion, " Tyler too " appointed him to the American Consular agency at the beautiful island of St. Thomas. He held it for some years. Since his return he has been in commercial business, but more recently has become deeply interested with insurance agencies.

Daniel E. Delevan is a fair sample of a New Yorker. With an integrity, political, commercial and social, that has never been questioned, Mr. Delevan unites a fine old school personal appearance, that wins with all who approach him.

He has been connected, directly or indirectly, with everything that could add to the strength of the city, or do her honor.

For a long time he was connected with her military matters, and hence his designation of colonel and general. He made a splendid officer.

In politics he has ever held a commanding influential primary position, but used his influence more for the benefit of others than himself.

At one time the Federal government of Mr. Pierce made him naval storekeeper at this port.

Since that time he has received and now holds the important position of city inspector.

For many years he has been connected with the Tammany Society or Columbian Order. We have few more ancient or more useful, and it has numbered among its members some of the first men in the nation.

On several elections Mr. Delevan has been chosen Grand Sachem. I find in former years that much more was published about this society than now. Its Sa-

16

chems had a particular designation. There was the
Sachem of the New York, or Eagle Tribe ; ditto of
the New Hampshire, or Otter Tribe ; ditto of the Massachusetts, or Panther Tribe ; ditto of the Rhode I-
land, or Beaver Tribe ; ditto of the Connecticut, or
Bear Tribe ; ditto of the New Jersey, or Tortoise
Tribe ; ditto Pennsylvania, or Rattlesnake Tribe ; ditto
of the Delaware, or Tiger Tribe ; ditto of the Mary-
land, or Fox Tribe ; ditto of the Virginia, or Deer
Tribe ; ditto of the North Carolina, or Buffalo Tribe ;
ditto of the South Carolina, or Racoon Tribe ; ditto of
the Georgia, or Wolf Tribe, etc.

Mr. Delevan was in mercantile life until within a few
years. He did not leave his hardware store in Broadway until 1850, and for more than one third of a century he has lived in the Eighth Ward. He is a man
any party may be proud of, and in his hands any interests of the city, no matter how important, are perfectly
safe. Few possess his general knowledge of the city
and its interests.

Mr. Daniel E. Delevan was for many years promin-
ently connected with our militia system. He served for
fifteen years in the First Division under Gen, Sandford,
holding the first position of a staff officer — brigade inspector. He was elected major, and afterward was lieutenant colonel and then colonel in the Second Regiment
of Gen. Storms' brigade, and he did active military duty until within the last few years, when the new con-
solidation took place, which rendered him a supernumer-
ary and took him from active service.

Colonel Delevan used to be one of the old Knickerbocker Club. It met in Fulton street, at Stoneall's. It
had among its members such men as Joseph C. Hart.
Levi D. Slamm, who was President of the Club, was

then editing the New York *Daily Plebeian.* Gen. Henry Storms, John J. Cisco, Charles A. Secor, Emanuel B. Hart, and Thomas Jefferson Smith. There were some fine fellows in it, and all New Yorkers. Jo. Hart was a lively person in such a club. He died many years ago, at Santa Cruz, Teneriffe, to which place he had been appointed United States Consul by President Pierce.

Gen. Henry Storms was an old New Yorker, and a merchant. Daniel E. Delevan took an active part in supporting this old military worthy some years ago, when an attempt was made to stop the celebration of Evacuation Day, in this city, on the 25th November. Gen. Sandford, who was an Englishman by birth, wished to abolish it; Gen. Storms, on the contrary, insisted that it should be celebrated by a military parade, and took strong ground for it, going so far as to say that if it was decided not to celebrate the day, he would do it on his own responsibility. There was a great time made. Gen. Storms, however, carried his point, and the day has been celebrated every year since then. The view he took was deemed so patriotic that it was determined to give him a massive silver salver, and two silver pitchers, all appropriately inscribed. There was a grand dinner on the occasson, and I recollect that Col. Delevan made a very happy speech upon the occasion. The Mayor and all the principal people were present, and there was a gay time generally.

The Delevans came from the good old Dutch stock. Their ancestors came out here from North Holland two hundred years ago, and went and settled in Westchester county. Col. Delevan's grandfather fought all through the Revolutionary war, together with his eight brothers, including the father of Col. Delevan. He finally rose to be a colonel, and was afterwards a general in the war of 1812.

There is probably no politician of modern times who has passed through the trying ordeal of party change and fluctuation, who has preserved a greater degree of consistency than that which has marked the career of the Colonel. As a leading member of the Democratic party he is governed by those principles of upright dealing and manly candor that mark his character in private life, and which have established for him a reputation that any man might envy. Had his counsel been listened to at the Charleston Convention, it is more than probable that Horatio Seymour, instead of Abraham Lincoln, would to-day have been President of the United States.

It is as an officer of the City Government that Col. Delevan has made himself conspicuously known to the inhabitants of our city. Without questioning the ability of his predecessor, it is but justice to the Colonel to give him a front rank by pronouncing him one of the most thorough-going and efficient City Inspectors that New York has ever possessed. And this efficiency would have been even greater, were the Department over which he presides, placed solely under his control and management, without being interfered with by outside politicians and managers, the bane of all good government. But we must take the world as it is, and make all due allowance for these political *contre temps* that follow in the wake of office, the necessary consequence of our "peculiar institutions." The Colonel is yet a young man, comparatively speaking, notwithstanding we have placed him under the head of " Old Merchants," of which be it known, he is but a junior member.

CHAPTER XXXVII.

I have never mentioned the name of a prominent old merchant, even incidentally or accidentally, without intending to give, sooner or later, a full sketch of him. In the first series I mentioned among the wealthy contributors to the loan of 1814, Isaac Clason, who loaned to Government $500,000. I have intended to give a complete history of this once eminent merchant. A man who could loan this sum, fifty years ago, was a great merchant — for $100,000 was a greater sum then than a million is now. On one occasion Mr. Clason wished to get a large loan ($200,000, I believe,) in specie, from the Manhattan Bank, to send out in the ship " Francis Henrietta " — which he was fitting out to China — without an endorser. To obtain it, he swore he was worth $750,000.

Originally he was a grocer, and kept his store, " Flour and Grocery," at 14 Albany pier, as early as 1789. His dwelling was in Smith (William) street. He had a clerk named John Duffie at one time. The latter had a clerk named Samuel Tooker. The last started in business on his own account as early as 1798, at 13 Coenties slip, in the very store formerly occupied by Isaac Clason, who moved to No. 51 Broadway. Samuel Tooker did an immense business, and had several clerks. One was Ralph Mead; another was Benjamin Mead. Mr. Tooker lived at No. 3 Bridge street, in an old two-story wooden house, that belonged to Peter Kemble. He afterwards bought a lot and built a fine house at No. 5 Bridge, next door to the house he had in 1802, and first occupied. He occupied the store at 13 Coenties slip until 1816, when he moved to 20 South street.

In 1806 he took in as a partner Benjamin Mead, and the firm was S. Tooker & Co. That house went largely into the privateer business in 1812, as did many other houses of that day. One vessel that he fitted out had a singular career, and I will give a detailed account of her to show how the business was done at the time. Mr. Tooker fitted out a brig called the " Arrow " with fourteen guns. He selected for her commander Captain Conkling, a favorite captain, who had been in the East India trade. The stock was $65,000. The shares were $1,000 each. As soon as it was known that Conkling had charge, they were all taken, for it was known that Captain Conkling's East Indiaman had been captured by the British, and that in the " Arrow " he would do all in his power to injure British commerce and property. The supercargo or purser was to be William Bogardus, who had been a clerk with Mr. Duffie, but had started on his own account in 1800, as a salt merchant, and after a few years failed, in 1808. Mr. Tooker determined to give him a start and chance. Mr. Tooker was the agent who got up the privateer, and if she succeeded would have the selling of her prizes, thus earning large commissions, besides owning the principal shares. Everything looked bright for the privateer " Arrow." She eventually was destined to hit the mark. Just as she was ready to sail, a United States vessel of war discharged her crew. One hundred and twenty of them went at once on board of the " Arrow," that bid fair to do well. Of course the harbor was blockaded closely ; but one dark night the " Arrow " and her gallant captain and brave crew, sailed. Two other privateers left the same night, one named the " Whig," and the other the " Warrior." They returned successful, after some weeks, but the " Arrow " was never heard of from that day until this. Of course she was a total loss. No insurance.

Mr. Tooker was from Newberg. He had no children. He adopted Ellen, a daughter of Henry Laverty, by his first wife. He and Laverty married two sisters named Smith. She always went by the name of Ellen Tooker. She married Joseph Hudson, one of the old importing firm so well known to old New Yorkers as J. & D. Hudson. I think she had two children, a son who married Miss Johnson, and a daughter that married my friend Henry Robinson, a son of Morris Robinson, the famous cashier of the Bank of the United States. His sister, by the way, married Alexander Slidell, brother of the famous John Slidell, now rebel minister in France, and son of good old Knickerbocker John Slidell, president of Mechanics' Bank. Mr. Tooker was a great old merchant in his day. He died about 1820. His partner, Benjamin Mead, carried on the firm of S. Tooker & Co. until the law compelled its change in 1834, at 20 South street. Afterwards the same house was kept up, and he took into the concern Mr. Rogers, who had been a clerk in the house, and its style was Mead, Rogers & Co. The company was Seelah Reeves, a nephew of old Samuel Tooker. They kept in South street, No. 20, until 1842, when they moved to 61 Water street. The house ceased in 1854.

The old Benjamin Mead had retired some years before, and *this* Mead of the house was his son Joseph S., now in Chicago.

Old Samuel Tooker the founder, in religion was an Universalist. He was the head of the church. Isaac Pierson was another leader of the church. After 1815 Mr. Tooker was the financier in renting ground, corner of Duane and Augustus streets, now City Hall Place, where he erected a brick building for a Universalist church, at a cost of about $20,000. In 1837 this church was sold out to the West Baptist Church, and subsequently to the Roman Catholic Church. In 1820, S. Tooker was alderman of First Ward.

Benjamin Mead, the partner of S. Tooker, was a splendid man. He died in 1860. There had not been a death in his or his father's family before for 62 years, and then it was his elder brother, who died in 1798. These Meads are all from Greenwich Ct., once known as Horse Neck, and made so memorable and so named from Gen. Israel Putnam, who in the early years of the · Revolution, rode down the height closely pursued to its brink by British soldiers. The father of Benjamin, Ralph, and Staats M. Mead, was Edmund Mead. He was an only son of a wealthy farmer, who married a highly respectable lady — named Theodosia Mead — of the same name. The first Meads that came from England settled in Greenwich. Edmund and Theodosia Mead had ten children, all in the eighteenth century, seven of whom were living in 1860, and whose aggregate ages at that time exceeded 500 years. Their names were Benjamin, born April 24, 1780; Sarah, born Aug. 22, 1782; Obediah, born March 10, 1785; Mary, born June 1, 1787; Ralph, born April 24, 1789; Staats M., born April 28, 1791; Brockhurst, born Aug. 8, 1797.

Edmund Mead, the father, by his extravagant tastes and habits, made shipwreck of himself and property, and his wife with her large family returned to her father's house, where they were cared for until old enough to do for themselves. Five sons came to New York. The sixth was left at the farm and homestead on the death of his grandfather. The eldest died as I have stated, shortly after he came to the city, in 1798, of yellow fever. His name was Solomon, and he was a clerk of Joseph Eden, a merchant of this city. Benjamin and his brother Ralph, who was only fourteen years old, went as clerks with Samuel Tooker, who always prophesied that the Meads would have a brilliant success. Benjamin, who became his partner, retired about 1847, and built a country seat. He died in 1860, leaving six children and a large number of grandchildren. He died Dec. 10, while attending a Union prayer-meeting, in Newark, N. J., aged 81. He was a Methodist, and worshipped in the old John street church forty years ago, and "Father Mead" will long be remembered by those Christians, as the meek and quiet man who was prompt as punctual in his devotions, and so continued to the close of his life. When he died, he was in company with his wife, of whom I shall have something romantic to say before I have finished. He was taken to the residence of his son-in-law, Dr. Annin, when it was found that he was quite dead.

Ralph, the next brother, who was born in 1789, went into the store of old Samuel Tooker, when he was fourteen years old, in 1803, with his brother Ben. Staats M., a third brother, came to the city two years later, and went to learn the trade of cabinet making with Jacob B. Taylor, who started cabinet making business at No. 94 Broad street in 1804. Mr. Taylor was Alder-

16*

man of the Eighth Ward from 1817 to 1826. He was
the father of the celebrated merchant, Moses Taylor.
Old Alderman Taylor was a sort of chief business man
for John Jacob Astor. Staats M. Mead made a magnificent fortune in the cabinet making business, and retired rich, built a splendid house on Fifth avenue, and
afterwards resided in Europe, where he had been enjoying himself for the past two years. He died a few
days ago. He left one son and two daughters. The
son is a Methodist clergyman. The eldest daughter
married Amos Mead Sackett, of the house of Sackett,
Belcher & Co. The youngest daughter married William Belcher, of the same house.

Ralph Mead clerked it with S. Tooker seven years,
until he had thoroughly learned the business, and then,
in 1810, left him to go in business on his own account.
His capital was this thorough mercantile experience, and
what he had saved out of his small salary. This is, by
the way, the best capital for a young merchant to possess, when he commences in this city. Mr. Mead took
the store No. 74 Pearl street, corner of Coenties slip ;
one of those old Dutch buildings (to which I have so
frequently alluded) with the gable end to the street. At
that time it was 129 years old, for the date on the house
was 1691. October 22, 1813, a few years after he had
started into business, he married Miss Sarah Holmes,
of West Bloomfield, New Jersey. It was then called
Cranetown. She was born there in 1792. Her father
was William Holmes, and her mother Abigail was a
daughter of Matthias Crane, from whom the place derived its original name.

Old Matthias Crane and his wife were both members
of the old Presbyterian Church. He was a merchant,
did a large business, and had but one child. She was

very beautiful, and, of course, had many offers for her
hand, and there were many applications for the situation
of son-in-law to her father. Her father had in his store,
as a clerk, a dashing young fellow named William Holmes,
a young emigrant from Ireland. His industry and honesty won the respect of her father. His gentlemanly
manners won the affections of the daughter. He called
one evening at her father's house, to have the matter
settled in the prompt way that Irishmen usually prefer,
when he found several rival suitors there, all of whom
were candidates for the hand of the unquestioned belle
of the place. He sat awhile, joining in social inter-
change with his rivals, and then he made up his mind
that something had got to be done, and likewise concluded to do it immediately.

" Miss Abigail, will you get me a small piece of the
cake you made yesterday ?"

" Certainly, Mr. Holmes ;" and she went out into
the hall. He followed her.

" Abigail, I love you ; will you marry me if I get the
consent of your father."

" I will, William."

The cake was forgotten, or postponed until the wedding. She married the young Irishman before she was
sixteen, lived with him sixteen years more as his wife,
and died at thirty-two, leaving several daughters. Sarah, who married Ralph Mead, was at the time her
mother died, only seven years old. And now I am
going to tell one of those curious facts, that if told in a
romance, would be regarded as proper subjects for fic-
tion.

The eldest daughter of the successful Wm. Holmes
was named Eliza. She was courted, and married Benjamin Mead, the eldest brother, and partner of Samuel

Tooker & Co.   Of course she moved to New York city,
and they went to housekeeping.   Sarah, who was a
beautiful girl, with dark eyes and expressive forehead,
went to visit her sister.   She was fond of dress, and
loved to array herself in a style that set off to advantage her handsome features and graceful form.   There
she met Ralph Mead, and in 1813, at the age of twenty-
one, became his wife, and went to housekeeping with
him over his store, at 74 Coenties slip, in which neighborhood, with the exception of brief intervals, he kept
it fifty-seven years.   Her younger sister Lydia afterwards married Staats M. Mead, the third brother, making three brothers husbands of three sisters.

These three families resided in the same locality.
Staats M. and his young wife at No. 2 Coenties slip, in
1816, where he commenced business ; Ralph at his
place, and Ben, at 12 Monroe street, where he resided.
Not an evening passed that they did not spend in each
other's society.   This was broken up in 1820 by the
death of the youngest of the sisters, Mrs. Staats M.
Mead.   All of these sisters were among " those women
whose children arise and call them blessed, and their
husbands trust and praise them."

During the war of 1812, Ralph Mead, then doing a
large business, served two years in the military defence
of his country.   He belonged to the second Regiment
of New York State Artillery.   The entire regiment
volunteered for the war, and it was stationed at the
Battery Fort, now called Castle Garden.   During the
continuation of the war with England, speculation ran
very high.   The price of everything ran up.   Sugar
was forty cents per pound by the quantity.   Molasses,
$2 per gallon.   Hyson skin tea, $3 per lb., and other
qualities of tea in proportion.   Indigo was $6 per lb.

Nutmegs, $12 per lb., by the case. Things continued at these high prices until the arrival of a Russian sloop of war, " Bramble," with the offer to mediate. Although it did not amount to anything, it had the same effect upon the market as if peace had been declared. Every article fell at once, and at least one half of the merchants of the city failed, and many of those who failed had previously been very wealthy. The banks got alarmed, as they would not discount for any one, but gave the merchants until 5 o'clock P. M. to pay their notes, instead of 3, as was the usual custom. If peace had happened at once, it would not have distressed the merchants so much. Peace took place about six months after the time to which I allude, and many kinds of goods advanced instead of falling, the demand was so great, and there were so few goods in market.

These were days that tried merchants' souls. When banks refused to aid their customers, and would hardly discount the best of paper, and there were then only eight banks in the city: Bank of New York, Manhattan, Merchants', Union, Bank of America, City, and New York Manufacturing Company (Phœnix.) Money was very scarce, and some of the leading merchants would act in a family manner with their customers. Ralph Mead was doing business in a small way, on the corner of the slip. He needed money, and went to Jonathan Goodhue, and said to him : " Mr. Goodhue, I wish to borrow your note for $2,000, for sixty days."

Mr. Goodhue knew Mr. Mead, felt that he could trust him, and at once drew his note for that sum, and gave it to the young merchant.

Fifty years ago, and even at a later period, it was customary for the old wholesale grocer merchants to club together, and purchase whole cargoes of sugar, rum, brandy, coffee, &c., and then divide them up. On one occasion, a Dutch house in the city had received a cargo of gin. When it was landed from the vessel, the old importer fixed his price for the article. He lived out of town, a little above where the City Hall now stands. It was under custom house lock and key, and the shippers abroad had limited it at a price above the current market rates. Still, some of the grocers constantly called to ask the Dutch consignee, if he was ready to sell his gin. He would say, " when the market prices reach the price at which I am limited, I will then be ready to sell."

By the arrival of a packet ship, that came into port during the night, information was received that gin had advanced very materially in the European markets. As this news reached the grocers, they at once conceived the idea of buying the gin of the Dutch importer before he received his advices. As I have said, he lived out of town. They all tried to intercept him on his way down, but missed him. Each made his way to the counting house of the old Dutch importer, which was in Coenties slip, and there he found congregated all his associate neighbors, the grocers. An exchange of glances was sufficient for a mutual understanding between the parties — mum being implied, and a division of the spoils understood. The Dutch importer and gin owner soon made his appearance, when the usual question was propounded to him, to which he replied as usual, that when the market prices reached his limits, he would sell the cargo. The grocers, finding him still in the dark respecting the advance in the article abroad, labored hard to purchase the gin at sixpence a gallon less than his limit. Not succeeding, they agreed to adjourn without purchasing — each, however, with the intent, as it afterwards appeared, of getting rid of his brother grocers, that he might privately return and secure the cargo for his own account. With this view, the parties left, each taking a different route ; but after-the lapse of a few minutes, they re-appeared in rapid succession in the office of the gin importer, neither having had the chance to buy ahead of his neighbor. They then selected one of their number to purchase the gin at the price demanded by the owner, leaving him to discover the rise at his leisure. They made a splendid profit by the operation. Ralph Mead was always very popular among the grocers. He remained a few years in the corner of Pearl street and Coenties slip, living over the store, according to the old Dutch fashion years ago, when real and domestic comfort and happiness stood in place of the fashionable frivolities of the present age. While in that store, April 18, 1818, he lost his eldest son, whom he had named after his old and much respected employer, Samuel Tooker.

In 1822 he bought the old stand 13 Coenties slip, where he had served seven years' clerkship with Mr. Tooker, and then he removed his family to a snug little house at 27 Stone street. He prospered and made money. His business increased, and he bought the store next door to 13 Coenties slip. After taking down the old buildings he erected a large and substantial store on the same ground. At different periods he took into partnership his two brothers-in-law Holmes. In 1813 he took in Hugh Holmes, and the firm was Mead & Holmes. This was only for a year or so. In 1815, when he formed the firm of Ralph Mead & Co., he took in Israel C. Holmes. He remained some time in the firm, but is now a Presbyterian clergyman out West.

Ralph Mead had in his employ at different times as

clerk, and afterwards took into the firm, his nephews,
young men of good business talents and habits, also his
son and son-in-law.

In 1827 he purchased a residence at No. 45 Pearl
street, near the Battery. Both he and his charming
wife joined the John street Methodist Church, soon after
the loss of their eldest child in 1818. In 1834 he went
up town with the emigration that commenced about
that time, into No. 254 Fourth street, opposite Washington square. That was a long way to go to church
every Sunday in John street; so several of them got
together, to see if they could not get up a Methodist
Church, with family pews, " up town." They succeeded, and erected the Mulberry street Methodist Church,
and old Dr. Bangs dedicated the church. The John
street folks were terribly down upon the arrangement,
and they prophesied that it would not prosper, and that
never a revival would occur in the new concern. This
did not prove so. The Rev. Robert Seeny was their
clergyman, and shortly after a revival occurred that
furnished the new church four hundred converts. Daniel Drew and Ralph Mead were the leading men in this
business, and are now. There would have been no em-
barrassment in the finances of the new church if they
had sold the pews, instead of renting them. But for
the liberality of Mr. Mead and Mr. Drew, the prophe-
cies of the opposition to the Mulberry street Church
would have become true. They annoyed Mr. Mead so,
that on one occasion he took Bishop Emory to survey
the new church. When he had examined the superb
pews, and the finished mahogany pulpit, the Bishop said :
" It is beautiful, it is just what the Lord has made and
man has polished."

In 1838, while Mr. Mead was residing in the Fourth

street house, he purchased lots on Second Avenue, a
healthy and pleasant location, and there he built a fine
house, in which he resided for twenty years. There,
too, he sustained a heavy loss, in the death of the lovely woman he had married 30 years previous, and who
had shared his cares and prosperity. She died October
5, 1842, leaving six children, — two sons, and four
daughters.

The eldest son is Samuel Holmes Mead. He married
a daughter of F. T. Luqueer, who once did a large
hardware business in Hanover Square. They are trav-
elling in Europe.

Melville Emory Mead, who was named after the
Bishop that praised the pulpit in the new church, is one
of the firm of E. & R. Mead & Co., at No. 13 Coenties slip, where the old business has been so long conducted. He married Elizabeth B. Hyde, a daughter of
Joseph B. Hyde of Auburn.

The eldest daughter, Elizabeth, married Edwin Hyde,
who is a partner in the above firm. They have nine
sons. He and I had an exciting night of it together
about twenty-seven years ago, when we were neighbors
in Exchange place, and were saving goods out of the
great fire of 1835. He was with David N. Lord, whose
store was blown up at No. 50 Exchange place — a capital old merchant by the way ; and I was factotum for
Rogers & Co., No. 46 Exchange place ; heavy East India house.

Another daughter married Nathan J. Bailey, formerly of the large grocery house of Hoffman & Bailey.
They have three daughters.

Harriet, another daughter, married Philip A., the
only son of James Harper, by his first wife, who was a
daughter of Philip J. Arcularius, who lived in a house

that stood at No. 11 Frankfort street, upon the very lot where the *Leader* building is now located. This daughter left one son, a fine lad now of twelve, and a grandson of the old mayor, who always called me colonel. The mother of the lad is dead.

Caroline, another daughter, married the Rev. Archibald C. Foss, now Professor of Middleton college.

On October 21, 1846, Mr. Ralph Mead married Ann E. Van Wyck, a daughter of Gen. Abraham Van Wyck, of Fishkill, with whom he lived fifteen years. This lady died September 18, 1860.

This venerable old merchant remained in business at Nos. 13 and 15 Coenties slip, until he retired from mercantile life in the year 1859, having done business in one spot for nearly 49 years, leaving it to be continued by his nephews, his son Melville, and son-in-law Edwin Hyde, under the firm of E. & R. Mead & Co.

In November, 1859, Mr. Mead purchased the elegant house No. 29 West Thirty-fourth street, where this venerable patriarch now resides with his eldest daughter, enjoying a hale and happy old age, the result of a well spent and well regulated life, in the society of a numerous and loving circle of grandchildren. His brother Brockholst is an aged bachelor in the vicinity. He once was a clerk in the City Bank.

In the year 1857, the Mulberry street M. E. church was sold, the congregation removing to Eighth Avenue and 22d street, where they erected, through the influence and perseverance of Messrs. Mead & Drew a beautiful white marble church, one of the finest in the city.

CHAPTER XXXVIII.

I have had frequent occasion in this work to speak of an old mercantile family in New York of the name of Woolsey. There have been great merchants of that name in this city, from the time of its first foundation to the present hour. George Woolsey came to this city in 1623, with the first Dutch emigrants ; probably he was a boy 13 years old at the time. Nine years later he became a merchant, or trader, as was the more proper designation in the early years of this city, when it was called New Amsterdam. George kept in business in this city until 1647, when he retired, having bought a country place on Long Island, where he died in 1698, aged 86. He was not a Dutch boy, but was English, and a relative of the great Thomas Woolsey, of massive intellect and ambition, who was Prime Minister to King Henry the Eighth. The grandfather of George was named Thomas, after the Cardinal. His grandson, Benjamin, was exiled to Holland in 1610, when he had the son George born to him, who afterwards became a distinguished New York merchant, as above stated. This George had a son, also named George, who was born in this city in 1650, and is mentioned in the patent of Governor Dongan of 1686. He died in 1741, aged 90. He had a son Benjamin, who was born in 1687 and died

in 1756. Hugh Gaines, *Mercury* for August, 1756, has
a long obituary, in which it speaks of him as a very remarkable man, and that " his intellectual powers were
much above the common level." His son Benjamin
was born in 1717, and died in 1751. His second wife
was a daughter of Doctor George Muirison. His sons
by her were Benjamin Muirison, John Taylor, George,
William, Walter, and George Muirison. One daughter,
Sarah, married Moses Rogers, of whom I have written
a sketch ; and another married the celebrated William
Dunlap, the historian, theatre manager and writer. Of
course these last were brothers-in-law of William Walton Woolsey. This latter was called after one of the
William Waltons, a connection by marriage.

B. M. Woolsey was born February 17th, 1758, and
died at Bridgeport in 1813. John Taylor Woolsey was
born in 1762, and died in the West Indies in 1798.

I think George Woolsey died early. If I am not
mistaken, he was with Daniel McCormick as a clerk
about the time of the War of the Revolution, in 1780.
I have his receipt before me, signed January 30, 1781.

William Walton Woolsey, the eminent merchant for
many years, was born Sept. 17, 1766. In 1792 he
married Miss Dwight, of New Haven. He was in business in the house of Rogers & Woolsey, at No. 235
'Pearl street, as early as 1795. Mr. Woolsey was doing
an immense mercantile business for a great many years.
He had several children. His daughter Mary Ann
married George Hoadley, of New Haven. Elizabeth
married Francis B. Winthrop ; one of the children of
this marriage is the gallant Major Winthrop, who was
killed near Newport News, and who had so distinguished
himself as a writer. His death was as widely lamented
as that of any officer who has been killed in this war.

OF NEW YORK CITY.

William Cecil was born in 1796, and married Catherine, daughter of Theodorus Bailey; died in 1840.
John Mumford, twin brother of William Cecil, married
Jane Andrews, and lives at the West. Laura, another
daughter, married William Samuel Johnson, who was
a lawyer in this city, and in 1834 was Assistant Alderman of the Third Ward. He also ran for Congress
that year. Mr. Johnson had children, one son and a
daughter Susan. I believe the family has removed to
the West. Another daughter, Sarah, married Charles
F. Johnson, of Oswego. Another son was Theodore
Dwight Woolsey, who was born in 1801, and is a Professor of Greek in Yale College, New Haven.

Mr. Woolsey was one of the most prominent members
of the Chamber of Commerce in this city. He was
elected its secretary in 1796, and held it some years.
In 1825 he was elected Vice President, and continued
to be re-elected until August 18th, 1838, when he died,
aged seventy-three. He was engaged in every benevolent and useful work. He was elected Vice President
of the Manufacturing Society of this city as early as
1797. In 1803, the Merchants' Bank was started, and old Oliver Wolcott (afterwards Governor of
Connecticut), was made its first President. The Bank
was not incorporated by act of the Legislature until
March 26, 1805, and then W. W. Woolsey was named
as one of the Directors, incorporated with such other
strong names as Joshua Sands, Isaac Hicks (that
brought up Jacob Barker), David Lydig, Henry A.
Coster, and others. The Bank obtained a charter to
save it from the operation of an " Act to restrain unin-
corporated Banking Associations " that had passed the
previous Legislature. Joshua Sands succeeded Oliver
Wolcott as President of the Merchants' Bank, and Mr.
Woolsey remained a Director many years.

As an evidence of the speedy manner in which justice was meted out in old times to criminals in this city, I will relate the following :

On Monday night, the 1st of February, 1803, the store and counting-room of Woolsey & Rogers, No. 235 Pearl street (Moses Rogers was the partner with W. W. Woolsey), was broken open, and a red morocco pocket book was taken thence.   It contained a bill of exchange for $2,500 sterling, one for £100, one for £173, one for £326, one for £67, and two notes of the Bank of New York for $5 each, and a note of hand for $50.   There was also stolen ten dollars in silver, a ticket in the South Hadley Canal Lottery, and a steel mounted pistol.   The house offered a reward of $40 for " apprehending the person or persons."   It was successful. On the 5th four negroes were taken up.   On the Monday afternoon of the 7th February, in the Court of General Sessions of the Peace, held in this city, and then adjourned that same evening, came on the trial of these four colored thieves.   After an hour's trial, they were convicted on two indictments.   Three of them were sentenced to be imprisoned in the State prison, at hard labor, for seventeen years each, and the fourth negro for eight years.   In these times it would have been a year, if not three, before these thieves would have been tried or punished.

An eminent merchant in these days, if he was robbed of a lottery ticket, would keep shady, but in the old time, there was hardly a merchant of note, unless he belonged to the church, who did not speculate in lottery tickets.   Such accounts as this were quite common. " The ticket No. 11,508 which drew the prize of $15,000 in the lottery No. 1, for encouragement of literature, drawn on the 13th of February, 1803, was sold by T.

B. Jansen, bookseller, No. 248 Pearl street, to Messrs. Tomlinson & Co., merchants of this city." The last firm was one of the most eminent in this city.

As Moses Rogers, who started the sugar refining in the old Liberty street prison in 1804, was once a partner of the Woolseys, I presume that is the way the Woolseys became so extensively engaged in sugar refining in later years.

He was also one of the prominent Governors of the New York Hospital; was elected in 1799, and continued until 1802. He was re-elected again in 1829, and continued to 1834. Mr. Woolsey was one of the most prominent citizens as well as most enterprising of merchants, sixty years ago. He belonged to a popular club of that day, as did his brother George Muirison Woolsey, Charles Brockden Brown, Samuel L. Mitchell, and William Dunlap, his brother-in-law.

In 1807, Mr. Woolsey became president of the Eagle Fire Insurance Company, that had been started under very favorable officers a few years previous. When Mr. Woolsey dissolved with Mr. Rogers, the latter paid him a very handsome sum not to go into the iron monger trade in this city for a stipulated number of years. Mr. Woolsey became sick of having made such an arrangement, so he went to New Haven and started a hardware store in that city. He was also president of a bank, (Eagle I think.) He remained in the Elm City until* 1815, when he came back to New York and started business again at 227 Pearl street, under the firm of W. W. Woolsey & Co., the term for which he had agreed not to do business (ten years) having expired. His partner was Abraham W. Woolsey. While at New Haven the bank did well, under his management; Mr. Winthrop, his son-in-law, and Mr. Hoadley, another son-

in-law, were both directors. The latter was made president after Mr. Woolsey returned to New York. • Mr.
Hoadley broke the bank, I believe, by issuing post notes,
and used the funds in speculation. Mr. Woolsey must
have had unbounded confidence in the bank, for I think
he was a Treasurer of the American Bible Society, and
he placed the funds of the sacred society in the New
Haven Bank. By some action of W. C. Holly, of the
firm of Irving, Smith & Holly, the amount was saved.
Mr. Winthrop lost a large sum by that bank. There
was a long law suit in connection with the sum that
was secured by Mr. Holly. In 1818, Mr. Woolsey
moved to 61 Greenwich street. I believe he owned 57,
59 and 61 in that street, for he lived many years at 59.
The house stood on the corner of an alley way, was
large, and in its palmy days was one of the most desirable houses in New York. It was the abode of good old
fashioned New York hospitality. In 1825, Mr. Woolsey presided at the great Erie Canal meeting held in the
city. His son, W. C. Woolsey, for some time lived at
59 Greenwich. In 1832, he was of the firm of Woolsey, Poor & Convers at 16 Hanover street. W. C.
Woolsey did business at No. 161 Pearl street. W. W.
Woolsey was president of the Merchants' Exchange
Company for some years.

George M. the brother of W. W. Woolsey, and who
was intimately connected with him in business, was born
in April, 1762. He went into business in 1797, and
that same year married Abby Howland, a sister of G.
G. & S. S. Howland, the famous merchants. She died
in London, in 1833. They had a son named Charles
William, who was born in 1802, and lost in the " Lex-
ington " steamer when she was burnt in Long Island
Sound, January 13, 1840. He left seven young daugh-

ters, and a son born after his decease. Another son of George M. was Edward John Woolsey, who married Emily Phillips Aspinwall.

George Muirison Woolsey was an extensive shipping merchant for many years. After he married in 1797, he resided at 32 Greenwich street, and later at 56 same street. He has only been dead a few years. During the embargo he had several ships that carried cotton cargoes abroad, evading the blockade. He was under heavy bonds to the Government for each vessel that left to go to another domestic port, that she should not go to Europe. He did manage to send several vessels to Perth Amboy, and by some understanding with the Collector of the Port, those ships did go to sea, and made immense fortunes. Mr. G. M. Woolsey had to go abroad also to save property from confiscation and himself from confinement, for violating the embargo. He went to Liverpool, and resided there for some years, or until the Custom house at Perth Amboy was burned and the bonds with it.

The Woolseys, at a very early period, became largely interested in the sugar refining business. They made immense sums of money in it. They commenced up near the old tobacco warehouse, in South street, between Clinton and Montgomery streets, on the East river side of the town. I think the business was chartered under the name of the New York patent sugar refinery — at any rate it was made a stock company. I believe George Muirison Woolsey was the founder of it, and then it was conducted under the firm of Woolsey & Woolsey. G. M. Woolsey owned the property of Green Hook on Long Island. This old cotton merchant left a large property to his sons, and they are among the most respected of our citizens. The Wool-

seys were among the first that carried on the sugar refining business on a very large scale, although early
there was a stock New York sugar refining company as
early as 1804. It was about the middle of the block in
Church street, west side between Franklin and Leonard. The company owned nearly all the block. They
sold off portions of it,—at first to the French church
on the north corner, and then to the old Italian Opera
company on the south corner. That company carried
a large amount of property, but closed their affairs
without loss to the stock holders about thirty years ago.
Towards the close Benjamin Strong was the president.
About that time the Woolseys commenced the business,
but carried it on in a much more extensive manner.

W. W. Woolsey was at one time in the firm of
Dwight, Palmer & Co., as a secret partner. The senior
was one of his New Haven relatives by marriage.

One of the sons of W. W., went to Augusta, Ga.,
and established himself in mercantile business, but did
not remain there long.

In the early days of Mr. Woolsey, or about the commencement of this century, all the principal merchants
would go out to the country to Hardenbrooks, to dine
every Saturday, and once a month they all took their
families. It was a great day for the junior members of
the family, who looked forward to this day of jubilee
when they could go and room in the country. This
Hardenbrook had a place of public resort on the East
river side, that would be about Twenty-fifth street.
You turned down a lane from the Boston high road,
and there found the house buried in trees. Several
acres of ground were attached. Only a limited number
of merchants would belong to this set. Another set
was composed of Englishmen, headed by John J. Glo-

ver. They bought a place and called it the Belvidere House. When the club broke up Mr. Glover bought the place for his own account.

These were good old days in 1797, and on to 1812. In every case one of the partners used to live over the store, no matter how extensive the business. They dined at different hours. One partner got his dinner at one o'clock; when he returned, the other partner would then go and get his dinner. This was done, so that one of the partners should be at the place of business constantly.

Merchants, during business hours, used to go and get their drinks at the Tontine Coffee House. The Exchange was held there, and there was a splendid bar kept. Upon it was a large bowl of punch, and another of lemonade. There were crackers, cheese and codfish. The merchants called it lunch, and from eleven o'clock to one, the bar of the Tontine would be well patronized.

END OF SECOND SERIES.

INDEX.

NEW BOOKS

And New Editions Recently Issued by

CARLETON, PUBLISHER,

(Late RUDD & CARLETON,)

413 BROADWAY, NEW YORK.

N.B.—The Publisher, upon receipt of the price in advance, will send any of the following Books, by mail, postage free, to any part of the United States. This convenient and very safe mode may be adopted when the neighboring Book-sellers are not supplied with the desired work. State name and address in full.

Les Miserables.

Victor Hugo's great novel—the only complete unabridged trans-'ation. Library Edition. Five vols. 12mo. cloth, each, $1.00.

The same, five vols. 8vo. cloth, $1.00. Paper covers, 50 cts.

The same, (cheap ed.) 1 vol. 8vo. cloth, $1.50. paper, $1.00.

Les Miserables—Illustrations.

26 photographic illustrations, by Brion. Elegant quarto, $3.00

Among the Pines,

or, Down South in Secession Time. Cloth, $1.00, paper, 75 cts.

My Southern Friends.

By author of " Among the Pines." Cloth, $1.00. paper, 75 cts.

Rutledge.

A powerful American novel, by an unknown author, $1.50.

The Sutherlands.

The new novel by the popular author of " Rutledge," $1.50.

The Habits of Good Society.

A hand-book for ladies and gentlemen. Best, wittiest, most en tertaining work on taste and good manners ever printed, $1.50

The Cloister and the Hearth.

A magnificent new historical novel, by Charles Reade, author of "Peg Woffington," etc., cloth, $1.50, paper covers, $1.25

Beulah.

A novel of remarkable power, by Miss A. J. Evans. $1.50

Artemus Ward, His Book.
The racy writings of this humorous author. Illustrated, $1.25.

The Old Merchants of New York.
Entertaining reminiscences of ancient mercantile New York City, by " Walter Barrett, clerk." First Series. $1.50 each.

Like and Unlike.
Novel by A. S. Roe, author of "I've been thinking," &c. $1 50.

Orpheus C. Kerr Papers.
Second series of letters by this comic military authority. $1.25

Marian Grey.
New domestic novel, by the author of " Lena Rivers," etc. $1.50.

Lena Rivers.
A popular American novel, by Mrs. Mary J. Holmes, $1.50.

A Book about Doctors.
An entertaining volume about the medical profession. $1.50.

The Adventures of Verdant Green.
Humorous novel of English College life. Illustrated. $1.25.

The Culprit Fay.
Joseph Rodman Drake's faery poem, elegantly printed, 50 cts.

Doctor Antonio.
A charming love-tale of Italian life, by G. Ruffini, $1.50.

Lavinia.
A new love-story, by the author of " Doctor Antonio," $1.50.

Dear Experience.
An amusing Parisian novel, by author " Doctor Antonio," $1.00.

The Life of Alexander Von Humboldt.
A new and popular biography of this *savant*, including his travels and labors, with introduction by Bayard Taylor, $1.50.

Love (L'Amour.)
A remarkable volume, from the French of Michelet. $1.25.

Woman (La Femme.)
A continuation of " Love (L'Amour)," by same author, $1.25

The Sea (La Mer.)
New work by Michelet, author " Love" and " Woman," $1.25

The Moral History of Woman.
Companion to Michelet's " L'Amour," from the French, $1.25

Mother Goose for Grown Folks.
Humorous and satirical rhymes for grown people, 75 cts.

The Kelly's and the O'Kelly's.
Novel by Anthony Trollope, author of " Doctor Thorne," $1.50